Also by Michael Russell

The
CITY of
GOD

The
CITY of
GOD

MICHAEL RUSSELL

CONSTABLE

CONSTABLE

First published in Great Britain in 2023 by Constable

A CIP catalogue record for this book
is available from the British Library.

ISBN: 978-1-40871-586-4 (hardback)
ISBN: 978-1-40871-587-1 (trade paperback)

Typeset in Dante by SX Composing DTP, Rayleigh, Essex
Printed and bound in Great Britain by Clays Ltd, Elcograf S.p.A.

Papers used by Constable are from well-managed forests and
other responsible sources.

Constable
An imprint of
Little, Brown Book Group
Carmelite House
50 Victoria Embankment
London EC4Y 0DZ

An Hachette UK Company
www.hachette.co.uk

www.littlebrown.co.uk

For Cecily Ware
1912–2012

Krv je moje svjetlo i moja tama.
Blaženu noć su meni iskopali
Sa sretnim vidom iz očinjih jama;
Od kaplja dana bijesni oganj pali
Krvavu zjenu u mozgu, ko ranu.
Moje su oči zgasle na mome dlanu.

Blood is my darkness and my light.
Blessed night they clawed from my face
With the lamps that gave me joyful sight;
Now blood-black eye-pits spear my head
And scalding fires take my tears' place.
My eyes lie in my own hands – dead.

Jama – The Pit
Ivan Goran Kovačić

PART ONE

ANGELIS HOSPITIO RECEPTIS

ANGELS UNAWARES

We refer to our telephone conversation today, concerning the transport of labourers from Italy to Germany. We thank you for your willingness to provide support for these transports. The labourers will be taken to Germany in special trains from Milan or other stations. Initially the schedules as established in Zürich on 23 March 1943 can be used.

German Railways to Swiss Federal Railways,
September 1943

Referring to the Swiss Posts and Railways inquiry into the disappearance of 26 Italian labourers from a sealed transport passing through Switzerland, we inform you that since July 1943 there have been no such German transports. The incident was created out of thin air. It did not take place on our railways.

To the Director-General, Swiss Federal Railways,
October 1943

1

ZÜRICH HAUPTBAHNHOF

Zurich, Autumn 1943

To begin with, the funeral Mass in the chapel of the Irish College in Rome was over. The man had been decently sprinkled with water and incensed and the choir had sung the *Dies Irae* and the *Libera Me*. At the close they had all sung the Irish national anthem, *Amhrán na bhFiann*, which brought tears to those eyes that had not yet shed them for the man in the coffin. Detective Inspector Stefan Gillespie didn't follow the other mourners to the cemetery to see the body interred. There was a taxi waiting to bring him to the Stazione Termini, where he would take the train no one knew he was taking to Switzerland, instead of the one to the French border he was meant to be on. He registered that the big, black car was still outside the Irish College, as it had been when he'd arrived. The Gestapo made no secret about watching the funeral. It was a matter of interest, given the dead man's connections, though they knew no one who really interested them would be there. A list of some of those who attended the Mass would go to the Gestapo offices in the Via Tasso, where it was likely to end up on the desk of the man Stefan knew as Hauptsturmführer Ritter. It was the last time he would be on such a list, for what it was worth. It wasn't worth much. Stefan Gillespie was lucky to be alive, but there was a list of those who hadn't been so lucky. If that wasn't such a long list, it was one he might have been on. It was also one he had contributed to.

Stefan's train arrived at Zurich's Central Station around three in the morning. From Rome to Florence the train had stopped, intermittently, randomly, pulling into empty rural stations and isolated sidings for other trains to pass. Sometimes the wait might be ten minutes, sometimes an hour. A train would pass on the mainline, north or south, but mostly south towards the lines the German army still held against the Allies advancing through Italy. Wooden freight cars and cattle trucks, endlessly repeated; flat wagons carrying tarpaulined tanks and artillery; troop-packed carriages. The traffic was going to and from Germany, through the Salò Republic, the puppet state Hitler set up for Mussolini after Italy deposed him and surrendered to the Allies. When the other trains came close, he often saw the German Railways insignia, Deutsche Reichsbahn. But there was no Blitzkrieg about these passing locomotives, however many came and went; only the rhythm of increasingly empty necessity. It has to be done. It has to be done. Rails rattled with it and the wagons rumbled to it. The whistles of steam engines sounded bravely. The tracks were full of motion. Yet it was somehow almost sluggish.

The war in Italy was a German war now. The Italians still fighting were mostly on the other side. The only role for what was left of Axis Italy and the now decrepit Pact of Steel, that had so recently united Germany and Italy, was to stop the British and Americans. But Italy wasn't an empty space. There was as much work policing the Italians as fighting Allied armies. As much brutality to expend on that as on holding back the enemy. Stefan had seen what that meant in Rome. Even if there was, quietly, cautiously, a sense, not only that the war could not be won, but that it could be lost, there was still faith in the crumbling New Order. There were still unbelievers to be punished; still those whose death the New Order demanded for reasons as inescapable as they were, ultimately, inexplicable. Didn't the fact that the war was not being won as it had been, unstoppably, gloriously, triumphally, prove the necessity for faith above all else? Hadn't it always been a war for survival? Hadn't they been told that from the beginning? With enough determination, with the body-count ever-higher, wouldn't the Allies be forced to negotiate? Wouldn't they be at each other's throats soon anyway? Wouldn't Britain and America see the foe wasn't Germany but Russia, not Hitler but Stalin?

That last thought floated in and out of Stefan's head as the train travelled north and he watched the traffic of war from the carriage window. It surprised him how often he had heard it in Rome, and not only from Germans. But coming from Ireland, and knowing England, it wasn't a bet he would have made himself. He had no horse in the race, of course, or at least his country didn't, though neutrality didn't always feel like that. If he watched from the outside, he had seen too much to be indifferent. What had taken him to Rome meant almost nothing, but what happened there was different. He carried away a scar. None of it should have surprised him. Irish as he was, his family was part-German. The signs were there, just unread. Perhaps all that was truly surprising was how little it surprised him.

If the scar was in his head, it was also in a briefcase that was, since he would enter Switzerland on a diplomatic passport, a diplomatic bag, and by all the diplomatic niceties unsearchable and untouchable. But the contents were not for the Irish ambassador in Berne. The papers were not on their way back to the Department of External Affairs in Dublin. No Irish diplomat knew what he carried. He was going to Zurich

3

only to change trains for Geneva. As far as Irish diplomacy was concerned, he was off the radar. It was easy enough, on a continent at war, where returning to Ireland involved circuitous and uncertain routes, either through occupied France into Spain and Portugal or north through Germany to Sweden.

The train took its own time. After Florence there was less traffic, but it was dark. Near Bologna something else was in play. The sound of bombs came early, heard first in the distance, but getting louder and more frequent. They headed away from the city on winding rural tracks. The guard told him the Allies were bombing the marshalling yards in the city. For a time, looking into the darkness, Stefan could see the misty, ethereal light that came from the explosives and the smoke of the flares that showed the bombers the way. In moments of silence in the blacked-out train, moving slowly, almost tentatively into the night, he could hear the drone of planes and the pumping, irregular beat of anti-aircraft guns. The guns achieved nothing. But it was all there was. The Allies had long controlled Europe's skies.

At Milan, most passengers got off. The train had not been crowded. There was little reason to travel unless your business was war. And along the platform, as the train waited, that business was evident again. German soldiers sat on packs or lay uncomfortably on blankets on cold stone, trying to sleep. Whether they were returning north from the front or heading south to fight was unclear. They looked different from the soldiers Stefan had seen in Germany two years earlier. It was hard to say what had changed. It was as if the men were unclear themselves.

A trio of black-shirted Fascist police moved through the carriages, checking the documents of the remaining passengers. They seemed more bullish than the German troops on the platform. They had a little authority and that was enough. The fact that it was only a shadow of the authority they and

4

their comrades possessed so recently made it all the more precious, perhaps. They were puzzled by Stefan's passport and began to fire questions at him. He spoke no Italian. He answered in German. As he had learned in Rome, good German was never wasted on bullying Italian policemen. The one Fascist who spoke German inspected his passport with a more professional demeanour, returned it to him and saluted stiffly.

The train travelled on in darkness, inside and out. Blinds were down and the only lights were so dim that it was impossible even to read. But they kept going now. There were no more delays. He was unsure what would happen at the Swiss border where he would change to a Swiss train. He had crossed several borders in the past month and his neutral status, though it attracted interest, had not been questioned. But he was closer to the heart of the war than he had been. There were a lot more people trying to escape German-controlled territory than to get in.

In the end, crossing into Switzerland was easy enough. It was almost one in the morning. The Italian police and customs officers got on the train as it stopped before the border at Chiasso. They glanced at his passport and moved on quickly. They were gruff and irritable, but only because there were trains coming through so late. They were followed by two men in plain clothes who inspected passports and visas again. They were German. He couldn't place them, but fine distinctions didn't matter in their line of work. Gestapo or Sicherheitsdienst of one variety or another. They were more polite than the disgruntled Italians, once he answered them also in amiable German. If good German had a disarming effect on Italian Fascists, it had a different effect on the German military and security services. The better your German, the more obvious it was, neutral or not, that you must be on Germany's side. Although the men examined some people's papers in intimidating detail and questioned them at length, they asked Stefan nothing.

As the Italian and German officials disembarked, the train moved slowly along the tracks into Switzerland, where it stopped again and the inspection of documents was repeated. He walked across the platform to the waiting Swiss train. The windows of the carriages were bright, the blinds defiantly up. There was no need to travel in shadows. Even the smell of the train was somehow bright. No smoke or smut or steam; all the filth that went with the sticky sludge that passed for coal in Europe. The engine that would take him to Zurich was electric. It had no camouflage and it carried no men in uniform, except for a chatty conductor who was sitting at a table with three passengers, beginning a game of cards. And as Stefan Gillespie watched the blacked-out Italian train pushing back, shrouded in its cloud of grubby smoke, he felt, for the first time in weeks, that he was free of the cloying dark, that he had no need to examine every face, that he was unwatched.

The Swiss train pulled away from Chiasso. The carriage lights dimmed, but there were no instructions to close the blinds and shut out the night. Stefan shaded his eyes to block his own reflection and looked out at the high peaks of the mountains, marked out in white. Sometimes the track was hemmed in by tight stone cliffs, but the cuttings would open out abruptly and the white peaks would be there again, sitting on top of black slopes, one behind another, receding into what felt like endless space. And lower down, scattered against the darkness as randomly as the stars are scattered across the sky, there were the lights of farms and villages; small, reassuring points of warmth that gave a shape to all that space. Then, unexpectedly, it all disappeared. The train dived into the mountains themselves, at the Gotthard Pass, running beneath them on slow inclines for miles.

Two hours later he was standing under the great glass canopy of the Central Station in Zurich. He was almost alone. There were a few cleaners moving along the platforms and through the concourse. Other passengers who had missed connections sat on benches or stretched out on them and tried, unsuccessfully, to sleep. It was not so cold in Zurich yet, but it was cold enough if you'd just got off a train from Rome. A few people walked monotonously up and down, chain-smoking for something to do. A policeman walked across the concourse shortly after the train arrived. Nothing was open. No bars or cafés. The waiting rooms would not be unlocked for hours. He sat on a bench on the platform where his connection for Geneva was due to leave at six-thirty. Over three hours to wait.

'Guten Morgen, mein Herr.'

He had almost dozed off. A man in a dark, heavy overcoat and a trilby was looking down at him. He saw, also, that further along the platform, the policeman he had noticed earlier was smoking a cigarette, self-consciously looking the other way. He didn't need to register this not too nonchalant back-up to work out that the man in front of him was also a policeman. Well, a policeman of sorts, as he was a policeman of sorts. Stefan was out of place. The detective, in whatever passed for something like Special Branch in Zurich, already knew that.

'Guten Morgen,' he answered, smiling. 'Eine miserable Tageszeit!'

'Miserable indeed,' said the Swiss detective. 'You've come from Italy?'

'I have. You'll want to see this.'

'Thank you.' The man took the passport. He looked at it. He registered neither interest nor surprise, which was surprising in itself. An Irish diplomatic courier in the middle of the night couldn't have been such a common occurrence.

'Herr Gillespie. Stefan Gillespie. Irish.'

Stefan nodded.

'Diplomat?'

'Nothing so grand. A courier.'

'And it's Inspector Gillespie, is that right?'

'It is. And what about you?'

The man looked puzzled. Stefan grinned.

'I don't know what you use here. Sergeant, Inspector, Captain?'

'Captain. I'm Captain Batz.'

'Did they call you from the border or are you just quick on the uptake?'

The Swiss policeman didn't answer. He returned the passport.

'I assume we're both in the same line, Captain, as policemen.'

'Quite possibly, Herr Gillespie. But if we are, then it's a line I'm qualified to pursue in Switzerland – and you, whether you're a diplomat or a courier, are not.'

Stefan laughed.

'Are you waiting for a train?' continued the captain. 'To where?'

'For Geneva. I should have been here earlier this evening. There was a connection. But it turned into a long journey. What with one thing . . . and another.'

'I can imagine.' Batz took out a packet of cigarettes. He offered one.

Stefan Gillespie stood up. He bent as Batz lit the cigarette.

'And your reason for travelling to Geneva?'

'To see an old friend.'

'I'm sure you know that under the present circumstances I have every reason, and naturally every right as well, to ask you for more detail than that. Your country has a consulate here in Zurich. I would have thought someone would be here to meet you. I'm sure your ambassador has the use of a car.

Hanging about on a station platform in the early hours of the morning seems, well, if you were English rather than Irish, I might be tempted to use the word eccentric. Your passport is in order but it's routine to check identity with your embassy in Berne.'

'It's a bit early in the morning. I doubt Mr Cremins will be up yet.'

'Your old friend in Geneva, what's his name?'

There was no choice but to say it.

'Mr Lester. Seán Lester. You'll know him, I imagine.'

Captain Batz showed no surprise, but he was more puzzled now.

'Yes, the Secretary-General of the League of Nations.'

'I'm stopping off to see him. Then France, Spain and back to Ireland.'

'That seems an odd journey. The League of Nations, I mean.'

'Does it?'

'Not in the past, Inspector. But these days . . . it's not a popular destination.'

'No?'

'No.'

'Well, all the more reason he might like to see a friendly Irish face.'

The Swiss detective looked at Stefan for some seconds, more dissatisfied.

'Is there a problem with me going to Geneva?'

Batz dropped his cigarette and looked down to stub it out. He looked up.

'No. But noteworthy. It's still a free country.' He grinned. 'More or less.'

'More or less sounds just like home, Captain.'

As the Swiss policeman walked away, Inspector Gillespie

stubbed out his cigarette and sat on the bench again. The uniformed policeman who had shadowed Batz walked past him and gave a curt nod. Stefan had drawn more attention to himself than he had wanted. Had the train kept even remotely to time, he would have arrived at a busy early evening Zurich Central Station and easily caught another train to Geneva. He had no doubt that now the Swiss police would contact the Irish embassy to check his identity. The ambassador had no idea he was in Switzerland. And he had no business being there without the ambassador knowing, even if he wanted to claim he was only travelling through Switzerland to make his way out of Europe and back to Ireland. A visit to Seán Lester at the now redundant and diplomatically isolated League of Nations wasn't going to go down well, certainly not with the Department of External Affairs in Dublin. Lester had always been regarded as too anti-Nazi before the war. Now he was barely regarded at all. For Stefan to visit him was questionable. The fact that the visit was being conducted in secret would take considerable explaining.

For a moment Stefan smiled. He had spent several years wanting his boss in Garda Special Branch, Superintendent Gregory, to sack him from a job he had never had any love for. His requests for transfer had always been refused. Even his worst misdemeanours and infractions had been forgiven. Maybe because he was useful. Maybe because he knew too much. He wondered idly if he had pushed things too far now. Maybe someone higher up than Gregory, someone in the Department of External Affairs, would want him out. He smiled again. No such luck. A bollocking would be about it. A bollocking, then back to the bollocks.

Another hour passed. Stefan Gillespie was colder and he was hungry. The buffet would open eventually. There would be hot coffee. It might be real coffee. He had been told that

Switzerland still had real coffee without recourse to the black market. He looked up, hearing the slight trembling of rails that came before the noise of an engine and the clatter of carriages. He watched the engine approaching, smoke hanging round it in the cold air. It pulled into the station slowly, across the track from him, on the other side of the opposite platform. A long, weary hiss of steam. It was a German train, black and wet and gleaming. He looked back towards the high, pitched arches of the glass roof. It must be raining now, raining hard.

The train was made of two passenger carriages and a line of half a dozen cattle trucks, the battered wooden workhorses that carried everything, everywhere. For a moment nothing happened. There was another hiss of steam from under the engine and the train shuddered to a second halt. Stefan looked up and down the platform. He looked towards the concourse. It felt as if he was alone in this great space. The cleaners had gone. The porter who had pushed a trolley full of mail sacks past him minutes before had gone. The wandering policeman had gone too.

Then there were voices. They came from the cattle trucks across the tracks from him. Men were shouting. The noise was muffled. He looked, for a moment almost idly. There were more shouts. He heard no words, but it was Italian. Then another sound. The doors of the carriages. German soldiers jumped on to the platform. A line of them, running the length of the train. They had their backs to him, facing the goods wagons. They didn't hold rifles, but rifles were on their shoulders. Stefan recognised the uniform. The all-pervasive field grey was enough, but they weren't ordinary soldiers. They were Waffen SS. There was nothing remarkable, until it struck him that there was. This was neutral Switzerland.

The shouting was growing louder. Stefan heard more Italian and some German. A tall, thin officer and a heavy-set NCO strode rapidly along the train. The NCO hammered on the cattle-truck doors, snapping out irritated commands in German. The officer followed, echoing them in quieter but equally petulant Italian.

'Quiet, you Eyetie fuckers! Keep it shut in there!'

It didn't change anything, but the noise was surly rather than angry now.

'We move in ten minutes! There'll be food in Germany!'

Stefan Gillespie took out a cigarette and lit it slowly, unmoving.

By one of the wagons the officer and the NCO stopped. There was more noise coming from this than any of the others. The NCO banged and shouted. There was some kind of conversation going on, through the doors. They were talking to the men inside. The NCO shook his head. The officer shrugged. The conversation, unheard by the Irish policeman on another platform, continued. The officer beckoned two soldiers. A pin was pulled from a bolt on the cattle door of the goods wagon. The soldiers heaved it sideways. The door opened a few feet. And now there were rifles in the hands of some of the Germans. Stefan could see the men in the wagon too, crowding round the opening, pushing at one another.

'Get back, you bastards,' shouted the NCO, holding a pistol.

Soldiers pointed the barrels of their guns towards the doors.

Stefan simply watched. The men in the doorway were Italian soldiers. The uniforms were ragged and filthy, but he had no doubt what they were. Then there was movement. Some of the Italians stepped back. Through the gap came a body, manhandled down to German soldiers on the platform. A man was dead. The SS soldiers laid him on the platform with some alacrity. The officer and the NCO stood over him. No one seemed keen to stand close to the body.

The officer bent down. He stood up, shaking his head, laughing.

Stefan Gillespie stood and dropped the stub of his cigarette. He walked closer to the edge of the platform, trying to hear something. He didn't need to hear. But he was drawn to it. Everyone by the train, across the tracks, was drawn to it.

There were a few more words and then the officer walked away.

'It's not typhus!' shouted the NCO. 'Non è tifo! Got it? No typhus!'

Most of the shouting had died down. Indistinct words came from some of the other wagons. The soldiers lined up along the platform were looking away, talking, lighting cigarettes. Their concentration had gone. Then, with the doors of the cattle truck almost closed, a man, dark and thin, leapt out. He was through the gap in the line of soldiers instantly. He was down on the tracks, running to the opposite platform. He was trying to pull himself up. But the energy he had found was gone. He was clawing at the stone lip, pulling, pulling and now not moving.

The Germans by the train had turned. In a line as before, but facing the Italian, who was still clawing at the platform. There was a roar of voices from the train. The Italian soldiers inside were shouting, cheering. Some of them could see something. They hammered on the walls of the cattle trucks.

The officer pushed his way through the line of men.

'No shooting! Under no circumstances shoot! You hear me!'

The NCO called several of the SS men across to him.

'Any man who fires a shot,' screamed the officer, 'any man who shoots—'

Stefan stepped forward, to the edge of the platform. The Italian was only feet away. He bent down and stretched out his hand. The man cried out.

'Hanno sparato ai – nostri – ufficiali – siamo schiavi!'

He was telling this stranger the Germans had killed their officers. They were being taken to Germany as slave labour.

The words meant nothing to Stefan, except as the sounds of someone crying for help. As the man grasped his hand, he pulled him up onto the platform. The Italian looked at him for only a second. There was an arch next to the bench Stefan had been sitting on. The man saw it and ran. German soldiers were clambering on to the platform, four of them. Behind them their heavy-set NCO, screaming orders, breathing fire.

Stefan stood between the soldiers and the arch. He moved, unthinkingly, until he was almost blocking it. As one of the SS men ran towards the arch, he put out his foot. The man fell. It wasn't something Stefan had intended to do. A mad instinct had taken over. He would give the Italian a few more seconds. Maybe it would be enough. The other SS men stopped, staring at the man in a coat and dark suit with surprise. One raised his rifle. The officer roared from the other platform.

'A single shot and I'll fucking shoot you! Just get the Italian!'

The NCO grabbed a rifle from one of his men. He swivelled it round and smashed the butt into Stefan's head. As Stefan collapsed, the German he had tripped was getting up. For a few seconds none of the others moved, waiting to see what the NCO was going to do. He looked up, calm, and shrugged.

'You heard the officer. Get the Eyetie and bring him back.'

The Waffen-SS men raced through the arch.

The NCO looked down. Stefan lay on his back, barely conscious.

'You're lucky, my friend,' said the German. 'My officer says no shooting.' He kicked Stefan hard in the ribs, then he kicked again. He brought the rifle butt close and held it over Stefan's outstretched hand. He slammed it down. 'Arsehole!'

He lifted the rifle again, higher this time, but the blow didn't fall.

'Unlike you, I don't have any orders not to shoot, Scharführer.'

The NCO turned to see a man, this one in an overcoat and a trilby. The detective who had questioned Stefan. He held a pistol. Behind him were two uniformed policemen, looking nervously across the tracks at the row of SS soldiers.

'Your government isn't going to thank you for a diplomatic incident.'

Captain Batz smiled. This was his territory. No one would thank him for a diplomatic incident either, but he wouldn't be sent to a concentration camp for it.

'Your choice. But I'd recommend you get back on the fucking train.'

The SS-Scharführer wanted to do what he was used to doing. In the world he had lived in for so many years, there was never anyone to stop that. He wasn't angry. What he felt was surprise, even bewilderment. And he had lost face. His men would remember it too. That wasn't how it should be. Something was wrong. In this small, insignificant moment something had changed. He looked from the Swiss detective to the SS officer watching from the opposite platform, silent, furious at the mess he might have to answer for and unable to clean it up the way these things were always cleaned up.

'Scharführer! Get back over here, you clown!'

There was an unfamiliar sound. It wasn't loud, but it could be heard. The cattle trucks were quiet. The station was quiet again too. Two Waffen-SS men approached their NCO from either end of the platform where the Swiss detective still held a gun on him. The other two emerged from the dark arch, empty-handed, more Swiss policemen walked behind them. The NCO looked at his men. They didn't need to say anything. They hadn't found the Italian. They wouldn't say they'd been told to fuck off to their train, but that was the gist of it. They were waiting for some serious bollocking. But it didn't come then. They had an unusual sense that it wouldn't come at all. The SS-Scharführer crossed the tracks, back to the

German transport. He didn't look at the unconscious man with his bloodied head and broken hand. As he climbed up on to the other platform, his men were making their way to the carriages at the front of the train. Then the unfamiliar sound again. Quiet laughter. The Scharführer knew they were laughing at him.

2

PALAIS DES NATIONS

Seán Lester stood where he stood most days when he walked from the flat above the house that was called La Pelouse, that looked out to the lake of Geneva and the French mountains beyond. He stood inside the main doors into the League of Nations Assembly Hall. He looked at the empty rows of seats. He looked at the square proscenium at the far end and its rising dais and its high, carved seats. He took in the emptiness and the silence that had been all this hall had known for over three years. The only sound today was the electric floor polisher as the cleaner moved it idly back and forward across the parquet. He didn't often see the body that had once lain almost exactly where the polisher's brushes circled now, but today he did. The body of the man who'd shot himself in the middle of a debate about Danzig five years earlier.

Danzig was often in Seán Lester's head. Danzig, where the war had started. Danzig, where he had once been the League's High Commissioner, trying to defend the democratic constitution of the tiny German-speaking statelet that the Treaty of Versailles established at the end of the Great War. Danzig, that had been taken over by National-Socialist politicians who created a miniature version of Hitler's Reich, with the sole purpose of causing the dissention that would reunite the Free City with Germany. With the destruction of Poland, that happened. Danzig, where the League of Nations had failed in everything it was established to do; to find a way to foster peace by reason and respect and mutual regard; to bring an end to the desire for war. It was where Lester had failed, above all, at least that's how he felt. If nothing could stop the fading of the light in that small space, what could be done anywhere else? Now his failure had been institutionalised, in the sprawling, elegant halls and colonnades of the Palais des Nations, where he presided, Miss Haversham-like, over the wedding feast that had never taken place.

The end had begun a long time before anyone saw it. It was already there when Mussolini marched his troops into Ethiopia. Everyone cared, but no one cared enough. And there were too many other failures on the list. This morning he was thinking back to 1936, and one of many days on that list of failures that should have pointed to the end. That day a young man stepped out of the press boxes on to the floor of the Assembly, in front of the proscenium. He pulled out a pistol and shot himself. His name went round the world, but who remembered it now? Seán Lester did. He had always remembered it. Štefan Lux. The man came forward just as he had stopped speaking. Silence descended on the Assembly as the delegates registered the gun. And Lester still remembered the words Lux shouted before the shot. 'C'est le dernier coup!' The last blow. The last blow for what? The words of a madman the Assembly said and adjourned for lunch. The dead man was removed. The cleaners cleaned. The Assembly resumed its debate two hours later.

As the League's great and good had gazed at the body and the hall had exploded back into sound, Seán Lester had picked up the dead man's briefcase. The letters inside would go unread by the world leaders they were addressed to. But he read them.

They called on the world to put a stop to what was going on in Germany, to everything that was going on there. But above all Štefan Lux had seen a vision of something happening to the Jews that there were no words for. Yet however real their problems were, who could take something that wild and fanciful seriously?

Those old letters were still in a filing cabinet in Lester's office, where his predecessor as Secretary-General had put them. He remembered, whenever Štefan Lux came into his mind, how quickly the body had been moved and how spotless the floor was afterwards. Nothing remained. There was not a speck of blood left. Nothing to see. Nothing to say. And nobody said it. But there was a new joke. He heard it in the bar in the Palais de Nations that evening, from members of the Nazi delegation that had come from Danzig to express its contempt for everything the League of Nations stood for. He heard it now in his head, remembering that day. The League of Nations might not be good for much, but they certainly knew their business when it came to making a dead Jew disappear in the blink of an eye.

Danzig was in the Secretary-General's head this particular morning, along with the body of Štefan Lux, because of an unexpected telephone call from a man he had not spoken to in years. It came from the Vatican, from Bishop Edward O'Rourke.

Seán Lester knew that Edward O'Rourke had lived behind the walls of the Holy See since 1939, when he was driven out of Poland after the German invasion, barely escaping what would have happened if the Gestapo or the Sicherheitsdienst had caught up with him. For the Nazis, even in the brutal chaos of Poland, killing Catholic bishops was generally frowned on, though priests were game for a bullet in the back of the head or, if they were lucky, incarceration in the Priests' Barracks at

Dachau. But a disappearance wasn't difficult to arrange. The Church had shown wisdom in silencing O'Rourke's resistance to the Nazi takeover of Danzig, but his opposition was not forgotten. The lists of sinners who had to be reckoned with were long. Unlike Catholicism, National Socialism didn't offer any absolution.

'It's a long time, Edward.'

'My dear friend.' The voice at the other end was frail. Lester remembered a very vital man. A round, often mischievous face. Intense eyes. The laborious, hard-won English was the same, but he could almost see a thinner, more fragile face.

'How are you? How is Rome?'

'I'm old. That says enough. And Rome is older. Too old for what . . .'

'I understand,' said Lester, answering a question that didn't need asking.

'Oh, Rome will survive. I won't say the city's seen worse, but it knows the routine. You know enough yourself. Who doesn't? I don't leave the Vatican now. For me, it's simply infirmity. I think the days I was worth a bullet have gone. So my friends tell me. Or there are just too many other things to do with the bullets.'

Something of the mischief was there again, but quieter, emptier.

'Though I think you are isolated in Geneva too.'

'Oh, probably more so, Edward. I have only the illusion of freedom.'

There was silence. The line hissed and crackled.

'I am not here to chatter,' continued the bishop. 'That is for another time. I say time, I mean age, another age. So, we count on that. We'll remember when such a time comes . . . For now, someone will be listening to this. A German in the Via Tasso at least, but very probably someone at the Vatican exchange too.' O'Rourke laughed. 'Who needs the confessional? But I spent the afternoon with Dinneen's dictionary, making bad English worse Irish. Almost as good as a code!'

'I don't understand. You've lost me.'

'You'll follow, my dear friend.'

The bishop spoke next in Irish that was more laboured than his English.

'An cuimhin leat an póilín Éireannach?'

Lester could hear O'Rourke was reading. He replied in Irish.

'I'm going to struggle with this . . . do I remember the Irish policeman?'

For a moment the words meant nothing.

The fragile voice continued, sounding even older and slower.

'You remember the Irish policeman. In Danzig. There was a woman. I don't remember all the story now. How he came. Why. Didn't the Nazis try to kill him?'

Lester answered in his own slow Irish.

'The Irish policeman. Must be eight years.' He laughed. 'Die Meistersinger!'

'Die Meistersinger?' Now the bishop was puzzled.

'The open-air theatre, in Sopot. That's where I met him.'

'Not so much detail, Seán. I won't understand.' O'Rourke paused. 'All that matters is that you know him. And you remember him being with you in Danzig.'

'Yes, I remember him. I'm not sure I recall his name though.'

'He will be with you in a couple of days. He will leave soon. No one will know about it. He has a diplomatic passport, but the Irish embassy won't know what he's doing, not here, not in Switzerland either. He will bring you something from me. It's something . . .' There was silence. The line crackled. 'I don't have the words. A dictionary isn't enough. Something no one wants to see. Wants anyone to see. Even here, behind our holy walls. No one wants to look. But you will, my friend, you will look. He will come by train. Three days, did I say? It's old work,

Seán. Our old work. But now much darker . . . we both saw the dark, but only part . . .'

Seán Lester left his thoughts in the Assembly Hall or did his best to. He walked to his office along empty corridors past empty offices. He signed some letters and had a conversation about the bills the League could no longer pay, as he did almost daily. He went out again, into the park, down towards the lake. Most days were the same. A tour of his estate and time to reflect, always, on the pretence that there was still a League of Nations to lead. The Palace of Nations was his palace. Its airy colonnades were his domain. As Secretary-General he presided over these elegant spaces. He cherished the crisp, new buildings that had been an architecture for a new world and were barely built before war emptied them of purpose. Where the world had gathered, no one came. Where international delegates and diplomats collected in their thousands and an army of administrators and experts planned a better future, only a handful of people remained. Guards in uniforms no one beyond Geneva recognised; a few clerks and typists; a librarian in a library no one used; a telephonist in an exchange that received hardly any calls; cleaners with little to clean; gardeners who husbanded empty grounds. Most of the rooms and halls were shut up. Money was short. Heating was a hard-won luxury. In winter there was ice on the inside of the windows of shuttered conference rooms. But for the Secretary-General the palace still echoed with what once was and with what might have been. And with quiet bloody-mindedness, work went on. Reports no one read travelled to and from the League's offices in America, as if they meant something. Sometimes Seán Lester almost persuaded himself they did. But there would be an afterwards. And somewhere in that afterwards some of this would matter. He was not a religious man, but he thought sometimes what it must have been like to chant the hours, day and night, in an isolated Irish monastery in another Dark Age, knowing the world beyond was in flames and destruction could come at any time. No one to listen, no one to know if the offices were sung or not. No one except God. On Lake Geneva's dutiful shores, there wasn't even God.

It was as he turned from the lake towards La Pelouse that Lester saw his daughter walking towards him across the grass. Ann Lester, just nineteen, was the only other inhabitant of the apartment that took up the first floor of the house. Only a year earlier she'd made a difficult journey from Ireland to Switzerland, through a Europe taking a few last breaths before the war it had spread across the globe returned, as now it had. When she'd arrived she said she wanted to make sure he was all right, as if she was going to stay for a couple of nights and get the train home. He knew his wife had sent Ann to keep him sane. She was making a good job of doing that.

'Daddy, there was a phonecall. It was Mr Cremins in Berne.'

He was surprised. The Irish ambassador wasn't far away. The company of another Irishman in a country where Irishmen were thin on the ground had once made them close. But Lester's last stand as the last Secretary-General of the League of Nations had left an aura of isolation about him and the Palais des Nations. It was hard for anyone to go there without reliving the mistakes of a past that was too close to home to generate affection. It was an uneasy place to be.

'Well, dear old Francis T. Has he finally got round to that lunch he never delivers on?' He laughed. 'Am I no longer persona non grata at the Irish legation?'

They walked back slowly towards the house.

'If you ever were, it's your own fault. You choose not to see anyone.'

'Only because no one wants to see me. The spectre without even a feast.'

'Never mind that.' She stepped firmly on the merest hint of self-pity, even when it manifested itself as a joke. 'He's not in Berne, he says he's in Zurich.'

'And he wanted me to know that?' He was laughing. 'Why on earth—'

'I haven't finished yet! He said he needs to talk to you.'

'You should have told him to call the office. I only just left.'

'He said it was something that needed . . . delicacy. He was quite flustered.'

'Delicacy! Jesus, isn't that Francis all over? And what is so delicate?'

'He said it's about Mr Gillespie. Something happened in Zurich, at the station. Isn't that the man . . . you said was coming from Rome? The one you call . . .'

'The Irish policeman, yes.' He finished her sentence, smiling. Then his expression changed. He was puzzled, recalling the conversation with O'Rourke.

'There's no message really, just that you call him urgently.'

'How the hell does Francis know about Gillespie? Was there any more?'

'Only that there's been some kind of . . . accident. I think it's serious.'

*

Standing by the hospital bed in Zurich where the Irish policeman lay unconscious, Seán Lester didn't think he would have recognised him without knowing who he was looking at, even without the bandages and the drips and the black bruises on the cheeks. It was eight years since the two men had met in Danzig. However exceptional the circumstances then, he had known Stefan Gillespie only for days. And there was a lifelessness in the face now. It was hard and unmoving, mask-like.

'Has he come round at all?'

The doctor beside Lester nodded, but somehow in the negative.

24

'For a few seconds in the ambulance . . . but since then, no.'

'Is it his head? Is that where he's hurt?'

'His head is what matters. It's all that matters. For the rest, some broken bones, quite small, hand and finger. The ribs and stomach are badly bruised. I don't know how the ribs are still in one piece . . . but that will all heal easily enough.'

The list of bones and bruises was a diversion.

'But what about his head? Do you know what damage has been done?'

The doctor shook his head.

'Not really. I know what I can see. There's no fracture. There's no obvious pressure on the brain. There was a blood clot but it's been drained and as far as I can tell it's stopped bleeding. There will be bruising internally, but I can't tell much from the X-ray. In short, what's going on in there . . . the concussion is severe, but right now that's all we can say.'

'So, what next? I mean . . . the outcome?'

Lester spoke quietly, looking down again. He hardly knew this man, but there was a connection. Old work, Edward O'Rourke had said, our old work. What he knew made that true enough for the Irish policeman as well. Old work and old ways. It was an unsettling serendipity. Unrelated incidents but somehow they touched. Nazi stormtroopers in Danzig in 1935. German soldiers at Zurich Central Station.

'We have to trust the head is . . .' The doctor gave a slight shrug. It said he didn't know. 'Is as solid as it seems . . . that there's not something we can't see.'

By guess and by God, thought Seán Lester. That's what the man meant.

'The nurse talked about an "accident" just now, Doctor. It's an odd word. There was nothing accidental, was there? It was not any accidental rifle butt.'

'I'm not sure of the details, Mr Lester. A heavy blow, that's all I know.'

The words were spoken in the doctor's same low, considered voice. There was the same non-committal tone. The slightly apologetic smile was full of concern. The doctor showed no outward sign of evading Seán Lester's question, but he had no intention of answering it. He had no views on why an Irish policeman was lying in his Swiss hospital. No one had seen any German rifle butts.

'How long before you know, Doctor?'

'If he comes to, he has a chance . . . if not . . . a prayer would do no harm.'

The doctor walked away.

The Secretary-General gazed down at the figure in the bed.

'I'm not much for prayers, Mr Gillespie, but I'll maybe risk one for you.'

3

STAZIONE TERMINI

Rome, Two Weeks Earlier, Stefan

It needed several trains and a lot of railway to take me from Madrid Atocha to the Stazione Termini in Rome. It was slow, always slow across Spain to Barcelona. I knew that already. From Barcelona there's a short run to the tunnel at Cerbère and the change to French gauge. Then France, and not much faster either, with all the stops and starts and changes that took me from Perpignan and Montpelier to Marseilles and Nice and Monaco and on into Italy, to Genoa, Pisa, Leghorn, Civitavecchia. All names I knew, somewhere in the back of my head, for no real reason except that the back of your head is where the half-forgotten, shapeless, inexplicable stuff of however many years you've seen is left. It's no great claim for those years that so little accompanied knowledge of the names. A port. Roulette wheels. Sunbeds and beach umbrellas of the rich, whatever that meant now. And a tower, of course. The platforms and the station buffets I spent my time on in those cities were indistinguishable and unremarkable. Some stations were big and others weren't. That was about it. I saw groves of olives. I saw vines on the hillsides. I saw the things you'd expect to see. If there was anything unexpected I must have passed it while I slept. But I saw the Mediterranean when the trains ran along the coast. I don't know what magic the summer sun worked on the Mare Nostrum, but I didn't catch anything very blue. It was the same grey mix you see on a calm day looking out from Dún Laoghaire. If I'd wanted to be there, I might have noticed the beauty that was passing. Maybe the reason you travel determines what you see.

What I didn't see much of was war. I spent a night in Barcelona at the start. And even in the walk from the station to the hotel, I saw more destruction than I saw again in France and Italy. The Civil War in Spain was over, but Barcelona was the last city to fall to the now all-powerful Generalissimo Franco. The price for that was everywhere in the rubble-strewn streets and broken buildings. In France, though the trains took me to the coast and the German military zone, I only really saw war in the field-grey uniforms and the German officers who sat next to me in the carriages, meticulously polite and deter-minedly good-humoured. There were a lot of them, no question about that. If they weren't inspecting the passports and train tickets, they were watching over the people who did. In Madrid, the Irish ambassador told me the Riviera was the soft under-belly of Europe waiting for attack. But it felt as if nobody was expecting anything, except the next train. The French and Italians kept to themselves. It was very noticeable. An unex-plained foreigner who seemed to speak good German wasn't an attractive proposition for idle conversation. If I could keep myself to myself, I did. An Irish passport raised eyebrows, whether French or German or Italian, but the diplomatic stamp precluded questions, even inside the military zone. Only once was I quizzed with any serious intent, by a Frenchman, between Marseilles and the Italian border.

I don't know that he was French at all. He started in French but shifted into English so seamlessly that I barely had time to say my French was limited to asking platform numbers and ordering a beer. He knew I was Irish before he opened his mouth. He wasn't bad at not looking like some species of secret policeman, but he moved too quickly from cheerful chat about Ireland to the Italian surrender, the Allied invasion of Italy and what I thought the possibilities of peace were, almost whispering, as if he was trusting me with great confidences. I made sure my ignorance of everything he said was profound. I bored him into giving up.

I had no idea why I was going to Rome. I had been sent to Spain to sort out a problem the Department of External Affairs, in the formidable shape of its Secretary, Joseph Walshe, had with the Irish ambassador in Madrid. The polite version was that Mr Kerney had lost the run of himself. He had too many friends who were German spies, though he seemed to reckon that was no bad thing. A couple of years earlier that might not have mattered. But times were changing, even for a country so far up the arse of holy neutrality. The job wasn't a diplomatic one, which was why Walshe sent a Special Branch inspector. I had to find out whether the ambassador was stupid or dangerous, or both, and slap him down.

Mr Kerney proved only fairly stupid. However, the fact that he thought he knew what he was doing and believed he knew more about Irish interests in Europe than any fucker in Dublin, didn't help him. He wasn't wise in his choice of friends. Some of those friends had friends who rarely attended ambassadorial balls. The two people who ended up dead had nothing to do with the Irish embassy. It was a coincidence that one of them was Irish. At first glance he looked like a hard-done-by businessman the ambassador owed belated consular assistance to. Mr Kerney didn't even know him. But he did know someone who knew someone who knew someone in the very undiplomatic line of business that got two people killed.

I was never quite sure why they were killed. They were innocents in a way, even if there wasn't much innocent about what they did. But they chose to be there, the two of them, selling a way out of Europe to desperate people. Sometimes they delivered, other times they took the money and didn't. It was easy to do. There were no refunds. Selling your customers back to the people they were running from was definitely pushing it, but there were plenty who did worse without ever ending up on a slab. And if people sometimes found themselves paying for things they didn't get, no one was going to shoot you for creative accounting. As it turned out though, there was no guarantee on that last point. But that was another story. The two bodies complicated things for the Irish embassy in Spain, but it was nothing that cash in the right quarters couldn't keep out of a Spanish courtroom.

Meanwhile, in Madrid, the rap over the knuckles was delivered to the Irish ambassador. Mr Kerney's extra-curricular activities had been curtailed. I thought I was on my way to Lisbon and then home to Ireland. Then a message came from External Affairs in Dublin. I was to go to the embassy in Rome. No explanation.

Kerney took some small pleasure in delivering the news.

'This was in code, Gillespie. I don't know why. The world and his wife can read our codes. What's the point? If the best secret we can come up with is an Irish policeman on a train to Italy . . . it's almost as if someone out there gives a fuck.'

The last words were not for me. They were directed west, far west, to Iveagh House on Dublin's Stephen's Green, to the desk of Joe Walshe at External Affairs.

'But Rome should be interesting, Inspector. It's in German hands in the wake of the Italians surrendering to the Allies. At some point the British and the Americans will have to take it from them. If you stay long enough, who knows?'

He was trying to find something clever to say. It wasn't his strong point.

'I'm sure . . . a bit of Irish neutrality will see me through, sir.'

He smiled. The thought allowed at least a smidgeon of doubt.

'Anyway, you'll have two ambassadors to piss off there. Mick MacWhite at the Quirinal, representing Ireland to a government that doesn't exist anymore, and Tom Kiernan at the Holy See, representing us to the Almighty. You'd almost think the country actually had some money. But do see the sights. Good luck, Inspector.'

I won't say Kerney was hoping I'd need luck, but somewhere in his head, for a moment, I wondered if there was a picture of bullets flying past my ear as I ran for shelter in a bombed-out Roman street, with maybe the dome of St Peter's in the background, and him sitting in the red-plush peace of his favourite Madrid restaurant, sipping a good amontillado. It was one way to put me in my place, at least in his head. If something like that was going through his mind, who could begrudge him? He knew he wasn't going to come out of it well when my report landed in front of Joe Walshe in Dublin. It wouldn't finish him now, but it would damn him for the future. The longer it was before I got back to Ireland, the more diluted the detail in that report might become. It would be a hard man who blamed the ambassador for entertaining, for a few seconds, a scenario in which the report didn't arrive at all. If it went missing in action, so to speak. But I was being uncharitable. Too long working in Superintendent Gregory's Special Branch. As if a thought like that would enter a diplomat's head. And an Irish diplomat at that!

Most of the way into Rome I was half asleep. It was late morning, but I'd spent the early hours of that morning pacing a platform in Genoa, after a night journey from Nice in a carriage full of German soldiers too drunk to sleep or let me sleep. It was the least comfortable of the trains I had taken since leaving Madrid and the one that most reminded me I was travelling into a war. The polite good humour I had seen from the Germans further west was no longer there. It certainly hadn't survived an excess of alcohol. For the most part they left me alone, even if their singing didn't. You couldn't say the same for the civilians on the train once we got into Italy, or the Fascist police and soldiers who were all that remained of the Pact of Steel. The Germans were loud and insulting. Their contempt even for the Italians on their side was the main topic of conversation and an endless source of amusement. If it didn't feel much like anybody was waiting for anything as I travelled along the French coast, here it was different. The raucousness had a tension. It wouldn't have taken much for an Italian who answered back to meet a German fist and be lucky it was only that. Here there was a sense that something was coming. The fact that no one could believe that was true, made it more dangerous. Behind all the bluster, there was edginess and uncertainty. Something men who had known nothing but certainty could not begin to think about, let alone talk about. I saw it on the faces of the ones who stayed sober. I had nothing to do but watch them.

From Genoa it was quieter. The soldiers disappeared. The next train, the last one, was emptier and quieter still. It ran faster too. I drifted in and out of sleep. The country was flat and grey rather than green, bleached of colour. At times we ran along the coast again and there was an hour when the sky was clear and blue and the sun shone on the water of the Mediterranean just enough to let me see it could be blue, as it was supposed to be. The pines were few and far between as the train rattled through the outskirts of the Eternal City, scraggy more than elegant. It was like any outer-city sprawl of tin-roofed sheds and warehouses and factories. If there was more to see of the Rome than I might have expected, I drifted back into sleep before it flashed by, waking only as we pulled into the Stazione Termini. I was in time to see, across the maze of lines that led to the goods yards, groups of men clearing an area of brick and stone and twisted steel debris. It wasn't much and it was quickly passed, but it was the first bomb damage I saw.

Walking out to the station concourse, I registered the uniforms and the mix of civilians. It was a habit you picked up quickly. Mostly the soldiers were German. The police were Italian. As I had seen across France and through Italy, when there was something to be checked, a German usually stood somewhere in the background. Here they were more obvious. But even so, mostly the station was full of people going about the ordinary business of catching trains and getting off them. The cafés were busy and there were long queues at the ticket offices. There was a buzz, too, of ordinary noise that had the echo of any great railway terminus.

I stood for a moment, looking where to go. I assumed there were taxis.

'Mr Gillespie?'

A woman was standing in front of me. She was dark-haired, in a dark suit, not quite short and not quite tall. I was out of the habit of being struck by a striking woman, but it seemed no bad thing to be struck just then, after a night with a couple of dozen drunken German troops. The smile was refreshing in itself. I was conscious that after almost four days without a change of clothes, I wouldn't be.

'I'm from the embassy.'

'Do I look that Irish?'

'You're holding an Irish passport.'

'Ah, right, I am. I thought someone might want to look at it.'

'I have a car outside, Mr Gillespie.'

She reached out her hand. I reached to shake it. She laughed.

'No, your case.'

I shook her hand anyway.

'Stefan Gillespie.'

'Vittoria Campana.'

'I can manage the case, Vittoria.'

She shrugged in a way that said more than you'd expect a shrug to say. Something like, if you want to do my job, don't expect me to thank you for it.

She walked on and I walked beside her.

'I don't know how you guessed the train though.'

'By coming to the station three times yesterday and twice already today.'

She didn't say, I thought you were a detective, but I heard it.

Outside the station there was a mulberry-coloured car. She opened the back door. I thought I'd rather sit in the front, but I was sure that wasn't the way the job was done. Two put-downs in the space of a couple of minutes would do for now.

She started the car and pulled out into the traffic.

'You had a good journey?'

'A long journey.'

'The way things are if you arrive it's a good journey.'

She had a solid line in conversation stoppers. Was that a joke?

For now the city itself took over. Whatever reason I had for being here, Rome was not any city. Just looking out at it from the car was unavoidable. There was nothing I recognised immediately, except that somehow it was all recognisable. Church after nameless church, but not needing names. And then, as the car pulled out into a wide avenue, there was the Colosseum. I almost said something, as if what I was looking at needed comment. I shut up. By now I had concluded saying nothing was a better option when it came to stating the obvious.

The car stopped just past the Colosseum. I had been aware of the uniforms in the streets. Outside the station they were carrying machine guns. I had seen tanks at several street corners, though the crews were standing in front of them smoking. But now there was a roadblock. An armoured car at a junction.

A wooden barrier and a string of barbed wire, funnelling vehicles and pedestrians into a narrow gap. German troops with rifles slung on their shoulders. Two men with machine guns, looking slightly more serious. A raised barrier where black-shirted Italians were checking documents. I assumed they were police. Behind them, as always, the Germans, in this case a group of SS men and two others in plainclothes. I knew them for what they were, Gestapo. With little traffic, we soon reached the barrier.

Vittoria wound down her window and held out a document. She spoke briefly to the Italian policeman, who nodded, looking back at me several times.

'He needs your passport, Mr Gillespie.'

I wound my window down and passed it out. He looked at it for a moment, then walked away, handing it to one of the SS men. They spoke for a few seconds. The SS man walked to the car, smiling broadly. He handed me back the passport.

'Vedo che vieni dall'Irlanda. Posso chiedre dove?'

'Non parla Italiano.' It was Vittoria who spoke, without looking round.

The German ignored her but he changed his language.

'Sprechen Sie Deutsch, mein Herr?'

I answered in German. He told me he had an uncle who worked in Ireland before the war. He didn't know where, but he was there for a year with Siemens. Was it a power station they were building? I told him it probably was. His aunt had shown them the photographs of a holiday they'd had in Kerry. Was it Kerry? He thought it was. Was that a place? Beautiful beaches, she always remembered the beaches. Beautiful beaches and they had them to themselves. Good days though!

He stopped as suddenly as he started. His Irish anecdote was done.

'Are you staying in Rome long?'

'I don't know.'

He looked round, then leant in closer to the car, grinning.
'Who does?'

The SS man waved the car on. Vittoria engaged gear and continued driving. I was conscious that her silence was somehow more silent than before. That was the only way to describe it. Before it had simply been silence, now it seemed to suggest something harder. I saw her glancing at me in the rear-view mirror.

'Is there a lot of that? Roadblocks, I mean, document checks?'

'Enough. It depends on their mood.'

I nodded. She was looking in the mirror again, curious.

'You speak very good German, Mr Gillespie.'

It wasn't a compliment. I shrugged and said nothing. I could see a conversation about my mother's family wouldn't endear me to her. There was already a lesson though. When in Rome, be careful not to overdo the German.

4

VILLA SPADA

The car was skirting the city to the south, avoiding the centre. Too much traffic, too many checkpoints, Signorina Campana told me, as if it would give me some bearings. The further out, the easier. I had no bearings at that point. I watched the unknown streets go by. There was no shortage of grand buildings. Heavy stone, square and triumphal, I assumed from the new regime that had now become the old regime. Ugly, you had to say, set between the pale plaster of older villas and apartments. A lot of that plaster in need of a coat of paint but looking like it would gleam anyway when the sun shone. I thought the sun must do a lot of the heavy lifting when it came to smartening the place up. For now, clouds closed in. It was warm and sticky. So the plasterwork was peeling. I liked that. It was probably always going to look a lot better than the Rome they had just stopped building.

Vittoria had given up on any commentary. Maybe she didn't think there was any more to see. Or she'd done enough. Or everything I said made me sound like an ignorant fecking Irishman. But she spoke as we crossed the Tiber. That would be something, I thought, but not as much of something as I expected. Like a lot you think you know, the river was smaller.

It was shut in by stone walls like the Liffey in Dublin, though it was lighter and brighter and lined with trees. There was no great backdrop of the city where we crossed, but it still put the view of the Liffey from a room on Wellington Quay in the shade. And it had come up in the world since it was the dumping ground for Ancient Rome's executed criminals, assassinated politicians and secret policemen. I didn't doubt that two thousand years on, Rome kept up to scratch with assassinations and secret policemen, but the river was tidy enough. They must have found somewhere else for the bodies.

Wide, leafy streets brought us to a big house set in a garden of tall trees.

'Villa Spada,' said Signorina Campana. 'The embassy.'

The Lancia stopped at the front door. It was another building that if not quite grand was heading in that direction. White plaster, elegantly peeling too, and red roof tiles that hadn't changed in more than two thousand years. An Irish tricolour drooped from a pole across the garden, by the iron gates, in need of a breath of air.

As she opened the rear door of the car, Vittoria leant in and picked up my suitcase. She smiled. That was something. She would not let me beat her this time.

The front door of the house opened and a West Highland White Terrier raced out, barking enthusiastically. Until it saw me. The bark was replaced with a growl.

Vittoria bent down and scratched the dog's head, laughing now. I assumed at me.

'This is Finn. You're safe enough.'

'You mean his bark's worse than his bite.'

'I don't know, Mr Gillespie. He's never bitten me.'

She walked into the house. Finn waited for me to follow her, then followed me, barking, but definitely not with any enthusiasm. At the door was a woman in a black dress. Her grey hair was scraped back severely, but her smile was simpler than Vittoria Campana's. At least it didn't seem to ask any questions.

'Mr Gillespie, welcome to the Villa Spada. The ambassador is coming.'

'Thank you . . . signora.'

As I entered, Vittoria was heading upstairs with my case. She called back.

'It's Signora Rosselli! If she likes you, Finn will . . . eventually.'

Eventually was some way off. Finn continued to bark at me.

'Silenzio!' The barking stopped. Finn slunk under a table. I didn't blame him. It was a word of profound authority. But he still watched me suspiciously.

A man walked into the hall. He was tall, balding. I thought in his sixties. He wore a heavy pinstriped suit that seemed out of place. The sun had reappeared now. The hall was bright. It was cooler inside. The stickiness of the day had gone.

'Gillespie! You made it. And Vittoria found you?'

'It seems I was easy to find, sir.'

The ambassador, Michael MacWhite, shook my hand.

'There's a room upstairs. But first things first. Some food!'

We ate in a dining room at the front of the house, at a long table that made it feel as if we were waiting for more people to arrive. But the food was good. I hadn't eaten anything except cold meat and half-stale bread since leaving Madrid. I don't know if the wine was good but after four days of smoke-filled carriages and station platforms it tasted like the sunshine beyond the window now. I needed it.

'You know the situation here?'

'More or less.'

The ambassador was giving me the kind of expansive description of events that he might have sent back to Dublin. I thought it was likely to be his version of small talk. I thought he also had almost no one to say all this to most of the time. Whatever I was there for, he clearly welcomed the opportunity to deliver his remit.

'The Italians were never as enthusiastic about this war as most of them claimed. Very different from Germany. But when it looked like all they had to do was hang on to Herr Hitler's coattails to be on the winning side, why not? There'd be great victory parades, extra territory in Europe, more colonies. All at little cost.'

'But not that simple.'

'Not at all. Disaster after disaster. And last year the disasters weren't only Mussolini's. The British routed Rommel in North Africa. The Russians did the same at Stalingrad, but with a finality that is only whispered in German circles. And then came Sicily. The British and now the Americans. And next the invasion of Italy itself. It wasn't the stroll to triumph that the Italians thought they'd signed up to. So they locked Benito up, whisked the king out of Rome, then promptly surrendered. A couple of weeks ago the Italian government in the south declared war on Germany. And it's that government, headed by the king, that Ireland recognises. Or do we? Silence signifies . . . whatever. We're used to talking out of both sides of our mouth and saying nothing. It's the speciality of the neutral state. Meanwhile, the government the Germans set up after they rescued Mussolini, doesn't exist outside the Duce's imagination. It's a German war. Rome is under German occupation. It might not look like that all the time, but that is the reality.'

'It looked like it to me,' I said.

'Not that you won't be able to find time to see what you want to see.'

'But I assume Joe Walshe didn't send me here to sightsee.'

'No, he didn't. What he wants . . . I don't know why it matters if I'm honest. But he thinks it does. He calls it house-keeping. I don't even know what he means.'

The ambassador stood up.

'You go upstairs and settle in. We'll talk in my office. An hour?'

I finished the last of the wine and pushed back the chair.

'Is there a bath?'

'There is, Gillespie.' He laughed. 'And it's probably not a bad idea.'

An hour later I was as spruce and as fresh as I could manage with one clean shirt and no clean socks. When Signora Rosselli knocked on the door to see if I had any laundry I was able to tell her that was pretty much all I had. She shook her head and said she was very sorry. I thought I'd have to work on the humour a bit more.

I had brought nothing in the way of diplomatic baggage from Madrid except a letter, from Leopold Kerney to Michael MacWhite. He read it. He was amused.

'How did you get on with Leo?'

I gave a shrug that was as non-committal as I could manage.

'He says I need to watch you. He says you're an arsehole.'

'It's probably my lack of diplomatic training.'

'Is he right?'

'That you need to watch me or that I'm an arsehole?'

He screwed up the letter and dropped it into a wastepaper basket.

'An arsehole may be no bad thing.'

It was his opening gambit on why I was there.

'I had a message from Joe Walshe. Coded, as if you're some kind of secret, though anyone can decode the bloody things. In this case, they'd be none the wiser though. I don't know what you know, but you're here to do this . . . housekeeping.'

MacWhite opened a cigarette box and took one out. He pushed the box across the desk. I shook my head. I didn't want one just then. If I felt sweeter outside, I still had the smoke from that carriage of German soldiers in my lungs. He lifted up an onyx cigarette lighter that could have doubled as a paperweight.

'Flotsam and jetsam. I suppose that's what Joe means by housekeeping. Things to tidy up that no one ever considered might need tidying up. It's the nature of war. Our stuff doesn't amount to much in the scheme of things, but there's been a little debris along the way. For a lot of countries these things can be matters of life and death. It's maybe a sad state of affairs that our concerns have more to do with embarrassment somewhere down the road. There are some . . . I don't know what they are myself . . . let's say anomalies. The powers that be in Iveagh House and the Taoiseach's office have decided that, looking ahead, some things need getting in order and some things that aren't in order need getting out of the way.'

'Well, it makes no sense at all to me, sir. Does it need to?'

'No.' He liked that response. I didn't need to understand anything.

'Looking forward meaning . . .' I smiled. 'An end to the war.'

'I'm not holding my breath, Gillespie, but it's out there. I assume something that needed sorting out was what made you so very popular with Leo in Madrid.'

He would have loved to know about Madrid. He knew I wouldn't tell him.

'I'm a policeman, Mr MacWhite, not a diplomat, not even an Intelligence officer. Whatever it is you want me to do, I'll do. For the rest I follow Dublin Castle's rules of engagement. If you don't know, it's not my job to tell you, sir.'

He laughed. I almost wondered if it had been a test. I thought we'd get on.

'Right, Inspector, no gossip at all. You'd be hopeless as a diplomat. So, business. A little bit of Irish flotsam that's collected up in Rome is a man called Charles Bewley. He's an ex-Irish diplomat. One time Minister to the Vatican.'

'And Berlin after that. Sacked just before the war.'

'Good, you know something about him then.'

I knew more than something.

'I've met him. I was in Berlin in 1940.'

MacWhite was surprised. He wasn't sure what to do with what I'd just said. I could see he didn't like knowing less than the people who worked for him.

'It might have been useful if Dublin had told me.'

'It'll be in a report somewhere, but it's not anything anyone would remember. We're not old friends. When I met him I was with a German policeman who was asking him what he knew about a man who'd had his head blown off.'

The ambassador was even more surprised, but this time he smiled.

'Sounds memorable enough. And did he know anything?'

'No.'

'And that was it?'

'More or less. He seemed to think I must be there to send a report on him to Dev. He said I might want to tell Mr de Valera he had an important job with Josef Goebbels and he was the only Irishman in Berlin with the ear of all the top Nazis.'

MacWhite shook his head. He liked this story.

'Now that's very Charles. What did you make of him?'

I hadn't thought about any of this in a long time. I wasn't with Bewley long but I recalled a few things I'd noticed. Wherever this was going, I guessed they might be useful if I met the man again. Such small things you keep to yourself.

'Not much that I remember, sir.'

The ambassador pushed a file across the desk.

'So, here it is. He lives in Rome now. He has for some time. The Germans found him less useful than he led them to believe in Berlin. I think he offered himself as an expert on Ireland. But I'd say after they'd had their fill of his inside knowledge about Irish politics – the totality of which was that he thought

Dev was a British spy and if he wasn't, well, he was a cunt anyway – they jettisoned him.'

I took a cigarette. I could cope now. The pleasantries were
done.

'I don't know if it's a good thing or a bad thing, that you've
met him,' said MacWhite. He was looking at me hard. 'Will
Bewley remember who you are?'

'There wasn't a stream of Garda detectives in and out of his
flat in Berlin.'

'I don't know. You might find it useful. It might even be the
way . . .'

'The way to what?'

'The job is to burgle his apartment. That's why you're here.'

It was my turn to laugh. 'Just like that.'

'I don't know about just like that. What you have to get
out . . . isn't small.'

'What is it?'

I was asking the question as if the thing was already
underway, as if somehow the only thing that needed discussing
was the size of what I had to steal.

'When Charles left the embassy in Berlin, he took a lot with
him. I'm talking about papers and documents. It wasn't an
amicable departure. He cleared his office, you might say, with
malice aforethought. He's said since that he only took personal
papers, but he took a great deal more besides. No one's very sure
what, except there was plenty of it. He was a man who made
decisions without any reference to anyone. When I say anyone,
the truth is he was more likely to discuss his decisions about what
he did in the Irish legation with someone in the German Foreign
Office or pals in the Nazi party than with anyone on his staff, let
alone with the Department of External Affairs at home. He was
not well supervised, to put it mildly. But at the time it didn't seem
to matter much. Looking back, a lot of what he did doesn't
reflect well on us. How, isn't your concern. It doesn't matter.'

In Dublin they must have thought it mattered a lot. Why else was I there?

'This is what . . . over four years ago, Mr MacWhite?'

'Sometimes it takes a long time to recognise the significance of a mistake, especially a mistake that it's not very easy to rectify . . . by conventional means. As I said, no one knows exactly what he's got, but he made some strange decisions. There's no doubt he has material that could be awkward for Ireland, even after all these years. I'm not saying it's important in itself. We're not talking state secrets.'

'Do we even have any?'

He smiled more easily. A bad joke seemed to offer relief.

'You do know he has all this stuff?'

'How do you mean?'

'That it exists. That it actually is somewhere in this flat?'

'A few times, he has almost said as much . . . a boast . . . a sort of threat.'

'This isn't about some kind of blackmail? If it is, you should say, sir.'

The ambassador's mood changed. He had said enough. Whatever it was the Irish government wanted out of circulation wasn't my business and he was close to talking as if it was. I didn't need to know more. He wanted to get back to business.

'The point is simply that Bewley has boxes of documents that he took from the embassy in Berlin, without authority. It seems likely he used the material to impress the Reich Propaganda Ministry or to polish his credentials as an expert on Ireland. But it's what he might do in the future that has become more . . . pertinent.'

He wanted to say urgent, but he avoided the word.

'We know enough to believe the material is in the study of his apartment here. People have been in there. It's a while ago now, but he produced something . . . to prove a point, what-ever. He is more cautious now than when he was first in

Rome. I think he believes he has something to get out of what he has.'

'And I have to do what? Break into his flat and get this stuff out?

The ambassador took another cigarette. He grinned.

'That's it.'

'Why now?'

'He's thinking of leaving Rome. He has been in here, trying to renew his passport. Like everyone else, he can smell the beginning of the end. He wants out.'

'But not yet.'

'I don't know. But he'll wait a long time for an Irish passport.'

'Or at least until you have what you want?'

MacWhite shrugged.

'So, a city I don't know. A language I don't know. A war all round us. And I walk into this man 's flat and clear out his study. How do I know what to look for?'

'Charles is a very meticulous man.'

He lit the cigarette. He nodded as if he had answered the question.

'Does that help?' I said.

'He also thinks he's the cleverest man who ever came out of Ireland.'

'That's better.' I smiled. 'Unless of course he is.'

My mind was working now. Mostly it was telling me this was something I should not even try to do. But that wasn't an option. This was why I was in Rome. And maybe the way Rome was, would make it easier. Did anyone much care what went on now? I didn't know what passed for a police force, but I didn't think the theft of old papers was high on their list of priorities. But how? A simple break-in wouldn't be the way. I would have to come from a different direction. I'd need to find out more about Mr Bewley. There were things I knew. It was coming back.

'How long have I got?'

'As long as you need, Gillespie. Just do it before the Allies arrive.'

A joke to end, but he had to work at it. I could see he didn't much like this. He was doing what he'd been told to do. Me too. I took the file he had given me.

'I'll need money.'

'Naturally.'

'That may include the kind of money that buys . . . well . . . assistance.'

'I understand. And you'll have no need to keep a record of where it goes.' He meant he didn't want to know. 'But a word of warning. Your man keeps unhealthy company. I presume he acts as an informer for the Germans. I have it from a number of sources, including a reliable Vatican contact. Low-level, I'm sure. Not any more than gossip probably. But he's in and out of the Via Tasso.'

'What's that?'

'The Gestapo.'

He threw it out as if it was Charles Bewley's Stephen's Green club.

The bedroom was at the front of the house, looking down at the drive and the gate. The ambassador's dog followed me up the stairs and sat, watching. He was no longer growling, but he kept a wary eye on me. If Finn and I hadn't hit it off, I had a feeling for his importance and his presence. It would be an empty house at night, with a lot of empty rooms. It would be quiet, even lifeless. I knew who the Villa Spada contained. As we left the dining room after lunch, MacWhite ran through the short list of people working there. The list of those who lived there was shorter.

Lavish was never the word for Irish embassies. None I'd seen. Here, there was Michael MacWhite himself and the one permanent member of staff the Department of External Affairs had given him, his secretary, Mrs Butler. I didn't meet her straightaway. He shared her with the other Minister in Rome, the ambassador to the Vatican. She did live at the Villa Spada, but apart from her and the ambassador, and Finn, there was only Signora Rosselli, the housekeeper. Her husband, Salvatore, was the gardener. I had seen him for only a minute, bringing in wood for the kitchen, I never saw him do much else. Mostly he sat in the kitchen drinking coffee. When I glimpsed him in the garden, coming in and out, he was smoking a pipe and peering at some tree or shrub as if it puzzled him. I think he spent a lot of time planning what he ought to do. Or maybe there wasn't much that needed doing. Whenever he saw me he said something cheerful in Italian and laughed. I never knew what he said, but I laughed too. I felt he thought we were both sharing a joke. As far as he could see, it looked like I didn't do much either.

The striking but sharp Signorina Campana drove the ambassador's car and worked in the office with Mrs Butler, whose Italian, according to MacWhite, wasn't as good as she thought. But his was worse, so he left the women to it and assumed anything he had translated bore some relation to what he had written. After the staff rundown, he gave me a list of churches where I might want to go to Mass. I nodded as if I'd think about that. He said they had a chaplain who came over from the Irish College, but only to scrounge a meal and play chess with him.

He laughed. He found that funny. I smiled as if I did too.

'He should be in now, I think.'

The ambassador headed across the hall. I followed. He opened a door into an office. At a typewriter a young priest typed with two slow fingers. A mop of light hair, a round face, younger than his years. In his late twenties. He stood up.

'Donal, there you are.'

'I am.'

'This is Mr Gillespie. Stefan Gillespie. You remember?'

'I remember he was coming.'

'This is Father Hyde.'

The priest walked forward and we shook hands.

'Donal is the real ambassador. Maybe not ambassador, but consul. Which is far more important. He's the one who keeps me in touch with the Irish community here. He knows where they are and what they're doing. If they need help, they go to him. They know better than waste time with me. And he's a deadly chessman!'

The priest shrugged a self-deprecating shrug.

'Am I right, Donal?'

'I like to think you're right about the chess, Michael.'

'I am, unfortunately. Nine times out of ten he beats me, Gillespie.'

My nod suggested a level of interest I didn't intend.

'Do you play chess, Inspector?' said MacWhite, fixing my gaze.

I had a vision of long evenings with the ambassador, the chaplain and the dog. Finn, I suspected, would offer the nearest thing to entertainment, even with a bottle of good wine. I lied and said I didn't. I detected a faint smile from the priest.

Meanwhile I had a map of the city now and the address of the curious Mr Bewley. I needed to get to know Rome a little and to see where this feller lived.

Upstairs, I opened my suitcase to put a few things in the wardrobe. I'm not a tidy man by nature, but I have routines. I do things the same way, out of habit. The case contained shoes and polish, a bag with a razor, hairbrush, toothbrush, soap, cufflinks. There was an overcoat and a couple of ties. Books and a carton of Spanish cigarettes that were too much for my lungs. Most of my clothes were with Signora Rosselli. There was nothing so very odd about the case, except that it didn't look quite the way it did when I took the dirty clothes out earlier. Nothing was exactly out of place, but it wasn't packed the way it had been. Someone had looked through it while I was with the ambassador. I now opened the briefcase that passed, when locked, for an Irish diplomatic bag. All it brought from Madrid was the letter telling MacWhite what an arsehole I was. There were punched train tickets and travel warrants, my passport, railway timetables that had proved useless anyway, a notebook with the erratic scrawl I often couldn't read back myself. There was money in an envelope, sterling, dollars, French francs, lire. I knew what was there. Nothing missing. But like the case, the briefcase had been searched.

I couldn't think of many reasons why anyone at the embassy would want to search my belongings. Theft was the first thought. I hadn't seen much of Rome but these were hard times. Anything was possible, but it didn't seem likely. Besides, everything was there. The money, most of all, down to last small-change notes.

I closed the case and locked the briefcase, puzzled more than troubled. I walked to the window, pulling on my jacket, trying to imagine what interest my belongings could have for anyone in the embassy. I looked down to the front of the house. The Lancia was parked. Vittoria Campana was getting into it. As she did, a man came from the back of the house, wheeling a bicycle. It was Father Hyde. He came to the car. Vittoria got out. They didn't speak, or if they did, there were no more than a couple of words. He took an envelope from his jacket and gave it to her. He turned immediately, got on the bike and rode off out to the street. Vittoria went to the back of the car. She opened the boot and put the envelope in, pushing it under something as she did. It didn't occur to me that she was making sure the envelope was hidden, but if you'd asked me afterwards, I'd have nodded.

I was still watching as Vittoria slammed the boot, took a key from her pocket, and locked it. She tried the handle to check it was secure. She walked back to the open driver's door. She got in and drove out. An odd transaction. I could say no more. It held my attention. I had no reason to keep watching, but something about what they were doing was out of place. The lack of words, the way they moved, the peculiar care for a plain envelope, the unlocked boot that needed locking. There could have been a thousand reasons for it and a thousand more for why it meant nothing. However, two strange things had happened in the space of minutes. If the second one wasn't my business, the first was. Yet when small things are out of place, there's always something more to know. At the very least it suggested more going on in Michael MacWhite's embassy than he knew. I hadn't spent nights as a boy reading Sherlock Holmes under the bedclothes with a torch for nothing. If anyone had gone to search my room, except the people who lived and worked in the villa, we would have known. Finn would have made sure of it.

5

CENTRO STORICO

I set out with a map of the city and no clear idea of what I was doing. I had the address of Charles Bewley's apartment. Nothing more. I had to see what that looked like, though the idea I would be shinning up a drainpipe in a mask to break in, if that's what the ambassador had in mind, was not a very likely scenario. Whatever I did, I knew that it would be down to me though. MacWhite did his best to look as if he was engaged, but if a ewer of water had been available when he finished speaking to me, he would have washed his hands very thoroughly. The short version of what he didn't say was, 'Don't tell me and don't get caught.'

For now I needed to know the city. The best way was to walk it, from the west side of the Tiber into the centre, the Centro Storico. Bewley's flat was somewhere there, between clusters of ancient monuments and the Stazione Termini. I had seen something of that en route to the embassy. I knew already that the centre was where the German administration based itself. It wasn't so hard to get in and out, but it was full of soldiers. There were roadblocks and document checks. It was patrolled. There was no curfew according to MacWhite but at night the German patrols were thick on the ground. It wasn't encouraging that the Gestapo HQ in the Via Tasso was only a few streets away from where Charles Bewley lived. It wasn't going to be a great place to get caught doing anything suspicious after dark. As I walked over the river into the Centro Storico, I wasn't sure the best bet wouldn't be to return to the embassy and say it couldn't be done. I had a feeling Michael MacWhite wouldn't mind, whatever Dublin's instructions.

I did have a kind of map of Rome in my mind already. It was a version of the one I'd stared at for five years as a boy, in the Classics room at Wesley College. The Forum, the Colosseum, the Circus Maximus, the Pantheon, the Domus Aurea. It was a start. And since most of these things were still there, whatever shape they might be in, they were there to steer by. They pegged out the shape of the city for me as I worked my way around it. They were like stars for an ancient navigator. I was never far from something I knew, something I had a picture of in my head, a couple of blocks east or west, half a dozen streets north or south. And for now, marking out these things took over. Walking over the brow of a steep street, I saw the Forum. I knew it. I didn't even remember I did. But there it was. Heaps of rubble and grassy mounds that had names I recognised written on them but were still unrecognisable as anything other than mounds of grass and stone. But there was enough to hold on to, even in a row of columns or a pedestal, enough to see what had been. The Temple of Saturn, the Temple of Vespasian and Titus, the great Arch of Severus, above all the plain square building that was the Senate. There were greater monuments to see, the Pantheon and the Colosseum, and I saw them that afternoon, with the map in my head as an excuse to forget the thing that had brought me into the Centro Storico. But in the Forum there were voices. I knew them too. They belonged to my childhood, but they were still there.

There weren't too many people doing what I was doing, but walking the city, ancient and modern, staring at everything, scribbling notes on a map, wasn't unexceptional. It was what the German guards and the Italian police expected, where in Berlin or Paris, even in London, you'd have found yourself questioned about what exactly you were doing. Here, there were German troops, in all varieties of field grey and black, doing the same thing as me. In the Forum and by Trajan's Column I was stopped and asked to take photographs for soldiers to send home. We exchanged idle conversation about Rome as if we were all on holiday.

It was late afternoon when I reached the street where Charles Bewley had his flat, in a row of simple but elegant apartment buildings. There was nothing in the road to warrant much attention from a tourist making his way from one ancient monument or church to another. There were a few shops, but mostly it was residential. One shop sold cameras. I bought one and loaded a film. It was more prop than tool, but a few photographs of the street and the houses would be useful. And a little way from Bewley's flat, on the opposite side, was a small café. I got a beer and sat at a pavement table, with the leisure to take the building in. I knew from MacWhite he was on the second floor, facing the street. There was a door to a hallway, glass and heavy wood. A little further on was an archway into a courtyard. I could see little walking past, but sometime I would take a closer look.

For now I had seen all there was to see. It was as unsurprising and unpromising as I could have expected. I walked across the street and ambled past the apartment building one more time. At the entrance to the arch a car horn blasted. I stepped back. A convertible was coming out, clearly with no intention of stopping for a pedestrian. It was a red Alfa Romeo. Very red and very bright and very polished. I only knew what it was because it was one of the few facts about Charles Bewley's life in Rome mentioned in the embassy file. It was driven by a young man in a grey uniform, multi-buttoned and topped off with a snappy peaked cap. He was as elegant as the car. And that was another oddity among the sparse facts. Bewley had a chauffeur who lived in the flat. Even reading the notes it had seemed a remarkable indulgence for an ex-ambassador who was still writing to the Irish government to demand the pension he had never been paid after he was sacked, claiming that he had no income. Seeing the car and its nattily coordinated driver, it was even more remarkable. I watched the Alfa Romeo pull away. I wasn't likely to create any curiosity by looking. The car and uniform were for admiring.

Maybe it was the peak on the cap and a little bit too much tailoring, but I was reminded of MacWhite's words about Bewley's association with the SS or the Gestapo or whoever it was he popped in to see round the corner. The Via Tasso was only a few streets away. All that suggested, whatever the ambassador thought, a level of familiarity, even protection, you'd treat with some care. But it was probably worth taking a look at the Via Tasso. Just to sniff the air around Charles Bewley. I wondered if that was part of what I was there for, to find out more about what he was. If he had material that might embarrass the Irish government, was he still embarrassing it in some way? That Bewley file was certainly thin on detail.

I turned round to take one more look at the street. It wasn't busy, but further along a man came out of a shop doorway. He took a few steps in my direction, then turned, more quickly than I just had, and walked briskly away. I watched him, as he took the next left turn and disappeared. It was the movement that caught my eye, unnaturally abrupt, a bit of panic. My change of direction had caught him out. I knew the dark clothes and that mop of hair. Father Hyde. He was following me.

Two strange things were now three, and two of them involved Donal. I had no idea how long he had been following me, but he hadn't just stumbled on me and decided to do it. I had walked all over the centre of the city that afternoon, but

I had no reason to think I needed to take care. I was preoccupied anyway, never mind the job in hand. I had been lost in Rome, my head full of just that, Rome. It wouldn't have been difficult to keep me in sight, even for someone who didn't know the ropes, though to be fair, he was better at it than I'd have expected.

Passing the street the priest had turned into, he was gone. I carried on. I walked slowly. If he was going to try and find me again, I wouldn't make it hard. And he found me. I caught his reflection in a shop window, looking round a corner. Now I knew he was there it was easy enough. He would keep me in sight.

By now I had reached the Via Tasso. It was another street like Bewley's. The buildings were a tad grander, palazzo-sized rather than apartment blocks, but that was all. There was a barbed-wire barrier as I approached it, but it was pushed to one side. The German soldiers who stood next to it looked me up and down. One of them nodded and I took it there was no reason not to walk through.

There were more soldiers in the street itself, most of them outside a couple of cafés, most of them officers. There were plenty of riding boots propped up on chairs that had never been anywhere near a horse. Black SS uniforms mixed with field grey. But there were shops in the Via Tasso too, doing business as armed men wandered by, looking in the windows more than at the passers-by. They looked bored. A daily routine maybe. A more vigilant group guarded the entrance to one of the palazzo-sized buildings. That had to be the lair of Charlie's familiars, though it was hard to imagine the familiarity amounted to a lot, even if he was a regular.

I didn't pause as I passed the Gestapo building, but I glanced back. My tail hadn't followed me. Maybe he'd given up. Maybe the Via Tasso wasn't a street he felt comfortable in. As I was wondering if he'd gone, there was a soldier in front of me. He asked me in German for identification. I presented my passport. The glance was peremptory once he registered what it was. He nodded me on and gave a courteous tap to his cap. It seemed casual, but this street was well-watched.

Leaving the Via Tasso I began to head back to the river and the embassy. It wasn't long before I was aware of my companion. He had watched me go into the Via Tasso and decided to avoid it. He must have taken a parallel street and waited till I emerged at the other end. By now I'd had enough. I took several sharp turns. I moved faster, without giving any appearance of it. I didn't need to know Rome to negotiate a couple of blocks and come back on myself. I didn't need to know where I was going to get behind him. I saw him by the Colosseum, looking around blankly. As Donal abandoned the search and walked on, I was now following him. It wasn't difficult and all the easier because it was beginning to get dark. It looked like he was taking the route I wanted as well, towards the River Tiber.

I kept only half an eye on the dark figure ahead. This wasn't the way I had come. From the map I assumed he was taking a different bridge to the one I had used earlier. My mind was still marking out the city, as best I could, with ancient points of reference. I had run out of the ones I knew but coming up was the Theatre of Marcellus. There would be more columns, Doric and Ionic, and more broken arches. Nothing much changed along the priest's way back, at least nothing I noticed. The buildings were a little smaller, a little shabbier. Then ahead there was a straggling line of people. There was a military truck and a small, armoured car. The clusters of German soldiers looked purposeful for once. It was a checkpoint.

I slowed down to let Father Hyde join the back of the queue. I needed to wait till he went through or I'd find myself standing next to him. But as he walked towards the line an SS officer beckoned him on, past the queue and the checkpoint. It seemed a priest didn't need his papers checked. I didn't have that advantage. I joined the line. I'd lose him, but no matter. I would find him at the Villa Spada.

The SS officer was patrolling the length of the queue, looking hard at the men and women in it. There were Waffen SS troops with rifles unslung from their shoulders. But there were no Italian police, none. It was somehow more intense than anything I had seen so far, even at Gestapo HQ in the Via Tasso. And it was slow. Ahead, at the checkpoint, there seemed to be a lot of questioning. It was very laboured. One officer leafed through sheets of paper. I thought they must be names. I noticed that no one in the line met the gaze of the SS man walking past. They either looked away or looked at the ground. Glancing at the map again, I saw what I had not noticed before. Beside the Theatre of Marcellus was the Great Synagogue. I caught, looking up, the top of a square-domed building in stone.

I took my passport out. The SS officer had noticed me. In some way I stood out. I met his look and nodded. It made me stand out more. He came closer.

'Che passaporto è?'

I answered in German.

'I don't speak Italian. It's Irish.'

No one looked round. No one looked up. I felt the silence.

'Let me see.'

I handed him the passport. He flipped through it and handed it back.

'You can go on through. The queue is for Jews.'

I stepped out uncertainly. But I nodded. I did as he said.

'Do you have some business in the ghetto?'

'No, just aiming for the river. Heading back to the Irish embassy.'

'You'd be wise to choose another way. Don't you know that?'

'I do now.'

He wasn't impressed by my answer. He shrugged and moved on. I saw there were questions that needed answering and questions that did not. That one did not.

I walked through the checkpoint unimpeded, round a corner towards the white building that was the synagogue. Now I had the smell of it, there was a different atmosphere here. If nothing else, it was quieter than the rest of the city. People I passed glanced at me and looked quickly away. I felt uneasy. They knew each other here. I sensed that if you weren't known you needed to be avoided. And then I saw Donal Hyde again. I hadn't lost him after all. He was coming out of a building just past the synagogue. I slowed down again to create the necessary distance. I took in the brass plate beside the door he had come out of. The words were Italian and Hebrew. *Biblioteca Ebraica* was easy enough to read.

Father Hyde was moving faster. He looked at his watch at intervals. He crossed the river and I tailed him at a pace that matched his. I assumed he was making for the Villa Spada. When we got there I would ask him what the fuck he was doing. It didn't seem an unreasonable question. I also wanted to know if he had anything to do with the search of my room. If so, why? Who told him to do it?

Suddenly the priest changed course.

He turned off the main road once we were over the river and very quickly I was following him through a maze of narrow streets that took unexpected directions. Short passages and twisting alleys. Every so often a square or piazza opened up. There might be a church, a fountain, a few tables at a café. Donal moved through these intervals of space and sky and into more narrow passages. I just kept in touch. If he'd been going much quicker I'd have lost him a dozen times. There were plenty of people. Wherever we were, it was lively, noisy. This was a different place from the Rome across the river. I had no idea where I was. No monuments to mark my way here. It was almost dark. Lights were few and far between. I was as much on the priest's tail to find an exit as for any other reason.

I came into another square to see Donal walk past a table of men playing cards and go into a café. It wasn't more than an open door with a bright window and a tiny bar beyond. He sat at a table by the door and I saw him talking to someone. On the other side of the square was a church with a wide colonnaded portico. The doors were open here too. There were people standing outside and on the step under the portico. I was suddenly visible. The square wasn't big and there were lights. I walked up the steps to the church. There was a Mass on. The smell of incense was strong by the door and there was the droning monotone of Latin.

As I knew from Spain, Mass, with all its trappings, could be a casual affair. Men stood around the bright doorway, smoking and talking. Even inside there were groups of men standing at the back, holding whispered conversations. The women took the thing more seriously, but some of them were wandering out with their children, taking a breath of air, engaging in a few minutes' conversation, and turning back again into the church. It was more offhand than even an Irish priest would have tolerated, let alone the stolid Protestant ministers who'd glowered over my Sundays as a child. Here, they moved in and out of the church as casually and as perfunctorily as they breathed, but then breathing did have a lot to recommend it.

I stood in the shadow of the columns and smoked a cigarette, invisible enough since no one was looking. In the café, Donal Hyde was drinking a glass of wine. The wine seemed like a good idea. I had been walking Rome for several hours. It wasn't a bad time to ask what the game was all about, as well as to get some assistance in finding my way out of the maze this priest had led me into.

I took a last drag on the cigarette and stubbed it out. I was about to emerge from the portico when I saw something that stopped me. A car had driven into the square. It pulled up outside the café. It was the ambassador's car. The mulberry Lancia that had collected me from the station. Naturally it was driven by Vittoria Campana. As she got out, Donal came out of the café and opened the passenger door. A big man was almost wedged in the seat. He struggled to get out and Donal took his arm and pulled him. The man was bigger out of the car than he was in it. He towered over the priest. He could have been six and a half feet. He was wide as well, not fat, but heavy. Something said all that heaviness was muscle. If that size and strength was notable in itself, so too was the long robe that contained it and reached to his sandalled feet. Even in Holy Ireland the distinctions of the religious orders weren't always clear to the outsider, but the rough brown of a Franciscan friar was unmistakable. However, they didn't often come this big.

The friar clapped his arm round the priest's shoulder, laughing. As he moved towards the café he stumbled and laughed even more. Donal took his arm again, this time to steady him. Either there was something wrong with the big man or he was drunk. The way Vittoria's eyes followed him into the bar didn't call for any commentary. There was exasperation and anger. The friar was clearly drunk.

The signorina stepped to the table where the men were playing cards. Two of them immediately got up and went into the café and disappeared behind the bar. I don't know that she spoke more than a couple of words. It was as if the men were doing something that was pre-arranged. Or obeying an order of some kind. That's what it looked like. I imagined Vittoria would probably be good at giving orders.

Mass was ending and people were drifting out of the church. I stayed where I was, in the shadows under the portico.

The crowd of Mass-goers chattering in the square kept me even more securely out of sight. I pulled out another cigarette and sat down on the steps. They were an interesting pair, Signorina Campana and Father Hyde. Entertaining, certainly, and here was more. It wasn't the first time I'd seen a priest or monk pissed, but there was something about the way they wanted to keep him quiet that was more than just embarrassment. It wasn't quite right, any of it, even somewhere I didn't know or understand. It didn't feel that this was a sensible place to tackle Donal Hyde, let alone Vittoria as well. This wasn't the airy, open city I had walked though that afternoon. This was a closed-in space. I had the feeling that the German soldiers who slouched against their tanks on street corners in the Centro Storico or meandered up and down the Via Tasso asking for identification, would not be so easy coming here. There was nothing wrong with my sense of smell, in any language. Nothing much was happening at all, yet I knew it was the kind of nothing that shouldn't be seen.

6

TRASTEVERE

Vittoria walked to the back of MacWhite's car and unlocked the boot. As she did so the two men who had gone into the bar reappeared. One carried a big square basket. It was the kind of basket you might use for bread and there were loaves piled high on top. But the way the man held the thing, bending to push it into the boot, it was heavy. Heavier than bread, anyway. The second card-player held two jerrycans. Vittoria opened one of the Lancia's rear doors and he shoved them in. I guessed that was petrol. Difficult to get everywhere if you didn't have an army to hand, even in Ireland. But I thought that however the Irish ambassador fuelled his car, a backstreet bar was unlikely to be the source. What was going on wasn't hard to read. In some shape or form this was the black market. So far, in what I'd seen all across Europe, so normal. We even had our own version at home. It was Lilliputian, but it was one area of war that we engaged in with some enthusiasm.

With the breadbasket and the jerrycans stowed, the men who had brought them from the bar, along with the other card-players, walked away, into a dark alleyway off the square. It was sudden and silent. A job was done, it seemed. At the same time the crowd in front of the church was dispersing, the buzz of conversation fading. But then there was a loud, echoing laugh. The big Franciscan came out of the bar with a glass and a bottle of wine. Donal Hyde followed him, looking like a man looks when he's sober and he doesn't know what to do with a drunken friend who's about to make an eejit of himself. The friar sat at the table the card-players had vacated. He shouted something at Vittoria who was locking the car boot. She liked to keep that boot shut. He held up the bottle, offering her a drink.

Signorina Campana didn't want a drink. She spoke to Donal as he sat down next to the friar. Her words were few, but I didn't need to hear them to know they were sharp and purposeful. She was more than irritated by their pissed companion. She was holding back anger. It felt as if she was worried. The Irish priest nodded and said little. Again, this was a woman giving instructions. The Franciscan had forgotten about offering her a drink. He was filling up his glass.

Vittoria said something to the friar. It was shorter and sharper still. He looked up and grinned. Then he stood and stepped forward, shakily enough, and clasped her in his arms. Pushing him away was not easy. His words were loud.

'Grazie! Grazie! Dio ti benedica! Come un angelo! Grazie!'

I got the gist. Probably a lot of people in the surrounding houses got it too.

The big man finally let go of Vittoria. He held up his hand to bless her as she moved back to the car. She gave Father Hyde one final look, raising her hands in exasperation, and her parting words were in English, as if to hammer them home.

'Get him to the palazzo! I have to drop the car at the villa. Get him out!'

She got in the car and drove away. Donal Hyde stood up. He was impatient, but he wasn't relishing his task. He said something in Italian. The Franciscan laughed, turning to the table and picking up the bottle. He filled the glass and thrust it

64

at the priest. Donal shook his head. I could almost hear, 'For fuck's sake!'

The friar shrugged and drank the contents of the glass in one. He poured more wine and then clapped his arm heavily on Donal's back yet again. He was laughing in a way that bore no relation to anything except what was in his own head. A stage of drunkenness incomprehensible to anyone unfortunate enough to be sober. He raised the glass as if he was toasting the night sky and called out something I couldn't understand. Not that I thought it was there for understanding. There was some Latin. I got a bit about drinking, about the soldier drinking, the priest drinking, everyone drinking. Then some language I couldn't even guess at.

'Bibit miles, bibit clerus, bibit ille, bibit illa . . . blagoslovi vino . . . vino . . . i blagoslovi molitve koje Bogu upućujemo . . .' He sang in a deep bass. 'Amen!'

The owner of the bar appeared in the doorway.

'Silenzio, cagacazzo!'

I didn't know what the second word meant, but I improvised.

The friar looked round and threw his empty wine glass on to the cobbles.

'Fuck off!

So, he knew some English. Father Hyde grabbed him by the arm and pulled him away. The big man chose to go. No one would have shifted him otherwise. He had lost his glass, of course, but he still had the bottle of wine, as yet unfinished. The barkeeper spat on the ground and went back in. The door slammed. The light went out. Now the square really was silent. I got up and walked out from the church's colonnades. In my head the idea of talking to Donal Hyde, and now Vittoria Campana, was taking a shape that was about more than finding out what was going on. I had a job to do and no sensible idea of how to do it. The priest and the driver moved in unexpected circles. There could be something there. But that was for another day. For now, I was lost in a warren of narrow, empty streets and dark alleyways. Though I knew I couldn't be far from the embassy, there was no chance of finding my way without some help. I decided to keep following the Irish priest and his noisy friend. It wouldn't be difficult. Whatever Donal was doing, he was following Vittoria's orders. She was going to the embassy. He had to do something with the Franciscan. I thought I might as well get some idea what that was. The more I knew, the more a conversation with the two of them might prove useful. I set off, following Father Hyde a little less cautiously than I should have.

If it wasn't hard to follow Donal, even in the dark, it was that much easier because of the chatter the friar kept up as they walked. He was still cheerfully drunk and loud enough that I didn't need to get too close. But I was deficient in information about the Franciscan that might have made me more careful. You don't expect a drunk to have some corner of his mind that's thinking clearly enough to notice anything very much, let alone that he's being tailed by someone who knows what he's doing. You don't expect a drunk to find that kind of alertness. The exception might be a drunk who hasn't quite forgotten that one of the reasons he's pissed is because he's got an idea there's someone out to kill him. I didn't know the big man was being taken somewhere to hole up. But that's what was going on. That's what Donal and Vittoria were doing with him. And he thought he was safe. But there was still that voice in his head, emerging out of the stew of alcohol, that told him to watch, to listen, to sniff the air. And somehow he had got the sniff of me. Maybe I did get too close to them. Maybe I took it for granted I was too good at all this.

I should have noticed that the big man was quieter. It didn't happen all at once, but little by little the laughter stopped, and the garbled words were fewer. I could still hear footsteps.

I could still glimpse them every so often under a light or crossing some junction of winding passageways. Then it was suddenly still. I'd lost them, when only moments before they had been there, a little way ahead. I stopped, listening hard. There was nothing. I realised they must be there, very close, but now standing completely still, just as the friar's voice rang out at me.

'Hai bisogno di aiuto, amico?'

I didn't understand the Italian, but I knew it was for me.

'Cosa vuoi?'

I said nothing. I would have to go. But where? Behind me was a narrow alley, leading back to more narrow alleys. I would be more lost than ever.

'Un povero frate e un prete? Nienti soldi qui!'

He laughed, then spoke in German.

'A poor friar and a priest? No one worth robbing!'

I heard Donal's voice, hissing, indistinct, probably telling him to shut up.

'Cosa vuoi? Perché non vieni qui?'

The big man stepped forward. I could just see his shape, the dark robe.

'Zar ne razumiješ, gade!'

That other language now, whatever it was. Then German again.

'What do you want? Not a thief then? Maybe a fucking spy!'

Something came flying through the air towards me. It smashed only feet away from me. It was the empty wine bottle. Not a bad shot for a drunk in the dark. A drunk who couldn't see me but knew where I was standing. The next words were in German too. They were louder, angrier. They were delivered on the run.

'Come here! Come here, so I can break your fucking neck!'

I was running as well, with no thought of where I was going.

I heard Donal Hyde's voice, shouting helplessly in English, then Italian.

'Come back! It doesn't fucking matter! Ritorno, Luca!'

There was enough light to see a turning. I took it. I didn't know whether I was going back the way I'd come or not. All I knew was that this big man was not far behind me. And all that size and heaviness was in my head. Drunk and furious. And something else. I sensed fear in his voice, even as he declaimed at the darkness. That was more dangerous than the alcohol or the anger. I couldn't know what it was about, but I knew it wasn't going to end well if he caught me. There were a few dim lights in windows above the street. Enough to see something by, but not much. Another turning, another alley. I plunged into each one I came to. I only needed to keep going. I had to maintain what speed I could, but it meant I could be heard. And I heard him. Something had sobered him. He was still close.

As I ran out through a stone archway, I knew where I was. The little square. The bar in darkness. The fountain bubbling. The portico of the church with its colonnades. I had gained some ground. But I had to give him the slip. Another street might do it, but I couldn't guess how well he knew the area. He wouldn't need to know much to know more than me. I had seen enough to realise there were dead ends in this maze. I had been lucky not to take one. That luck might not last.

I ran to the church. I could hear his feet echoing. I moved into the darkness of the colonnades. The Franciscan entered the square. He was running, breathing hard. Maybe he wasn't fit, but neither was I, and he had stamina. He would keep going. He stopped as I had stopped, looking round. He stood by the café, listening intently. I stayed where I was. Surely he had to assume I had run on and taken one of the streets out of the square? There were two besides the one we had both entered from. I had to hope he was too drunk to wonder if I was hiding. That he would choose one exit or the other, drunkenly, blindly, and keep blundering on.

He walked slowly round the fountain, still listening, still hearing nothing. If he came towards the church steps I would have to make a decision, to risk staying hidden, or to run, straight past him to the alleyway opposite, trusting I was faster. He sat down at the edge of the fountain. He reached into his robes and took out a cigarette. I could see him lighting it. I think the alcohol had caught up with him more than anything. He had used up what energy he got from whatever had driven him to pursue me. But now I was trapped. As long as he sat there I couldn't move. And I didn't know what he was going to do. His mind might be moving slowly again, but there was no reason he might not suddenly decide to search the square.

The friar looked up. He had heard something. Maybe I was concentrating on him too much, but there was nothing wrong with his senses. I had heard nothing. But now someone else entered the square. It was Donal Hyde. He saw the Franciscan standing by the fountain and hurried across to him. He was relieved, I could see. He spoke quietly. I thought in Italian. I couldn't hear anyway. For a moment the big man said nothing. But he was still agitated. When he did speak, that combination I had heard when he first spotted me was there again. There was anger, frustration, but behind it fear of some kind. I couldn't understand what he was saying, but that camaraderie I saw when Vittoria Campana delivered him to the café was gone. This was a man who was not in control. It was no longer about being drunk. Donal Hyde was trying to calm him down, but now he was almost sobbing. His voice wasn't as loud as it had been, but it echoed around the square.

A shutter opened. Yellow light shone from an upstairs window. The Italian words that followed didn't need translation. They were variations on *shut the fuck up*. Father Hyde took the Franciscan's arm, but the friar was still in no mood to accommodate anyone. He was up for lashing out as he had wanted to lash out at me. He answered the abuse thrown at him from above in the spirit with which it had been thrown. Another window opened. Someone else started to call down at the square. The big man gave this newcomer an equally voluble response. Donal again tried to grab at the Franciscan and drag him off. The friar shoved him to the ground and stormed across the square, swearing, still screaming out at the people shouting at him, presumably telling them to fuck themselves. The Irish priest got up, brushing himself down, now alone. A third window opened and the beam of a torch shone out. It lit the colonnade of the church as it swept across the portico, accompanied by another furious voice. For a few seconds I was in the beam. Donal Hyde was looking straight at me. I could think of nothing to do except smile and shrug. The torch moved on. Donal was running out of the square, following the friar, it seemed more spooked by me than anything else that had happened. Above me windows and shutters closed. The lights went out. The square was black again. It felt safe to come out of hiding. Now all I had to do was find the way back home.

I took the same exit from the square as my new friends, except that where they left at speed I dawdled, smoking a cigarette and making sure they were gone. It was the way I had followed Donal Hyde into the square earlier. I didn't know that I could remember the route, short as I was on the proverbial ball of thread, but it was a start. And as I walked, it felt as if the alleyways were getting wider. There was a little more light, not just from the occasional window but some street lamps on the walls. Then there was noise. Some music on a radio. There were people talking and laughing. I came out into a much larger square, bright by comparison with the alleyways behind me. There was a café and a restaurant. And no one took any notice of me. I was back in something like the city. I sat at a table and ordered a beer. I discovered I was already at the edge of the warren that was simply marked as Trastevere on the map. The waiter had enough English to direct me out to the road that would take me back to the Irish embassy.

The Villa Spada. There was a light on downstairs, dimmed by a blind, another one upstairs. I hesitated as I approached the front door. The car must be back by now. If Vittoria seemed to be on a loose rein as far as driving it around all day, it must be in the garage for the night. I retraced my footsteps and walked round to the back of the house, keeping away from the villa, close to the shrubs in the garden. There was a courtyard of rough cobbles. There were no lights from what I knew was the kitchen, just a pale bulb in a window higher up, a landing on the stairs. On the other side of the courtyard was a low building with several sets of double doors. Stables once but now the villa's various outbuildings and garaging. I walked across and examined the doors. The first set were half open. Inside was a stack of cut firewood. There was a padlock on the next set. There was also a small window. It was dirty and cobwebbed, but I could just see the back of the car. I needed the torch from my case, but I didn't want to go into the house to get it. I didn't know who I'd meet, but I did know I'd encounter the bloody dog, Finn, and that would be that. I would make do. There'd be light to see what I wanted to see, whatever that was.

The padlock was so feeble it hadn't been worth the effort of snapping shut. I didn't have a penknife with that peculiarly popular tool for getting stones out of horses' hooves, but there was a thin, pliable blade that served well enough to pick the lock. Inside the garage the boot was no harder to release. As I opened it the first thing was the smell of coffee. I couldn't see, but I could feel some sacking on top of the basket that had been carried out from the bar in Trastevere. I flicked on my lighter. The bread was gone. I could see small, tightly packed hessian bags of coffee beans. I knew that was a familiar black-market currency.

Then I noticed, sticking out under the basket, a white envelope. I assumed it was the one I saw Donal give Vittoria that morning, that seemed to call for locking the boot. I pulled it out and opened it. It contained two new, blank Irish passports. I pushed the envelope back. The flame on the lighter was flickering. It would soon go out. I moved a couple of coffee bags to one side. There was another smell now, oil or grease and then something sour and metallic. There was more hessian too, a big heavy sack, folded and stuffed down into the basket. I lifted it at one end.

Underneath, at the bottom of the basket, was an automatic, a Luger. I shifted more coffee. There was something bigger and heavier. I saw a curved magazine first, then a steel stock folded back on itself, then a barrel. It was a machine gun.

7

L'APPARTAMENTO

The mulberry Lancia was pulling away from the Villa Spada as I came down the next day. Signora Rosselli was sweeping the dust from the hall through the front door out to the drive. She looked up from her broom and nodded. Finn lay on a gilt chair, watching me. His teeth were bared, but he wasn't barking. A step forward. I walked out into the morning sun. The car moved through the gates and was gone. The guns that had spent the night in the ambassador's garage would be gone too, I assumed, wherever they were going. It was hard not to feel that Mr MacWhite gave his driver a lot of latitude. Access to petrol was obviously a problem – so maybe he didn't ask where it came from – but it seemed at best generous, at worst indulgent. Vittoria drove his car as if it was her own. I had yet to see him in it. Still, appearances suggested the signorina had more pressing business than her boss.

Turning back into the house, the signora had gone. Finn was still in the chair. He growled and closed his eyes. Almost a welcome. He opened his eyes again briefly as the door from the kitchen corridor opened and Father Hyde came in. No growl for him. As the priest still had bicycle clips on, I gathered the flush on his face was from the ride to the embassy, but he went a shade redder seeing me. There was no question. He did see me and recognise me in those seconds in Trastevere. He knew that his attempt at surveillance had resulted in me following him, with all that followed in the shape of the drunken Franciscan. I had my own botched surveillance to contemplate too, along with relief that the big man hadn't caught up with me. I also had the contents of the ambassador's boot to reflect on. I couldn't guess how much the priest knew about that, but he knew something. I wasn't sure what I would do with it, but I wondered if I could make use of it.

Donal had known he was going to see me at some point. He must have known it wasn't going to be comfortable. The only way of dealing with it he had come up with was to pretend nothing happened. It was possible he hadn't recognised me in his torch beam, but the odds were against it. Still, I wasn't going to let him off.

'How's it going, Father?'

He looked relieved. Did he think I was going to pretend too?

'Mr Gillespie, good morning.'

'Stefan,' I said genially.

'Is the ambassador about . . . Stefan? We have a meeting—'

He was hoping Michael MacWhite would appear to end the conversation.

'I haven't seen him yet.'

'I'm early enough. I'll just . . . I need to sort out . . .'

He tailed off with an awkward smile and opened the door to the office, abruptly acquiring the air of a man with a lot to do. He was about to shut the door but I was at his heels. I followed him in, then shut it behind me. I grinned at him.

'We should have a chat, Donal.'

Silence. A slightly hunted look.

'Did you get your friend home in one piece last night?'

He frowned, on the verge of asking me what I was talking about.

'The big feller, I mean. And, Mother of God, big is the word.'

He shook his head. If he'd brought any lies with him, they were defunct.

'I'm not sure I'd be in one piece if he'd got hold of me. Well oiled! But that's only half of it. An angry man? A frightened man? What's the story, Father?'

It was a moment longer before he said something. He was weighing what I might know and might not. What was the minimum he could say? But he was no better at this than following me through Rome. He didn't see I was testing him.

'I'm sorry. You're right, Stefan, he had been drinking.'

'Let's leave the big feller for a minute. I was following you because I saw you following me earlier. You do need to up your game on that front, Donal.'

I could see his mind racing, but he had no answers.

'I don't think following me was your decision. And I can't see why Mr MacWhite would want to know what I was doing, when I was doing what he told me. I can't think why Signorina Campana would want to know what I was doing either, but working on principles akin to Ockham's razor, and not multiplying available entities unnecessarily . . . well, she's there when you hand over the passports you filched from the embassy . . . I doubt anyone gave them to you.'

He was getting more worried about what I knew. Now, a very hunted look.

'She's there to drop off your sozzled Franciscan in the embassy car. She's also picking up a delivery in Trastevere that I don't think Mr MacWhite would feel happy storing overnight on what passes for Irish soil. So, Vittoria's in this, right?'

The passports had hit home, but he avoided those.

'Everyone uses the black market for something. All of us do. It's the way people survive. Petrol, coffee, even bread's hard to get. It's the same for Vittoria.'

'And passports are worth a lot of money, especially neutral ones.'

I wasn't going to let him off that easily.

'It's not about money!'

Donal was moved. A flash of anger. A thief maybe, but an indignant one. And I didn't sense guns in that indignation. For now the guns would remain silent.

'Well, let's put the motives to one side, Father. I don't know how many passports Mr MacWhite keeps on hand, but whatever your reasons for giving them to the signorina, I wouldn't overdo it. Let's just say, for now, it's about a few jerrycans of petrol. Seeing how she runs around in the embassy car, it's only fair.'

Now he was confused. He had believed, and why wouldn't he, that I was about to go to the ambassador and denounce him. He could see I wasn't going to.

'Let's start with following me. Why?'

'I just wanted . . . to see . . . I knew you were a policeman . . .'

'Begin at the beginning, Donal. Who told you to do it?'

'She thought . . . Vittoria thought . . .'

That was better. She'd been the one giving orders at the bar.

'The passports are to help people escape . . . or hide . . . there are Allied prisoners of war in Rome . . . and people on the run from the Fascists . . . they need documents . . . identity papers. It's only a few passports. They can save lives . . .'

Definitely no whiff of gun oil, I thought.

'Where do I come in? I still don't get that.'

'She thought the ambassador . . . had become suspicious.'

'And I was here to investigate?'

'Yes.'

'Seems a bit extravagant. Couldn't he just lock them in the safe?'

He shrugged as if he had explained enough. He hadn't.

'Unless there's more to come out.'

'I don't know what you mean.'

'More at risk, with me sniffing around. Maybe more than you know.'

He didn't like that. I wondered if he didn't like it because there might be truth in it. Even a priest might turn a blind eye to a lot for Signorina Campana.

'There is a system for helping people. Of course there are risks.'

Too pompous. He was giving me the holier-than-thou.

'Donal, I'll buy that you're on the side of the angels. I won't buy there aren't times you'd look away and cross yourself if you saw something you didn't want to see. Vittoria wouldn't ask you to ride round Rome on your bike with a machine gun in your communion set, but how surprised would you be if one found its way into the boot of Mr MacWhite's Lancia? She wouldn't want a policeman stumbling on that, wherever he came from. So it's worth knowing what I'm up to, isn't it? Black market or no black market, isn't she using the Irish embassy for cover? And as long as you don't see anything, Father . . . that'll do for you. What do you say?'

He shook his head. He'd fucked it up. Fucked it up for her. It was easy to read why that mattered. If he was on the side of the angels, Vittoria was the angel.

'The great art, Donal, is to know when to do fuck all.'

'What do you mean?'

'It's not why I'm here, not at all.'

He couldn't make any sense of that. I wasn't going to explain.

'So what now, Stefan?'

'I don't care about the passports. Unless the ambassador notices he's been robbed, it's nothing to do with me. If someone's using his garage to move . . . whatever . . . around Rome, that's nothing to do with me either. No one's really asked me to inspect the embassy's security. Until someone does, if you think it's worth it, do what you like. But the job I do have to do . . . I'll need help with it.'

'I don't understand.'

'Not help from you, Donal. From Vittoria. Or from people she'll know . . . because I'm sure she'll know the right sort of people . . . or she'll have friends who do. If that doesn't make sense to you, it will to her. You might tell her that. Say I don't give a fuck what she's doing . . . but there's a small price for that. A favour.'

At that moment the door opened and a woman I didn't know came in.

'Ah, Father Hyde, the ambassador's waiting for you.'

He left, muttering something indistinct, and relieved to get out.

'Mr Gillespie, I'm Mrs Butler, the ambassador's secretary.'

She reached out her hand and shook mine. She was in her fifties, thin and unfussy, with quite sharp features that I could see probably reflected a sharp mind.

'You had a reasonable journey? I won't ask if it was good.'

'It got me here. I'm told that's good enough.'

'I'm sorry I didn't see you yesterday. I work for Mr Kiernan at the Vatican Legation as well. I was over at the Via dei Corridori. If there's anything you need, let me know. I know you've settled in, but you will need some expenses, I assume.'

'I think Mr MacWhite has sorted that out, Mrs Butler.'

She pursed her lips. I wasn't sure whether the bad marks were mine or the ambassador's. I didn't tell her I wouldn't be accounting for any money MacWhite gave me, however I ended up spending it. He wouldn't be accounting for it either.

'So, Mr Gillespie, what you will have to do is tell me precisely what you need to see, in terms of documents and records and anything else that's going to be relevant to your security audit. I'm not quite clear yet what it actually consists of.'

I could tell Mrs Butler, despite the smiles, didn't like not being quite clear what my security audit would consist of. I imagined that in the general run of things, she knew more about what was happening in the embassy than anyone else, including the ambassador. I was an anomaly and she didn't know which filing cabinet I belonged in. And since I didn't know what my non-existent security audit was going to consist of either, I was in no position to help her.

'I'll let you know, Mrs Butler. It will be a very . . . general . . . look.'

She was unimpressed. As explanations went, I wasn't impressed myself.

'I see. Well, when you know what you want, I shall be here, Inspector.'

Later that morning I left the embassy, heading into the city. The ambassador was coming in from a walk with Finn. I heard the dog barking round the corner of the Via Giacomo Medici before I even saw MacWhite. Finn must have smelt me, bath or no bath. The dog appeared, straining at the lead. I was the object of his attention.

'Shut up, Finn! For God's sake!'

Finn wasn't intimidated by God's name. Now he was growling.

'He'll get used to you,' said the ambassador, cheerfully.

'Maybe he just doesn't like policemen.'

'No, it's anybody, he doesn't like anybody much.'

I thought I'd better say something that showed I was working.

'I'm going to see Mr Bewley. Is that all right with you?'

MacWhite frowned as if he'd rather I hadn't bothered.

'Is that a good idea?'

'It's the only one I've got at the moment.' That wasn't entirely true, but if any other ideas proved useful, they would do so without the ambassador knowing. 'I need to see inside the flat. I need to know what happens there. At first glance the outside isn't promising. I want at least to get some idea of the interior layout.'

79

'You still think he'll know you?'

'I'm sure he will. But if my visit's official, it makes me more credible.'

'What do you mean official?'

'He's waiting for a passport no one's in a hurry to give him.'

MacWhite looked puzzled. Finn continued to strain at his lead.

'You did say he wanted it badly, sir.'

'More badly than he did. Presumably because he wants to leave Rome.'

'What does he think the delay is?'

'Bureaucracy.' The ambassador smiled. 'My stock reply.'

'The Department might have some queries then?'

'The only query Joe Walshe has got is giving him a passport at all, Stefan.'

'I've looked through the file, sir. I can find enough questions. About what he was doing in Berlin, after he was sacked. It doesn't matter what the answers are.'

The thought amused MacWhite, but he wasn't quite easy with it.

'He will love the attention. He'll be unpleasant though. And very pissed off that I haven't asked him to come into the embassy or gone to call on him myself.'

'Well, he'll enjoy putting me in my place.'

The ambassador laughed. 'I think you have him, Stefan. To a tee.'

Finn was still straining on the lead, but rather than trying to get at me, he wanted to get away. MacWhite was pulled towards the gates of the Villa Spada, slightly off balance and at speed. But Finn wasn't the only one who wanted to retreat. The parting laugh had been more awkward than the ambassador meant to show. He didn't much like what I was there to do. Whatever his feelings for Charles Bewley – uncharitable to say the least – I sensed he probably believed diplomacy shouldn't stoop to the grubbiness I was there to engage in. I wasn't sure that kept him at the coalface of what I'd glimpsed of diplomacy, but having delivered his instructions as ordered, I could see that now he didn't want to know anymore. He wanted it done, out of sight and as far as possible out of mind. That was no bad thing. Where I was heading, I already knew he wouldn't want to come.

'Did you have some coffee this morning, Stefan?'

The ambassador called back, turning as Finn pulled him on.

'We just got some. The real McCoy!'

So were the guns. He disappeared into the Villa Spada. But first things first. At least the embassy was getting something out of Signorina Campana's sideline.

I risked a tram from the Viale di Trastevere, still finding out what was useful in making my way around the city. I got off close to the Stazione Termini. It was further than I needed go, but I wanted to come at Charles Bewley's apartment from a different direction and take in the streets close to it. The exercise provided nothing more than increased familiarity but I had to acquire that quickly. In Bewley's street I walked past the entrance to his apartment, I looked up again at the smooth, flat walls and the impenetrable windows of the second floor. Not even a balcony. Just past the doorway was the arch I had already noted, leading to a courtyard. I wandered in with the unsure gait of someone who must be lost.

The courtyard was small. It was paved and there were wooden tubs with flowers along one side. Walls stretched up, as flat and plain and unaccommodating as the front of the building. There were heavy doors at the back of the yard and another wall, older than the apartment block, black stone and a few barred windows. Some sort of warehouse. There were also three sets of garage doors. One garage was open. The red car inside was Bewley's. The apartments themselves formed an L-shape. There were few windows at ground level and they were small and barred or boarded up. There was no way to reach the bigger, higher windows. There was no fire escape. There were three doors into the block. Two of them were heavily padlocked. They would lead somewhere, but it looked like somewhere a long way from the apartments with windows on to the street. The wall that formed the back of the street-front apartments had a short run of stone steps that led to a bigger door. Clustered round the steps were high metal rubbish bins. Boxes and crates were piled up by them. There was nothing else. This door might be the one.

I was looking up at the windows above the door when it burst open, outward. A man emerged, carrying a box of empty wine bottles. He was in shirtsleeves but I recognised him immediately as Bewley's chauffeur. He stopped on the steps. The expression on his face wasn't particularly suspicious, but it was definitely far from welcoming. I gave him my best innocent-abroad smile.

'Cosa vuoi? Privato!'

I got the gist, the tone provided the detail.

'Do you speak English? I'm looking for Mr Bewley's apartment.'

He carried on down the steps. He put the box down next to one of the bins.

'Is there something wrong with the front door?'

'I wasn't sure which . . . the directions the Irish embassy gave weren't . . .'

This seemed to mollify him. I was speaking in English and I'd been sent by the Irish embassy. I could read that it was enough. An idiot sent by other idiots.

'Go back to the street. Left and then the double doors on the left.'

'Thank you.'

'Do you have an appointment with Signore Bewley?'

82

'Do I need one? Either he's in or he's not.'

The chauffeur didn't bother to answer. He was less sure I was an idiot though. He shrugged, went back up the steps and slammed the door behind him.

I walked round to the entrance to the apartments. The hall was cool and elegant. There was a floor of bright tiles, flowers and acanthus. There was a wall of a dozen rectangular letter boxes, above a table scattered with newspapers and magazines.

There was a corridor off with several heavy doors. A wide staircase took up half the hall, with white marble steps and black cast-iron banisters with more acanthus. There was nothing to see here either. I registered Signore Charles Bewley's name on one of the mailboxes. I climbed up two flights of stairs to the second floor.

As I reached the landing a small door opened at one end. The chauffeur came out. That was the staircase that led to the courtyard. I smiled at him again. He walked past me to a door further along. He pushed it open. Only then did he turn.

'Your name, signore?'

'Gillespie, Mr Gillespie.'

'From the embassy?'

I nodded.

He stepped back to let me in. It was a small hall, but it had the same elegant tiles and high walls that made it feel bigger. There were prints of Rome on the walls. I thought if I knew about prints, these would be the expensive kind. The chauffeur walked on down the hall and through another door. He didn't tell me to wait. It felt like that was what I was supposed to do. Another door opened, almost without noise. An elderly woman in black, wearing a spotless white apron.

'Your hat, signore?'

She gestured at the hat I was now holding.

'Thank you. I'll just hold on to it.'

She smiled but it wasn't the right answer.

'Has Alfredo informed the signore?'

I assumed that was the chauffeur's name. I nodded. He reappeared.

'The signore will see you, but he says do you have a card?'

'A card?' I laughed. 'No, I don't have a card.'

I could see Alfredo was a stickler. He didn't like me laughing.

'Under the circumstances, as he doesn't know you . . .'

'Don't fret, Alfredo, I might surprise him. We're old acquaintances. But he's very lucky to have you. It's not every ex-ambassador who has a head of protocol.'

As I walked into the room, I heard the woman's voice, very soft.

'Chi è? È irlandese?'

Alfredo's reply, fired at my back, didn't bother with softness at all.

'Sì, è irlandese, un bastardo irlandese!'

8

IL SOGGIORNO

I entered a big, bright living room with big, bright, old furniture. No prints here, only paintings. I doubted they were old masters, but they were respectable impersonations. The room was empty. I stepped further in, towards another door on the far side. The door was open. Charles Bewley came through it. He smiled, but it was a smile that mixed a little puzzlement with slightly more irritation. He didn't know me and he already didn't think I looked like someone important. In that respect he wasn't a bad judge. But I knew him. A brief meeting three years earlier. The receding temples had receded a little more. The toothbrush moustache was too dark not to have been given a bit of help. I had forgotten about the moustache. Maybe he should have done. The fashion for toothbrush moustaches was waning.

'Mr Bewley.'

I nodded. He nodded back, still sizing me up.

'Mr Gillespie.'

I could see behind him, though the open door, the room he had just left. Bookshelves, part of a desk, a filing cabinet. That was the study. That was where, according to the only information I had, the material I was meant to get out of this apartment resided. Nothing I had seen so far suggested there was a simple way.

'Mr Gillespie, I don't know you, do I? Are you new?'

'I'm new enough.'

He was looking at me more quizzically. I guessed a memory stirred.

'Your position?'

'I don't know that I have one.'

'Second secretary, third secretary? Attaché?'

He sniffed slowly as if to say I didn't fit any of those grades.

'Since when did the embassy run to more than one man and a dog?'

He was going to be big on put-downs. I thought that wasn't bad.

'You know the dog then, Finn?'

He wasn't going to let me play games.

'I assume you're here to do more than pass the time of day.'

'It's about your passport, Mr Bewley.'

He almost looked pleased. That interested him.

'Sit down then, Mr Gillespie.'

He gestured at an armchair. It was plush stuff. Lemon velvet with too many cushions to sit on it properly. Despite its size I was perching more than sitting. Bewley sat on a sofa. The same velvet. Even more cushions. It was all plush. And a little too much of everything, from the cushions and the ornaments and the tapestry curtains, to the gold stripes on the wallpaper, the pale carpets and the tassels on the gold lampshades. Joe Walshe might have stopped his pension, but it hadn't cost much more than his dignity. He had some money, no doubt about that.

'We do know each other, sir.'

He arched his eyebrows as if he doubted that.

'We met in Berlin. Three years ago. I was assisting the German police with an investigation. It happened to involve someone in the Irish community there.'

I didn't know if he remembered anything. An Irishwoman who nearly went to the guillotine for killing a man. But I knew the memory wouldn't suit this room.

'I have some vague . . . weren't you some sort of policeman?'

He used 'policeman' as he might have used 'swill'. But sometimes so did I.

'I'm seconded to the Department of External Affairs.'

'Have they run out of diplomats?'

'I'm looking at security, that's all.'

The vaguer the better. Details would be beneath him.

'So you're nobody in particular.'

'That's about right, sir.' I smiled as if admiring his perception.

'So, where is my fucking passport, Mr Nobody-in-Particular?'

I enjoyed the next bit.

'Mr MacWhite has some questions.'

He stared. His face was sour. He thought I'd brought it.

'Concerning the passport.'

He made the best of the defeat.

'Well, there's no point me rehearsing the length of time this is taking, but I'm glad the man has finally got off his arse to set the bloody thing in motion. It can't be easy with all the aimless activity involved in being an Irish ambassador in a city where nobody gives a toss for you or your country. So where is the thing?'

'It's still held up . . . due to some queries from the Department, in Dublin.'

'You mean Joe Walshe.'

I shrugged my best what-would-I-know-about-that shrug.

'Dear old Joseph. What an old woman. And of course, a profound cunt.'

I took out my notebook. I had no interest in what the man said. But a notebook smacked of something demeaning now he knew I was a policeman. 'Is that something you'd like me to pass on to the ambassador?'

'Save your wit for the public bar, Mr Gillespie. You can pass that message on with pleasure, as long as it reaches Iveagh House. Get on with your questions.'

I looked down at my notebook as if I wasn't making it up as I went along.

'You worked for Reichsminister Goebbels, at the Ministry of Propaganda?'

'I was consulted on Irish matters. That doesn't make me an employee.'

'Were you also consulted by the German Foreign Office?'

Bewley sat back. He didn't dislike the questions. They fed his ego.

'Ribbentrop offered an Auswärtiges Amt job. That is the Foreign Office.'

I looked grateful for the translation. If he thought I was a fool, good.

'Again, I felt a salaried role was inappropriate, as an ex-ambassador.' The ex-ambassador still relished that title. You could hear it. 'I was happy to give advice and provide a depth of knowledge about Irish affairs that no German could hope to possess, naturally. But I was never concerned about money. I had enough to live modestly. And I'd done rather well selling a very luxurious Packard I owned to a friend. You couldn't buy an American car then for love nor money.'

I don't know why he thought selling a car would impress me, but he waited for a moment, as if he expected me to congratulate him. There probably wasn't much Mr Bewley did that didn't remind him of his acumen. I smiled. It sufficed.

'My aim was very simple. I wanted no particular rewards beyond the proper recognition that belongs to any field of expertise. I wanted to be useful to Ireland and to Germany. But I was determined that if I was to have any influence on the fate of Ireland after a German victory, it was essential for me to keep my independence. I did. That didn't always sit well with the less perceptive Germans.'

Bewley stopped, as if he had explained everything that needed explaining. He leant forward to open a silver cigarette box. He took out a cigarette and lit it. He sat back again, drawing on the cigarette, as if there was nothing left to say.

'A long time ago now, Mr Bewley.'

'What is?'

'That German victory.'

He didn't like that, but it was hard to argue with.

'Perhaps, as they saw it then. But the thing is by no means played out.'

I thought I'd keep him going. I was starting to want to irritate him.

'Well, it's not finished. We can all see that.'

He summoned a little more contempt for the smile that accompanied his next declamation. The idea I was venturing any opinion at all really did call for a smile.

'We can. War is still war . . . and the Tiber still foams with much blood!'

He laughed. Not at the words but at watching his quote fly over my head. But at least there was someone to hear. Any fool would do. For a moment, I thought he had forgotten why I was there. This was a man with something to say.

'Germany was never the real enemy for Britain or America. Herr Hitler always knew that. But English arrogance and American ignorance . . . the blind leading the blind. Where else can democracy lead you but into the ditch? And the real enemy is still there, masquerading as a friend. I'm sure even Stalin can't believe his luck. He's got the very clowns he intends to destroy fighting on his side against the only power on earth that sees the Bolsheviks for what they are. All that Messrs Churchill and Roosevelt are missing are the funny hats and the red noses.'

89

I felt this could go on some time. He was mostly looking through me as he spoke. I was still looking idly across the room through the open door to the study, but I'd seen all I was going to see of it. It wasn't helpful. I closed the notebook.

'I think we can leave the questions there, sir.'

'And the passport?'

'Mr MacWhite will send the paperwork to Mr Walshe.'

'And how long is that going to take?'

I shrugged, giving him my best I'm-only-the-messenger smile.

'It's a pity there's nobody with the wit in Dublin to recognise that far from hurting Ireland, my connections with the National Socialist Party, and with powerful politicians and diplomats, military men too, could have been extremely beneficial. But I was undermined, always. Another reason they didn't listen. De Valera saw to that. He did a remarkable job on some very gullible Germans. You can't credit him for much, but you can for that. But despite everything, I could have helped Germany make sense of Ireland, even help Ireland. If the Führer had taken the chance to crush England in nineteen forty, when he had his hands on its throat—'

He spread his hands expansively to express that lost opportunity.

I stood up. I had wondered if getting into Bewley's apartment might be hard. Was he too suspicious about the embassy? I was wrong. It was harder getting out.

He gave a world-weary sniff, a new variation on his repertoire.

'The Germans are an admirable race, but they don't respond well to anyone who knows better than them. But I never intended to stay in Berlin indefinitely. My connections here go deep. I was Minister to the Vatican before Berlin, of course.'

'I'm sure you've kept your connections everywhere, sir.'

The look he gave was more contemptuous than defensive. If I was unable to understand his importance when it should have been self-evident, there was little he could do for me. But the sore was still there. And he couldn't stop picking at it.

'My views were on record. I had nothing else to offer. Nothing they wanted. Nothing they understood. But then they didn't know what they wanted. It wasn't worth my time. The depths of their ignorance about Ireland weren't for me to plumb. They could do it themselves. I wrote a few articles for the Berlin dailies, sketches of diplomatic characters before the war, short stories about the idiosyncrasies of English life. They were rather well received. But I was bored.'

He sniffed his bored sniff. I was bored too, but it still seemed worth pressing the button in Mr Bewley's pier-end panorama. A penny in the slot and he'd be off.

'And you wrote a book about Mr de Valera, of course.'

I put a hap'orth of real respect into my voice. A book, bejesus!

Bewley smiled more indulgently. True, a whole book.

'Rather less well received. Literalness is another German fault. It goes with a lack of imagination. When they encounter the phrase, England's difficulty is Ireland's opportunity, they think de Valera has it carved over his bedhead, next to his portrait of the Sacred Heart. My book was an honest analysis of the man. Something no one else has managed. Honesty didn't suit Berlin and no one in Ireland knows what the word even means. I'm told it offended the Department of External Affairs. I'm surprised anyone could read it. It was published in German. I suppose Joe Walshe found some hack with enough school Deutsch to get the gist.'

'It wasn't very complimentary then, Mr Bewley?'

I knew he wanted me to say something like that. Well, why not?

The next sniff was a clear sniff of engagement. It brought him to his feet.

'The full story has yet to be told, believe me. And it is not unrelated to my scandalous dismissal from post in Berlin.

The reason I was put out? Simple. I recognised the threat the Jews pose to Europe. I didn't need to be in the middle of Germany's great awakening to that fact to see it. I had always seen it. But the rise of Adolf Hitler, and all that meant, sharpened my focus. I knew what I already felt was true on a far greater scale. A world stage. It was impossible to be at the heart of the National Socialist revolution and not experience that. And it was impossible for me, as an Irish patriot, not to act on it. So when the Jews came knocking at my door, as Jews always come knocking where they sense weakness, when they came to ferret out a way to bring their poison to Ireland, because Hitler would not let them poison the Reich any longer . . . they found no weakness. The door was shut.'

Bewley was walking from sofa to window and back, now much stirred.

'And I made damn sure it stayed shut!'

I had put more pennies than I'd intended to in the slot.

'But there were those who wanted it opened. Not too much. A crack. Just enough to accommodate a couple of sob stories. Nobody really wanted more Jews in Ireland. But you had to pretend. You had to stand at the League of Nations and tut the dastardly Germans. But you still kept most of the buggers out. And the filth that came with them. That's what democracy's done to us. That's the great lie. I was honest. I paid for it. The truth has always been a problem for de Valera and his cronies. But why so difficult when it came to this issue in particular, you ask?'

I wasn't asking, but this was a speech now. He had said it all before.

'Why was I pushed out for slamming the door in the face of Jew-boys queuing to get into Ireland? You know the rumours. Everyone in Ireland knows.'

He stopped and stared, waiting. My puzzled look was answer enough.

'Not a drop of Jewish blood in my veins, says Dev. I am descended from Catholic stock on both sides, says Dev. Be decent and stop this vile propaganda, he protests. Why does he need to protest? And why does he need to protest so much?'

He gave a slow and satisfied QED nod. Hadn't he proved his point?

Then he seemed to shrink in on himself, deflated. I almost felt sorry for him, reduced to declaiming his long-incubated vision to a Garda inspector who was only there to size up his flat for a burglary. I did consider asking him if he thought this particular spittle-flecked line of argument was the ideal way to win over those in the Department of External Affairs who weren't just delaying the issue of his Irish passport but were looking for reasons not to let him have one at all. I had already gathered the Department's attitude to Mr Bewley wasn't so much about diplomatic failings and disagreements as unadulterated spite. But after half an hour in his sitting room, I couldn't honestly say that spite didn't have some real merit.

I moved towards the door. I reckoned I'd earned my release.

'I'm sure Mr MacWhite will be in touch, Mr Bewley.'

Not even a sniff of annoyance now. After the spittle, words of wisdom.

'The art of the lie is the Semitic sine qua non, mastered over thousands of years. For those with eyes, history has told us. But we see it acted out in our own time, endlessly. It was only last week here . . . the Jewish gold. You know about it?'

I opened the door to the hall.

'I'm afraid not. Jewish gold is not my forte.'

He laughed and shook his head, as if amused that he had just wasted his arcane words on a potential acolyte who was simply too stupid to comprehend.

'The lie, the lie in perpetuity. Never mind, Mr Gillespie. But remember, no one should assume too much about this war.

93

There will be surprises ahead. There is, after all, still a lot of water to flow under the bridge as they say! That is war!'

I left a parting shot. The words he had sent over my head, back at him.

'Bella, horrida bella, et Thybrim multo spumantem sanguine.'

The Tiber flowing with blood silenced him. I should have used it earlier. He was frowning as we entered the hall. I didn't fit the slot I'd been put in. But then his attention shifted to a uniformed man sitting, waiting. The man stood up.

'Ah, Charles, ich sagte dass ich hereinrufen würde.'

A German officer. Dark-haired, maybe thirty, a cheerful face that went with enthusiastic hand shaking. He did some of that as Bewley greeted him. He wore what looked like an ordinary uniform, but I knew enough to recognise SS flashes.

Bewley answered in German.

'Dietrich, I hadn't forgotten. Are you coming in?'

The German took an envelope from his pocket and handed it to him.

'I can't stay long. But this salutation is overdue. And extra petrol coupons!'

'Wonderful. More precious than manna from heaven!'

The officer was smiling at me, unsure whether I was some-one he would be introduced to. Bewley remembered I was still there. He spoke again in German.

'This is Mr Gillespie, from the Irish embassy. In fact, he is Inspector Gillespie of the Garda Síochána. A policeman. You are in the same line of work.'

Garda Síochána was spoken as if in quotes, a joke the German missed.

'This is Hauptsturmführer Ritter,' said Bewley in English.

German hierarchies always provide information. It was an SS rank.

The Hauptsturmführer stepped across to me and reached

out his hand, resuming his hand-shaker smile. He shook my hand with irresistible enthusiasm.

'A pleasure, Inspector. A great pleasure. Not a police force I know.'

He spoke in English, struggling a little for the words.

'Well, we keep ourselves to ourselves. The wages of neutrality.'

He smiled but didn't understand. Bewley translated. He laughed.

The ex-ambassador wanted me out of the way. The fit had passed.

'I shall expect to hear from MacWhite, Gillespie. Soon. Very soon.'

Soon was unlikely. Bewley knew that as well as me. But I grinned amiably, as if MacWhite might actually give a fuck. I nodded at Hauptsturmführer Ritter.

The housekeeper appeared as if from nowhere and held the front door open. It closed on laughter and the start of a cheerful conversation in German. I walked down the stairs. I had not achieved much. What I had seen of the apartment confirmed that this was not somewhere to break into easily. There was limited access. The only sensible way in was through the front door. The study was at the front of the house, facing the street. The staircases, front and back, were no place to shift boxes out of the building unobserved. But I did know more about Charles Bewley and his domestic arrangements. I knew more about his views on the world. He had treated me to a display of self-importance undiminished by the Irish government's sacking of him in Berlin. His opinions I could forget, gratefully, but his ego might be more useful. That, anyway, had been worth observing in the wild.

I also knew that Michael MacWhite was not wrong about Bewley's relationship with the Germans who now occupied Rome. His chirpy visitor was an SS officer of some kind.

Whatever he did, Intelligence wouldn't be far from it, neither would his colleagues in the Gestapo. I had no doubt what was in the envelope he'd delivered with those petrol coupons. Money. But money for what?

9

VIA TASSO

Ihad been walking from Charles Bewley's apartment for barely five minutes when I was aware of someone at my shoulder, close, closer than was comfortable.

'Herr Gillespie . . . Inspector . . .'

I stopped to find Hauptsturmführer Ritter, beaming cheerfully. He was a little breathless, not much but enough to show he had hurried after me. Enough to indicate he had some sort of purpose. He was looking for me.

'I hoped . . . to catch you.'

'Well, you did.'

'You will have perhaps coffee?'

The English words came again with some effort.

'We are close . . . in the corner . . . or is it round the corner? My office. Via Tasso. An interesting talk . . . chat . . . a better word, no?'

Coffee and a chat at Gestapo HQ. It was hard to resist, but I did.

'I have to get back, Hauptsturmführer, but thank you.'

'I shall not hear it. The coffee is real, I advise you!'

I thought it would be quicker in German and that's how I answered.

'The ambassador is expecting me back and I need time to find my way. Chances are I'll get a tram in the wrong direction and take all afternoon anyway.'

'Ah, you do speak German. Charles didn't know that.'

'I'll set him straight next time I see him. I think he likes to stay informed.'

'Ah, he does, he certainly does.'

It was said as a compliment. Irony wasn't Ritter's strong point.

'But this will make it all the more enjoyable. Your German is excellent!' He clapped me a hail-fellow-well-met slap on the back. 'And I won't accept a no!'

I should have known better. Good German made me a fast friend.

'So, let's go. Only a few minutes away. I'm Dietrich by the way.'

It was a question as well as a statement.

'Stefan.'

I had accepted the invitation. Cheery as he was, the Hauptsturmführer was determined. He wanted that chat. And I could see the when-in-Rome approach covered a lot of ground now. In a city that told you at every corner that nothing ever changed, there would always be a mad emperor somewhere, and a Sejanus whose invitation for a beaker of Falernian wine it would be unwise to refuse.

I followed my new friend through the unassuming door into the offices of the Gestapo and the Sicherheitsdienst in the Via Tasso. It was, as I had seen the day before, a fortress. But we negotiated only one roadblock. They felt secure here.

Inside there was an entrance hall that had once been grand. There was some dirty stucco and peeling paint, but apart from that the space was empty and echoing. A marble staircase led upstairs. Two uniformed women sat on the bottom steps smoking. There was a bare reception desk with two telephones and nobody at it. I thought if you needed to ask directions this was probably a building you shouldn't be in. Ritter walked through a baize door into a long corridor. The only sound was the clatter of typewriters and from somewhere laughter. Suddenly a door opened along the corridor and a young man in an SS uniform emerged. He was dragging another man out, a man in a dirty, torn shirt, much older, who was half supported by a second SS officer. Together the two Germans held the old man up. He was close to collapse. His legs were barely able to prop him up unaided.

'Back to the fucking cells and think about it!'

The words were shouted into the prisoner's face.

'Pensaci, pezzo di merda!'

The man's legs gave way. For a moment he was on the floor. The SS officers pulled him up, suddenly laughing, to carry him down the corridor. It was only now that one of them looked round to see Ritter. He smirked sheepishly.

'Sorry, sir. We're in the way.'

Ritter had stopped. I stood behind him. He was irritated.

'The front office is not for this shit. You know that!'

'He just got a bit frisky, Hauptsturmführer.'

The two young officers exchanged grins, still holding up the old man, his head sagging. They looked like schoolboys who had been caught out of bounds.

'Don't piss about! Keep it in its place!'

The grins disappeared. The young Germans dragged the prisoner away.

Hauptsturmführer Ritter walked a few steps further on and opened a door into an office. He made no comment on what had just happened. As I followed him into the room I saw the trail of blood left on the corridor floor by the old man.

It was a high, airy room. The windows looked out to a yard somewhere at the back of the building. It was barred outside.

Inside a blind was pulled part of the way down. A ceiling fan revolved slowly, though the day wasn't particularly hot. There were shelves of books and files. A desk that was neat and ordered. Behind the desk a map of the city. Ritter gestured at a chair in front of the desk. He moved round the desk and sat down, facing me. As I sat, he picked up the phone.

'Two coffees. And strong ones.'

He sat back and smiled.

'It is real coffee, very good coffee. Did I say?'

'You did, Hauptsturmführer. But everyone says it. Where's the chicory?'

'Ah, the black market. The Italians were born for it. But it's true enough, you can get anything for a price. Coffee included. Still, the black market is a dangerous game, even if the Italians love to play it. And naturally enough, some commodities are more dangerous than others. The consequences are not pretty.'

I didn't know if that was a reference to what I'd seen in the corridor or some kind of oblique I-know-more-than-you-think-I-know throw of the dice. Sitting in Ritter's office, it was hard not to have Donal Hyde and Vittoria Campana in my mind. I pushed it away. What could he know? Wouldn't he say that to everyone?

The door opened. A young woman entered with a tray and the coffee. Her blonde hair was so severely plaited and her uniform so sharp and well pressed that she looked like she had been sent straight from the League of German Maidens.

'So, you're taking the opportunity to see the sights, Stefan?'

'What I can, yes.'

'It's a strange time but in many ways a surprisingly good one. In the old part of the Centro Storico, you can walk through the Forum and there's hardly anybody there. You can feel Ancient Rome in a way that would have been unthinkable even a couple of years ago. In the evenings, so many buildings come alive, I think. You see the columns and the lintels melding together out of the shadows. The temples and basilicas and bathhouses fill up the darkness without any crumbling masonry in sight. The gap-toothed ruins form into something solid. Even when you're looking at a row of brick foundations, everything's softened. You see the ancient city rising up around you. You walk through it in the silence and you start to hear the noises Juvenal heard. The plays, the music, the roar of the crowds from the Colosseum, that from a certain angle looks the way it looked on an October evening just after it was finished. Stand in the emptiness of the Circus Maximus and you hear the clatter of the chariots and the whinnying of the half-mad horses. Some nights you've Rome almost to yourself. Maybe it was worth a war for that.'

I wasn't sure whether that was a joke or not. I decided it was.

'But maybe not worth the Italians changing sides.'

'Does anybody really care?' He grinned. 'They'll be no more use to the Allies than they were to us. And as for Rome, it deserves better than the Italians.'

'And the Partisans? How do they feel about you having Rome to yourself.'

He let a smidgeon of tight-lipped irritation show. He didn't like that.

'A much-exaggerated problem. Take an evening walk, Stefan. You'll be perfectly safe. Juvenal describes the thieves and cutthroats who thought Rome belonged to them. We don't use crucifixion, but we do keep the streets clean.'

'Crucifixion's always an option, Hauptsturmführer. When in Rome . . .'

A patient smile. He was indulging me for some reason. He would have one.

'It's good to talk to someone who's no part of it. Any of it.'

I felt he meant that, not that it changed what he had to say.

'I know Rome. I lived here for a time in the thirties. I like the Romans more than I have cause to these days. On a good day, I'd almost say they have the virtue of not being entirely Italian. The Italians produce good food and nothing else.

Not long ago they produced great music. But it only tinkles when you set it beside Beethoven or Wagner. Further back they produced great art and poetry, that's if you've got the stomach for Dante. Would anybody put him next to Goethe or Shakespeare? As for the Renaissance, I think they stole it from the rest of Europe.'

He chuckled. He amused himself anyway. It was his party piece.

'But Rome is a beautiful city, there's no denying it. There is something about the way the architecture of over two thousand years has come together and fallen apart and mixed up ancient and modern, that is unique. You can weary of churches, but the Vatican has its splendours, though mostly inside rather than out. Yet it's all a trick, a trick of nature too. Wake up in the morning on a bright, clean Roman day. Look out over the city. A wonder. But what makes the wonder? The sky. A sky that's so blue nothing beneath it can look anything less than beautiful.'

He stood up and turned to the map on the wall, gazing for some time.

'So there it is. The perfect city that on a perfect day sits under its perfect sky.' He looked back at me. 'And from that sky the Allies are bombing it. Yet it's their city more than ours. Their civilisation. So they'd have the world believe. And good luck. We don't need to doff our caps to the past. But they might want to look at their civilisation, especially what they're dragging along behind it in the desperate attempt to prop it up. After the chocolate and the chewing gum has been distributed in whatever corners of Europe the British and the Americans manage to grab, there's more to come than Hollywood.' He shook his head. 'The beast they think they've tamed. The Bolsheviks and Morlock Slavs. Barbarians to eat them alive.'

Hauptsturmführer Ritter was satisfied that had put the lid on that.

I nodded. He expected something for his trouble. It was literally the least I could offer. I didn't know how much of what he said he believed but I did him the courtesy of not raising my eyebrows at those 'corners of Europe'. Half of Italy struck me as roomier than that. But faith without belief was a German trick. I'd seen it in my cousins years before. Momentarily they were in my head. I wondered how many wore my new friend's uniform. I wondered how many were dead.

Dietrich was sitting down again, drinking his coffee, more thoughtful. Then he sat up quite brusquely. A different mood. Polite and businesslike.

'I wonder if I could look at your passport, Stefan.'

'Of course, Dietrich.' I could be polite and businesslike too.

I took it out and handed it to him. He sat down, leafing through it. There was nothing that would tell him any more than he knew, except where I had come from.

'Ah, you were in Spain?'

'Our embassy in Madrid.'

He didn't pursue it. He had no real interest in the passport.

'Inspector . . . unusual. Is the Irish embassy really in need of a policeman?'

'It's not. I'm just a messenger, a courier for my government.'

'But also taking a look at the embassy's security?'

Bewley had told him that in the few minutes they'd had. For what it was worth, which was nothing. Oddly, the SS man thought it was worth something.

'Maybe not before time, Inspector.'

I didn't know what he meant but he seemed to think I did.

'Security is overstating it. I'm sure you know the embassy is quiet enough. The only real risk to Irish neutrality is the ambassador's dog. Now, if he got out . . .'

'I see you have the English habit, Stefan.'

'What habit would that be?'

'A joke for every occasion that doesn't require one.'

'You have that the wrong way round, Dietrich.'

'In what way?'

'You'll find that's a habit the English picked up from the Irish.'

It wasn't bad, though banter never quite works in German. It didn't work for Hauptsturmführer Ritter. He couldn't decide whether I was a fool or taking the piss. Either way he wasn't going to play the game when he didn't understand the rules.

He reached down and opened a drawer. He brought up a folder. He put it on the desk and pulled out a collection of passports and papers. The papers looked like identity documents of various kinds. The passports belonged to different countries.

'You can see what these are?'

I could.

'All false in one way or another. Collected over a period of weeks.'

The word 'collected' carried a lot of weight. I saw the man in the corridor.

'My own love of Rome doesn't mean it's not an odd place to be just now. In a war and not quite in a war. There are those who do like to think it somehow sits outside what's happening. The foundation of our civilisation and all that. They forget how shaky those foundation were. A city of exquisite ruins but ruins, nevertheless. German tribes brought it down and gave a corrupt and decaying empire the energy that allowed the civilisation of the west to survive and triumph.'

'And you're still at it, Hauptsturmführer. A long job.'

If the businesslike Dietrich remained, the polite one was struggling. As a man who cared about history he looked at me with an expression of sour contempt that suggested he had discovered why the English always wanted to screw Ireland.

'These are less amusing, Inspector.'

He pushed three Irish passports across the desk. I examined them.

'What do you think?'

'I think they're Irish passports.'

'Two of these were used. The first by an American. He escaped from a prisoner-of-war camp after the Italian guards deserted their posts. He was recaptured in Rome. I say a POW. Maybe he was. It's not entirely clear. He could also have been an Intelligence operative. He is still under interrogation. The second passport was used by a British officer we believe is now hiding in the Vatican. His identity isn't in doubt. And he is unimportant. The passport was going to be recycled for someone else before it was intercepted. The third has the photograph of a man who never got to use it. An Italian terrorist who used a variety of these IDs. He was captured and shot before he needed to pretend he was an Irishman.'

He gestured at the pile of documents.

'All fake, as I said.'

I pushed the Irish passports back at him.

'We're in good company. How many countries have you got there?'

He shook his head as if my lack of indignation was disappointing.

'Too many, Stefan. These are valuable documents. You might even say that in the wrong hands they can become weapons of war. In the hands of terrorists and saboteurs and spies of assorted denominations, they're worth a great deal. And naturally enough the ones that come from neutral countries are the most valuable. Switzerland, Sweden, some of the South American countries, and, of course, Éire.'

I said nothing. It was a statement of the obvious.

'There is a little game that goes on in Rome, Stefan.'

He was back to the smiling and confidential.

'The consequences of the Italian betrayal in part. Allied prisoners of war were released by Italy as the Duce's government collapsed, or if they weren't released they simply walked out when the guards deserted. Like the American I mentioned. Most of them weren't difficult to round up again. But there were a lot left, soldiers, airmen, sailors . . . if they couldn't get through the battlefront to the south, they made for Rome. Because . . . because they thought they could disappear here and because there are people who think it's some act of resistance, whatever that means, to hide these men. As if they matter, as if we could really give a fuck about them, as if we care much whether we feed them or the starving Italians do.'

He stood up again and half turned to the map of Rome on the wall. Now he was in another mode. No more close confidences. A lecture instead.

'You'll find them all over the city. And that's where the city gets odder still. Because we have this little make-believe country in the middle of it, the Holy See.'

He jabbed his finger at the map. The Vatican was circled in red.

'And this miniature Ruritania is, of course, a neutral country. We tolerate it. We tolerate the presence of so-called ambassadors from enemy states, Britain and America and even countries that haven't existed since we occupied them. Now we tolerate the fact that the Vatican is providing bed-and-breakfast for escaped Allied prisoners of war, as well as assorted Italian politicians, spies and a choice selection of Jewish bankers with the money to buy their way through St Peter's Gates. I don't say the Holy Father and his cardinals want these people, but there are a number of idiot priests who smuggle them in, and once they're in, they turn a blind eye. And it doesn't stop there. All over Rome there are Vatican buildings. Churches, palaces, offices, convents. Italian soil but extra-territorial properties of the Holy See. The Italian police can't go in. Here and here and here! A joke!'

He stabbed at small, red-ringed spots all over the map.

'They've got people in these as well. It's not hard to find out what's going on. We have names. We have lists. If we want to reel them in . . . but for now, we turn a blind eye too. Berlin likes it that way. Why not? Since we don't give a shit, not giving a shit is the Reich policy. As long as Germany has nothing serious to lose by it. As long as they don't overdo it. As long as the Pope sticks to praying.'

I realised I was supposed to laugh. I didn't. It took me too long to decide the last bit was meant to be funny. If Dietrich had got to England in those heady days when it was there for the taking, he might have said something similar about Ireland. We'd be grand if we stuck to eating our potatoes and saying the rosary.

'It'll keep you busy anyway, Dietrich. Making sure he does.'

He'd decided to let jokes in the wrong place slide. He sat down at the desk and picked up one of the Irish passports again. He leafed through it slowly.

'Vatican identity documents are a problem. They give them out too easily. They don't even know who's issuing the things. It's not a question of forgery. They're genuine. But worthless. We wouldn't always take them at face value. Swiss passports are the cream of the crop, obviously. A train ride to the border. But the Swiss keep a cold eye on these things. They need to work with Germany. They're not sentimentalists. But an Irish passport's good too. We like the Irish.'

'Doesn't everybody?' It was the best I could do.

'If there's a dog-collared do-gooder smuggling an English airman into the Vatican or getting him through a checkpoint to hole up in Maria Maggiore, well, we have better things to do. But some of these priests have odd friends for men of peace. And they're used, make no mistake. The car that brings some Italian traitor or Jew-so-called-convert into the Palazzo Callisto, with a nod and a genuflection on Sunday, can be carrying guns or explosives to Italian terrorists on Monday.'

For the first time I felt there was more direction in Ritter's words than I had seen. I knew the things he had just brought together were common currency in the Via Tasso, but priests and cars and guns were closer to home than I liked. I had a good line about men of God being full of surprises. But I saved it for another day.

'This was signed by your ambassador to the Vatican, Mr Kiernan.' The SS man held up the passport he had been reading. 'In that sense not a forgery. Except that it is. Filled in after signing. The photograph added later. Perhaps a mistake?'

I gave him my these-things-happen look.

'An interrogation last week suggested an Irish passport, a blank one, could be obtained if it was . . . urgent. With the right connections. For the right price.'

'You told me, Dietrich, that's the black market. For a price, anything.'

'Well, since you're in Rome to take a look at security at your embassy, I assume both your embassies . . . you might want to make sure the passports are securely under lock and key. I hate to say that might not always be the case . . .'

'I will certainly look into it.'

The Hauptsturmführer smiled. He was enjoying this more now.

'Neutrality is a valuable protection. But it can be fragile. My instructions, and we all have the same instructions, are to avoid diplomatic incidents at all costs. It tries our patience, especially with the damn Vatican. But patience has limits. Not every priest who has an Irish passport has diplomatic protection. If some of them choose to act in ways that conflict with German interests, or flirt with people who claim to be liberators but are no more than killers and terrorists, well, as I say, there are limits. The fog of war is thick, even under Rome's blue skies. Anyone can disappear into it. I'd be sorry to see more Irish passports getting into the hands of criminal elements, however they find their way out of the Villa Spada. And since you are a messenger, Stefan, perhaps that's a message you might pass on.'

I don't think he had a clear idea whether or not I knew what he was talking about. I doubted he had the solid information his words suggested. He was pushing it, hoping I'd reveal something that would help him. But those Irish passports had started something. If the Irish embassy wasn't being watched, there were clearly people who were. That might include Donal Hyde. For the moment the SS man was watching me, almost quizzically. I thought he was waiting for my parting joke. I hadn't got one. That was probably a mistake. He grinned lazily as he stood up. I could see that it gave him considerable satisfaction to have silenced me.

He thanked me for my time. He said how much he'd enjoyed our talk. I thanked him for his time too, but I left it at that. He said we should meet for a drink. I nodded, I think. But I assumed that having taken half an hour to gauge whether I was important in any conceivable way, he would have come to the conclusion I wasn't. He had wanted to know something about me. Now he knew there wasn't a lot to know. It was understandable, even familiar. All information was useful information until you knew it wasn't. You could only discard what you had. In that sense, unpalatable as it felt now, we were both in the same business.

Approaching the door to the street, a small, very old Italian woman was mopping the floor, cleaning away the blood that had been left there earlier. I nodded as I walked round her. She didn't look up. She didn't seem to register me. As I walked on I heard a sharp, liquid spurt. I didn't look back. I knew what it was. The woman was spitting at me. Fair play to her. I needed to keep better company.

10

PALAZZO SAN CALLISTO

I came away from the Via Tasso and Dietrich Ritter's office not much wiser than I went in. I decided to take a tourist's route back to the Tiber. I consulted the map and found my way to the Trevi Fountain. I threw a coin in. I got out the camera and took pictures. I took another picture of the house where John Keats died and wished I had another reason for being in this city and something better to think about than the shite that brought me here. I had no sense I was being watched but if I was it wouldn't be by the likes of Father Hyde. It seemed no bad idea, for the sake of the performance, to play the tourist again. I was more unsettled by the Hauptsturmführer than I'd realised. I had plumped for the easiest explanation, idle curiosity, but I wasn't sure. Was it that idle? Was he trying to find out what I'd made of his visit to Charles Bewley? He didn't refer to it, but maybe he wanted to see if I would. I doubted our ex-ambassador had said much about my conversation regarding his passport. It wouldn't look good that he might have been better buying one on the black market himself than waiting for Dublin's decision. No, Bewley had appearances to keep up for his Nazi connections. His line would be that he still counted for something in Ireland. But maybe some remark he made about me had intrigued the

SS man. Or was Ritter showing off? We're in charge, feller, just so you know. Pearls before Irish swine, surely. Hardly worth the effort. Or was there a threat behind what he was saying, something more specific? We know someone's getting these Irish passports out. He had made a point about the passports. Was that the gypsy's warning? A small step to being helpful. Sort it out yourselves and we won't have to. No one wants a fucking diplomatic incident. Or was he fishing because that's what he did, and he simply happened to bait the hook better than he realised? I found myself wondering if the Villa Spada was watched, as any embassy might be, and whether that chance visit to Charles Bewley's apartment was chance after all. But whether there was a threat or not, a warning or not, a lucky guess or not, my knowledge of what was being carried around in the Irish ambassador's Lancia needed acting on.

When I arrived back at the Villa Spada I kept to my room. There was only a lazy snarl from Finn as I entered. It wasn't welcoming but I felt he was becoming bored into accepting me. The sight of Mrs Butler crossing the hall into the office had been less reassuring. There was a smile of expectancy rather than a welcome. Whatever her word for it, she was under the impression I was arsing about, wasting the Department of External Affair's shilling. She was waiting for that list of whatever it was I was supposed to be asking for, to inspect, check and audit. Since I had no idea what went on in the embassy, it was hard to know where to begin. I did know that if there was a tally of blank passports anywhere, it wasn't likely to match the numbers they had on file. I could almost have claimed I was on the case already, however inadvertently, except that the only people I was intending to discuss the discrepancies with for now, were the ones smuggling out the passports.

'If you're looking for the ambassador he won't be back till this evening.'

From our conversation that morning, I already knew Michael MacWhite wouldn't especially want me to catch up with him. Charles Bewley was now my problem, until such time as the problem was solved. Only then would he reclaim it. But I thought he could at least give me something intelligent to ask Mrs Butler for.

'I'll catch him when I can, thank you.'

She gave me a few more seconds of that expectant look, then gave up.

Vittoria Campana was in the office as Mrs Butler entered. I saw her through the door. She glanced round as I was heading for the stairs. She registered me. That was all. There was nothing to tell me whether Donal Hyde had spoken to her. I would find out. All I was doing upstairs was waiting for her to leave for the day.

It was only an hour later, looking down from the bedroom window, that I saw the signorina outside, walking to the road, presumably heading home. I came down the stairs. The dog opened one eye, no more, and closed it again. That degree of acceptance would make coming in and out less of a show. I gave Vittoria enough time to get away from the villa, then I hurried to catch up with her.

'Buonasera!' I thought it was more amusing than it sounded. It wasn't.

'That's very good. You must be taking lessons, Mr Gillespie!'

She laughed but she was looking at me harder than the laugh suggested.

'It's Stefan. And I thought we might have a drink.'

'Is that Irish? No preliminaries? Not even a little flirting in the office?'

'It wouldn't be Irish, no. The Irish way would be definitely no flirting, God save us, and I'd never ask anything, ever. Nothing would happen. And the only drink I'd have would be in a bar with a bunch of other fellers in the same boat.'

She laughed again, but she was waiting for something else.

'I'll take it Father Hyde has played the go-between.'

'Yes, he has, Stefan.'

'So, a drink?'

She nodded. We walked on in silence. She was wary but she showed no concern. She was very cool, I had to say that. However, the advantage was mine. She didn't know what I wanted. She didn't know what I knew. She didn't know what to make of me. She would have got no more than confusion from Donal.

She turned into a street that led into the alleys of Trastevere. I was conscious this was her territory. It had been last time I saw her there. We didn't go far. She went to a café in a bright, busy square. We sat at a table. She asked the waiter for wine.

'Do you start or do I, Vittoria?'

She took out a cigarette.

'It's your party.'

'What did Donal say?'

'You were in Trastevere last night. You were watching him.'

'And you, don't forget the bread basket.'

'Shall we get on with it, Stefan.'

'You mean what do I know?'

'I mean what do you want?'

'No, first some questions. When I got to the Villa Spada, my room was searched. When I went into Rome, Donal followed me. I was slow to spot him, but it wasn't what I expected. At home, priests wait for you to tell them what you've been up to, at Confession. They don't follow you about to check up in advance.'

She managed a smile for that.

'So, once I'd spotted him, I repaid the courtesy. I followed him. I thought it might help me work out what he was up to. Then there was you, of course, and the drunken friar and . . . a miscalculation on my part about quite how drunk he was.'

And a laugh, a more genuine one. She had heard the tale.

'I'm not sure it would have been funny if he'd caught me.'

'Possibly not.'

'You don't seem very bothered.'

'Probably not.'

'Thanks.'

The waiter reappeared with a bottle. Vittoria nodded and he left it.

'So, why follow me at all? It wasn't his decision. It was yours.'

She didn't answer. She filled the glasses.

'If you hadn't drawn attention to yourself . . . we wouldn't be here.'

'Perhaps that was my miscalculation, Inspector. That's the thing, I knew you were a policeman. I thought you were here because . . . I thought the ambassador was looking at . . . there are a lot of things that make what I can do . . . very helpful.'

'Helpful for some black-market trading?'

'That's not what I mean.'

'No. I know. Let's forget the coffee. Everyone's at that, I take it. Let's say passports, to be used for moving people around who don't want to encounter any Germans. And the other things in the basket that I'd say sooner or later are going to encounter Germans, because that's what they're for. Or is it for duck shooting?'

She was clear enough about what I knew now.

'I don't know what you call it, Partisans, resistance . . . war, anyway.'

She shrugged. She wasn't impressed that I could state the obvious.

'But I don't think Donal's in the same war as you, Vittoria.'

'He's helping to get people away, to hide people. Passports and identity documents mean life and death. There are many in Rome who need that help.'

'He might not be in the same war, but he could end up against the same wall. Wouldn't that be about it? Irish passport or not. You're not telling him half of it.'

She said nothing, then she shrugged. She looked harder.

'Does that mean it's worth it?'

'You won't understand.'

'I don't need to. Father Hyde's big enough to make his own mistakes. He'll have his reasons for making them too. Only some of them appropriate for a priest.'

That didn't amuse her. I thought she was going to slap me.

'Come on, the blind eye's as much about you as his fellow man.'

She pushed that aside. She was steely again.

'There are too many things you don't know. There are a lot of secrets in Rome. If there were things Mr MacWhite knew . . . I don't know what he would do. It's not simply about stopping it . . . or finding other ways. That happens all the time. But it's about people. Just to say something to the police . . . to the wrong person at another embassy. I had to know what you were doing, what you were looking for. Nobody knew. Even Signora Butler . . . and she knows everything.'

I picked up the bottle. I filled her glass and mine.

'That's because none of that has anything to do with why I'm here. I'm not investigating anything. I'm not here as a policeman, only as a thief. I kid you not.'

I raised my glass. She was unconvinced. I couldn't blame her.

'As for what you're doing, I don't have to tell the ambassador anything. I have a job. It's not one I want. To tell you the truth, I'm pissed off being here. I thought I'd be home by now. And there's only one thing I want from you. I want you and your friends, whoever they are . . . and I'd say some must be in the line of work required . . . to help me break into the apartment of an Irishman in Rome and remove a couple of boxes from his office. That's the only thing I'll be having a conversation with the ambassador about. I don't care about the rest, not Donal's passports, not your guns. It isn't my war, after all. So, you can all get on with it.'

She drank slowly, looking at me. She was weighing me up. It was all true. There was something I wanted from her and connections I guessed she must have. As for her business, it was no business of mine. I wished I'd put that better. 'If anybody thinks I have any principles, don't worry, I haven't', wasn't my best look.

'It doesn't make much sense,' she said warily.

'It does to someone in Dublin. Maybe to Mr MacWhite. He knows what it's for, some of it. I don't. But he doesn't want to be involved. I have to get it done. I guess I'm in your world, where some things just have to get done. Isn't that right?'

'Yes, because it's a war . . . is that hard to understand?'

I didn't bother to answer. I wasn't going to try to persuade her Irish diplomacy counted for much in the middle of her war. But there was more to say.

'These things that have to get done . . . I'd say there's a bit more to it than the ambassador giving you a free rein with his car . . . and you using it for some cover.'

'It's like the coffee.' Vittoria smiled. 'I can get him extra petrol.'

'Well, if he's turning a blind eye too . . . it won't be to the guns.'

She knew that. She didn't think it needed saying.

'You should take care, Vittoria. More care than you have been.'

'How do you mean?'

'It could be no more than a coincidence . . . let's leave aside how I know . . . but you might want to let things settle . . . or do whatever it is you do when you need to shut something down. I don't know about the weapons . . . I assume there are all sorts of ways of moving those about the city . . . but I think there's a lot of attention on passports and where they're coming from. And that includes Irish passports.'

'Whose attention?'

'My knowledge is limited to SS Hauptsturmführer Ritter. Know him?'

She shook her head.

'He has an office in the Via Tasso, as you might expect. My suggestion would be for you and Father Hyde to get rid of anything you shouldn't have and for now just resume the roles of driver and chaplain to the Irish ambassador.'

'How can I know if . . .'

Trust was the word she didn't say. She put down some cash and stood up.

'I'll have to talk to someone.'

'Start with Donal.' I drained my glass and stood too. 'I wouldn't say he's a man you'd want in the hands of the Gestapo for long. Is he at the Irish College?'

'No. He's very close. It won't take long.'

She walked off. I went with her. She had made the decision to trust me.

I didn't know whether I was starting to know where I was going in Trastevere, or if it was that one cobbled street looked much the same as any other. Maybe I recognised something, maybe I didn't. I wasn't planning on making a habit of getting lost there. What I did recognise was that Signorina Campana knew her business. She was confident in a way that confirmed what I'd seen the previous night. Whatever the pecking order in her world, she wasn't at the bottom. She knew what mattered and she knew what she should leave alone. She asked me no questions about how I knew what I did. She knew that if I'd wanted to say more about Ritter and the SS I would have done. I'd said what I needed her to hear. She didn't waste her time on anything else. That didn't mean she didn't want to know. For now, she responded by telling me what she thought I needed to know. That wouldn't include those guns she stored overnight on what counted as Irish soil. Since I was ready to shrug them off, she was going to behave as if we'd never had the conversation. I didn't know how sure she was about me though. If it looked like she was trusting me with something, she was also keeping me very close.

The conversation was an uneasy replay of the one I'd had with Dietrich Ritter in the Via Tasso. Only from the other end. Her Rome, like his, was full of people who needed hiding or spiriting away. They had to have places to stay. They had to have false identities sometimes. Father Hyde was a great help with that, not just with a few Irish passports but with Vatican identity papers and passes. She explained, again as the SS man had explained, about the Vatican properties all over Rome where there was some kind of safe refuge, since the Germans were still going through the motions of respecting the neutrality of the Holy See. But getting people into these places was getting harder. It would have been churlish to ask her if she kept her machine guns in the Vatican's extra-territorial buildings. What she was describing was a humanitarian crusade. We both knew it was only her day job.

'And the friar who'd been at the Communion wine?'

'He's a problem.' She laughed then shook her head. 'Still a problem.'

'Thankfully, not mine now.'

'You'll meet him again. Donal is with him now.'

'And I thought you trusted me, Vittoria?'

'His name is Luca, Luca Horvat. I brought him from where he'd been hiding in the city and Donal was taking him to the Palazzo San Callisto. That's where we're going. It's a Vatican building. There are people sheltering there. Donal had to wait till it was late and there was no one about. It's not so hard to get in and out of these places, but it needs to be done with the minimum of attention, obviously.'

I laughed. She smiled.

'Well, hopefully by the time he got there . . . however as it turns out . . .'

'You mean it didn't go to plan? If I'm supposed to be surprised . . .'

'It's more complicated than that. It's something Donal got me involved in, that I'd have to say I wasn't looking for. A Franciscan shouldn't need hiding in Rome. I don't even think the Germans are looking for him . . . they have no reason. He went to Donal because he was afraid. He was in a Franciscan house. I don't know that he was hiding as such, but someone told him he was going to be killed.'

'Is that normal in Franciscan circles here?'

'It's not a joke.'

I nodded, waiting to find out why it wasn't.

'He's a Croatian. Croatia has its own Fascist government and its own little Hitler. They have their own little party, the Ustaše. Do you know what that is?'

'I haven't got any further than Hitler and Mussolini.'

'Well, the Ustaše has its own take on who they want to kill. They don't like the Jews, of course. But they're Catholics and Catholic is what you have to be to get to Heaven, or anywhere on Earth, if that's in Croatia. And since they've got millions of Serbian Orthodox who didn't get the message, it's a problem. It ceases to be a problem if you kill them. They've been doing that for a couple of years.'

'I didn't know. I mean . . . I've seen nothing . . . I've read nothing . . .'

'You should complete your education, Inspector. Ask Mr MacWhite. He won't have much to say though. It's not a popular topic at diplomatic receptions.'

'I see.'

'We all live in the real world . . .' She smiled. 'Maybe not in Ireland, yet.'

I felt the sting in that yet.

'And your friend Luca?'

'He came to Rome to tell the Vatican what was happening, in its name . . . if not in its name, well, in something remarkably like it. He was a Croatian nationalist himself. I think he'd been a member of the Ustaše. I know Italian soldiers who were in Croatia and they . . .' She stopped. She was going to say more, but she checked herself. 'Let's just say they're not short on priests in the Ustaše.'

We were now in another square, facing a high, grand building that took up the whole of one side. This was the Palazzo San Callisto. It could have been any palazzo in Trastevere, but over the doors hung the white-and-yellow flag of St Peter. A small sign at the door, in German and Italian, said this was the territory of the Holy See. At home, some joker would have scribbled 'Queue Here!' on it.

I followed Vittoria inside, to a wide, elegant hallway. At the door stood a man in a deep-blue uniform that looked like he was in an opera. A short Hussar-like tunic, epaulettes out of the Foreign Legion and a triangular hat that stuck out on either side of his head. The last one of those I'd seen was on Napoleon's head in a picture. He carried no gun, but a sword hung at his side. I wasn't sure what he was, but he nodded politely at Vittoria. It wasn't courtesy. It felt like he knew her.

There were not many people about. It was getting to the end of the day. The corridors that led off the hall suggested offices of some kind. But as we walked on and headed out through some glass doors into a cloister-like courtyard, there were groups of people standing and sitting, talking, smoking. There were a few smiles and greetings. Again, it was clear Vittoria Campana was known to some.

'Don't imagine I care much what goes on in the Vatican, Stefan.'

Her words wouldn't have gone down well at the Irish embassy.

'I think the short version of the story is that Brother Luca's information was news to nobody, whatever he thought. He was dispatched to a monastery or a friary, or whatever they call these places, and that was that. He'd betrayed all sorts of people, friends, priests, his Franciscan brothers in Croatia, for nothing. But it hadn't gone unnoticed. After all, he had betrayed more than his country, if you believe what they believe . . . and God, as they say, can move in mysterious ways.'

We walked through another set of doors, across a corridor, into a garden. There were high walls round it, but it was full of shrubs and neatly tended trees. Through the trees, against the far wall, there was a tiled roof and a series of sheds.

'And those mysterious ways are why he's in hiding?'

'If you believe what he says . . .'

'Don't you?'

'Donal does. Maybe he's spoken to him sober.'

Vittoria didn't much like the Franciscan. I could sympathise.

'Anyway, the Ustaše found out where he was, and either they sent someone to kill him or there's someone in Rome already who'll do it. There's enough of them about. They worked with the Fascists here and they work with the Germans now. I don't doubt you can bump into them in the Vatican. That's the message Luca got.'

'Is he safe here, then?'

'He might be if he kept his head down. He was drunk again earlier. He got into an argument with someone else who's taken refuge here. I don't know if it was a Serb or another Croat. Some man thought he recognised him. Luca hit him.'

I didn't offer any comment. I knew how big the friar was.

'So, we've got to get him out . . . and take him somewhere else. Ideally out of Rome. He's trouble. Donal came over to find him. They've moved him out of the building. We'll find him in one of the garden sheds. But before we do anything else, Donal needs to know what you told me. If he's under surveillance at all . . .'

She stopped and took out a cigarette. I took out my lighter, but she had produced a box of matches. She grinned. It said, don't bother with the gallantry.

We walked through an arch in a high hedge. There were the sheds, scruffier than what surrounded them in the palazzo, but better made than many houses.

Vittoria went to one of the doors. She knocked. No one answered.

'Donal, Luca? Vittoria!'

She knocked again.

'Maybe they've gone for a drink.'

She didn't think any more of my jokes than Dietrich Ritter. She turned the handle and pushed open the door.

'Donal?'

Vittoria led on into the darkness. I followed. It smelt of earth and there was a sort of fragrance. Herbs, thyme or marjoram. There was no window. She felt the wall for a switch but couldn't find it. She got out a small torch. In the narrow beam I could see garden tools, more piled terracotta, a bench, a lawn mower. There were bunches of dried herbs hanging from a beam under the low ceiling. There was a camp bed. Someone had been sleeping. She turned the torch and found the light switch.

It was a dim bulb but it showed immediately what we had not seen in the torchlight. Stretched on the floor was a body, face down. A dead body. As I stood there, gazing down with Signorina Campana, neither of us needed to see more to know that. There was a black jacket and black trousers. It could have been the body of any dead priest you might have stumbled on in Rome. But the thin frame was familiar, even to me. More familiar was the fair, tousled hair. Donal Hyde.

PART TWO

SOCIETAS ANGELORUM

THE COMPANY OF ANGELS

Why should the Church not use force to coerce her wayward sons to return? Is it not the shepherd's duty of care, whenever sheep leave the flock, even though not forced by violence but enticed by soft seductions, to restore them to his master's fold, by the exercise of fear, or even the pain of the whip, if they resist?

St Augustine, Letter to Boniface, c. 416

There are those in Croatia . . . who would impede the role entrusted to it by Providence as a Catholic bulwark against the East. The Croatian people have a natural right to rid their organism of such poison. The Ustaše movement would prefer these hostile elements to be freely assimilated . . . but if not, Catholic morality gives the state the right to annihilate them by the sword. These principles are founded in natural law and every Catholic is obliged to carry them out . . . to fight for a state in which the Church can achieve her supernatural mission unhindered.

Ivo Guberina, Croatian Review, 1943

11

LA CASETTA DA GIARDINO

Neither of us spoke. Vittoria's arms moved slightly. The sign of the cross. I knelt beside the dead priest. Between the shoulders his black jacket was sticky. There was a kind of shallow dent. The wet fabric pressed into him. It was an entry point. He had been stabbed from behind with something thick, sharp, heavy. It had gone in deep. The blood had not yet congealed but it had thickened and grown darker.

Vittoria stood over me. I looked up. I gave a kind of shrug that said no more than that there was no more to say. The light caught her face. She was shocked, of course, horrified perhaps. She knew him after all. I didn't. But she wasn't afraid, I could see that. It crossed my mind that she had probably seen the dead before, whatever that meant. There seemed no need to say anything about that. It was what it was. And as I looked down at Donal and back up at her again, I could see that the shock was receding. Her face was harder. I hadn't even got to the first question about how to deal with this. She was there before me. She had a lot to think about in a very short time. I could only start to see the complications, but, as I stood up, I knew she was making a list. It would be longer than anything I could come up with. But even in a garden shed at the back of a Roman palazzo, I was a policeman. There was a dead man and it was unlikely he'd stabbed himself between the shoulder blades. There was a procedure. She knew that too, but it wasn't a procedure she wanted. I already knew she wouldn't want to be part of it.

'You've got no reason to think anything like this . . .'

'Of course, I haven't. Madre di Dio!'

There were some tears she needed to stop. I didn't know how inexplicable this was. From her face, I reckoned inexplicable enough. But I couldn't know enough about the world she'd pulled the Irish priest into to guess whether she felt any responsibility, or whether this connected to her. I had seen, only moments before, that the Church wasn't exactly dear to her heart, but she reached for it, like a lot of us, when there was nothing else available. No, she couldn't comprehend it.

'Who do we go to, Vittoria? Who calls the police?'

'I don't know. I know the priest in the Chiesa di San Callisto . . . and Monsignor Venuti . . . at the Sacred Congregation . . . he'd be the most senior . . .'

'We'd better find him. Are there any police in the building?'

'When we came in . . . the man at the door . . .'

'In the Gilbert-and-Sullivan hat?'

She didn't understand. I didn't know why I'd said it. One of the habits you pick up as a policeman that you wish you never had. It marks you out as a bollox.

'The Vatican police, the Gendarmerie.'

'I thought they came with striped pyjamas and halberds.'

'No, they don't.' Now I'd pissed her off. 'Is that the best you can do?'

She looked down at Donal Hyde again.

'Maybe the best I can do is to stay, signorina, while you get out.'

She held my gaze. That was what she was thinking about.

'You probably should. I'm just a feller from the Irish embassy who was looking for Father Hyde. I don't need much of an explanation. He told me to meet him here so we could go for a drink or go to Mass, whatever. I needn't have the faintest idea why he was here. I don't need to know he was calling on his friend the friar. Here I am. There he is. And I know fuck all about anything. That's the story.'

I could see she was going to take my offer. She didn't like doing it.

'You'll probably make a better job of explaining than I will.'

'I assume I'll find someone with some English. Or I can just point. I'm fine on "buonasera", but I haven't got to the lesson about the body in the garden shed.'

A moment of disbelief swept back over her.

'How did this happen? Donal wouldn't have hurt . . .'

'You'd know a lot more than me, Vittoria.'

I didn't think she did, but it was her world, not mine.

'Meanwhile, you were never here.'

'I'm sorry, Stefan. I still don't know what you know . . . what you're doing . . . but if I end up in a Fascist police station . . . being questioned about why I was here, why Donal was here, who the man hiding here is . . . I wouldn't be well known to them but they can connect me to people who are. Even as a witness to this . . . it gives an excuse to look harder. Where would it go? And there are the Germans.'

There were the Germans. And maybe they already knew something.

Vittoria still hesitated. She felt Donal's death. And she had a reason. She was in there with whatever other reasons the priest had for what he was doing. If she didn't know why he was dead, it was hard to believe it wasn't her business.

'Can you get out without being seen again? It won't matter to Donal.'

'I can get out through the church.'

There was still no fear. If there was, she hid it. She bent

down and touched Donal Hyde's head, almost stroking his hair. He would have liked that, I thought.

'Mi dispiace tanto.' She was speaking to him. 'Non capisco perchè . . .'

'I'll give you five minutes or so,' I said. 'Just go home as quickly and as quietly as you can. I'm sure there are people you will want to tell . . . your people. I wouldn't rush to do it, that's all. Give it a few hours. If you have to go out to contact . . . whoever you need to contact . . . don't come near here. And when you go to the embassy tomorrow, it'll be the first thing that hits you. You need to be prepared to be unprepared. No shortage of shock and sorrow. But don't overdo it.'

She gave me a look I'd seen before. She didn't need lessons.

'Just one thing, Vittoria.'

'What's that?'

'Where's the fucking friar?'

I could see she hadn't thought of that. She shrugged.

'Whoever your friends are, someone might try to find out. The police will want to get hold of him. Did Donal find him? Did he see him here? He's meant to be hiding. Where is he now? If he's in the city, well . . . he's hardly inconspicuous.'

Vittoria nodded. Then she was gone.

I gazed down at Donal Hyde again. I didn't know why he was dead. Why would I? But I doubted it was over a few Irish passports. But Irish passports were in the mix. However genuine the ambassador's grief was going to be when he got the news of his chaplain's murder, he wouldn't want those passports in the hands of the police or the Gestapo, not when they could be directly traced back to his office. There were practicalities. My job was to know when things needed tidying up. It came so naturally that I just did it. It was something Vittoria should have thought of too. Was he carrying anything incriminating? If she was a professional, and it felt like she was, he was an amateur in deeper than he knew. And while I didn't imagine he walked around with his pockets stuffed full of blank Irish passports, I wouldn't be thanked for not taking care of anything embarrassing.

I crouched down and felt in the side pockets of his jacket. In one there was a small book. It looked like a prayer book. It was in Hebrew. I remembered him coming out of the Jewish Library only a day ago. Between the pages were three small photographs, the kind that would go into a passport or some other document. There were two pieces of paper, folded. They weren't passports but they were identity passes of some kind. They bore the emblem of the Holy See, the mitre and the keys to the kingdom. They were signed and stamped but were otherwise blank.

There were only the inside pockets of the jacket to search now. I pulled him over. The body was still limp and mobile. He had not been dead long enough for rigor mortis to set in. It was as I turned Father Hyde on to his back that I saw, not his face, but the two black-red, glutinous pits that pierced his head. He had no eyes.

*

It took some time for the Palazzo San Callisto to produce anyone I thought it was right to fill in on what was waiting at the bottom of the garden. I did find a key hanging next to the door as I left the shed and I locked in Father Hyde's body. I intended to go to the man in the hat who was some sort of policeman, but when I tried to speak to him, he had neither English nor German. The hall was busy with people coming and going and the man seemed to think I was looking for directions to Mass in the church. The idea of trying to offer up an explanation in dumb show and pointed gestures didn't feel like a good one. I found a priest who spoke German but he didn't work at the palazzo. He spoke to a nun who got the message that I had something serious to say that wasn't for public consumption. She realised that whatever I had to impart

131

was unpleasant in some way. She disappeared and ten minutes later a round, bald, elderly man arrived, half dressed in robes that showed he was about to take part in a Mass. He was irritated, though less with me, I thought, than the nun who had been concerned enough to extract him from the church. She stood behind the priest, probably already wishing she had just told me to wait. German was what we had in common. He wanted a quick explanation.

'I'm Monsignor Venuti. The sister tells me you have a problem.'

'I don't know if problem is the right word.'

'What is it? I was preparing for Mass.'

'There's a dead body . . . an Irish priest . . . in one of the garden sheds.'

He stared at me. Now it was serious. He didn't know how serious.

'Who?'

'Father Hyde. He's from the Irish College.'

'I think I know him . . . but he's a young man . . . was he sick?'

'You might do better to come down there yourself, Monsignor. And find someone to make sure the building is kept secure. It will be a matter for the police.'

I spoke the next words quietly.

'He was killed. Stabbed in the back.'

I left it at that. He would see soon enough what went with it.

For the next hour I sat in a small office off the Palazzo San Callisto's entrance hall. Monsignor Venuti had little to say after seeing the body. I couldn't blame him. He locked the door again and produced another guard with a cocked hat and sword. I had explained my connection to Donal Hyde briefly. The monsignor asked nothing. Some of that was shock. I could also see he had a lot of other things on his mind. Back in the palazzo I said I would obviously wait until the police arrived. He didn't answer immediately. He nodded and pointed me at an open door, then left.

I couldn't work out what was happening for the next hour. I did notice that the entrance hall was suddenly empty. When I got up and walked out to the cloister to smoke a cigarette, that was empty too, where before it had been full of people. I could hear the sound of voices singing. The Mass was underway, but sound was all there was. There was an entrance to the church from the street. That was the way Vittoria had exited the palazzo. The Vatican policeman at the door looked distinctly uneasy, even after he was joined by a colleague. I assumed that, whatever my intentions, and maybe the monsignor's, some news of Donal's death had found its way out. The result was a hush and an emptiness that had come quickly. I might have expected the opposite, a buzz of curiosity and conversation, but I remembered why many people were in this place. They were hiding. This was a place of safety and refuge. Suddenly it couldn't have felt as safe as it had done.

The silence was broken by the sound of cars and a siren in the square outside. The two gendarmes looked even more uncomfortable. One of them walked to a table and picked up a telephone. The other stood in front of the open door. And when the first re-joined him, he had slung an aging Mauser rifle on his shoulder.

It was dark now. Car lights lit the square. I stood and looked out from the room I had been left in. Beyond the door I could see several dark uniforms. The police. A couple of men in suits and hats pushed their way through. But the two gendarmes simply stood where they were, blocking the entrance. The words that started amiably in Italian, were quickly louder. I then saw Monsignor Venuti, hurrying into the hallway with two young and surprisingly large priests at his heels. I doubted the Palazzo San Callisto ran to a rugby team, but they would have been useful in the front row. The monsignor pushed his way outside, followed by the priests. The gendarmes stayed in the doorway. The voices got louder. The monsignor's, loudest of all, was sounding far from priestly. If I couldn't get the words, it wasn't hard to slot in some likely English equivalents. For whatever reason, the police were there, with detectives in charge, and Monsignor Venuti had no intention of letting them inside. If I didn't understand the ins and outs of what Vatican ex-territorial meant in Rome, it did seem that he could do exactly that.

The three priests came back into the palazzo. The monsignor barked an order at the gendarmes. They pushed the heavy doors shut, leaving the throng of police, abruptly silenced, outside in the square. Monsignor Venuti walked away, pausing only to glance at me sourly, as if the whole thing was my fault. While one of the Vatican policemen pushed the bolts shut on the doors, the other laughed, breaking out a packet of cigarettes. He walked across the hall and offered me one, laughing.

'Polizia! Figli di puttana, eh?'

I was none the wiser, but whatever it was . . . so much for the Polizia.

Half an hour later I was back in the shed, looking at Donal Hyde's body again, now with a young officer of the Vatican Gendarmerie, who had introduced himself as Commissario De Angelis. He was barely out of his twenties. He wore the same blue tunic as the guards at the palazzo doors and the same bicorn hat. He held it awkwardly as he gazed at the priest's face, turning the points on one side between his fingers. He showed almost no emotion, but it was costing him not to.

He had listened to my story as we walked to the garden. I adopted the approach recommended in the Superintendent Gregory school of lying. Keep it simple, never too much detail. Use whatever of the truth you can. Don't twist what it is you don't want to say, just avoid it completely. He asked few questions to follow up. I thought it was lack of experience. As time went on I wasn't so sure. He knew I was only telling part of the truth. He assumed he would get more later.

'You'll have to excuse me if my questions come in no particular order, Mr Gillespie. I'm feeling my way, as you say. I'm here only because of my English.'

He smiled. It was too early to call it disingenuous, but it was odd that he said nothing about the mutilated body in front of him. He had already seen it on his own but it didn't improve with viewing. I felt sicker in my stomach than the first time.

'You didn't say why you came here to find Father Hyde.'

'He was taking me to eat somewhere. I think it was near here.'

'Of course, you're new to Rome.'

I hadn't told him that. Maybe it didn't take much working out.

'He told you to meet him here?'

'He had a friend he was visiting, staying here.'

'Staying in a shed?'

'I asked when I got here. Someone said to go out through the garden.'

'You knew the man? The Franciscan, Brother Luca?'

'No. I know he was hiding out, whatever you want to call it. I've been in Rome long enough to understand something of what's going on. Donal was helping the man. I don't know what that amounted to. You'd know more than me.'

'B&B, that's the English joke. Bed and breakfast at the Vatican.' De Angelis laughed. 'We've all picked up that, even in Italian. Some of the men are Allied prisoners of war who were released, or escaped anyway, after the Italian surrender.'

He turned to the body, crouching slowly.

'As you say, Brother Luca was also on the B&B. No one knows why.'

I hoped I looked like I didn't either.

'This is very nasty, Mr Gillespie. Even nowadays when we all know . . .'

Commissario De Angelis didn't finish. He shrugged. It was enough.

'Why would a Franciscan friar need to hide in Rome?'

It felt like my turn to shrug.

'Why did you turn the body over?'

I was about to say I hadn't but he saved me making that mistake.

'It wasn't to see if he was still alive.'

I avoided a real answer.

'I wished I hadn't when I saw him.'

De Angelis didn't push it. He was better than I'd anticipated.

'I have found his eyes, by the way.'

He stood up and went to the workbench. He picked up a small saucer.

'They were in his hand. Someone put them there. I'd guess after he was dead. What would have been involved in doing it before that must have created more noise than even this quiet corner of the Palazzo San Callisto might have stomached without attracting attention. Even with a full choir in the church.'

I looked at the bloody mess in the saucer, the eyeballs were still solid enough to almost look up. The commissario was watching for my reaction. An attempt to shock me into saying more than I intended. It was theatrical, but nothing more. But he had a cool head. I didn't think he'd seen many bodies, let alone anything like this.

'So, Inspector.' He put down the saucer and looked at me quizzically. 'Is there more?'

'More what?'

'More here.' He gestured around the shed.

'Maybe.'

'Maybe not,' he said quietly. 'I think the body can be taken to the hospital mortuary in the Vatican. We have no forensic pathologist, of course, but we'll see if there's anything to find. This is what you'd call, I think, a fucking mess, no?'

'I don't understand, Commissario.'

'It's Giulio, please. It will be easier. And you?'

'Stefan.'

'Let's go outside. I need a cigarette. I can't look at this any longer.'

He walked out. I followed. There was a scent of herbs in the night air. He lit a cigarette and passed one to me. He was silent. No, he wasn't used to this at all.

'I mean what I say when I tell you I have no experience. We have no experience. The Gendarmerie is a police force, but our job is protecting the Holy Father along with the Vatican and various buildings in Rome. We're not the Swiss Guards. We do deal with crime but we normally work with the Italian police. Something like this, a murder, we'd hand over to them and follow their lead. We are not detectives. We don't have that sort of training. But these are strange times.'

He walked on into the garden. I needed some of that air too.

'The first thing my boss did when this came through was to phone the city police. I was supposed to meet them here and liaise with their investigation. But it has to be said our relations with the Polizia aren't what they were . . . who do they even represent now? We've got two Italian governments in the war . . . one on each side. Anyway, the next thing is a very senior cardinal appears in the Ispettore Dirigente's office. There's all hell. The outcome is that under no circumstances do the Roman police, who the cardinal now refers to as the Fascist police, set foot in the Palazzo San Callisto or touch this investigation. But they were on their way.'

I laughed. 'I saw all that. They weren't very happy.'

'You can see their point, Stefan. I doubt they were bothered about a dead Irish priest, but here's a building full of all sorts of people in hiding, in hiding from them, for God's sake, and the Gestapo. And there's an open invitation to walk in and interrogate every single one of them. And perhaps that's only the start. Who knows where else . . . I'm sure Father Hyde had a lot of friends. Wouldn't you say?'

It was subtle, but it was there, another question for me.

'I couldn't tell you, Giulio, I've only been here a couple of days.'

'Time to forget the politics. You get the picture, Stefan. Know it and ignore it. It's not pretty. Not pretty even in the Gendarmerie barracks. If there are two sides in Italy, they both find their way into the Vatican. But we can leave it alone, I hope. There is a dead man, an Irishman. We will try to find out what happened. Even if I'm not sure my superiors want to know. So, just me, who knows fuck all.'

I hadn't yet picked up how the commissario was using 'we'.

'Isn't that how you say it? Fuck all – about any of it?'

'They were right about your English, Commissario. It's not bad.'

'Not bad means excellent, no? So, we understand each other. What I need is someone who knows more than fuck all. I think you do. I think you are that sort of policeman. A detective. Who knows what we have to do? But we begin with where he was, who saw him, yes? Working backwards from here. Besides the palazzo, besides people in the Vatican, there'll be the Irish College, where he lived, and the Irish embassies. Both of them, Villa Spada and Holy See. Signore MacWhite and Signore Kiernan. Interviewing these people is something I shall need help with.'

I could see where 'we' was going. I wasn't sure it would do much good. I looked back to the garden shed and thought of the bloody body lying on the floor.

'I don't know what answers you'll get. What happened in

there is a long way from any embassy or any college. It's a long way from anything I can think of.'

I could see he recognised that himself.

'But don't you start with people? What else is there?'

'I guess you do, Giulio.'

'And with luck, and work, you find people who know more than they say.'

He was looking at me harder. He was certain I knew more.

'It's not a time when people are going to pay a lot of attention to another dead body, but I've been told to find out what I can, Stefan. It's my job. I have to do something. And I think – I'm sure – with your help, we can do something else.'

Somehow I had just agreed to something he hadn't even asked me.

'I'm working on the assumption you didn't kill him, Stefan. Is that OK?'

I dropped my cigarette and stubbed it out. I nodded.

'A good start, Inspector.' He grinned. 'Now we know more than fuck all!'

12

UFFICI GENDARMERIA

Next morning the embassy at the Villa Spada was silent. I had given Michael MacWhite the bare facts of Donal Hyde's death the night before. He had few questions then and not many more when I saw him now. He didn't directly ask me why I was looking for Donal in the Palazzo San Callisto. Incomprehension was enough to be going on with. He struck me as a man who didn't only restrict himself to what he needed to know but also had a strong instinct for avoiding what it wasn't helpful to know. Maybe that was the art of diplomacy. I knew his silence wasn't simply about the real distress and shock he felt. I could see that had hit him hard. But his knowledge of the good Father's extra-curricular activities, however far that extended, had to be in the mix as well. I had seen the ambassador for only a few moments that morning, as he walked out of the dining room and I walked in. Both of us were relieved we would not have to hold a conversation over breakfast. Even Finn seemed to have got the message. There were not even any bared teeth.

Signora Rosselli served me some coffee with a few words in Italian that I couldn't understand. I didn't know whether she didn't have the English for what she wanted to say or it was easier not to attempt a conversation. I thought the latter, but I didn't want one either. Mrs Butler was at her desk, typing with an energy that was pouring out her own feelings through her fingers. It sounded like anger. I stood in the hall, looking through the open front doors to the garden, hearing her heavy staccato. It stopped abruptly. She came out from the office.

'Does anyone know what happened?'

I had offered the ambassador my short version. Just the stab, not the eyes. Her question wasn't asking for more information. She didn't mean what, she meant why. The answer to that didn't require prevarication on my part. It was easy.

'No.'

We both looked round as Signorina Campana came in. She was not going to pretend she didn't know. That was good. Less of a performance required.

'What's happened? I don't believe . . . Salvatore told me . . .'

Not bad. She had avoided the need for the first moment of shock. The gardener's version would have been elliptical enough through the pipe always clenched between his teeth. Mrs Butler knew that. She went into something like motherly mode. The job of explaining was hers. She swept forward and put her arm round Vittoria. She gave me a no-nonsense, I-think-it's-best-I-deal-with-this-Mr-Gillespie nod. They went into the office and the door closed behind them. As I turned back to the front door, I saw Salvatore looking at me from the drive. He shrugged. It wasn't without feeling, but it was still all he had. It felt like the best response so far. I shrugged back at him. He looked away. He pointed down the drive. He walked off, cupping his hand over the pipe bowl and striking a match.

I heard the car as he pointed. I went to the door. An open-topped German staff car. In the back, Hauptsturmführer Dietrich Ritter and a slight, dark man in black. He wasn't SS. I already recognised the uniform. An Italian police officer.

*

Ritter didn't exactly say, 'I'm sorry for your trouble', as he shook my hand, but if he'd known the formula he would have done. His face expressed great seriousness and concern. He said how shocked he was, shocked, by the death. Shocked was the word. He said it several times more in introducing his companion, Capitano Penna. The Italian echoed the sentiment. He was also shocked. They spoke in English. The Italian was more fluent than Dietrich. He added his take on the shocking events of the previous evening to leave me in no doubt about his fierce indignation.

'An attack of such unimaginable savagery. And on holy ground!'

They had called to see the ambassador, mainly, it seemed to express their shock to him too. I knew MacWhite wouldn't thank me for wheeling these two into his office, but there was little choice. A few minutes later we sat round his desk. There was more conversation about the terrible nature of what had happened, but it didn't last long. The capitano could have gone on at greater length, with a lot of head shaking and a good English vocabulary when it came to the thesaurus entry on barbarity. However, even the Hauptsturmführer could see that too much distress at the idea of brutality could be overdone by an SS man and a Fascist policeman. Besides, when they had gone through the motions, it wasn't why they were there.

'The killer must be caught, Ambassador. Be assured, he will be.'

Ritter took the lead. The Italian nodded in almost fierce agreement.

'That's for the police in Rome to do. But they will have the assistance of the Gestapo and the German army, as required. We will give them our fullest support.'

Capitano Penna nodded again.

'And the killer has already been identified,' continued the SS man.

'We are on top of it, Ambassador,' said the Italian. 'He won't get away.'

The simple, almost casual certainty of this came as a surprise to me. I could tell I must have shown it. And in return, the grin I got from Dietrich Ritter showed he had noticed my surprise. He thought I was impressed. The expression on Michael MacWhite's face, practised in showing surprise at nothing, didn't change.

'However,' said Ritter, 'there are some problems in . . .'

The ambassador merely raised his eyebrows.

'Inspector Gillespie may have explained . . .'

'He has explained that he found Donal Hyde's body.'

'I mean about the investigation . . . and its unsatisfactory nature.'

The SS man smiled at me again, as if expecting agreement.

Capitano Penna opened a briefcase and took out a photograph. 'This is the man.'

He put the picture on the desk. There was no doubt who it was.

'Luca Horvat. A Franciscan,' continued the Italian policeman. 'So, Brother Luca. Croat by nationality, wanted in Croatia for the murder of a senior Ustaše officer and another Franciscan friar, a man who was a chaplain with the Croatian forces. There may be other killings. According to the Croatian police the man is mentally ill. He escaped custody in Zagreb a year ago. And disappeared. We now know he was living in a Franciscan monastery in Rome. They had no knowledge he was a wanted criminal until he was recognised by a Franciscan who had come from Croatia. Horvat disappeared again. That was over two weeks ago.'

'I see,' was the ambassador's unembellished reply.

Hauptsturmführer Ritter and Capitano Penna expected more.

'Do you know this man?'

Ritter barked the question at me.

I peered at the photograph and shook my head.

'I don't.'

MacWhite looked at me oddly. He couldn't see why I would.

'That doesn't seem very likely, Herr Ritter.'

'Probably not, Ambassador. Unfortunately – very unfortunately as it turned out – Father Hyde did know him . . . Father Hyde was involved in some very misguided activities . . . I imagine under the false impression that there is something charitable in helping people . . . people who are the enemies of both Italy and Germany. I don't need to explain, do I? Hiding such people . . . is not uncommon.'

'Whether it is or isn't,' said MacWhite, 'it's not the business of the Irish embassy. Donal was not an employee of the embassy. He was an Irish priest working in Rome. I have no reason to consider him in any other way. If you had some reason to accuse him of some misdeed, perhaps you should have done so.'

'I think your Irish priest had been taken in by this man Horvat, Brother Luca. I think he helped get him into the Palazzo San Callisto after his identity was discovered and the Croatian authorities informed the Italian police. Father Hyde paid a high price for his foolishness. Let's say no more about that. The madman who butchered him must be brought to justice before anyone else suffers.'

Dietrich made a good job of the speech. I almost applauded. Capitano Penna had nodded throughout. Nodding seemed to be what he was there for. But at that point the Italian obviously felt he should do more, or at least feed Ritter's next line.

'The problem is a lack of cooperation . . .'

'In what respect, Capitano?' asked the ambassador.

'The investigation . . . I'm sorry to say the Vatican allowed my officers no access to the palazzo or to the scene of crime. We have not even seen the body.'

144

'Inspector Gillespie tells me the Vatican gendarmes are investigating.'

The capitano gave a snort of derision.

'No detectives, no forensic equipment. It's not a police force—'

Ritter didn't think derision was the way forward. He cut him off.

'I think the Vatican's decision, with respect, is a political one. The Polizia don't want to trample on their sovereignty, neither does the Gestapo. It's simply not helpful if witnesses can't be properly questioned . . . if the forensic evidence hasn't been properly collected.' He turned to me. 'You understand that, Stefan.'

I fell back on a non-committal shrug. He didn't think much of it.

'We would all appreciate it if you would approach the Vatican, Ambassador, and ask them to take a more cooperative approach. This is a very dangerous man. It is an Irish priest we're talking about, who lost his life in horrific circumstances.'

Michael MacWhite nodded, but what he was nodding about was unclear.

'But you've already solved this. What can the Papal Gendarmerie do?'

Ritter half frowned, half smiled as if he didn't grasp the question.

'You know who did it. All the capitano's men have to do is catch him.'

Capitano Penna nodded. Ritter glared. That was the wrong nod.

The ambassador stood up before the SS man could rewind. Hauptsturmführer Ritter and Capitano Penna stood, a little clumsily, slightly caught out. The conversation had ended more abruptly than either of them expected.

'I'll do what I can, gentlemen.'

I read that as an I-won't-do-anything conclusion. Ritter did too.

When the SS man and the Italian captain had gone, MacWhite picked up the photograph of Brother Luca. Penna had left it on the desk. He turned it to me.

'You wouldn't miss him in a crowd.'

'No.'

'Did Donal know this man?'

I nodded.

'And he was in hiding . . . from the Italian police, the Gestapo . . .'

'That's what I've been told.'

'But for political reasons, not because he's a murderer . . . or a maniac?'

He smiled because that story suddenly sounded absurd.

I smiled because it was only slightly less absurd than it sounded.

'Maniac's probably overstating it . . . he's maybe not altogether . . .'

Michael MacWhite held up his hand. Too much information.

'But do you know him?'

'I don't know him. I have seen him.'

The fact that the friar was chasing me through Trastevere at the time, maybe with the intention of breaking my neck if he caught me, wasn't helpful, I thought.

'Did he kill Donal?'

'I wouldn't say so. Commissario De Angelis wouldn't say so either.'

'And they know that, Hauptsturmführer Ritter and the nodding capitano?'

'No one wants Luca for Donal's death, sir. Someone just wants him.'

The ambassador sat at his desk again.

'I have to let Dublin know. I'm still not sure what. At one level it's simply a death. But it has to be said that he was killed. And there's a police investigation . . . though what the fuck that means . . . as we've just seen, is anybody's guess. The Department will send someone to tell . . . his parents . . . and I don't doubt they'll lean heavily on difficulties of communication . . . war . . . an occupied city. I'll talk to the Irish College, but he'll be buried here. There'll be no body going home. Is there more to say about how he died? I'm conscious you haven't told me very much. I shall write to his family myself. He was a friend. I do have to pass on what I can.'

Even the words meant for me were somehow addressed to himself.

'I'll put it in a report,' I said. That was always the way to postpone what was better postponed. 'Not all of it. But there'll be some sort of post-mortem from the Vatican. You can have that. No one need be sorry his parents won't see the body.'

It was not much later that I was heading along by the river with Vittoria Campana, towards St Peter's and the Vatican City, the little enclave at the heart of Rome that was another country altogether, only a few acres in size. I had seen the dome of St Peter's from a distance already. It was something else I carried in my head, like the ruins of what went before it. And like them, more than just a picture somehow. Another one of those places your imagination has already made you a visitor to. As Vittoria drove me towards the great circle of the piazza and the steps to the basilica beyond and the arms of the dark colonnades that held it all together, it was instantly familiar. Also familiar now, after only a couple of days, were the German soldiers who meandered up and down a painted white line that marked the otherwise invisible boundary of the Vatican City, Hauptsturmführer Ritter's irritating Ruritania. Not that the soldiers seemed to be doing anything. People were walking back and forward across the white line. The German troops took no notice.

The embassy car turned away from the piazza, round one side of the colonnades to a long wall and an open gate. Vittoria showed a pass to a soldier in a baggy grey uniform. A small dent in familiar expectations. No striped pantaloons and helmets. Even the Swiss Guards, the Pope's bodyguard, were dressed for war, after a fashion. We drove in with little more than a nod. The back of St Peter's gave way to buildings that looked like they'd been plucked from any of the streets I'd recently walked and set down again in a greener, quieter space, overpopulated by priests and nuns.

We said little on the way. She was still taking in Donal's death. Somehow, in the hours since we'd found him, I had become a policeman, even if in uncomfortable circumstances. It was easy to forget he had been close to her. But she wanted to know about the visit from SS Hauptsturmführer Ritter. I wanted to know what she'd found out from the Partisans she smuggled guns for. I wanted to know what had happened to the Franciscan. She had nothing to tell me, or nothing she was prepared to tell me, for whatever reason. I had no reason to keep anything from her though. It was simple enough. If the Gestapo or the Fascist police got to Brother Luca, the outcome wasn't in doubt. It might be quick or it might be slow, depending on what they wanted from him, but he would end up dead.

The signorina dropped me at a building fronted by a small garden and a fountain. The offices of the Gendarmerie were at one side. She said she would come back to collect me but I said I'd make my own way. I thought I'd done enough to make her trust me the previous night, but she was still uneasy. She wanted to know what I was up to, or at least someone had ordered her to find out. I told her not to worry, I would let her know. I added that a bit of quid pro quo would oil the wheels in that regard. She frowned as if she didn't understand.

'If anyone knows who killed Donal, it's Luca. We need to find him.'

I didn't stay in the Gendarmerie offices long. Commissario De Angelis worked in a room with four other officers. They were in uniform but he was in a suit. I didn't know if he had moved into detective mode or whether it was a good excuse to ditch the outfit. The offices were small and cramped. The scale was much the same as the Special Branch building at Dublin Castle, except that this was a whole police force. I was taken along a corridor to another room, where I was introduced to Giulio's boss, Ispettore Dirigente Caproni. He was short, round and inexplicably nervous. He spoke little English and our conversation was mostly in German.

'I'm grateful for your assistance, Inspector Gillespie.'

'I don't know what I can do, sir, but whatever I can . . .'

'Exactly! Exactly my point.'

The Ispettore looked oddly relieved, as if I had just provided a solution to some problem going round in his head that he hadn't managed to get out.

'I'm not happy with what we're being asked to do, not at all.'

He looked at Giulio and said something in Italian. Giulio shrugged.

He turned to me again, speaking in German.

'Crime, let alone something as serious as this, is not our remit. We work with the Polizia di Stato or the Carabinieri, as is necessary. They deal with such things. We have no expertise, no resources. My men are not detectives. But the Curia sends a cardinal, a bloody cardinal, for God's sake, to tell me I can't even let the police see the body! And we have to investigate ourselves. Mad, fucking mad!'

He spoke again in Italian. The commissario nodded, unconvincingly. Caproni turned back to me.

'We have no jurisdiction in the city. We are not in a position to find this man. We have no authority to arrest him anyway. So, a murderer is on the loose!'

Ispettore Dirigente Caproni pushed a photograph across the desk, not so much for me to look at, I thought, but as incontrovertible proof of everything he had said. I took a leaf out of Commissario De Angelis's book and gave a considered nod. I had already seen the photograph that morning, at the Villa Spada. It was the one Hauptsturmführer Ritter and Capitano Penna had produced.

Father Hyde's body lay on a marble bench in the mortuary of the Vatican hospital. A post-mortem had been carried out, with as much attention to forensic detail as the pathologist could offer. In a sense the lack of expertise didn't matter. The cause of death was a traumatic stab wound. A heavy-bladed knife had been plunged between his shoulders twice, maybe three times. Death would not have come instantly, but it would have come quickly. The eyes had been forced from their sockets at around the same time. Whether Donal was actually dead or not at this point was unclear. If not he would have been beyond awareness, maybe beyond consciousness. There was nothing to add to what had been obvious in the garden shed at the Palazzo San Callisto. The kind of work that might have found evidence of the killer, in blood or hair or fibres, was impossible, just as any serious forensic crime-scene examination had been. It was hard to think what was possible. It was even hard to see the point of what we were trying to do. Looking down at the body my cautious words to Ispettore Caproni seemed to sum it up. I didn't know what I could do. I didn't know what Commissario De Angelis could do either.

'I need some air again,' was all Giulio said as we left. 'And a cigarette.'

We walked back to the Gendarmerie offices but didn't go in. The commissario stopped in the neat garden at the front and sat by the fountain to light his cigarette.

'Outside is better, Stefan.'

I took a cigarette. I gathered the breath of air was about the absence of ears.

'Have you spoken to anyone at the palazzo?'

'I have. It doesn't help very much, so far. Maybe one thing . . .'

'So, what do you have?'

'The priest goes to the garden of the Palazzo San Callisto to find a man, the Franciscan, who is sleeping in a shed there. The man is in hiding, like many, all over Rome, here in the Vatican too. The priest has been sent to take the man somewhere else. He has smuggled him into the palazzo, but there's a problem. Someone in the palazzo says he knows this man, Brother Luca. He thinks he's a spy or he was a Fascist in Croatia, or both. It doesn't matter. There's a row, even a fight. Someone says get the brother out of here and Father Hyde, who is part of the underground that does this, that hides people from the Nazis and the Fascists, has to go back. He goes to find the friar. Does he find him? We don't know. Does the friar leave then? Has he gone already? We don't know. But someone finds Father Hyde and kills him. Is there a reason? Is it a mistake? Is it someone he knows? One person, more? We don't know. No one sees a thing, hears a thing. You arrive . . .'

He looked at me, smiling.

'In English, of course, I say "you", whether it's you on your own . . .'

He stopped. Whatever he suspected, or knew, he left it and continued.

'For such a busy place, witnesses are hard to find. There's silence. A lot of these people are afraid. And why not? They are already running from something. But they feel they have found safety within the Holy Father's walls. If someone can walk in and kill. Or maybe not walk in. If somebody who is already there . . . who's still there . . . and even if I'm from the

Papal Gendarmerie, I'm taking down names, making lists, asking questions. And there's reason to be suspicious. We're sitting here because anything my ispettore hears goes straight to the Fascist police. Anything the Fascist police get goes to the Via Tasso. There are three kinds of officers in the Gendarmerie. The ones who worked with Fascist Intelligence, SIM, from the moment Mussolini came to power, the ones who didn't but had to keep their mouths shut, and the rest, who did what they were told. But now it's complicated. If you're giving information to SIM, which one? The SIM that works for the Germans or the SIM that works for the Allies? If you're choosing sides, you need to see which way the wind is blowing. Ispettore Caproni is deeply religious, he tells us, but he should read his Bible more . . . and discern the signs of the times.'

'He seems to have discerned who killed Donal Hyde.'

'With a little help. We had visitors this morning.'

'Hauptsturmführer Ritter and Capitano Penna, by any chance? They came to the embassy as well, bearing gifts into the bargain. A photograph of Brother Luca.'

The commissario laughed.

'Very helpful. But we didn't get the SS man. Penna brought a Croat with him. I don't know him but I've seen him in the Città del Vaticano. He's a secretary to the Croatian representative. I think the name is Milić. He was in a suit this morning, but he's often in his Ustaše uniform. They're very big on black, like the Italian Fascists. They were in the office with Ispettore Caproni for a long time.'

'Was it the same message, the mad monk on a killing spree?'

'Not so much mad as bad. He's wanted in Zagreb for killing a policeman or soldier and another friar. But he's also a spy now. He was with the Croatian nationalists himself, so that's the Ustaše basically. Replace Ustaše with Nazi and you get the picture. However, that was all a front. They claim he was an agent for the Yugoslav government in exile . . . and was being paid by British Intelligence.'

This version of the murdering brother wasn't quite the one Dietrich Ritter had offered up at the Villa Spada. This friar seemed more manipulative than mad.

'What about the man at the palazzo . . . who recognised him?'

'He started to tell me something, but . . .' Giulio shook his head. 'He clammed up. It was fear. A lot of it. The man's in the Palazzo San Callisto because it's a sanctuary . . . then he sees a friar he thinks he knows from Croatia . . . who is a Fascist . . . then there's a dead priest . . . and no one knows where the Franciscan is. I think the man's locked himself up in a room now. Terrified. He's not alone either.'

'So, did you get anything?'

'According to him, Horvat was an Ustaše chaplain, a party member, which fits what Capitano Penna and Milić had to say . . . up to the point when Brother Luca turns into a spy. Croatia is a nasty business, whatever side you're on. There's a big population of Serbian Orthodox. But the Croats are very Catholic. When the Ustaše took over, they started forcing Serbs to convert to Catholicism. It was a test of loyalty, I suppose. I've heard from Italian soldiers that people who refused were killed. That's all I know. As you might imagine, it's not talked about a lot here.'

The commissario took out another cigarette and lit it. I thought he knew more than he said about all that, but he wasn't going to talk about it much either.

'The Croatian at the palazzo said Brother Luca was part of it. I assume he meant the forced conversions. But that was it. I couldn't get any more out of him.'

I still wasn't sure how much more De Angelis had wanted to get. He didn't like the subject. What he had told me only created more confusion about who Luca was.

'That turns it all upside down. Now our friend Luca's on both sides at once.'

The Vatican policeman laughed.

'Well, maybe he's a lunatic after all.'

Maybe a joke, maybe he was easier changing the subject. Then his name was called.

'Commissario De Angelis! C'è del lavoro da fare!'

Ispettore Dirigente Caproni was leaning out from the window of his office.

A stream of Italian followed before the window slammed shut. Giulio stood up.

'Now he wants to know what I got at the Palazzo San Callisto too.'

'Why?' I grinned. 'Haven't the Italian police solved it?'

'It means they can't find Brother Luca and they've got no idea where to look. That'll piss the Gestapo off. They won't want to waste their time on this. So, since I'm the only one who's talked to any witnesses, for what that's worth, the Polizia are scraping the barrel and hoping I might have something. Still, I haven't.'

'Do I get an invite to this conversation?'

'You don't.'

'Tell the Irishman to fuck off?'

'I wouldn't say it was as polite as that, Stefan.'

He took a piece of paper from his pocket and handed it to me.

'A pass. Come and go as you want. It'll be inconvenient for the ambassador to have you using his car all the time . . . inconvenient for Signorina Campana too.'

He definitely knew she was with me at the Palazzo San Callisto.

'I'll catch up with you, Giulio. Do you know the Via dei Corridori?'

'You're looking for your ambassador to the Holy See, Mr Kiernan?'

I nodded. I was following MacWhite's instructions now. Commissario De Angelis gave me directions, back out of the Vatican, then across St Peter's Square.

'He will be useful,' said the commissario. 'His wife perhaps more so. Tell them you want to talk to Monsignor O'Flaherty. They can vouch for you. Better I'm not involved in that. Ask the monsignor about Luca and Father Hyde. He will know.'

As I walked out of the Vatican gate, there was a group of boys playing with a football in the street. I noticed them only because one of the Swiss Guards was shouting at them and they were shouting back. It was something so ordinary that I found myself looking on to remind myself there was something ordinary, still out there, even after the last few days. It wasn't only those last days either. It was weeks and months of my life. And more than that. The thought took me somewhere else, if only for seconds. It took me home, to my son in Ireland. There was little point in what I was doing, it felt. In another time and place it would have mattered. A dead man should matter. I didn't believe he mattered here at all.

I watched for a few minutes. I watched the boys laughing at the Swiss Guard and, eventually, the Swiss Guard laughing at the boys and deciding to leave them alone. If I hadn't spent those moments looking at the boys, I wouldn't have fixed a picture of them in my head. And if I hadn't fixed that picture in my head, I wouldn't have noticed, later that afternoon, that one of the boys was following me.

13

COLÁISTE NA nGAEDHEAL

I walked across the open end of St Peter's Square, from one curved colonnade to the other, following the thick white line that separated German Rome and the Holy See. I carried on to a street that led away from St Peter's, with a long wall on one side and terraces of apartment houses on the other, in search of Ireland's second embassy in Rome. For a country that had few embassies, two here seemed extravagant, but if other missions mattered more in the real world, I knew none were more highly regarded than the one that gave the Irish Minister access to the Pope. Not that the embassy to the Holy See amounted to much. I walked up some stairs to a flat over a restaurant in the Via dei Corridori that was half the size of the one I'd visited to see our defrocked and unlamented ex-ambassador to Berlin.

There was no secretary and it seemed no staff in the room that served as the embassy's office. Mrs Butler, who was shared with the Villa Spada, was across the river in Trastevere. I was met by the ambassador's wife, who introduced herself as Delia and wanted neither Mr Gillespie nor Inspector, but only my first name. She made a point of being welcoming and offering up a few remarks about my journey and the weather and the mess the city was in. But I could see, however, she had been crying. The ambassador, Tom Kiernan, appeared and Delia left us alone.

Kiernan was also light on formalities. Michael MacWhite had begun to call me Stefan but expected Mr MacWhite or sir in return. Kiernan's style was Tom, for what it was worth. I wasn't anticipating lasting friendships with either of them.

The ambassador already had the basic details of Donal Hyde's death. Like his colleague at the Villa Spada, he wanted little more. I told him that Donal had been involved in smuggling someone into the Palazzo San Callisto, to hide from the authorities in Rome, Italian or German or both. Whether there was a direct connection between that and the priest's death or not, we couldn't tell. I could see he already knew something about what Donal had been doing. He didn't comment.

Since the consular duties devolved on MacWhite at the Villa Spada, there was nothing for Tom Kiernan to do. He seemed relieved the inquiry into the death didn't involve the Italian police or the Gestapo. Though he didn't say it, I could see he expected little to come of the investigation. I almost got the impression he thought that might not be such a bad thing. It wasn't so much that he didn't want to know, but that other things, unexpressed, undefined, unremarked, were better left unexamined. At the same time, I knew he was personally distressed. Donal Hyde had been a frequent visitor to the Via dei Corridori, as he had to the Villa Spada.

'Commissario De Angelis said I should talk to an Irish priest, Monsignor O'Flaherty. He's in the Vatican, but the commissario said it would be good if the contact came from you. You'd vouch for me.' I smiled. 'Whatever that means.'

Tom Kiernan nodded. He was slightly less easy.

'As it happens, Hugh O'Flaherty was on the phone to Delia this morning. About you. It's best I hand you over to her.

Hugh's not the easiest man to get hold of. There are also matters it's wise for me to be ill-informed about. The main thing is that the monsignor would like to talk to you . . . without your Vatican gendarme.'

Kiernan saw my surprise. Monsignor O'Flaherty was ahead of the game.

'There's not much he doesn't know. Whether he'll tell you anything . . .'

Tom Kiernan had left, to do whatever it is ambassadors to the Holy See do. Delia Kiernan took me through into a sitting room and produced a pot of tea. She didn't bother with the kind of conversation I imagined ambassador's wives were good at. She had done her best on that front when I arrived. She wanted to know more about Donal Hyde's death. She asked, not in the official, almost transactional way her husband had asked, but as a friend or family might ask. I told her what I felt I could. It was still the version that left the priest's eyes in his head, but it was brutal enough without that. She had tears left to shed for Donal, but she held them back. I heard them in her voice though. I thought they would be shed again when I left her.

Delia had no problem talking about what Father Hyde had been doing. I almost felt she needed to. She not only knew of his work helping people on the run from the Germans, she said bluntly that she was doing whatever she could to help too. There were a lot of blind eyes turned in and out of the Vatican, and those included her husband's. What she did was very limited. She couldn't take the risks other people took. I didn't ask her what she did and I didn't say what I knew myself. I did wonder whether those Irish passports had come from the Via dei Corridori rather than the Villa Spada. I wasn't sure why she was telling me this, but then I heard the catch in her voice again, and the tears that were waiting till I went. She wasn't sure if somehow, somewhere, there wasn't some blame attaching to her. She couldn't say that, but I saw it. She had supported him, helped him, maybe even encouraged him, from the safety of the little island of Ireland that was the embassy.

'We have no idea why he was killed. There's some sense this man he got into the Palazzo San Callisto, this friar, was . . . that it connects to something that happened in Croatia . . . to the war or politics. Donal was just in the wrong place.'

Delia Kiernan appreciated the gesture. She nodded. But I could see it didn't change anything. It didn't change why he was in the wrong place. She had a point. But she had said enough of what she needed to say. Her voice was sharper now.

'Did Tom mention Monsignor O'Flaherty?'

'Yes. I want to see him. It seems he wants to see me.'

'Are you going to the Irish College?'

'When I leave here. I need to talk to the people there. I have to look at his room. I don't expect to find anything significant . . . but there are basic questions . . .'

I wished I'd left the bit about the room out.

'Yes, I understand. Hugh said he'll see you there.'

I smiled and nodded. There really wasn't much the monsignor didn't know.

I had followed the map from the Via dei Corridori to the Irish College. And as I approached the college I saw a group of boys playing football, kicking a ball about between them as they moved along the road in front of me. It wasn't long since I'd watched another group of boys doing the same thing at the gates into the Vatican. Then I remembered another boy with a ball, bouncing it up and down in an archway off the Via dei Corridori as I was walking away from the Irish embassy. Now, as I turned in at the gates of the Irish College, one of this new group of boys collected up the ball and started to bounce it, slowly moving away, as the other boys shouted something at him and walked off. The boy with the ball was one of those I'd seen outside the Vatican. Probably the same one I'd seen in the Via dei Corridori. He had appeared in three places. Cleverly, he had got ahead of me by the third time. Following by staying just in front, but nevertheless following. I kept on through the college gates, but the moment he was out of sight I turned round and walked back. He was there. He wasn't expecting me to return. But he was quick. He saw I'd noticed him. And he was gone. I guessed he wouldn't come back. He was good enough for that. If it hadn't been for the thoughts that game of football put in my head outside the Vatican, I wouldn't have noticed him at all.

The Irish College was an elegant building in grounds that were filled with pines and had the regulation fountain at its heart. I hadn't learned where the line between a big house and a palazzo was drawn, but if the college didn't cross that line, it was close enough. It was also empty. Its job, which was to be home to Irish priests and seminarians in Rome, was on hold for the duration of the war. Only a few students had stuck it out, while the rector and his staff ran a skeleton crew.

My gut told me not to expect much. If anything, there was even less.

The rector was, not unreasonably, serious and sober. But he had nothing to say. By now I was used to the fact that a lot of people knew what Father Hyde had been doing in his spare time. Few would talk about it. Mrs Kiernan had been an exception. I got the impression that the rector of the Irish College had known enough to make sure he avoided finding out any more. He didn't have much to say about Donal at all, other than that he had been an excellent student whose studies at the Pontifical University had been disrupted by the war, as everything had been disrupted. He didn't elaborate, but I felt that something about Father Hyde had irritated him and even the shock of the priest's death hadn't quite got that out of his head, despite his best intentions. I didn't ask him directly about Donal's extra-curricular activities. I knew within five minutes that he would prevaricate or lie.

No one else had more to offer. Donal had friends in the college and they were deeply upset, but I felt as I spoke to those friends that he had left such friendships behind in some way, at least in recent months. In the college there was a feeling that the war ought to stop at the gates. It hadn't stopped there for Donal Hyde and that had created a distance between him and some of his colleagues. What was certain was that what had happened had nothing to do with his life there.

A look at Donal's room only confirmed that. He had few possessions except books. These had mostly to do with the Bible. There were versions in Latin and Greek and volumes of commentaries. There were also versions of the Old Testaments in Hebrew along with other Hebrew texts and dictionaries. Other than recognising what these things were, they told me nothing except that there had been another life that Father Hyde lived in his head. However, the dust on the books suggested he hadn't been living that life for some time. Apart from that, there was a drawer full of family letters. Again, it was only something to register.

I had left the door to the room open. I looked round, sensing someone was watching me. A tall man with a round face and round, thick-lensed glasses stood in the doorway, smiling at me. He was oddly dressed. He had on a long, dark priest's gown, a soutane, but wore a white linen coat over it, slightly grubby and stained.

'Mr Gillespie, Inspector Gillespie?'

'I am.'

'Hugh O'Flaherty. Good to meet you.'

The priest walked forward and shook my hand. I found myself looking down at the coat he wore. There was no question that the stains on the linen were blood.

'You're not long out of Ireland, I hear, Stefan.'

'Not so long, Monsignor.'

Among the many things he knew, he knew my first name.

'So long as it's still there, eh? And where are you from?'

'Wicklow, near Baltinglass.'

'Ah, Vallis Salutis . . . the Valley of Salvation.'

'Well, eight hundred years ago, Monsignor.'

'Not at all, salvation's always there. And Hugh will do! A Cork man.'

The ritual exchange of counties done, the monsignor wasted no more time.

He turned and shut the door.

'Tell me what happened. When? How? As far as you know.'

Something about this man disarmed me. I told most of what I knew and most of what I'd seen. I included the gouging out of Donal Hyde's eyes. I felt he knew even that. It was as if he was checking details rather than looking for information.

'The eyes are important.'

It was a strange remark. He already knew something I didn't.

'I shan't waste your time with what you know and don't know, Stefan. You have some idea what Donal was doing. We'll leave the games to the rest of them. He was working with me. You'll hear that. At some point you may even hear someone say the fact that he's dead is because he was working with me. I'm sorry to say I can't avoid saying it myself. I can't avoid facing it myself either. That's for another day. For now, why has this happened? Who did it? Most of all, what's it for?'

'I was hoping you'd tell me, Hugh.'

'Perhaps, I will. Maybe between the two of us . . .'

'Three . . . there's also Commissario De Angelis.'

Monsignor O'Flaherty smiled a wry, cautious smile.

'A good man, I think, but there are those in the Vatican Gendarmerie . . .'

'He knows that.'

The priest shrugged.

'I have been involved in hiding people from the Nazis, and the Italian Fascists, ever since Italy surrendered and changed sides. It started because there were suddenly Allied prisoners of war all over the place, trying to avoid recapture. Then there were Italians the Nazis wanted for betraying Mussolini or just for surrendering in the first place. Then there were others. They're all over Rome. Some in the Vatican and places like the Palazzo San Callisto that belong to the Holy See. They're at least reasonably safe. We play a kind of blind man's bluff. The Vatican won't let these people in, but once they're in, they won't kick them out. That's the game Donal played with Brother Luca. But it went wrong. I don't know why. Luca was unusual. He was running from the Croatian government . . . or their secret police . . . that's what he said, but still from Nazis by another name.'

'You know he's wanted in the city now, for Donal's murder?'

O'Flaherty nodded.

'Is there any possibility at all . . .'

'No. I don't believe that. But it's another way to find him. And it's probably a way to make sure he won't get back on to Vatican territory again. That's very certain.'

'None of it tells us why Donal was killed,' I said, 'and killed that way.'

'That's what I have to know, Stefan. Is this just about Luca Horvat. Or is it something else? Is this a way to attack the whole underground? If the Vatican thinks the people hiding on its territory are going to bring killers in their wake . . . that's one way to put an end to the blind man's bluff. If the people hiding feel they're not safe . . . that's already happened at the palazzo. Or if the people running escape routes start to feel they'll be murdered . . . that because the Gestapo can't just pick them up in the street, Herr Kappler has decided to send his people on to Vatican territory to kill them. Is Donal's death one terrible thing or the beginning of more?'

I shook my head. This was nothing I could help him with.

'I'm out of my depth already. You don't expect me to answer that.'

The monsignor smiled.

'No, but I think you can help me make a start in answering it myself. Of course, what I'd most like to do is to find Brother Luca, before the Fascists do.'

'You've no idea if Donal had already got him out of the palazzo?'

'He didn't. I think Brother Luca just ran, whether that was before or after they killed Donal, I don't know. What Donal intended was to get him out of Rome. The Irish College has a house in Tivoli. It's been shut up since the war started. No one goes there. I've used it as a stop-off for POWs. It's where I told him to go.'

'So what's happened to Luca then?'

'I have no idea. But we are looking for him . . .'

That was it. That was all the Irish priest had.

'So, what now?'

'I have an old friend for you to meet, Stefan, in the Vatican.'

'Do I have an old friend in the Vatican?'

'You do. And he can tell us more about Brother Luca.'

Monsignor O'Flaherty led the way out of the college building, but not back along the corridors to the entrance and the gardens. He took me down some narrow stairs and into the kitchens. We walked past two men cutting up meat and peeling vegetables and a woman piling dishes up in a sink. No one took any notice of us. They didn't even look as we passed. We came out in a small courtyard. There was a truck. The engine was running. A man in a white coat, grubby and stained like the monsignor's own, leaned against the driver's door, smoking a cigarette.

'Prossima tappa il Vaticano!' said Hugh.

The driver got into the cab. The priest pulled open the back doors of the truck. Inside was a row of butchered meat carcasses, hanging from a rail. There were whole sides of pork and lamb and quarters of beef. The smell of blood.

'Just find somewhere to sit.'

O'Flaherty climbed in. I followed. I sat against the side of the truck, between half a pig and a whole lamb. He pulled the doors shut and sat opposite me. The truck pulled away. The carcasses swung back and forth between us. The priest drew out a packet of cigarettes. He took one and leant across to give me one.

'I vary how I travel . . . have you met Obersturmbannführer Kappler?'

'No. I know a man called Ritter who must work for him, Dietrich Ritter.'

The priest sat back, drawing hard on his cigarette, grinning.

'Kappler is head of the Gestapo and Sicherheitsdienst. I've met him a few times. I've reached a point where it wouldn't be advantageous to meet him again.'

The butcher's van was oddly welcome. I was glad to be in it. I doubted that Obersturmbannführer Kappler and his subordinates sent kids with footballs to follow people through Rome's streets, but someone did. The van was no bad place to be.

14

CITTÀ DEL VATICANO

The butcher's lorry dropped the monsignor and me at the back of another big kitchen, this time somewhere off a street in the Vatican City. O'Flaherty disposed of his blood-stained overall and as the van doors opened we simply got out. The two men in dirty kitchen whites who were waiting to unload the carcasses gave a curt, respectful nod, as if a monsignor stepping out of a meat wagon was an everyday occurrence. I got the impression it probably was. We walked along an alleyway into the street and then to a quiet garden that extended out from the back of St Peter's. We climbed the stairs of a building full of broad, stone corridors. O'Flaherty knocked at a door and I followed him into a room that looked out over the garden we had just walked through. It should have been bright, but everywhere there were books and where there weren't books there were piles of documents and files, tied up in bundles, heaped on top of each other. In one corner was a bed, and that too, for the moment, was entirely covered in papers and docu-ments. I took this in before I saw the man in the wheelchair, who sat among the books and moved forward to greet us. He looked at me quizzically, as if not quite remembering something, and then he smiled. And it was when he smiled that I recognised him.

'Like old times, Mr Gillespie . . . is it Stefan, do I have that right?'

'It is, sir. It's good to see you.'

The face was still sharp. The eyes behind the glasses were still bright. But he was older, older than he should have been, it seemed. It wasn't so long ago I had met him. Eight years. The discovery of a long-dead body in the Dublin Mountains had taken me to the little German enclave that was the Free City of Danzig, a miniature country almost surrounded by Poland and full of people who wanted to be part of Germany, whatever the cost. I went to find a missing Irish woman whose bloody-minded determination had nearly got us both killed. That wasn't the only memory I had of her, but that was then, and eight years had passed. The man in front of me had been Danzig's Catholic bishop, and one of the only people left in the city who was resisting the Nazi takeover of his city. Edward O'Rourke was a Russian with an Irish ancestor from two centuries earlier, who had left him his very un-Russian name. He had fled Lenin's revolution in 1917, only to find himself, years later, in the middle of Hitler's. When we'd met in Danzig he'd been a vigorous, middle-aged man, bright and determined. He had got old before his time.

'An unexpected surprise,' said the bishop, who was, it seemed still a bishop of somewhere or something, if only in name. 'I've been shut in the Vatican for years. They pushed me out of Danzig, not long after you were there. They found a bishop who thought Adolf Hitler was a grand feller altogether, so that went well.' He laughed. 'Well enough, unfortunately, that the Nazis were able to start this war in Danzig and make my old city the excuse for it. I was never forgiven though.'

O'Rourke turned and pointed at a table.

'Hugh, there's a bottle and glasses. Pour some. The doctors say I shouldn't touch wine. It will kill me. But other things haven't. So, I do and I'm still here.'

The monsignor poured the wine.

'I got out of Poland when they invaded. They wanted to catch me, but I ended up here, helped by a German general looking for some insurance in Heaven.'

Hugh O'Flaherty passed round the glasses.

'So, you want to know about Father Hyde and Brother Luca?'

The bishop crossed himself as he spoke Donal's name. He was silent for a moment. He shook his head. There seemed to be no shortage of people who felt some kind of responsibility for what had happened. O'Rourke was another one.

'I asked Hugh to help Luca. It was done as a favour to me . . .'

'It was done because it needed doing,' said O'Flaherty quietly.

'The story, briefly,' said the old man with a shrug. 'Brother Luca came to me over a year ago. He had left Croatia because of what was happening there. When the Germans invaded Yugoslavia and broke the country up, they let the Croatians have their own state. They gave it to the Ustaše, the familiar gang of Fascist nationalists, who had their own little Hitler, a man called Pavelić. But the Ustaše had their own special take on things. Whereas the Nazis would quite like to destroy the Catholic Church, Croatia is a very Catholic country. And you can do a lot with what people believe, if you turn that inside out and upside down and set it against anyone who doesn't think the same way. The Ustaše had their own enemies. The place was full of heretics, they thought. Orthodox Christians, Serbs. There was the enemy. Millions. Not just an affront to Croatia, but even to God!'

Bishop O'Rourke crossed himself again.

'So, the thing to do was to make them all Catholics. And if they didn't want to become Catholics, well, there was a simple answer. Kill them. And that's what they set about doing. I'm sorry to say that the Church, for the most part, closed its eyes.

And it did worse. There were priests and bishops who supported it, who even called it a crusade. Villages full of people were murdered. Churches were burned with their congregations. Orthodox priests were tortured. And to prove that the puppet state had learned its lessons, there were concentrations camps. Why not?'

The bishop held up his glass.

'It can't be said on an empty glass, Hugh.'

Monsignor O'Flaherty refilled our glasses.

'I knew a lot of what was happening. I have made it my business to collect up information about what has been happening all over Europe. I have a room full. I live with it. I sleep with it. But what I have is only part of what my colleagues in the Vatican have. We gather it in, but we don't act to let it out. Never mind that. That is something else. Today, we are in Croatia. And in Croatia, even when the Church was appalled, it was very quietly appalled. But one of the most shocking things in all this was the role of the Franciscans, the servants of St Francis, one of the gentlest of all the saints. In Croatia, there were Franciscans who took it on themselves to lead this thing they called a crusade. They stood beside the Ustaše killers. They prayed beside them. They blessed them. And one of these Franciscans was Luca Horvat. And when he could take no more of what he saw, he fled his country. He came to Rome. He came to tell the Vatican what was happening. He came with places and names. He came with what he had seen himself. And no one wanted to hear him. He came to me because he could find no one else. But I already knew how few ears were open, how firmly the filing cabinets were closed.'

There was silence again.

'And what happened to him?' I asked.

'He gave up. He went to a Franciscan house and, I guess, prayed.'

'But he wasn't safe.'

169

'No, he was a traitor. I don't know the precise circumstances in which he left Croatia, but they hadn't forgotten. When they found him, they wanted him sent back to Croatia. Failing that, they wanted him dead. He went into hiding. He contacted me. I asked Hugh to get him somewhere safe. But it wasn't safe, was it? The Croatians have a long reach, longer than I would have believed. Even here.'

'You do think they did this . . . the Ustaše?'

The question was Monsignor O'Flaherty's. I already knew how important it was to him. He needed to know this went no further. It wasn't an easy thought, faced with the brutality of the murder, that somehow it could be contained as the revenge of Brother Luca's Croatian enemies. I could see O'Flaherty's discomfort.

'I'm very sure it was. The way Father Hyde was killed is very specific. It has a kind of uniqueness that belongs to Croatia and to the Ustaše . . . we won't call it a crusade, we won't give a name at all. But the method will send a message to Luca.'

O'Rourke wheeled himself to the bed and picked up a typed page.

'This is something Brother Luca wrote himself. "In Otočac I saw more than three hundred Serbs executed. The Orthodox priest there, Branko Dobrosavljević, was forced to pray before the dying. His young son was cut into pieces before his eyes. His hair and beard were torn from his face. Then his eyes were gouged out before he was killed by a knife between his shoulders." It's enough, I think. There is much more. Gouging out the eyes appears again and again. You might say it's a calling card. I am certain Luca would have no doubt who killed Father Hyde, or that it was done to send him a very clear message. This is what is coming to you.'

Monsignor O'Flaherty and I walked through the garden that had brought us to Edward O'Rourke. It was almost dark now and we both let the darkness silence us. There was little to say. In a sense, the priest had his answer. It might not be entirely conclusive, but it seemed to indicate that what had happened at the Palazzo San Callisto was about Luca Horvat and what he had brought with him from Croatia. Even the inexplicable barbarity had some kind of explanation. I had an answer as well, or at least something more I could share with Commissario De Angelis. But it was an empty answer. It pointed us in a direction that we couldn't follow. If there were Croatian agents of some kind in Rome and in the Holy See, they were in plain sight. After all, one them had been sitting in the office of Ispettore Dirigente Caproni that morning, announcing that Rome was being scoured for a psychotic killer who was already wanted in Croatia and who, in reality, was running from Donal Hyde's killers. It was more than likely the Ustaše representative knew who the killers were. It should have come as no surprise, but the simple truth was that even if the commissario and I put a label on the crime, and pointed a finger, that would be that. It was also probably true that Luca Horvat would be discovered and murdered himself.

I felt in my pocket to take out some cigarettes. I touched the small book I had taken from Donal's body at the palazzo, the Jewish prayer book with its photographs and Vatican passes. I had done nothing with it, but I knew it was not something that should get into the wrong hands. I knew it had something to do with the work the priest did for O'Flaherty. I took it out and handed it to him.

I explained how I got it. I also told the priest that I thought Donal had collected it from the library in the Jewish Ghetto when I saw he had called there. O'Flaherty looked at the photographs and then put the book into his pocket.

'I know one of these people. A Jewish politician. And I think his wife and daughter. We were going to get them into the Vatican. The Gestapo are looking for him. He was publishing an anti-Fascist newspaper. That's been closed down, but . . . I don't know where he is now. But hopefully we can still do something for him. Most of the people we've been hiding have been Allied POWs, but it's really the Jews who started me on this road. I had my own dislike of the Nazis before, but I didn't find it hard to step back and take the plague-on-both-your houses course. Like any Irishman, my feelings about the English don't encourage great affection.'

He laughed, but then he was quieter. We walked more slowly.

'But when the Germans occupied Rome, I saw how they treated the Jews. It wasn't that I didn't know. But I had averted my eyes, well, as so many of us have.'

He made a gesture with his hand. I wasn't sure whether it was meant to encompass some vague group of people, the Vatican, the city beyond it, or more.

'Anyway, I opened my eyes. I saw. I felt I had to act.'

'I saw some of it myself,' I said. 'In Rome, but in Berlin too.'

'I think Rome's Jews may be all right,' continued Monsignor O'Flaherty. 'There are those who are in danger, yes, like the man I just mentioned. But the Italians aren't like the Germans. They can be unpleasant about the Jews. They had their own laws that imitated Hitler's. But they don't feel it. Deep down they don't really believe that shite. And for all that Obersturmbannführer Kappler is a model Nazi, he's found a way to fend off the worst excesses and leave the Ghetto alone.'

I remembered the line of people at the checkpoint into the Ghetto.

'It didn't look much like that when I was there.'

'If it's no more than that, Stefan, it's hardly even a performance by their standards, however nasty. The solution was nasty enough in itself, but we have to be grateful. That's what people are reduced to. Kappler told the Jews they could buy their safety. The price? Fifty kilograms of gold. They found it.

It came from everyone who had even the smallest piece of jewellery. And Herr Kappler made the delivery as humiliating as he could, but people pray for even that, humiliation.'

The monsignor left me at the gate out to the city. I was conscious that the information he had now, and the investigation the commissario and I would probably be able to take no further, left a man hiding somewhere in Rome, pursued by the police, the Gestapo and the same people who'd slaughtered Donal Hyde.

'What about Brother Luca?' I said, almost as a goodbye.

'I hope something practical comes up, Stefan. Meanwhile, pray.'

I stepped across the strange, almost invisible Vatican border into the rest of Rome. I had gone only yards, getting my bearings for the walk to the Villa Spada, when a car pulled up. And Vittoria Campana was driving it. She wound down the window.

'A lift, Inspector?'

'I could ask for nothing better. I was just about to get lost.'

She smiled. To be honest, I was looking at that smile more than perhaps I should have been. I was thinking she might like a drink, maybe something to eat. I'd had a day that had got darker as it went on. I needed some light. There it was. I didn't notice that the car she was driving wasn't the ambassador's Lancia. It was bigger, a black limousine. I didn't register it and I don't know that I would have thought much about it if I had. It was a car. I was too busy looking at the driver.

I got in next to her.

'A drink? Does that sound like a good idea?'

It wasn't my best line, it had to be said, but I had no time to improve on it. The two doors at the back opened and a man got in on either side. I turned round. The rear doors slammed shut. The car was moving away, fast. The man directly behind me was holding an automatic. The barrel was only inches from my head.

I looked back at Vittoria.

'No drink then?'

She didn't move her eyes from the road.

'I'm sorry, Stefan.'

At that moment I felt hands on my head. I pushed them off. The other man was leaning forward, trying to get some kind of cloth or band tied round me.

'What the fuck . . .'

I lunged for the car door, with the idea of flinging myself out, whatever the speed, but as I did, the metal of the automatic hit me on the side of the head. It wasn't hard enough to knock me out, but I was dazed. I tasted blood on my lips.

'Jesus!'

Vittoria's voice erupted. She was still driving but she was screaming at the men in the back. They were giving as good as they got. As they all argued, I bled. I was struggling to focus my eyes. Vittoria shouted over the two men one more time. Silence. For a moment nothing happened. I could see now. My head only throbbed.

'He wants to put a blindfold on, that's all. I'm sorry.'

'Well, I'm glad you're sorry. If it matters that much to him . . .'

I sat back in the seat. Vittoria spoke a couple of words in Italian. Then my eyes were covered. The blindfold was tightened. I was in complete darkness.

15

LE CATACOMBE

The car drove on for maybe half an hour. I could tell nothing about the direction we were going in. The city around us wasn't very noisy, mostly there was only the sound of other vehicles. But after a while it felt quieter in a way that made me think we were away from streets and buildings. I had a sense we were driving somewhere more open. The car pulled on to a surface that wasn't tarmac. It was still smooth, but it felt different. I thought it was hard earth, maybe grass. Then we stopped. Doors opened. My arm was taken and I was pulled out. It was nothing particularly rough. It just meant get out and stand up. The voices of the men again, not whispering, but soft, and maybe another man too. Another arm took mine.

'Just walk slowly. Keep with me.'

It was Vittoria. I could smell her scent. It was familiar, a faint, light perfume that I hadn't noticed I already knew until now. And there was another scent, a pine-woody something that was in the air. I knew there were trees round us.

We walked for only a few minutes. The ground was still firm. Then we were squeezing through some sort of doorway. I could feel stone. I could smell stone too and then something earthy and musty at the same time. The air suddenly felt cold.

'There are steps. Very uneven. One at a time.'

The steps were hard to find. It was as if they were different shapes, wide, narrow, deep, shallow. There were a couple of dozen. Then we were on a sloping path, still going down. It was some kind of tunnel. The roof was low. The walls were close. I was brushing against them. Vittoria and I were pushed tight together.

She stopped. It felt flat underfoot. The slope we had come down had levelled out.

'You can take this off.'

Vittoria untied the blindfold.

I was standing in a narrow tunnel. It was dark, but one of the men from the car shone a torch ahead of us. As we moved on, Vittoria was in front of me. There was another man behind me. He carried a machine gun. When I glanced round at him he grinned back. I hoped that was as reassuring as it looked.

The tunnel widened slightly and on both sides there were small cubicles, a few feet long, carved into the rock. There was nothing in most of them, except for dusty piles of rubble, but then I saw bones, almost indistinguishable from the stone heaped around them. Bones, nevertheless. I knew this place too. The catacombs.

'You've an odd idea of a night out, Vittoria. I'd have gone for the drink.'

'Maybe another time,' she laughed.

Another time sounded reassuring too.

The torch picked out a wall ahead of us. The tunnel turned right and left. There was an archway on each side. There was a faint light too. The man with the torch stopped. Vittoria turned through one of the arches. I followed her into a small, square room. It was lit by several candles. Immediately in front of me was the back wall. It was hard not to notice. It was formed out of skulls. There were hundreds of them, piled in rows, one on top of another. Distinctly less reassuring.

A wiry man in a grey suit stood in front of the wall of skulls. He wore very dark glasses, which I assumed were at least a gesture towards disguise. They weren't functional underground. But there was little enough light anyway. What I could see, besides the skulls, were rows of rifles and packing cases that must have contained weapons or ammunition. He reached out and shook my hand.

'I'm sorry about the theatrics. I'm not very free to move around.'

'Well, it's something else to tick off my list.'

The man said something in Italian. Vittoria answered.

'You'll forgive me if my English is slow,' continued the Italian. 'Good but slow was what my teacher always said. Vittoria can fill in if you leave me behind.'

Nothing was slow about his English. As he spoke I saw why he kept looking at Vittoria. It was to check what I was saying agreed with what she already knew. He nodded at her and then smiled at me. He perched on the edge of a packing case.

Vittoria stood to one side of the room, in shadow. If he was relaxed, she wasn't.

'You've packed a lot into a few days in Rome, Inspector.'

'There's a lot to see.'

'Two visits to a man who collects information for the Gestapo. A small fish, perhaps, but swimming with some bigger ones. You went to the Via Ferruccio to see Bewley, almost straight away. I'm told he's an odd one, even for an Irishman.'

'The first time I was passing. I didn't stop.' It wasn't much of an explanation, but I could see I'd be giving him the rest anyway. 'I wanted to see where he lived, that's all. The second time, the ambassador asked me to talk to him about his passport. He needs a new one . . . and there are . . . well, a few problems.'

He wasn't impressed with that.

'There must be if they sent you all way from Dublin to sort it out.'

'The thing is he held on to a lot of papers from his time in Berlin, as the ambassador. The government wants them back. He won't give. I have to get them.'

'And the conversation you had with Vittoria, about a burglary?'

The man knew what he was doing. I could see from his face he wasn't interested in explanations. What he wanted was what I knew, what I'd seen.

'It struck me she might know someone who could help.'

'And why would that be?'

'Well, does the black market get all that coffee delivered by lorry?'

'This isn't about the black market. You found more than coffee.'

'Nothing much.' I risked a smile. 'Nothing I remember.'

The Italian didn't return the smile. What he gave back was something I had experienced a few times in my life, never in comfortable circumstances. In Italian, as in English, it was the is-this-man-a fool-or-does-he-think-I'm-one look.

'You remembered when you spoke to Vittoria.'

'I've got a job to do.' I shrugged. 'It's not important to anyone here. But I need help that I don't have. I was looking for a way . . . I thought I'd found one . . .'

The man's look had shifted a little. The is-this-man-a-fool end of his question was getting the upper hand. I wondered if that's what I should go for.

'Vittoria works at the embassy. It was clear . . . without going any further . . . that there were things the embassy was useful for . . . in what she was doing, in what Father Hyde was doing. It didn't seem such a stretch to look for something back.'

'This is a war, a real war. We're not for hire. If the Irish embassy provides something useful . . . we will use it. But I'm not a great one for neutrality, Inspector. I like it about as much as dog shit on my shoe. You can never get rid of the smell.'

'It's not a big deal,' was the best I could do. 'It doesn't matter.'

'No, it doesn't, signore. But what about the rest?'

'The rest?'

'You followed Donal Hyde to Trastevere. You saw Vittoria arrive with Brother Luca. You watched her take away . . . various things . . . that you later searched your ambassador's car for. You then followed the priest as he was taking the Croatian through Trastevere to smuggle him into the Palazzo San Callisto.'

'Buggins' turn,' I said.

'What does that mean?' The Italian looked at Vittoria. She shrugged.

'I followed him because he was following me. I wanted to know what he was up to. Professional curiosity. If you'd left me alone, I wouldn't have seen anything.' That wasn't the entire truth. It was near enough. 'I assume it was you.'

The man glanced at Vittoria Campana. Somewhere the instructions must have come from him. He thought the mess they'd made of it was down to her.

'The second visit to Signore Bewley's apartment. You left with an SS officer, Hauptsturmführer Ritter. Then you went to the Via Tasso with him.'

'He arrived when I was leaving Bewley's. Not because I was there, because he was dropping something off. Money, basically. He asked me to go to his office. He wanted to know why I was in Rome. Maybe like you wanted to know. I told him less than I've told you. Next to nothing, either about why I'm here, or about anything I've seen along the way. Mostly he gave me his views on Rome, ancient and modern. He prefers it ancient, by the way. Gestapo HQ wasn't on my list of sights to see, but it didn't feel like an invitation it would be clever to turn down.'

'You saw him again this morning, with an Italian police captain?'

'At the embassy, with the ambassador.'

The man looked at Vittoria. She nodded.

'And what did he want then?'

'He wanted to say they'd solved Donal Hyde's murder and the mad monk who did it was wandering around Rome, possibly looking for more priests to stab in the back. They'd get him soon enough but meanwhile would Mr MacWhite get on to the Pope and complain that the Gestapo can't get to interrogate people about the death. Oh, and the Vatican Gendarmerie are a bunch of clowns. More or less.'

There was something like a laugh. I saw Vittoria nod. She knew all that.

'They don't know anything about Vittoria?'

'I don't think they know she was there. If they do, it's not from me. But Ritter may have known something about Donal stealing passports. And he may know more.' I looked at Vittoria now. 'The embassy must be watched sometimes.'

She shrugged. Even Donal's death hadn't dented her confidence.

'And what does this man De Angelis know?'

'He doesn't know about Vittoria either. No one does.'

I didn't say the commissario suspected something. It wouldn't help.

'You know anything you tell him will go to his boss, Caproni?'

'And he'll pass it to whoever . . . Fascist police, Fascist Intelligence . . . I know all that . . . because the commissario told me. He won't say much to the Ispettore. But he knows damn well this Franciscan didn't kill Father Hyde. What it looks like, just from what I've found out, is that there's some Croatian link. Luca Horvat is wanted by the Croatians. That's what he's running from. If he's caught, that's where he'll end up . . . which probably means he'll get a knife in his back too.'

I could see this interested the Italian. It also made sense to him.

'And what makes you say that?'

'I spent some time with Monsignor O'Flaherty this afternoon.'

I saw he didn't know that. We'd got to the end of his information.

'I don't know if the kid with the football would have got on to that if I hadn't spotted him. Probably not. He was with me as far as the Irish College. But if you're looking for someone to vouch for me, I'd say the monsignor would do.'

The man got up and paced slowly. He had watched me intently so far. Now it felt like he had made his mind up about something and didn't need to say more. Behind him the grey, stacked skulls almost flickered in the candlelight.

'It makes sense, yes. The problem, Mr Gillespie, is that if they catch Brother Luca, what happens to him between getting picked up and being handed to his Ustaše friends? What does he tell the Fascist police? What does he tell the Gestapo? I don't know this man, but I gather he is not all there . . . is that how you say it? Simple, crazy, whatever, and a drunk into the bargain. I have better people to protect. People this friar may recognise. One of them is there, right in front of you.'

He pointed at Vittoria. She looked away, uncomfortable.

'You've met Monsignor O'Flaherty. A good man. A charitable man. And why wouldn't he be, sitting with the bunch of arseholes who run the Vatican? At least they have him. He saves a few people. He hides a few people. While they wait to see which side's going to win. Well, maybe they've an idea now, but they haven't got the wit to do anything about it. The dog shit again, Inspector. Not just neutrality this time, holy neutrality. That stinks, as you might say, to high heaven.'

He liked that turn of phrase. Fair or unfair, it wasn't bad.

'I'm not here to save Allied POWs, Mr Gillespie. I have time for some of the others. The politicians, the Jewish leaders.

But there's only so much you can do. War means killing. My people are here to do that. I don't know how long we have to wait for the Allies, but in the meantime we can make the Fascists and the Nazis pay for being here. And when the time comes, we will have the lists, long, long lists, of the spies and collaborators they'll leave behind. So, if you've seen guns, the guns are for firing. They will be fired. And Monsignor O'Flaherty and his underground? They're useful. One of the most useful things is that they keep the police and the Gestapo and the Sicherheitsdienst running around for nothing. But everything has its price, even nothing. And a lot of the time it is nothing. What happens when a British POW gets caught? He is sent to a camp. That's it. What happens to the Italian who hides him, feeds him, even gives him a coat? A bullet to the head.'

The man in dark glasses stood close to Vittoria. He spoke sharply in Italian. She looked him hard in the eyes, then let her head drop. He turned to me.

'I'm sorry about the Irish priest. And I'm grateful to you for letting her get out of there. But she should never have been there. She went too far in helping the Franciscan. She did it because the priest asked her. She did it because she felt sorry for this man Luca. Because he was such an easy man to spot and he had to be transported across the city. She should have left it alone. We don't do lifesaving.'

Vittoria was angry and upset. I could see her face. She glared at me as if I was part of it, tight-lipped, breathing deep. And she looked like she had heard it all before. She walked through the arch into the dark tunnel we had come down. The man took no notice of her exit. He smiled again and sat down on the packing case.

'We have to use Monsignor O'Flaherty sometimes. Like we've used your embassy. On our terms. But you can only do these things so many times without pushing your luck. Mostly we don't get mixed up in what the monsignor does. We can't play those games in the same way. And I see it as a game because for us it's different. Because we are all, each one of us, on borrowed time. We all have a bullet waiting if we're caught. The Franciscan saw too much because Vittoria ignored orders. There are three or four faces he could identify. Even the café you watched him drinking in . . . could cost lives. Wherever this friar is now, he needs to get away from Rome. He has to be put out of harm's way . . . one way or another.'

He looked sideways at the rifles piled against the skulls. He shrugged.

'I take no pleasure in necessity, Mr Gillespie. So, if you do find him . . .'

There was no blindfold on the way back into the city. I had passed some kind of test, even if it was only the one that marked me out as a fool who'd strayed into deep water without knowing it. The man who had slugged me outside the Vatican drove the black car. He didn't speak English, but he occasionally said a few words and glanced round to where I sat in the back with Signorina Campana and laughed. There wasn't going to be an apology, but he had concluded we were all friends. I smiled when he looked back. Since I only felt the pain when I moved my mouth, I was glad when he shut up. Vittoria was silent. She didn't like the way it had been done. She didn't like the bollocking the Partisan leader had given her either.

The car stopped at the Villa Spada. I wasn't sentimental about Irish harps, but I had to admit I was relieved to see the one at the gates. I got out with Vittoria. The black limousine drove on. We stood by the entrance. Starting a conversation wasn't easy. Most of the evening needed forgetting. But it wasn't quite that simple.

'Shall I come in and clean up your face? Some disinfectant . . .'

'No. It's not much more than a cut and a bruise. But lay off the jokes. It only hurts when I laugh . . .' And then I laughed. 'You see what I mean! It'll be grand.'

She nodded. She was about to go, but there was another apology on her lips, I could almost see the words. She shrugged and left it where it was. She had already said what was worth saying. She stepped closer and leant forward. She kissed my cheek. The apology she had left on her lips. I wouldn't have said it was worth the clout round the head with an automatic, but it was better than nothing.

16

BASILICA SANCTI PETRI

The next morning I sat in the dining room alone. Signora Rosselli brought me breakfast and said something about the weather. Her English didn't go much further than the weather, which took her a long way in the embassy of a country whose preoccupation with the weather was inexhaustible. She made no comment on my face. She didn't appear to have noticed. It still felt worse than it looked.

In the absence of anyone more interesting, the ambassador's dog had followed me into the dining room and sat watching me eat. I slipped him a bit of bacon, precious though I had been told that was in Rome. Finn and I had an understanding. As I didn't want his barking to advertise my coming and going, a bit of breakfast seemed a small price to pay. Mrs Butler came in, brusque and businesslike. I knew she didn't approve of me. She still couldn't work out why I was there. I still hadn't started my audit. Now I'd been caught feeding the dog.

'You shouldn't encourage him.'

I nodded as if I'd make sure I didn't do it again.

'There's a message for you. It's from Monsignor O'Flaherty.'

The statement was a question. Did I know him? I didn't

respond. But I could feel, somewhere in her tone, that she didn't altogether approve of the monsignor.

'He phoned just now. For some reason it's in Irish.'

I didn't respond to that either, although it was another question dressed up as a statement. But I knew the uses of Irish, where someone might be listening in on a conversation or a telephone might be tapped. It was likely the embassy's was.

Mrs Butler put a piece of paper down.

The message began, 'Aodh – fuair mé é.' Hugh – I have found him. It started with O'Flaherty's first name in its distinctly unrecognisable Irish form. And there was only one person he could have found, the friar. He went on to say he was hearing Confession in English at St Peter's from ten that morning. That was that.'

I smiled up at Mrs Butler. My approval rating hadn't risen.

'How do I go about . . . Confession at St Peter's?'

'I wouldn't have thought you were a man for the confessional, Inspector.'

She had me. She looked almost pleased, as if she had been hoping I'd give her the opportunity of saying that. Like any good Irish Catholic, she could spot a Protestant at fifty paces in the dark in a storm. Not that we couldn't do it in reverse.

'There's hope for us all, Mrs Butler.'

Her expression showed that she doubted that.

'You go into the basilica and turn to the left. In the far left aisle there are confessionals. And there are signs that tell you the language each priest speaks.'

'Thank you.'

I got up.

'Do you need any attention, Mr Gillespie? I can get a plaster . . .'

Not a question disguised as a statement, but one question for another. She was asking what happened to my face. I tried the truth, to fob it all off as a joke.

'A feller came up and smacked me with a pistol. You know how it is.'

She didn't think it was funny. On reflection, she was right.

'I hit my face. It was an accident, that's all, Mrs Butler.'

She appeared to make some sense of that. I could guess why. She thought I'd been drinking. She gave one more withering look over the top of her spectacles. Not only a gobshite and wise-arse but a clown. I imagined, as she went back to the office, she was reflecting on the sorry state the Department of External Affairs must be in. The fact that they had even let me out of the country spoke volumes.

If I had entered the St Peter's Basilica at any other time, for any other reason, I would have paused to be awestruck. As it was, I gave all the vast beauty of the space around me and above me, reaching high into the dome, only a few seconds of my time. There was a Mass somewhere ahead of me and voices that seemed to come from nowhere that were singing Mozart. I simply turned to the left and found a long wall where wooden cubicles in ornate mahogany had been placed at intervals, each with two curtained entrances. Printed signs announced the language the priests were listening to Confession in. Italian, Spanish, German. There was only one that said English. There was nobody waiting on the benches across from it. I pushed the curtain and went in. I knelt, facing the dark, latticed grill and the shadow beyond it that I assumed was Hugh O'Flaherty's head. I muttered the words I knew well enough, though, as Mrs Butler observed, I was not a man for the confessional. However, I needed to be sure I had the right priest before speaking.

'Bless me, Father, for I have sinned . . .'

'Consider yourself blessed, Stefan.'

'You've found our friend?'

'Someone has. A good thing . . . and not such a good thing.'

'In what way?'

'Yesterday he turned up at an apartment behind the Piazza Venezia. It's where he was hiding before we moved him to the Palazzo San Callisto. We had some British POWs there, but I'd a tip it was being watched. I don't know if it was true. It hasn't been raided. And it's empty now. That doesn't mean it isn't under surveillance. Brother Luca broke in. I guess he was sleeping rough before that.'

'Someone's seen him?'

'The priest at Nome di Maria. He was at Mass there.'

'Jesus! He's just walking around?'

'I think he feels safe there. For no better reason than he was safe there before . . . like going back is a problem solved. He could go out then. There wasn't such a risk. We didn't know the people who were looking for him were that serious . . . the Croatians . . . not the way we do now. I don't think he knew that himself. As long as he was out of sight, somewhere no one knew him, that was all that mattered. It's completely different now. The Italian police are looking for him, even the Gestapo. But he doesn't know that. And he doesn't know about Donal.'

'Didn't the priest tell him?'

'He didn't know himself till he talked to me.'

'So what now?'

'I need to get him away from where he is, then take him out of the city somehow. I think where I told Donal . . . the Irish villa at Tivoli . . . well, for now.'

I had held back my own addition to Brother Luca's problems.

'Something else, Hugh. I had a conversation about our friend last night myself. I don't know who I met, but he was a Partisan commander. He was concerned . . . put it that way to start . . . some of his people were involved in getting Luca into the palazzo. They moved him across Rome. I think as a favour to Donal.'

I didn't add what I knew, what I'd seen, who I'd seen, in Trastevere.

'Yes, I know. I didn't ask for that. Donal panicked. It was unnecessary.'

Monsignor O'Flaherty was taking what I'd said in. It was news.

'This man's worried that Luca can identify some of his people . . .'

I sounded vague, but only one of those people was in my mind.

'We do cross paths with the Partisans, Stefan, but we keep our distance. We go our own ways. I'm not in the business of guns. They are. I'm not in the business of killing. They are. I can have nothing to do with that. I will have nothing to do with it. We avoid each other because it creates complications. For them as well.'

The priest may have known that Donal Hyde had probably created such complications himself, by getting pulled into what Vittoria Campana was doing. He may have known she'd done the same by helping Donal hide a fugitive. But none of it needed saying. It was the problem that was left behind that mattered.

'The complication for Brother Luca is that the feller I met in the catacombs doesn't want to wait for the police to pick him up. If you don't get him out of Rome, and the Partisans find him, they have a simple solution to the problem.'

'I see,' said O'Flaherty. 'He has to be moved today. We'll do it.'

'How much of this do I tell Commissario De Angelis.'

'For now . . . nothing at all. Not till it's done.'

I could see I never would find out who murdered Donal Hyde.

'I'd still like to know what Luca saw, Hugh . . . before he left the palazzo. Something made him run. So, if not Donal's death, he could still know who . . .'

'Well, you can always ask him.'

The confessional voice was almost impatient. Now was its focus. He couldn't spend his energies on what was over.

'I would if I could . . .'

'There's isn't much time,' said the priest. 'Someone has to get to Luca and tell him to stay where he is. Not to go into the street, not to look out of the window, not to move, until I get some transport to him. That someone must be you, Stefan.'

'I'm just another complication, Hugh. I've done what I can.'

I felt I could see the smile on Monsignor O'Flaherty's face.

'Aren't you investigating this with the Vatican Gendarmerie, my son? As I understand it you've even got a Vatican pass that says so. If you get yourself into any trouble, I'll have Commissario De Angelis come and pull you out of it. I mean you're only delaying telling him you're on to something, isn't that so, Inspector?'

Curiosity had led a number of people to follow me around Rome for a few days, to no real end. All they'd discovered was that I was doing something I didn't even understand that nobody, outside an office full of filing cabinets on Stephen's Green in Dublin, gave a fuck about. As far as anything else went, I was out of my depth. Now that Monsignor O'Flaherty had provided a reason to follow me, I was pretty sure they'd all give up. But I didn't take that for granted. I knew the Piazza Venezia already. I'd walked through it before and stopped for a drink. It was big and busy, and busy was good for staying invisible. I took the tram he told me to take, but I took one the wrong way for two stops and then took one the other way. I jumped on the trams as they pulled away and I got off as they left the stop I wanted. It was easy to see if anyone else was suddenly doing the same thing. No one was.

I made no show of hanging about. I had the directions and the map was in my head too. I walked two blocks and took two more turns. I was in a street of terraced apartments, four or five storeys. There were a few shops, but no crowds. I walked past a coal lorry, pulled up by two open flaps that led to a cellar under one of the buildings. I passed an ironmonger's that filled the pavement with its goods and a tailor's that had suits hanging in the window that looked like second-hand clothes. I almost felt well dressed. There was a grocer's with dirty windows and half-empty shelves. The Piazza Venezia had been left well behind.

I found the entrance and the number. I went up the steps and straight in. If I was wrong I'd find out but hanging around outside was a bad idea. There was a dark, narrow hall and a staircase leading to the floors above. There was little light. The air was stale, like years of cooking smells that had never found a way out. It was very different to Charles Bewley's apartment. And it felt very empty. But I couldn't be sure of that. As I climbed the stairs there were doors that had boards nailed across them. But on the next landing I could hear some music on a radio. However, I saw no one. I heard nothing else. I reached the last landing. There was only one door here, only one apartment, high in the building's sloping roof. The door was shut but I could see the lock was broken. There was splintered wood in the jamb. The splinters were fresh and white. It was recent. I pushed at the door gently. It didn't move. I pushed harder. There was a scraping sound. There was something holding it. I kept pushing, slowly. When there was enough of a gap I slipped in. An armchair had been pushed against the door to keep it closed.

The apartment was silent. There was a corridor and a couple of rooms. The roof sloped steeply, making the whole space feel tight and claustrophobic. Through the open doors I saw some beds and a few chairs. There was a small kitchen, no more than a galley with a pile of dirty crockery in a sink. The place was not really furnished. People had been sleeping there, O'Flaherty's English soldiers and whoever else had passed through. But the place wasn't lived in. And it was empty. But when I went back to the kitchen there was food on a plate. Sliced sausage, some tomatoes. There was an open bottle of milk. I smelt it, it was fresh.

It was only when I was in the kitchen that I saw a small door. Through it there was an equally small set of cast-iron stairs, almost a ladder. I looked up and there was open sky above. There was a trapdoor to the roof. I climbed the stairs.

I came out on to a flat area between a couple of slated gables. And I saw the big man I was looking for. He was sitting on a deckchair, looking out over the city, smoking a cigarette and drinking wine from a bottle. He didn't look like someone who was being hunted all over the city. But then he didn't know that he was.

I moved quietly and slowly. I had forgotten how big the Franciscan was. Looking at his head and his back in the chair, I realised that an introduction would need to be handled carefully. I hadn't thought about how I was going do it, except to say Hugh O'Flaherty's name. I didn't know what language to use, since Italian wasn't available. German didn't seem great for an introduction. I didn't know if he spoke English, but I guessed that a bit of English would at least offer some kind of reassurance.

'Brother Luca, Monsignor O'Flaherty sent me . . . the monsignor . . .'

He stood up, startled for a moment, but only a moment.

'O'Flaherty?' was all he said.

'Yes, Hugh O'Flaherty.'

He smiled broadly. It seemed that was reassurance enough.

Brother Luca was out of his Franciscan robes now. He was in a suit that was almost clownishly too small for him. It was a credit to the trousers that they held together. High, broad and bursting out of what he was wearing, he was unmissable.

'Sorry, no English, signore. Italiano?'

I shook my head. 'Das Beste was ich kann, ist Deutsch.'

German was fine now he trusted me. Brother Luca walked forward and shook my hand. It was a surprisingly gentle grip for such a big man. He held out the bottle.

'Have a drink.'

I shook my head.

'I've got another bottle, don't worry.'

'Maybe later.'

He took another swig.

'They gave me four, four bottles. And cigarettes. For nothing. I went into the café because I knew them, from when I was here before. I said I couldn't pay and he said take these. People are good here. They look out for each other. I thought, here I am, just like St Francis, begging for his supper. It's not bad wine either.'

Not only had the friar been out to Mass, he'd been shopping.

'Monsignor O'Flaherty is going to get you out of Rome. He's going to find a way, some way. And they'll come to get you. But you can't leave this building. You can't be seen. You have to keep quiet and keep out of sight. It's not safe here.'

'It was safe before. With the others. But when they took me to the palazzo . . . that was going to be the safest place of all . . . but it wasn't . . . it wasn't . . . there was a man who said he knew me. And then there were two Franciscans . . . Croatians . . .'

For the first time I saw fear.

'I had to run. Donal said they'd move me again. But I couldn't wait. I left. I couldn't tell Donal. I know he was coming to get me. I came here . . . this was safe.'

Luca took another swig of wine. Suddenly, the fear was gone.

'What's your name?'

'Stefan.'

'Do you know Donal . . . are you from Ireland too?'

'I am from Ireland, yes.'

'He has been so good to me. I couldn't wait at the palazzo though. It wasn't safe for me. But I'm here now . . . I'll do what he wants, of course. Somewhere away from Rome, he said. So whatever he wants, whatever the monsignor wants.'

Brother Luca held out the bottle again. I shook my head again. When he offered me a cigarette, I took it. I didn't know what to do with him. I thought I could just deliver the message from Hugh O'Flaherty and leave them to it. But it wasn't that easy. The man was capable of wandering out to the street again if the mood took him. He felt safe in a way that had no connection to his real situation. I could tell him the police were searching for him, but I didn't believe this was any time to tell him why. He didn't know about Donal's murder. It might fix his mind if he did, but it could also create the panic that made him run from the Palazzo San Callisto. It was the idea of people from Croatia that had terrified him in the palazzo, and since I'd seen what they did to Donal Hyde, with good reason. If he got even a whiff of that, what were the chances he would wait for O'Flaherty?

'The police are looking for you, Luca. You have to stay out of sight.'

I had to hammer it home, even without more explanations.

The Franciscan nodded and smiled. He went back to the deckchair.

'Here I stand! With such a view and with such good wine, why not!'

He sat down. He picked up a bottle of wine and a corkscrew. There was certainly nothing wrong with the view. We were looking across the roofs of the city, with its domes and towers glowing in sunlight that had broken through some white and well-formed clouds. And catching that sun was the biggest dome of all, St Peter's. Luca sat back cheerfully and pulled out the cork.

There had been a buzz of traffic and the occasional sound of voices while I had been on the roof. It was barely noticeable. Nothing more than the background noise of the streets below. The sound of the city. But there was something different now. Sounds that made me listen harder. There were louder voices and there were noisier engines. They weren't drifting in lazily from nowhere in particular, they were close. There was something about them that was sharp, even aggressive.

I walked cautiously past the deckchair where Luca Horvat was now starting on the next bottle of wine. I moved to the low parapet at the front of the building. A sloping roof of red tiles hid me as I looked down. I crouched beside it. I could see the street below clearly enough. At both ends there were police cars. Black-uniformed Fascist police stood in twos and threes. As I looked to the left, a truck pulled up. Soldiers jumped from the back. Italian, I thought. But behind the truck was a German armoured car. I knew the troops getting out of it were Waffen SS.

17

LA CARBONAIA

I took in what I could as I looked down at the street below. To look for too long would risk being seen. There was now a checkpoint at each end. There were few people exiting. There seemed to be no problem with that. The police were checking papers, but they stopped no one leaving. To the right the coal delivery carried on as if nothing was happening. The two coalmen were heaving sacks off their lorry and carrying them down into the cellar as they had been when I walked past them. The other end of the road, to the right, was where the business was serious. Two groups of Italian policemen split off from the rest. They entered the first house on each side. The others looked on, including the Germans, with no great interest. The pace was unhurried. There was no urgency, but there didn't need to be. The street was sealed. I walked across the roof to the other side of the building, past Brother Luca, still clutching his bottle of wine and gazing at the view. At the back of the house was a courtyard and some outbuildings and sheds. Versions of the same untidy layout were repeated on either side. I focussed on a break where a patch of waste ground led to the next street. Two men stood there, German soldiers. There would be more I couldn't see,

SS men and Fascist police. The back of the building would offer no escape.

Apart from a resolution to let priests carry their own messages in future, I could do no more than offer up the opposite of a prayer for Monsignor O'Flaherty and make a fast decision about what to do with the friar. There were a dozen or so houses to go before the search reached us. It wasn't a lot of time. There was one simple option. I could leave Brother Luca, climb back into the apartment, walk down the stairs, and exit the building. The police were letting people through. I'd seen that already. I had the papers to pass. This was no random search, no general sweep. They were looking for someone. They didn't know the building, but they knew the street. They had it shut. They would work their way along methodically.

It wasn't hard to guess who they were looking for. If the priest at the local church had seen Luca Horvat, so had other people in this neighbourhood he felt so safe in. A solid bet was likely the café owner who had generously loaded the Franciscan down with wine, doubtless glad to do anything to get rid of a mad killer. Luca's description was circulating in Rome. No one needed a second look. And maybe that was the one thing to hold on to. They knew what they were looking for. That's why people passed through the document checks so easily. None of them were six and a half feet and built like an armoured car. There was a way. And even as I thought about it, I cursed O'Flaherty for the gobshite Irish priest he was. Walking out and leaving the friar was the one option I couldn't take.

I walked back to the front parapet. At the far end of the street the coal lorry was there, and still with a lot of sacks to go. I turned back to Brother Luca. This was either going to be very easy or very hard. If it was too hard, if I could not get him to do what he had to do, then I might have to leave him behind. But I owed the man a chance, that's how it felt. He had to take that and to take it fast.

Luca was watching me now. He wasn't more than puzzled, but he could see something was wrong, or at least that something was worrying me. I looked at the back of the terrace. The flat roof we stood on joined the next house and the next. There were tiled gables at intervals but the parapet formed a wide gutter all the way. The destination was six houses further on, where the coal cellar was.

'It's this simple, Luca. Down in the street there are police and some SS and Gestapo. They're looking for you. Why the fuck they are, I don't know. But they are. The explanations can come later. We have ten minutes, a bit more if we're lucky. There's a chance. You can sit here and wait for them or you can take it.'

He stood up, without the wine bottle. That was a start. He took a couple of steps across the roof. I stood in front of him, blocking his path. I shook my head.

'You don't need to see, because if they look up and see you . . .'

He seemed suddenly almost sober. There was no panic. He nodded.

'We move along the back of the roof. Between the gables and the parapet. The gutters are wide enough to crawl along. They run along the whole terrace. Six houses along, we have to get in, through the roof, a window, whatever we can do.'

He frowned and then grinned broadly.

'Is that all?'

'Not exactly. But it's a start.'

He shrugged. He turned to the trapdoor that led back into the apartment. He pushed it down. There were some iron bands across the top. He looked at them and picked up the deckchair. He held the wooden frame and snapped it with his foot. It would have taken me five minutes stiff work with a saw. He pushed two of the pieces into the ironwork of the trapdoor. It would take a lot of opening from underneath. It might be enough to stop an unsuspecting policeman even looking.

The two of us worked our way along the roof, crawling as fast as we could, keeping out of sight, below the parapet. At two points low brick walls ran the other way across the roofs and we had to risk being seen for the moments it took to clamber over. It didn't take long, but it seemed longer. And then we were there. A piece of flat roof with a trapdoor that mirrored the one we had left. I moved to the front parapet. We had the right apartment block. The coalmen were still there. But the trapdoor was shut, firmly shut, and almost certainly bolted from inside.

There was nothing around to use as a lever. There were no windows anywhere. There was a stretch of sloping roof further along. Tiles wouldn't be so hard to pull off. It would get us into an attic of some sort. It might be noisy though. I peered over the parapet. The apartments here had iron balconies. There was one ten feet below. There would be a window there, maybe a door. It was wide and solid. It looked safe. It wouldn't be hard to drop down on to it. A few seconds hanging from the parapet, that's all. But we would be fully visible.

I turned back, knowing it would have to be one or the other. The Franciscan was hunched over the trapdoor. He was pulling at it, holding an iron ring. He strained. Nothing was happening. The ring came off in his hand. The trapdoor stayed shut. He shook his head, staring down at the square of wood. He took a deep breath. He clenched his fist. He drove it down hard and fast. He smashed straight through it. He drew out his hand, covered in blood. He stood up, grinning almost childishly.

'Now we need to get down to the coal cellar,' I said.

'La carbonaia?'

'If that's the coal cellar, yes.'

Luca shrugged. Explanations later. He returned to the trapdoor. It was quickly opened. This one dropped us into a small attic. A door led out to the staircase. No one had heard us. The landings were empty. There was no sound. I headed down the stairs. Luca followed. As we turned on to one landing a woman was standing at the door to an apartment, putting a key in the lock. A child stood beside her. The woman was startled, not so much by the fact that we were there, I realised, but by the size and outlandish look of the friar. We slowed our headlong rush down the stairs. The child clutched the woman's hand and moved closer to her. Luca winked at the child and smiled at the woman. Neither of them looked reassured. We were an odd couple, very odd. And we definitely didn't belong.

'Siamo cercando la carbonaia, signora.'

The woman stared at Luca for a moment, then pointed down the stairs. I recognised the word I thought meant coal cellar. To be fair to her, you couldn't say asking for directions to the cellar from upstairs wasn't a little odd. The Franciscan smiled again and then raised his still-bloodied hand to make the sign of the cross.

'Grazie! Dio vi benedica entrambi.'

The woman pushed her front door open. She pulled the child inside and slammed it shut. We ran downstairs, picking up speed. Now Luca was laughing.

The door into the cellar took us into a narrow, black corridor. I didn't look for a light. I couldn't know where the coalmen were, but I didn't want to give them any warning that they weren't alone. I felt my way along the corridor in pitch blackness. There were openings off it, a series of small rooms. Then the corridor ended with a closed door. I pushed it open and finally there was some light. It came from a single dim bulb that lit a much bigger space. A great heap of coal massed up against the far wall, sloping to the low roof. There was more light to one side, where the doors to the street were thrown back and daylight came in.

I stood in the doorway, where it was still quite dark, with Luca behind me. Below the trap to the street one of the coalmen waited, looking up. A sack thudded down, dropped by the man above. The coalman dragged it across the floor to empty it onto the heap. The plan was vague. I had no idea what we would find. It amounted to not much more than grabbing the two coalmen and silencing them. It had to be fast. The Franciscan didn't wait. However big, he moved with speed.

The first coalman looked tiny in Luca's arms, held too tight to even try to struggle. The friar's big hand was clenched over the man's face. Another sack thudded down from the street above, spilling out coal as I crossed the cellar.

'Tell him we're taking his truck. He'll be left here. He won't be hurt.'

Luca hissed out some version of this in Italian. It went on for some time. At intervals the coalman nodded. Another sack crashed down through the opening. Then Luca took his hand away from the coalman's mouth. The man smiled at me.

'He's happy to help,' said the Franciscan. 'He says it's an honour.'

'What did you say?'

'I said you're an American spy.'

I wasn't sure what that meant if we were caught, but it had worked.

'We need to get the other one down here.'

Another sack fell through the trap. The man above shouted down. Something like, 'What the hell are you doing?' He could see little, except work had stopped.

The first man was looking at me, puzzled.

'Perchè parla Tedesco?'

'Non parla Italiano,' Luca laughed. 'Sta spiando i nazisti!'

'Ha qualche dollar?'

'What's the matter?' I could see the man was suspicious.

'I'm telling him why you and I are speaking German. Have you got dollars?'

'What?'

'A few dollars would satisfy him.'

I did have some dollars in my wallet, along with a few pounds and francs. I got it out and produced a two-dollar bill. I held it towards the man. He took it and peered down at it. He nodded and smiled. It looked good. So good he folded it and put it in his pocket. He walked to the street opening as another sack came through it, accompanied by some words I guessed were now more curses than questions.

'Vieni qui, Giacommetti! Un problema!'

Luca whispered across at me. 'The other one's coming.'

Feet appeared on a ladder leading down into the cellar.

'Che problema?'

Then the rest of the body. And as the second coalman reached the cellar floor, he was folded, as his comrade had been before, in Brother Luca's embrace.

He made some attempt to struggle, but it lasted only seconds. The Franciscan gave his explanation for the second time, in a tone so quiet and reasonable that it felt irresistible, even if I couldn't understand what he was saying. The first coalman added his own comments at intervals and finally produced the two dollars, which seemed to quell any remaining doubts as far as the second was concerned. Luca let him go. The man then spoke for several minutes, and this time Luca was nodding.

'We need to tie them up, Stefan. We can use their belts.'

'Whatever, that's fine. But we need to move . . .'

The coalmen both had pieces of sacking tied round their shoulders. One wore a corner piece that formed a pointed head covering. I pulled off the sacking. I gave one piece to Luca. He draped it round him. I put the loose sacking hat on his head. I took the other man's sack and covered my own shoulders. We both took some fistfuls of the coal slack from the floor and smeared hands and faces black.

The friar gave me one of the belts. The two men put their hands behind their backs and we buckled them up tightly. The first man seemed satisfied, but the more businesslike second wasn't, not yet. He grinned, looking at Luca Horvat.

'Colpiscimi, compagno!'

The Franciscan frowned then shook his head.

'What is it now? For fuck's sake!'

'He says to hit him. Hard. I can't hit him. I wouldn't do that . . .'

'It's a good idea,' I said. 'But there's no time to argue.'

I walked forward and punched the coalman's jaw. He fell back, laughing.

I climbed the ladder up from the cellar. As my head reached the street I could see the Fascist police at our end of it. There were only four now. They stood in a group, talking. In the other direction I could see very little. I raised myself higher and I caught a group of policemen going into a building across the road. There was a German soldier with them and a man in a suit who was probably Gestapo. The search was still some way down the street. There was still no urgency. Everything was under control. It was thorough. There was something routine about it all. Whatever information they had, urgency wasn't required.

I stood by the coal lorry as the Franciscan clambered out of the cellar. He was barely recognisable as anything other than a large, grimy coalman, with his head half-hidden by the sacking over it. But size and shape would strike anyone with even a poor description of Luca Horvat. He got straight into the cab of the coal lorry. Once in it, his size was halved. He could lessen it more by sinking into the seat. We had agreed that he would drive. He had driven trucks before and if he didn't know the city well, he was more familiar with it than me.

He started the engine. I pushed some loose sacks down into the cellar and then let the two wooden doors fall flat to close the opening. I got into the cab.

'We just go?' asked the friar.

'We go, but slowly. They've been looking at this lorry since they got here. If they had anything to say, they'll already have said it. Slow, and give them a wave.'

The Franciscan seemed calm, calmer than I felt. The policemen barely looked up as the coal lorry moved past them and turned into the next street. There was a nod, but nothing more. We were away. The question now was where we were going and how much time we had. There was maybe fifteen minutes before the search party got to the apartment building we had just left. A bit longer till they found the coalmen in the cellar and worked out what had happened. I had no idea how efficient they were, how quickly the news of an escape would get across the city. I had the feeling this was not a major operation. I couldn't see the Italian police and the German military throwing up roadblocks left, right and centre. But that was no more than a guess. They would do something. If we had half an hour or so of invisibility in hand now, after that the coal lorry would turn into a liability. And on foot, so would the begrimed appearance that had got us past the police.

The idea in my head was to get Luca Horvat out of Rome. It was the same idea that took Donal Hyde to the Palazzo San Callisto the day he died. And since I knew nowhere else, it was the same place Donal had intended to take him. The Villa Greca was a house in Tivoli that belonged to the Irish College. It was shut up for the duration of the war, but Monsignor O'Flaherty felt it was safe to put Allied POWs on the run there. However, it was one thing hearing about it. I didn't know where it was. Even if I could find the town on a map, I could hardly turn up there, with the Franciscan in tow, asking for directions. And there wasn't much point trying to work out what might happen in Tivoli, when I had no means of getting out of the city. All I had was a coal lorry the police and the Gestapo would soon be looking for, and a giant wanted for murder who was dressed like a chimney sweep.

I had half an hour, if I was lucky, to drive through Rome without attracting suspicion. In that time I had to get rid of the coal lorry in some way that didn't mean it would be found almost immediately. I had to shake off anyone who came after us for long enough to find help in getting Luca out of Rome. If I couldn't do that, it was hard to see what I could do other than leave him to it. That was where I started. There were people who knew how to do this. I looked across at Brother Luca in the cab, humming to himself as if unaware of what was going on. His size didn't alter the fact that he seemed helpless. He didn't know what had happened to Donal Hyde. I had to give it one more try.

'The Vatican, Luca. Let's give it a go.'

He looked unsure. I knew he was thinking of the Palazzo San Callisto.

'Shouldn't we get hold of Donal? He had somewhere to take me.'

'That's where we'll go, Luca. But not in a fucking coal truck!'

He chuckled for some time, as if this was an explanation of something. But he knew where he was going. We were crossing the river now. The Castel Sant'Angelo was on our right. We were heading towards St Peter's. I was assuming a coal lorry could drive in to the Vatican without a lot of trouble. People needed checking, I had seen that already, but vans and trucks making deliveries seemed to be nodded through. Many would be known, but they couldn't all be. I had no sense that there were lists of vehicles to be clocked in and out, any more than the meat wagon that had taken me into the Città del Vaticano with

Hugh O'Flaherty. I did have a pass, but I didn't want to involve the Gendarmerie. If I got someone other than Commissario De Angelis, it could mean the opposite of assistance.

'It's a coal delivery, Luca. The tradesman's entrance.'

He roared with laughter, almost enjoying it. At least I entertained him.

It worked. At the Via Sant'Anna, Luca wound down the window and called out something that seemed to amuse the Swiss Guards who were standing there. They didn't even wave him on. He simply slowed down and then kept going.

I could still not risk Giulio De Angelis and the Gendarmerie. Now that Luca was publicly wanted for murder in the city, it was unlikely there would be any safe haven on Vatican soil. This wasn't somewhere he could stay. It wasn't even somewhere, as the palazzo had shown, he could feel secure. But it was a place to breathe and find help. The obvious recourse was to Monsignor O'Flaherty, but I needed to find him. The other thought in my head was Vittoria at the embassy. I didn't know what she felt she owed Luca. But in spite of the Partisan leader I met in the catacombs, I knew she would still feel she owed something to Donal Hyde.

The only building I knew, apart from the Gendarmeria, was the one Bishop O'Rourke lived in. And since I had no way to contact O'Flaherty, he was the best bet anyway. The Franciscan drove the coal lorry round to the back of the building. There was a yard with sheds and a stone outhouse and some heavy doors that could have led to the basement. It was somewhere a truck delivering coal wasn't going to look out of place. I thought it could sit there for a considerable time before anyone asked questions about it, hidden from the Italian police. However, it wasn't so easy for Luca and me to hide ourselves. Our disguise was the coal lorry.

There was nothing for it but to get to the bishop's room as quickly as possible. With the coal lorry at the back of the building, there was some answer to anyone who queried what we were doing. There was a caretaker to look for or a housekeeper, or someone vaguely responsible for whatever a couple of coalmen could come up with in the way of confused deliveries or wrong addresses. In the event, no one took any notice. We saw only a couple of priests, who saw only a couple of coal-stained tradesmen. We were soon in Edward O'Rourke's apartment.

The bishop was surprised by what appeared at his door, but he took the situation in quickly. He was good at reading between the lines and needed little explanation. If he was amused for a moment, he was less amused at the seriousness of the situation. I found a way to let him know that Luca Horvat was unaware of Father Hyde's death and so nothing was said. O'Rourke and the friar knew each other already, of course. It was the bishop who'd persuaded O'Flaherty to try to find a safe refuge for the Franciscan. It had been a costly exercise and it wasn't over.

O'Rourke's attempts to contact Monsignor O'Flaherty were unsuccessful. He tried several phone numbers and got no answer. When he got one it was to learn that something was wrong. There had been a number of raids in the city, like the one I had been caught up in. O'Flaherty was holed up somewhere until he could get back to the Vatican. Everyone was waiting for things to quieten down.

The first thing that was needed was the disappearance of the two coalmen who had arrived in the lorry outside. Brother Luca was dispatched to the bishop's bathroom, to clean off the coal dust. While I waited to do the same, the bishop said there could be no question of the friar staying in the Vatican. Although Commissario De Angelis was still collecting evidence for his investigation into Donal's murder, Ispettore Dirigente Caproni had already reached his own conclusion, as I knew. The killer was Brother Luca Horvat. Whatever the doubts of the commissario, they would not be enough, not now. The Vatican would not turn a blind eye to Luca's presence there.

With O'Flaherty out of action, I turned to the only other person who could help, Vittoria Campana, and the one thing she had access to that had already been used successfully to move Luca though Rome, the Irish ambassador's Lancia. I called the embassy. But I knew there could be someone listening, at either end.

Vittoria was in the office. She answered the phone.

'It's Stefan.'

She was silent for several seconds. She already knew something was up.

'Are you all right?'

'I wouldn't want to overstate it.'

'You know this line . . .'

She didn't need to finish.

'Get Mrs Butler on.' I laughed. 'Say she'll have to forget the conversation.'

The next voice was Mrs Butler's.

'How can I help you, Mr Gillespie?'

I spoke to her in Irish. It would have defeated anyone listening in to the call, which was unsurprising since it would also have defeated most people in Ireland. I told her to give Vittoria an English version of what I was about to say. She could do it bit by bit, making sure the telephone wouldn't pick up any of the English.

Even in Irish I referred to Luca Horvat as a package that needed collecting and delivering to the Irish College's villa in Tivoli. I didn't know what Mrs Butler would make of any of it, but I guessed that whatever she thought about me, she would somehow respond as if it was something that came within my remit. Since I had been sent there by the Department of External Affairs, however ill-advisedly in her view, it was still her job to do what I asked. And she did exactly that. She passed on each part of my message to Vittoria. She might have raised questions about why I was asking her to bring the ambassador's car to the Vatican and then drive on, complete with mysterious package, to Tivoli. She didn't. She could have said she needed to clear this with MacWhite. She didn't. It seemed she wasn't unaware of what had been happening. But she was aware that however little it was or however much, she was not supposed to see it. I thought that most of the time Mrs Butler had the sense not to look. Even when forced to, she wouldn't see.

Half an hour later, Signorina Campana arrived at Edward O'Rourke's rooms in the Vatican City. The bishop had done what he could. He only had prayers left now, as we set off for Tivoli and the Villa Greca, me in front with Vittoria, and Luca in the back. Brother Luca and I had been scrubbed up to remove most of the coal dust, apart from what we couldn't get from under our fingernails. I had been provided with a suit and a clean shirt. It was the kind of suit that a priest would wear, but without the dog collar it just about passed. The Franciscan had a long, full cassock on. It didn't reach anywhere near his shoes as it should have, but it had been made for a clergyman who was almost as round as the friar, if nowhere near as tall. It changed how he looked and the broad-brimmed clerical hat changed him even more, putting his face in shadow and hiding his hair. Certainly, sitting in a car, he looked very different from the man I had met earlier that day. He had a Vatican passport that gave him a new name and the identity of a civil servant in the Holy See. With my Irish diplomatic passport and the car's diplomatic plates, it should have been enough to get us past all but the most serious checkpoints, with barely a glance through the Lancia's windows. We were now going to find out if it was.

I left a note for Commissario De Angelis, asking Edward O'Rourke to make sure he got it and only he got it. I said only that I had found 'him'. I said I would be in touch when I had more detail. It was enough for Giulio to understand.

The car moved out from the Vatican into Italy and the Porta Angelica. For a moment Vittoria stopped. A red convertible, taking up as much of the other side of the road as its own, was driving in, forcing her almost up on to the pavement. There were a couple of muttered words that I could have found decent English equivalents for. She had more to think about and just continued. But I recognised the shining paintwork and the whitewall tyres, and the man in the natty uniform and cap. My chum, Alfredo, probably the best-dressed chauffeur of any defrocked ambassador in Rome. He was alone in the car, with no sign of Signore Bewley. I smiled at the pompous ex-ambassador's even more pompous driver. For a few seconds, as the Alfa passed, he saw me and recognised me. He wasn't a man to take a slight lightly. He didn't give me a finger in salute, but his look did service for it. I almost felt a tinge of fondness for Alfredo, so self-important, with little to be self-important about. Thank goodness there was still something that trivial out there. And thank goodness there was still something that absurd to laugh at.

18

TIVOLI

The journey from Rome was, in the end, far easier than any of us could have expected. More of that was down to Vittoria than I understood, but I felt it. The roads she took wove round the centre and through backstreets, villa-lined avenues and scruffy suburban sprawl. We crossed main roads but never stayed on them long. We were into something like countryside surprisingly quickly, and there too we travelled on small roads, sometimes little more than compacted dirt. We saw no checkpoints. Only twice did we pass some military vehicles, Italian and German, heading the other way, but without any sense of purpose that concerned us.

Brother Luca hunched in the back, looking out of the window as if he was on some kind of excursion. His moods were unpredictable. They shifted abruptly from fear and panic to a kind of benign indifference. I knew the lack of alcohol in the car contributed to controlling those mood swings, but for now he felt safe. He said little, but he asked more than once if we would see Donal when we got to Tivoli. I couldn't avoid a real answer much longer. I was glad to look round and see he had fallen asleep. Even though Vittoria and I spoke English, she didn't say much until she saw Luca was asleep too. We were some way out of Rome by then. She was less tense. I could see she felt we had put the riskiest part behind us.

For the rest of the journey we talked quietly, mostly about things that had nothing to do with where we were or what was happening. I thought it was a relief to her as well to be somewhere else, for however short a time. She talked about growing up not far from where we were going, in the hills above Tivoli, at the edge of the Apennines. And I saw them now ahead of us, rising out of the flat land all about us. I had my own hills, of course, in Wicklow, starting their own rise behind the farm at Kilranelagh. Maybe not so grand, but big enough for us to call them mountains in Ireland. The conversation picked a few things at random, some bigger than others. And sometimes a lot can be said in a few words. We had a sense of each other that didn't amount to much but was enough to put aside the real business of that drive. I knew that her brother had been killed fighting the British in Libya. She knew my wife had died a long time ago and that I had a son. We spent no more time on those things than the hills we had climbed as children or the fact that our parents were growing older than we somehow ever expected them to do. I knew that she, like me, was sorry when the sign for Tivoli appeared ahead.

It was almost dark as we approached the town. The land was suddenly very white on both sides of the road, spreading out around us. It was the hard, crisp stone that had been dug out of this landscape for thousands of years to build Rome. As night came in, patches of it shimmered in the headlights when the car turned a bend. It was something I might have imagined on the moon. Vittoria laughed. For her it was as familiar and unremarkable as any stretch of Irish peat bog was for me.

The Villa Greca lay on the outskirts of the town of Tivoli. I would see nothing of the town, just the house and the garden where the priests of the Irish College spent their summers, until the war meant shutting it up and putting it in mothballs. From that garden I would glimpse the long stone walls and broken pillars that told me that somewhere out there were the ruins of a Greek theatre and a great bathhouse and a palace built by Hadrian. They were not the things I would take away when I left the place though. I would remember the first, peaceful day in the garden. I would remember something else. I would also remember things better forgotten.

Arriving at night, the villa was still a welcoming sight. It was fronted by tall pines and the kind of tumbledown stone wall that looked as if it had been there for a thousand years and it had never occurred to anyone to repair it. The roof tiles were the familiar colour of red earth, but here they seemed to grow up out of the stone walls that were yellow and warm and had nothing hard about them. It was comfortable and reassuring and peaceful. Brother Luca, just awake, felt the same.

'Bella! Deo gracias!'

He crossed himself as he got out of the car.

We were welcomed by a man and a woman, old in the way the house was old, maybe crumbling slightly at the edges but with a kind of cheerful elegance in their lined faces. Somehow Monsignor O'Flaherty, or someone in his system, had got a message to the villa that we were on our way. The old woman introduced herself as Emilia and the old man as Claudio. He took us upstairs from the big hall where a fire burned in a high open grate, to some neat, bright bedrooms where there was white, crisp linen on newly made beds. The priests of the Coláiste na nGaedheal didn't do themselves badly in their holiday retreat and Emilia and Claudio had kept it ready for their return with scarcely a musty mothball in sight.

We came downstairs and Claudio took us through into a kitchen. There was a range full of saucepans and the smell of good food rising up from them. There was a huge table at the centre of the room. The back door was open to the garden.

There was the sound of laughter. The old couple shooed Vittoria and me outside. I looked round and saw the Franciscan had disappeared. I assumed he was upstairs.

In the garden, sitting round a brazier, were three men in their twenties or early thirties. They were scruffily dressed, slightly unshaven, drinking beer from bottles. They got up as we approached. They introduced themselves cheerfully, like a trio from a music-hall joke, an Englishman, an Irishman and an American. They maybe told us their surnames, even their ranks, but I remember them as Bob, David and Adam. We sat down and had some beer thrust into our hands. They were prisoners of war who had walked out of Italian camps when Italy surrendered a few months earlier. They had been on the run since, avoiding recapture by the Italian Fascist police or the Gestapo. Bob was the Englishman. He had been in an Italian camp for two years after he was captured in North Africa. David was the Irishman, from the North, Newry, captured in Sicily. The American was Adam, the officer in charge he claimed, to ridicule from the other two. He had been captured only weeks before the Italian surrender and escaped shortly afterwards. It was an oddly animated gathering, but I could see the three men needed to make it that way. They were not free in any sense. They were on the run and could be recaptured or betrayed at any time. During the day, they couldn't go outside, even though the Villa Greca stood on its own, in large gardens, it wasn't safe. Night offered the chance to sit by the back door and breathe some air.

There was suddenly a roar of laughter behind us. We all turned. The soldiers stood up, staring at the apparition that had emerged through the kitchen door. They had yet to meet Brother Luca. He was an unusual sight at the best of times. I had got used to being with a giant. I'd had a long day with him. Now, in his black priest's soutane, still with his broad-brimmed hat, holding a heavy wooden crate, and lit by the flames of the brazier fire, he was more than enough to startle anyone.

He spoke in a mix of Italian and German as he put the crate down.

'Hanno una cantina, a wine cellar! Full of wine!'

He introduced himself to the soldiers by taking bottles out of the crate and handing one to each of them, with a brief exchange of names and a handshake. He presented one to me and to Vittoria, then pulled out a corkscrew to open his own.

'Good stuff too. Ottimo vino, figli miei!'

He held up the corkscrew and made the sign of the cross with it.

I glanced across at Vittoria. She shrugged. I shrugged in return. One thing we were not going to be able to do was keep Luca Horvat sober. And as Bob, David and Adam waited with some enthusiasm for the holy corkscrew to come their way, there seemed little point doing anything other than join in the party.

The evening passed quickly, with a meal of good, simple food and the good wine that Brother Luca had decided, in a spirit of Franciscan generosity, the priests of the Irish College in Rome would be happy to share with their unlooked-for visitors at the Villa Greca. The friar and the soldiers sat in the kitchen late, very late if the hour they eventually appeared at the next day meant anything. Neither I nor Vittoria sat with them for long once we had eaten. I don't know when we decided that we would use only one of the rooms we had been given that night. I don't know that anything was said between us. Like all such moments between a man and a woman, the real decision was hers. It needed no words, no explanation.

The next morning was quiet at the Villa Greca. There was no sign of the revellers of the night before. The three servicemen had good reasons to stay in their rooms during the day as it was, but the empty wine bottles Claudio carried to their demise, somewhere at the back of the garden, had provided more. Vittoria and I had the villa to ourselves until the early afternoon.

Emilia worked in the kitchen and Claudio spent his time in the kitchen garden, appearing at intervals to bring baskets of vegetables and fruit to his wife. We spent most of our morning in the garden too. It was a bright day, for me more like summer than the Italian autumn it really was. We walked and sat about doing nothing and talked about nothing much, in the way that happens between two people and makes a closeness out of so much nothing that no one else outside can comprehend, although they have probably known it themselves. For everyone it's a different kind of nothing in particular. I don't remember what we said. But I don't forget being there. It is as clear as it was at the time. The garden, the scent of herbs, the yellow house, hills in the distance.

In the afternoon I found Luca. I couldn't put off what I had to tell him any longer. He was still asking about Donal Hyde, still wondering when he would see him. He felt a bond with the Irish priest that was both gratitude and friendship. I thought he was a man who gave friendship easily and honestly and that once you had it, you would always have it. I had to tell him his friend was dead.

He was in the small chapel, little more than a room with a wooden table and an altar cloth and a crucifix. It was a strangely simple place to be. Only the day before I had been in all the golden pomp of St Peter's. The friar sat on a chair, looking at the crucifix. He looked up and smiled. He tapped his head and shook it.

'The best cure for a hangover is prayer. Sometimes I need to pray a lot.'

I sat beside him. I told him what had happened at the Palazzo San Callisto. I told him what I had found. I didn't ask him what he knew. He sat in silence. All the time I had been speaking he kept his eyes on the crucifix. Only now did he look round. There were tears in his eyes, but there was nothing in his voice that said he was crying.

'Ustaše.'

'I don't know. Maybe.'

'I know.'

He closed his eyes for a long minute. I told him only about the body and the knife wound, nothing more. But I saw in his face that he had read more in mine.

'They were there.' The friar opened his eyes. 'I was going to Mass at San Callisto, the church. I came in by the door from the courtyard, the one from the palazzo. I stopped in the doorway. I saw two Franciscans at the back. It's such a small church. They were just standing, looking at everyone, even though Mass had started. I recognised one of them. I knew him in Croatia. We were ... brothers together. He left the order. But he had the robe on. I knew he was looking for me.'

'You told me about them,' I said. 'You think they were disguised?'

'One, yes, but it doesn't matter. Don't you see that ... it doesn't matter.'

'I don't know what you mean, Luca.'

He shook his head.

'They found Donal. They looked for me and found him. And killed him.'

'I think that's possible, yes.'

'It doesn't end. It never ends. Nothing I've done will ever end.' Luca stood up. 'I shouldn't be here, Stefan. It's the truth. I have no right to be in here at all.'

Brother Luca looked at the crucifix once more. He turned and walked out.

The second night at the villa was quieter than the first. Luca produced a crate of wine again, but he simply left it with the rest of us. He drank but he drank on his own. He didn't eat and he didn't sit with us. He sat by himself in a dark corner of the garden and then disappeared to his room. He drank a lot, but he showed no sign of being drunk. Only Vittoria knew about my conversation with him. It meant nothing to anyone else. But the mood communicated itself to the house somehow, and when Vittoria and I went to bed, Bob and David and Adam were talking about their own problems in ways they had pushed out of their heads the day before. They had been at the Villa Greca for over a week. They felt safe but the promise of getting them into the Vatican or some other Papal property in Rome was still only a promise. Even when their chance came, it had its own risks. It could as easily turn into a time to get caught as a time to reach safety.

The noise that woke me the next morning was sudden and unexpected. It brought Vittoria and me out of a deep, peaceful sleep. There were loud voices in the corridor. Not just loud but shouting. There was the sound of hammering on doors. I knew at once that some of the voices were German. I turned out of bed and went to the window. Looking down at the front of the house I saw the military vehicles. A heavy army truck, a small, open troop carrier, a black limousine, a motorbike and sidecar. German or Italian, or both, they were all in the same grey-green colours except for the car. Beside them stood German soldiers and the black-uniformed men I had become familiar with as the Fascist police. At almost the moment I took this all in, the door burst open. A German soldier walked in, holding a machine gun. There were two Italian policemen, one with a pistol, the other a rifle. Vittoria pulled the bedclothes back over her. I put my hands up.

We came downstairs to find everyone else in the hall. Lined up against the wall were the three servicemen, Emilia and Claudio, and Luca, his face black and bleeding. Whether he had put up some resistance or whether someone decided to let him know it wouldn't be a good idea, something solid had hit his face. The Italian with the pistol, who was an officer of some kind, pushed us into the line. Guns were trained on us. They had come quietly, as is the way, just after dawn.

I recognised a face I knew, as three men walked in through the front door. Hauptsturmführer Dietrich Ritter, complete with death's-head flashes and riding boots, along with a small, dark-haired man in some black uniform that wasn't SS and wasn't Fascist police. I wasn't that interested in another variation on black, but Luca, now next to me, knew what it was. He knew what it was and who it was.

'Ustaše. He's found me now.'

A German sergeant stepped forward and screamed at the friar.

'Shut up! Keep your fucking mouth shut, arsehole!'

Ritter looked along the line and nodded. I didn't know if the nod was for his own satisfaction or whether it was directed at me. He was certainly looking at me. He went first to the three escaped POWs. He looked them up and down. He addressed them in English. Slow as he was, it was better English than he'd claimed to have.

'Name, rank and serial numbers is all I'll get, I suppose.'

It was Adam, the American, who spoke. His seniority now meant something.

'That's all you have any right to get. You know that.'

'I have the right to shoot you as spies, since you're all in civilian clothes. But let's not get ahead of ourselves. You will identify yourselves and then I'll decide what to do. It will go easier on you if you cooperate when questioned.'

'We won't be answering any questions.'

Ritter shrugged and walked on along the line. He didn't pause to look at Emilia and Claudio. He moved on to Brother Luca. The size and strength of the friar wasn't about to be taken lightly. Machine guns and several rifles were on him.

'So, the mad monk. Certainly big, and probably crazy. Is that right?'

Luca was looking at the man who stood next to Dietrich Ritter, the one he had identified as from the Croatian Ustaše.

The man gazed back at the friar. I could see they knew each other well. There was familiarity and hatred in both their faces.

'You'll know Captain Milić, Brother Luca? A compatriot, even a comrade. He knows you anyway. He's been looking for you. I'm sure he's glad to catch up with you. When I've finished with you at the Via Tasso, he can have what's left.'

The Hauptsturmführer moved on. Milić spoke a few words to Luca in what I assumed was Croatian. The Franciscan didn't answer. He just gazed back at him.

'Stefan, I don't know what you're doing here,' said Ritter. 'I suppose you're going to tell me you fancied a few days in the country with the ambassador's charming driver?'

'There's a bit more, but that is about the gist of it, Dietrich.'

I still had to come up with what that bit more was going to be.

'I thought it might be, Inspector. You're a problem, I have to say it. That fucking diplomatic passport is a pain in the arse. I really have two choices. The first is you disappearing, with no one having any idea what's happened. That might work well, now I think of it. You've been driving around with a maniac. The other, well, let's leave the other one up in the air for the moment . . . we're among friends.'

He looked at me once more and shook his head. He moved on to Vittoria.

'And Signorina Campana. A job at the Irish embassy, but much more . . .'

She stared back at him. She wasn't unafraid, but I knew that somewhere in her there was something that had prepared her for this. She was reaching for that.

'You'll talk, signorina. I expect to get a lot from you. And I mean a lot.'

Ritter walked back to the three POWs.

'Let's waste no time on you clowns,' he said in English, then continued in German, giving orders to his sergeant. 'Get their names and ranks, all that shit. Load them on the truck. They can go straight to a POW camp. I'll clear up here.'

'Yes, Hauptsturmführer.'

The SS man called the Italian police officer over to him.

'Tenente, qui! Prendi gli altri fuori.'

He turned to two of the German soldiers.

'Go with the Italians. Take the rest of them outside.'

At the front of the Villa Greca, the three servicemen sat in a row in the back of the army truck. German soldiers hemmed them in and sat opposite them. The rest of us stood in a line behind the truck. Hauptsturmführer Ritter had brought us out to see them go. He wanted some spectacle. We didn't yet know what it was. We were simply standing there, me, Vittoria, Luca, Emilia and Claudio. The German sergeant was instructing the lorry driver as he started the engine. The two remaining German soldiers covered us with machine guns, along with two Fascist policemen carrying rifles. The other Italians were standing in a group, paying little attention to anything, just talking and passing round cigarettes. They seemed to feel the job was over and they could relax. The Italian officer was next to Ritter. With them was the Croatian. The SS officer and the Ustaše man seemed pleased with themselves. The Italian lieutenant was not pleased. I thought he was sweating.

Dietrich Ritter addressed the three POWs in his most pompous English.

'Gentlemen, the game is up, as you say. You will be returned to a POW camp. The food won't be as good but that's all. Unfortunately, for those who showed you such hospitality, the game isn't the same. It certainly isn't cricket.'

He turned to the Italian policeman.

'Fai il tuo lavoro, Tenente.'

The man didn't move. Ritter spoke again in German.

'They're your laws, man! Obey them! Do your job!'

The lieutenant unclipped his holster and took out his pistol. His men were silent, looking on. There was no more talk and cigarettes remained unlit. I saw that the German soldiers with machine guns had shifted slightly. The guns weren't pointing at us now. They weren't quite pointing at the Fascist policemen, but they were moving in their direction. The German sergeant had walked away from the truck. His hand was on the automatic at his side. Ritter was still staring at the Italian lieutenant. The struggle inside the man's head was brief. He knew it would be, even before he gave himself a few seconds to show at least some gesture of reluctance to his men. It hadn't lasted very long. He walked quickly towards the straggling line I stood at one end of. He went straight to Claudio who stood at the other end. It was too fast for the old man even to see what was coming. He looked up, almost smiling. The lieutenant pointed the gun at his head and fired twice.

The truck was pulling away from the villa. In the back the three POWs stood up, shouting furious and pointless curses. None of us moved, except for Emilia, sobbing as she covered her husband's body and kissed his already dead face. The German machine guns and the rifles of the Italian policemen were all on us now.

PART THREE

PASTOR ANGELICUS

THE ANGELIC SHEPHERD

How is it that we don't see any Emergency Acts directed against the Jews who crucified Our Saviour nineteen hundred years ago, and are crucifying us every day of the week? There is one thing that Germany did and that was to rout the Jews out of their country. Until you rout the Jews out of this country, it does not matter a hair's breadth what orders you make. Where the bees are there is honey, where the Jews are there is money.

Oliver J. Flanagan TD, Irish Parliamentary
Debate, 1943

God save Ireland; the Jews can look after themselves.

William Francis O'Donnell TD, Irish Parliamentary
Debate, 1945

19

VILLA GRECA

The wine cellar at the Villa Greca was a kind of semi-base-ment room. There was a low ceiling and earthen floor. There was only a little light from a window that was just above the level of the ground outside. It was barely a foot wide. There were shelves of wine, stacked in orderly rows. It was also the place Claudio had stored fruit and vegetables for the winter ahead. It smelled of earth and of apples. There was a heavy, studded door, now firmly closed, with a bolt on the outside.

Now we were three. Emilia had gone, in an undertaker's van with her dead husband. Dietrich Ritter seemed to think she would make the point better as a grieving widow than as a corpse. I sat against a wall with Vittoria and Luca. There was nothing to do but wait for whatever it was that was coming. Ritter had said only that he would question us before he took us back to Rome. He wanted the details, he said, before things went any further. That phrase stuck in my head. I didn't know what it meant but it suggested some kind of uncertainty. I got the impression that he wasn't entirely committed to this operation. I didn't think that meant he objected to rounding up Allied prisoners or people who might lead him to Partisans or terrorists, or whatever he wanted to call them. I didn't think it meant he was kept awake at night by seeing Italian civilians shot in the head. This business irritated him somehow. I didn't know what that was, but I knew I was part of it. Whatever he said about me disappearing, I remained a problem he didn't like.

We had been in the cellar for two hours. We had said little to each other. We had our own thoughts and our own doubts about what we had to face. I had some sense that I might have a way out. The more I thought about it, the more the idea that I was a loose end no one would know what to do with took hold. Taking me to Gestapo HQ for questioning wasn't straightforward. I knew that anything could happen in there. I had no illusions. But it was still a place of officials and paperwork and senior officers. I still had that fucking pain-in-the-arse passport. As Ritter had told me, I could be dumped in a ditch, but once there was a docket or interrogation or a superior to answer to, explanations would be required. Even here, there were Fascist policemen and an Italian officer who would be making his own report. He might report nothing if that's what he was told, but there were niggling problems piling up. I had a chink of light at least. But I knew there was none for Vittoria Campana or Luca Horvat. If they went into the Via Tasso, it was unlikely they would come out. I couldn't share that chink of light with them.

After a long time of looking into space, Vittoria took my hand.

'They say you have to think this time will come.'

I didn't answer. I didn't have an answer.

'Think it will and hope and pray it won't.'

'What do you think the Gestapo know . . . about you?'

She shook her head.

'Anything and . . . nothing . . . I'd guess not much, but I can't know.'

'Well, nothing is the best place to start. If it's more you'll find out.'

'I don't know if I . . . I'm frightened of what's going to happen. I'm frightened I won't bear it too. I'm frightened about what I end up saying. I think I won't say anything. But I don't know . . . I don't know what I can take, Stefan.'

I thought of my chink of light. It didn't have to be big to be something. It lay in how little anyone might know about anything except what was in their faces. Ignorance was all there was to hold on to. If I was wrong there was nothing else.

'Keep the story simple, Vittoria. And keep it about this. About being here. You know nothing else. No one knows you had anything to do with hiding Luca. Just assume that. No one knows you were at the palazzo. Believe it. I think that's true. You came here with me because I asked you to drive me. That's the only reason. You don't need my story. Just tell yours. It is what happened. You brought me here. You never saw Luca till we got here. There's no one to contradict that. The POWs have gone. Claudio's dead. They let Emilia go. There's only one story. If Ritter is just chancing his arm with you . . . you have to stick with it. He has some problems . . . with me. It might mean nothing. It might mean he knows a lot less than you think. Whatever the reason, I think it's Luca they're here for . . . at least that's what's been driving it. Why else would they turn up with some Croatian?'

'No.' She shook her head. 'The SS man has something on me.'

'That's his job. To make everyone assume he has something . . .'

'Well, he's good at it, Stefan.'

I could add nothing to that. The next problem was the Franciscan. He had to know how little to say.

I had some idea what I was going to say to the Hauptsturmführer now. It was all about peddling neutrality, not just Ireland but the Vatican, as hard as I could, to try to make it clear that somehow what happened at the Villa Greca, or in the Via Tasso, wouldn't stop with him and his three prisoners and a few Italian policemen. His next spectacle was going to be a public one and because of me, he wasn't going to avoid that. And if he got it wrong, he was going to piss off his superiors.

'Has Luca been drinking?'

Vittoria shook her head.

'That's something. He could say anything . . . nothing . . . everything.'

That truth didn't reassure me. I moved across to him. His head was down. I almost thought he was asleep. He wasn't. But I had to shake him to make him hear.

'You need a story, Luca. One story. You tell them one story.'

He looked up. I thought it was the first time he had really been sober.

'As far as what happened at the Palazzo San Callisto goes, you just tell the truth. Donal took you there. Someone recognised you. He was going to bring you here. You saw the men in the church . . . Franciscans, Ustaše, whoever they were. You ran because you thought they were there to kill you. You never saw Donal. But you knew he was going to bring you here. You just came yourself. You disguised yourself as a priest. You got here . . . just say you came on the train. No one knows.'

Then I thought about the Croatian, Milić. I remembered the hatred.

'Was this man Milić the one dressed as a Franciscan?'

'Yes.'

'And you know him?'

'We entered the order together . . . we were . . . friends, great friends.'

'When Ritter asks you, tell him. Tell him that. I'd give good money he doesn't know. I'm not saying it changes anything, but it takes it in a different direction. It throws in another kind of confusion. No, he can't know. And it's going to make him wonder what the fuck's going on . . . I'd say all Ritter wants is information about who helped you, who hid you. But if he's sitting next to the man who really killed an Irish priest on Vatican territory . . . what does he do with that?'

The friar nodded. He was thinking clearly. I had a hope he'd stay that way.

'You know nothing about Vittoria. You know nothing about anyone other than Donal. You say people in the Vatican helped to hide you at first. You don't know their names. They were priests . . . nuns . . . other people. You were moved around. You don't know where . . . except the palazzo . . . you found your way here.'

'What about the coal cellar?'

'The truth. Except for me. Didn't you tell the coalmen I was American?'

Brother Luca smiled. I had some faith in what he would say. But as soon as the smile formed on his lips, it was gone. He was staring up at the small window.

'We are the same . . . Laban Milić . . . and I . . . both killers.'

'Just tell what you know, Luca. Tell Ritter you saw Milić there. You saw him. Hammer it home. I don't know what it'll do, but put it in his head, all right?'

'He killed dozens . . . Serbs . . . men and women . . . even Orthodox priests. I say even priests . . . especially priests. And he was still a Franciscan. He was a chaplain . . . I was a chaplain. We were making our country . . . making Croatia . . . making a new nation . . . a holy Catholic nation that would show all Europe . . . and Laban and I . . . the big saint and the small saint they called us . . . the big killer and the small killer . . . always there with a joyful Mass to comfort the other killers.'

'You did what you could, Luca. You saw what was happening . . . you've risked your own life to do something. It's why you're here. Because you tried—'

'No, my son, I'm not here because I saw what was happening. I'm here because of what I did. I did my part. I did my part for my country and my Church. That was all I had in my head. That was my faith. We were saviours, crusaders. We needed to cut out the rotten wood. Someone had to. They were heretics. They were enemies of our country and enemies of Christ. And we had our creed. A third of the Serbs forced to convert and become Catholics. A third kicked out of the country. A third to be killed. That was it. If I have sometimes felt I was mad since then . . . it's nothing, nothing at all compared with the madness I knew then, the madness I think I loved. I was there when we burned people in their churches. I fired the bullets too. And I used the knife. A priest in Banski Grabovac. A priest in Kostajnica. A priest in Vojšnica. Maybe Vojšnica was where Laban and I said the Mass. I think Laban left the order then. Some of the bishops were taking a stand. Take it easy lads, they said. You mean well . . . but take it easy. And Laban didn't like that.'

He looked round, from me to Vittoria. We both looked away. If it wasn't easy for me to listen to what he was saying, it was harder to see what was in his eyes. Vittoria could hear his pain and see the anguish in his eyes too, though she understood little of Luca's German. It was enough to push her own situation out of her head for a few minutes. But I knew she wouldn't want a translation.

'Laban has come for me. It's only right. We belong together. I should never have run. I did kill two Ustaše in Croatia. I saw them beating a woman in the street. I don't why I had to stop them. I had done far worse. What did it matter? I don't know. But it suddenly did. There was a light in my head. Not a clean light. Not God's light. It burned. And I killed them. Then I had to run. And so I did. But I shouldn't have done. I should have died then. It wouldn't have been so hard. And then . . . there would have been an end to it. But Donal . . . why did Laban do that?'

He stopped and said no more. His head hung down again. I knew I had heard only part of what was going on inside him. Outside, all Luca had left was silence.

An hour later I stood in front of Hauptsturmführer Ritter in the hall of the Villa Greca. He sat at a table, leaning back in his chair. The day had produced a clear sky and a bright sun that we had been unaware of in the wine cellar. Ritter had his tunic unbuttoned and the heat had given his face a glow. The front doors were open and the light fell on me, still warm, as I looked down at the SS man. I thought of the light in the garden the day before and the lost moments doing nothing with Vittoria. Behind me was the Waffen SS sergeant, propped up on a sofa with a machine gun on his lap. The Croatian I now knew as Laban Milić sat next to the table in a heavy armchair that somehow made him look smaller than he was. He wasn't interested in me. I didn't think he would be interested in Vittoria either. He maintained a slightly bored smile, directed at no one. It was hard to relate him to the man Luca had described, but I had no doubt everything the friar had said was true.

Behind the German and the Croatian was a large oil painting. It almost framed the two of them. I looked at it as Ritter scribbled some notes down, probably for no reason other than to keep me waiting and unsettle me. He was working by the book. You think of odd things at odd times. Nothing mattered less now than a painting on a wall, but I found myself wondering what it was. Some trees and a horse and a man stretched out on the ground, bloody and almost naked, while another man, in some kind of turban and in rich robes of red and gold, bathed his wounds. The Good Samaritan. Unmissable now but I hadn't noticed it before.

'Gossip,' said Hauptsturmführer Ritter, 'is underestimated.'

Here we go, I thought. By the book. The idle banter beginning.

'It was your friend Mr Bewley, a phenomenal gossip, and not much else, who started the hare. He heard, in a call from an equally trivial friend he has in Tivoli, that Mr MacWhite's car had been seen at the Villa Greca, along with the ambassador's lovely secretary, or driver, or whatever needs Signorina Campana fulfils. Bewley mentioned it to his chauffeur, another jack-of-unclear-trades. The Irish ambassador and a young woman in a house he has no reason to be in? Why wouldn't the vengeful Charles want to spread that around the diplomatic corps? But it was the wrong rumour. Alfredo knew better. Hadn't he seen you in the car?'

'So, Charlie does some light spying for you and Alfredo spies on him.'

'Be careful what you eat in a thieves' kitchen, Inspector. I don't need to tell you that, do I? Alfredo has some surprising contacts of his own. I asked him to keep an eye on what you were up to with his boss. I didn't know it would be worth anything . . . but lo and behold, here we are! We did have some suspicion about this place . . . that Monsignor O'Flaherty and his friends had used it to store their Allied merchandise. At some point we would have taken a look. But suddenly, you're here, and we have a little heap of coincidences to dig into. Because one small piece of information our Italian colleagues picked up about this man Luca, he of the saint who had all those conversations with the birds, was that the late-lamented Father Hyde was planning to bring him here, to the Villa Greca, to get him out of Rome.'

'And away from your friend, the defrocked friar over there.'

The conversation was in German, but I had Milić's attention now. Ritter had no idea what I was talking about. The man he knew was simply an Ustaše officer.

'Isn't that right, Laban? But old habits . . . die hard . . . do you get it?'

'Luca always has a lot to say,' replied Milić. 'Lunatics often do, I'm told.'

'Let's get on with this,' snapped the Hauptsturmführer. So, time to move on from the idle banter stage. 'I don't much care about the friar, except as a source of information. The Italians want him for the murder of the priest. Captain Milić wants him for whatever it is he fucking wants him for. That's not my concern. But I want to know what you're doing here . . . and what the hell I'm supposed to do about it.'

I could see that Dietrich Ritter was pissed off. He wasn't only pissed off with me, though I thought I was at the top of the list. He didn't want to know about a dead Irish priest and he didn't want to know about Franciscans in Croatia. There was something about this job that it took a policeman of sorts to smell in another policeman of sorts. Orders from on high. Orders to blame the murder on Luca. Orders to do a favour to the Ustaše. He was probably used to orders he didn't like, but this needed delicate footwork. It was time to play the only card I had and give Ritter something else he didn't want and make him think a bit harder about his footwork.

'I'm here because of the Franciscan, Dietrich. You're right. I maybe volunteered for it with an eye on a couple of days with Signorina Campana, but you're not going to blame me for that. It's a lesson I should have learned at my age . . . think with your head, Stefan, not your dick. Still, we're all up for that, eh?'

It was my playbook now. First, enough bollocks to prove I was a fool.

'But Commissario De Angelis did think it would be better for me to do it. It's part of the Irish College . . . as an Irish diplomat . . .' I was stretching that, but it was there to be stretched. 'He wanted to persuade . . . that's the word . . . persuade Brother Luca to come back to the Vatican, so he could talk to him about Father Hyde's death. You know the commissario asked me to help with the investigation. But he

233

didn't want to ask the Italian police. I don't want to labour the point, Dietrich, but if we went down that road, we knew we'd never question Brother Luca at all. At least not in this world. I mean, between Capitano Penna . . . and Brother Laban . . . .'

I looked at the Ustaše man.

'You must have kept that old habit . . . didn't you have it at the palazzo?'

He didn't like that. I could see the anger. But he was holding it in.

'Do we have to listen to this bullshit, Hauptsturmführer?'

The SS man wasn't as comfortable as he had been. I was always going to be the problem. I had just made that problem bigger. He didn't give a fuck about the Vatican police, but the fact that a Vatican policeman knew I was there, wasn't something he could just shrug off. I was exaggerating what Giulio De Angelis knew, but he still knew something. It was one more complication Ritter could do without. And it gave me a reason to be at the Villa Greca that asked questions he couldn't so easily dump in a ditch. I couldn't know what he had on Vittoria, but my story didn't involve her in anything Luca had done. It didn't connect her to O'Flaherty and the POWs. It didn't even connect her to Donal Hyde. That was a dead end anyway, for obvious reasons. Unless Ritter had something specific, it connected her to nothing except me and Michael MacWhite's Lancia. If he was flying a kite, the story gave her a chance, at least. There was no chance for Luca Horvat, I knew that. But I had something left that was going to up the stakes on the SS man's irritation with Laban Milić and push it all back to Commissario De Angelis and the Gendarmerie. It might mean no more than embarrassment, but I had seen enough of Rome's diplomatic confusion to believe embarrassment could count.

'What Commissario De Angelis is looking into particularly . . .'

I took the opportunity to plough on. The Croat glared at Ritter, having got no reply from him. The SS man was frowning. It was getting even more complicated.

'He has evidence that Brother Luca left the Palazzo San Callisto before Father Hyde was killed.' Untrue, since the only evidence was Luca himself, but worth planting where it couldn't be contradicted. 'He also has evidence that two men entered the palazzo, shortly before the murder, disguised as Franciscan friars. I say disguised. One of them may have been a real Franciscan. The other one wasn't. Wasn't, but had been, if that makes sense. He was a Franciscan, a friend of Luca's, but he left the order . . . for whatever reason. He's been identified as a Croat, working as an Ustaše liaison officer with the Italian police or the Croatian representative to the Vatican. The commissario didn't have all the information. I'm just repeating what he told me. But I think even Giulio's boss knows he has two suspects who ought to be questioned.'

I stopped, turning to Captain Milić and smiling.

Dietrich Ritter followed my eyes. We were both gazing at the Ustaše man. The Hauptsturmführer had been silenced by how much more complicated this was becoming. He knew what was coming next. He didn't want it but he was no longer surprised. Whether it was true or not wasn't the point. It was a piece of shite that someone was writing a report about, somewhere reports couldn't just be binned.

'The evidence identifies the man as your colleague. Ex-Brother Laban.'

'Taking notes from Luca, Mr Gillespie?' Milić laughed. Not too much. He had the sense not to explode with indignation. He was right about my source, but he didn't know his old friend's words were all I had. 'He tells a very good story.'

'Where is this going, Inspector?'

If Ritter's curt question was directed anywhere, it was at himself.

I carried on. I still had the floor.

'As you'll understand, Commissario De Angelis wanted to make sure there was no mistake before the information went to the Polizia . . . or to the Gestapo. I don't know if the Gestapo is involved in the murder investigation or not, but as I'm working with the Vatican police, it's something both the Irish ambassadors will want to know, Mr MacWhite and Mr Kiernan. Their concern is that the murder is properly investigated. The Irish government owes that to Father Hyde's family.'

A good place to stop. It was almost as if we were real policemen.

Captain Milić stood up and took out a cigarette.

'Thank you for entertaining us, Mr Gillespie. What a tale!'

The Ustaše man was going to stick with contempt. He did it well.

'Sergeant, get the other prisoners. We're going back to Rome.'

Ritter's only response was an order. The sergeant saluted and walked away, heading for the wine cellar. The SS man got up and walked out through the front doors. He left me looking at Milić and the Croat looking back. The man didn't know what to make of me, or of what I had said. He didn't like it, but I guessed he didn't think it threatened him. He was almost certainly right. If he had killed Donal, no one would care. No one would get to question him. He walked away, heading to the kitchen. Unexpectedly, I was alone. It didn't make any difference. I had nowhere to go. But it felt as if all that confusion had blurred the edges. I knew why Dietrich Ritter was going back to the Via Tasso without asking any more questions here. He needed someone to tell him what to do next. I had a good idea he knew he was also going to be bollocked for fucking up. And he had fucked up. One way or another he was leaving the Villa Greca with complications that weren't there when he arrived. Nobody ever thanked you for that, anywhere.

I walked to the doors and out to the front of the house. There was no one to stop me. Ritter stood by his black car, looking at the tyres. They were flat. He took a few paces and looked down at the flat tyres of Michael MacWhite's Lancia. He walked toward the gates, where the troop carrier was parked by one of the elegant pine trees. More slashed tyres, as we both expected now, even the spares attached to a door on each side. It was thorough. The only thing untouched, or forgotten, was the motorcycle and sidecar. The Hauptsturmführer spun round, shouting.

'Tenente, dove sei? Dove sei! Lieutenant, where are you?'

There was no answer.

'Sergeant! Sergeant! Where is everyone? Sergeant!'

As I was the only one available, I answered.

'He's getting Vittoria and Luca from the cellar, Dietrich.'

'For God's sake!'

He stormed into the house without a glance back. I didn't know what he had in mind for me, I doubted he knew himself, but for now he didn't even think I needed a guard. If I'd wanted to, I could have walked out of the Villa Greca then and there. Still, the Hauptsturmführer had a lot on his mind. But I followed him in. I had plenty on my mind too. I had done what I could to create a mess in Ritter's head. It was having an effect, I had seen that. But was the mess any use to Vittoria?

The hall was empty. I could hear Ritter's voice, loud and angry, but I couldn't see him. Then he reappeared with the two German soldiers, from the direction of the kitchen. The men's rifles were slung on their backs but they were hurriedly buttoning up their tunics. Captain Milić walked behind them, eating a piece of sausage. It seemed as if he had already put my words out of his mind. He gave me a wry smile. He hadn't caught up with the fact that something was wrong. I knew, even if I had no idea what it meant. I returned his smile with a wryer one.

237

'Where the fuck is he? Where the fuck are the Italians?'

The soldiers clearly didn't know.

'Find them! Find the Eyetie wankers and bring them here. Now! Their arsehole of a lieutenant too. While they've been pissing about somewhere . . . and you two were stuffing your fucking faces, the tyres . . . all the tyres . . . find them!'

The two soldiers ran out through the doors. From the back of the house Vittoria and Luca walked slowly into the hall. Behind them was the sergeant, covering them with the machine gun. I shrugged at Vittoria. She looked at me quizzically. She had already felt the tension that told her something strange was happening. Ritter suddenly noticed I was there, standing on my own, unguarded.

'Get over there with the other two.'

I moved across the hall. The sergeant's machine gun followed me as I approached him. He pointed it at the sofa Vittoria was now sitting on. I sat down next to her. Luca was standing on his own by the wall. He was looking at no one. He was silently absorbed in his own thoughts and hardly aware of what was going on around him. Just outside the doors, Hauptsturmführer Ritter was telling the Ustaše man what had happened. It wouldn't have needed that many words. From where they were standing the vehicles, with their flat, slashed tyres, were visible enough. The two men came back in. Laban Milić sat down in the armchair. As he did so he unclipped the holster of the revolver at his side. Ritter stayed near the doors. He took his own automatic from its holster. He checked it and put it back.

It was ten minutes or so later that the German soldiers carried the body of the Italian lieutenant into the hall. His throat had been cut. An ear-to-ear job. You didn't have to get close to see that. They put him on the floor. And there he was, with all of us looking at him. Luca crossed himself. That was as much as the man got. Dietrich Ritter looked down for barely a moment. He turned to his soldiers.

'Well, where are his men?'

The two Germans shrugged.

'Where the fuck are they?'

'They've gone, Herr Hauptsturmführer.'

20

CINEMA PARADISO

Vittoria and I still sat in the hall at the Villa Greca. Luca still stood. The sergeant had pulled up a chair opposite us, cradling his machine gun on his lap. Captain Milić was in his armchair, smoking one cigarette after another. He was nervous, there was no doubt about it. Hauptsturmführer Ritter walked in and out of the house, one minute pacing the hall, the next outside. He was impatient, he was irritated, but he was calm, I had to give him credit. Each time he paced the hall, he had to step round the body of the dead Italian lieutenant. It might as well not have been there.

We were waiting for the two Waffen SS soldiers to return with some transport. Richter had dispatched them into the town on the motorbike, to find the police station and bring back men and vehicles. Failing that they were to commandeer any truck that came their way. 'Failing that' was a phrase that didn't inspire the two soldiers. They received their orders standing next to a body with the black-red decoration that had been cut into the neck. Whether Ritter's confidence was real or manufactured, he had plenty of it. He saw no problems. The policemen who had murdered their officer would be long gone and heading for the hills. I knew the SS man thought all Italians were cowards. There was the lieutenant's body to prove it.

Eventually, we heard the sound of the motorcycle returning. There was something else too. A deeper engine. Something heavy on the stones of the drive. Ritter smiled and walked outside. Confident as he was, there was some relief there. The sergeant stood up, relieved too, and gestured at the front door with the gun.

'Come on, my friends. Time to go.'

The Ustaše man got up and clipped his revolver into its holster. He had put his nervousness away as well now that he could. He said something to Luca in Croatian. It sounded as if it was meant to be funny. The Franciscan took no notice. He walked towards the doors slowly with Vittoria and me, as the sergeant followed behind. And then we stopped, all of us. Through the door came two men in their underwear, with their hands held on the back of their heads. Behind them was Hauptsturmführer Ritter. His hands were tied behind his back. A man in a German uniform that had been on one of the soldiers not long before, gripped Ritter's arms with one hand, while the other held a pistol to his head. There were two more men, one in the second German uniform, with the motorcycle goggles he must have arrived in still on, the other just in a suit. They held the machine guns the German soldiers had taken into Tivoli to convince those who didn't want their trucks stolen.

For a moment no one moved. No one spoke. The first move came from Laban Milić. He put his hands up. He might be the murdering bastard Luca Horvat said he was, but he was no fool. He knew one mistake would turn the hall into a slaughterhouse. I knew it too. The man I was watching now was the sergeant. His gun was pointing at the door. He had forgotten us already. The first voice was Ritter's. The credit I had given him for lack of nerves earlier, was nowhere near enough. I knew he was no Nazi fanatic, but I had to say he took his job seriously.

'Fire, Sergeant. Just fire.' He gave the order very calmly.

The man holding the pistol to Ritter's head was unimpressed. He pushed the muzzle of his gun hard into his hostage's temple. He spoke in good German.

'Move your hand and you're dead, Sergeant. And your officer too. In an instant. You won't even have time to take anyone with you. Put the fucker down.'

The sergeant did nothing, and now it felt like nothing was all he would do. And if he was still debating whether or not to go down in a blaze of pointless glory, the decision was taken away from him. I hadn't noticed Brother Luca move at all, but suddenly the big man was next to the German sergeant. He reached out and clasped one of the sergeant's wrists. It must have been a grip like steel. The sergeant cried out in pain and the machine gun fell to the floor. The Franciscan smiled at the German, then bent down and picked up the weapon. It was over.

After those hours inside, I was grateful to get out into the air. It was the same for Vittoria. For Luca, I don't know that it mattered. After taking the gun from the Waffen SS sergeant, he had resumed the silence and the distance he had been taken over by even before the SS arrived. The man who wouldn't stop talking, the man of so many violently changing moods, had gone. I might have put it down to the fact that he was sober, for the first time since I saw him with Donal Hyde in Trastevere, but it was something else. I knew only some of it. That was enough.

The Germans were outside too, sitting against the wall at the front of villa. Ritter, his sergeant, the soldiers, now with their uniforms back. With them was the Ustaše man. The Partisans who had captured the two soldiers had arrived with the motorbike and sidecar leading a small flat-backed lorry. The uniforms had got them close enough to the Hauptsturmführer to do what they needed to do. By the time he saw they weren't his men it was too late. He couldn't even produce his automatic.

While the Germans now took their turn under the gaze of men with machine guns, Vittoria and several others were deep in conversation by the truck. It hadn't started as an argument, but now voices were raised. I hadn't got any further than relief that it was over and that Vittoria was going to be all right. I had reason to believe I'd done enough to keep myself out of the hands of the Gestapo. I was too much trouble. I'd made myself too visible in a place where the Germans didn't want trouble. It was clear Dietrich Ritter had no issue with killing anybody for anything or for nothing, but his hierarchy was still squeamish about diplomatic niceties that hardly seemed worthy of attention. It was part of the Rome I'd come to know in only a few days. Vittoria hadn't qualified for those benefits.

As I sat on a bench, looking across at the argument, I realised what it was about. It should have been obvious straightaway, but I hadn't been thinking. What did they do with their prisoners? Did they shoot them or did they let them go? I looked round to see Brother Luca was watching the Partisans too. He spoke Italian, of course, and so he could do a lot better than hazard the guesses I'd just made.

'Will they kill them, Luca?'

The friar shrugged. He still had the machine gun he had taken from Ritter's sergeant. He stood and walked over to where I was sitting. He handed me the gun.

'Keep it safe for the moment, Stefan.'

The Partisans were suddenly much quieter. The man who had held the pistol to the Hauptsturmführer's head seemed to be the leader. He went over to the prisoners. He told them to stand. Vittoria was next to me. She was flushed and tense. It was passion and fury. Her voice had been loud as the Partisans argued.

'What's happening?'

'He has no orders to kill them.' I heard her anger.

I didn't say anything. My story, for those who were prepared to believe my version, made me guilty in German eyes of not much more than trying too hard to discover how a dead Irishman died. Watching a massacre of German solders was something else altogether. I couldn't say I didn't sympathise with what I saw in Vittoria's face. I could still see the old man, Claudio, too. And I knew what had waited for her and for Luca. But I wasn't in a place where I could have pulled the trigger. The thought that it wasn't my war was in my head. It made me feel cheap. These people had earned the right to kill. All I could feel was that I didn't want to be a part of it. I hadn't earned that right. I hadn't even earned the right to be there.

'I want them to kill Ritter. I've said I will do it myself.'

Vittoria was staring at the SS man. I had no doubt she would do it.

Brother Luca was now talking to the Partisan leader, quietly and intensely. The man nodded and shrugged. He listened to the friar again, looking puzzled. Then Luca walked forward and started to talk to Laban Milić. The Ustaše man was obviously afraid, as the massive figure towered over him in his clerical cassock, the round, black hat back on his head. But as he spoke, Milić seemed to relax. He even smiled. The conversation was in Croatian. Nobody understood it except the Franciscan and the man who had once been his friend, and a Franciscan too.

They talked for almost five minutes. I could see Vittoria was impatient. She had something in her head that needed no conversation. The Partisan leader was becoming impatient too. He looked at his watch. There was no sense that anyone was coming, but it was not a business that lent itself to staying in one place very long.

Brother Luca turned, smiling. He spoke in a mixture of German and Italian. His words were directed at everyone, the Partisans, the prisoners, and also at me.

'There is only one thing left . . . one more thing . . . for me to be reconciled with my old friend, Laban . . . I think that is why I am here . . . I don't expect you to understand that . . . but Laban and I have been brought together by God . . . to put an end to something . . . for me to take his sins and add them to my own . . . for the rest . . . you must let these Germans go . . . all of them, my daughter . . . every one.'

Luca looked hard at Vittoria. He knew what she wanted.

'If you kill them now, even one of them now, it will only be the beginning for this place . . . they will come back to this town . . . and they will kill . . . and they will kill . . . and they will kill . . . you have been saved and there are others to be saved . . . you must fight your war . . . you will fight your war . . . on other days . . . for now, this is our day . . . my day, my friend's day . . . we are the ones who cannot be saved . . . we can't be saved . . . we can be reconciled as the brothers we once were.'

The Franciscan turned to Laban Milić. He held out his arms. The Ustaše man was still nervy, I could see that. But I also saw he could hardly believe his luck. I doubt he'd given himself much chance with the Partisans. Now the man he wanted to kill, the man he had sought out to take terrible revenge on, was offering him brotherly love. It probably confirmed his conviction that Luca was a lunatic, but he wasn't complaining. I thought I could read his face as he looked up at his old friend's benevolent smile. If the fool wanted to bless him, bring it on.

Brother Luca put his arms round Milić. The big man almost folded the small man into him. He held him tight. He held him very tight. I could see the forced smile that the Ustaše man had produced changing. He was frowning now. He started to struggle. He wanted to get out of that brotherly embrace. But it got tighter. So tight that he couldn't struggle. So tight that he couldn't speak. Only a gasping noise came from his mouth. We were all gazing, yet not quite taking in what we were seeing. Then it was over, very suddenly over. I don't know whether I heard something snap, like bones breaking. Maybe I just thought I did. The Franciscan opened his arms. The body of Laban Milić fell to the ground. Dead.

The friar made the sign of the cross over the body. He turned to the Partisans and walked across to where I was standing with the machine gun he had given me.

'It's done. Ora è fatto. Portaverit hircus . . . omnes iniqui-tates . . .'

I didn't know if anyone else heard what he said. Sins and something else . . . a goat? Or did he say circus? I always had a good memory for these things, but it was too long ago. And he was talking to himself. No one was doing anything other than stare at the man whose life he had crushed out. Luca took the gun from me.

'If you want more, there is always more. Now, I leave it to you.'

He held out the machine gun, fixing his eyes only on Vittoria. She took a step forward. She reached out and touched the gun. She looked at me and then across at Hauptsturmführer Ritter and back to me. All the certainty that had been there only minutes before had gone. There was nothing of sentiment or sympathy in her face. There was nothing I could see that told her she shouldn't kill Dietrich Ritter. There was nothing that told her she didn't want to. But what she had witnessed had drained her ability to do it. It was as if she now needed someone to tell her to pull the trigger. I think if I had nodded she would have shot him. I shook my head. Even as I did, I felt I had no right to stop her. But I knew I had. I wondered if she would resent it. For in that moment, the decision had been made, not only by Vittoria, but by all of them. The Germans would go. And no one, on either side, would thank anybody for that. Vittoria turned and walked away, into the garden.

*

Dietrich Ritter had departed. It had been a humiliating departure too, four of them crammed on to and into the motorcycle and sidecar. They had been warned not to stop. The road out of Tivoli would be watched. It almost certainly wasn't, but they wouldn't stop till they reached somewhere on the road to Rome with a police station or German troops. The truck the Partisans brought to the Villa Greca was revving up outside. They were ready to go, heading for the mountains I could still see in the distance. They were the mountains Vittoria had shown me as we drove towards Tivoli, the mountains she had grown up with. And she was going there with the Partisans. For now, anyway, there could be no going back to Rome.

'Where's Luca?' she said.

'I don't know. I think he's gone.'

'Gone where?'

'One minute he was in the chapel, then he disappeared. I don't think he's running now. I think that's over. I don't know what he's doing. I guess he does.'

The sins . . . the goat . . . and the desert. Something had come back to me.

'I thought he'd come with us,' continued Vittoria. 'I don't know what else he can do. If he got to the north, someone could help him cross into Switzerland.'

'I'm not sure there's anywhere he wants to go, Vittoria.'

'They'll find him.'

'Maybe so. Maybe no one will want to now . . . outside Croatia.'

She nodded. I don't think either of us believed that. We would never know. We'd never see him again. That was a thought I could see was in her head as well as mine. It wasn't such an important thought, except that it wasn't about him at all now. It was about us. That was a different thought altogether. And we didn't have anything to say about it. She changed the subject. If she hadn't, I would have.

'Someone's coming from the town . . . with tyres for the Lancia.'

'And then I just find my way back to Rome?'

'You'll find your way. I'm sure you always find your way.'

'I wish that was true, Vittoria.'

She nodded again, for no real reason, except that we'd run out of words.

There was a shout from the truck, moving slowly towards the gate.

'I have to go.'

'Yes.'

I kissed her.

There was a loud blast on the horn of the lorry.

She kissed me once more, for only a second. She ran to the truck and one of the Partisans heaved her on to it. She sat on the back, waving a rifle and laughing.

'Come back when we've won the war, Stefan!'

And then she was gone. It was done. I took out a cigarette and lit it.

*

The weeks I had spent in Spain and Italy, on various diplomatic loose ends that Joe Walshe and the Department of External Affairs in Dublin wanted cleared away or explained or undone or erased or, from what was still left to do in Rome, referred to the filing-cabinet-of-no-return, hadn't impressed me much with the heights of diplomacy, Irish or otherwise. I'd never read what Machiavelli had to say on it, but I felt his reputation must rest on something other than the three-wise-monkeys school of diplomacy that drove most of what I'd seen so far. Like tightrope-walkers, the basic requirement was to stay on the rope and not fall off, that's all, whatever else was going on in the circus. Neutrality looked even more like that abroad than it did at home, where it was just how things were. There were presumably some principles that went with all that, somewhere, but they were for better times. For now, there was the rope. But I saw no more than anyone put in front of me, and I saw that from the outside. If Lilliput came into my head, and what I was doing seemed to matter less and less, the longer I was in Europe, maybe it was because no one had told me why it mattered. But maybe nobody even knew.

I got back to the Irish embassy very late. There was no one to ask me any questions. Only Finn was there, at the top of the stairs, now pleased enough to see me to get up and wag his tail, but it felt more like a gesture than real enthusiasm.

It wasn't that different the next morning. I explained nothing to Mrs Butler, who asked nothing. I was expecting a cross-examination. It wouldn't have been unreasonable after the Irish-English back and forth she'd provided between me and Vittoria. All she asked was whether we were both all right. She meant it. If she didn't like me much, she cared about Vittoria. She seemed unsurprised when I told her Vittoria wouldn't be coming back. She nodded, that's all. She knew a great deal more than I'd supposed. But whatever she knew, stayed where it was. All she offered, as I went in to see the ambassador, was the advice of any wise monkey.

'The minimum of detail is probably more than enough, Inspector.'

I took the advice. It certainly suited Michael MacWhite. The only note he took was about the bill for the four new tyres on his car. He was surprised by Vittoria's abrupt departure, but not surprised enough to push very hard at the edges of the vague explanation I gave him. It mostly consisted of telling him she would be in touch herself at some stage. That was enough. I did say that the Vatican Gendarmerie's investigation into Donal Hyde's death had produced more evidence and Commissario De Angelis was pursuing it. There seemed no doubt the man the Italian police had been looking for was not the killer. That was as far as it went. I wouldn't know how far it went till I spoke to Giulio. But I didn't have much faith it would go any further. The ambassador knew less than I did, but his instincts told him the same thing. There was nothing to know that people wanted known.

I didn't know what else was on the ambassador's mind, but I could see there was something. The conversation had drifted to an end. Not a conclusion, because almost everything was missing. It just stopped. I had given him my short version of what had happened and in my head all that felt more real than sitting in MacWhite's office while he fidgeted with a pen and the dog snored quietly beside him. But I waited for him to continue. There was something else to say.

'I'm pissed off with Dublin, Stefan. Joe Walshe gets a fucking bee in his bonnet . . .'

'Charlie boy?'

I hadn't forgotten. Bewley had been on my mind for other reasons. He had led Ritter to the Villa Greca.

'Another message. Joe's more agitated about this now. God knows why.'

'Tell Gillespie to get off his arse and rob the fucker?'

The ambassador laughed.

'More or less.'

'I haven't found any easy way, sir.'

'I know. I also know far more serious matters . . .'

He was about to step into a real conversation, but he stopped.

'One thing has happened. Bewley was in here yesterday. About his passport. Where the hell is it, and all that. I did the usual and passed the buck back to Dublin. But, there is a problem. He's definitely leaving Rome. Going north. He gave the usual blather about how boring the city is now. Jesus! I know he doesn't want to be around when the Allies get here. And "when" is definitely the word. I also suspect he wouldn't mind being close to the Austrian border if they get close to him there. Just that hop across. But the point is, when he goes, this stuff Joe Walshe is so determined to get hold of, is going to go with him. That'll be that.'

I nodded. But urgency didn't make it any easier.

'I don't know if it helps, but Bewley's away for a week, from tomorrow. A train to the Lakes, to look around for somewhere to move to. The place is empty.'

'If the chauffeur hasn't gone with him,' I said, 'it won't be empty.'

'Think about it, Stefan. If there's a way . . . if not, forget it. I'll tell Joe you've done what you can. It's not worth the risk. It's not a game here. He can sit there on Stephen's Green and send out his bloody instructions . . . he's got no fucking idea!'

I met Commissario De Angelis in a bar outside the Vatican. I told him everything that had happened in Tivoli. It wasn't evidence by any normal standards. Luca Horvat had told me he saw a Croat Ustaše officer in the church of San Callisto, disguised as a Franciscan friar, along with another man, around the time Father Hyde was murdered. Luca knew the Ustaše man. He also knew the Croatian authorities were trying to have him arrested or simply find him and kill him, for reasons that went back to his own activities as an Ustaše chaplain. That was why Luca was in hiding. Donal had been helping him and got caught in the crossfire. He was probably killed in fury or maybe because he wouldn't give information. Now the man Luca had identified as one of the murderers was dead, killed by Luca himself. If I believed the story, and I did, it amounted to not much more than one suspect kills another suspect and then disappears. There was no one to question.

Giulio's own evidence supported the story. He had found witnesses at the Palazzo San Callisto who saw two unknown Franciscan friars, not just in the church, but in the palazzo itself. The two men were behaving oddly, but that was about it. They had been seen close to the garden where Donal's body was discovered. One gendarme did recall them leaving in a hurry and speaking in a language he didn't know, which he described as having a Slavic ring to it. The commissario had also found that when Captain Milić arrived in Rome, a month ago now, as some kind of assistant to the Croatian representative at the Vatican, he called into the Gendarmeria to ask if they had access to lists of Franciscan houses and the friars living in them. There were no such lists and he was directed to the Franciscans themselves. Milić made no mention of Brother Luca during this visit, but Giulio had learned from a Fascist-police contact that Luca had been put on a list of Croat nationals wanted for crimes committed in Croatia. It was more hearsay. But it was enough hearsay to ask real questions about what happened at the Palazzo San Callisto. It was enough for Commissario De Angelis to point the finger away from Brother Luca and in the direction of the dead ex-Brother Laban.

'What will you do?' I asked.

'I'll put together a report. It won't mention what happened in Tivoli. I can't know anything about that, can I? But it will make the case that the man we need to talk to, who ought to be the suspect in Father Hyde's murder, is the Croat, Milić.'

'And what will the Ispettore Dirigente say?'

'Once he's finished shouting, he'll shut the investigation down. But it won't be easy. The report will be on record. He can't bury it without telling the Polizia, because he made the point of saying they should deal with it. But if it does go to them, they've got to take it on board and interrogate Milić. They won't want to, but they'll have to. The Vatican won't want them to either, but we'd have to insist. No one wants to go near an investigation, wherever it is, that means conversations about Franciscans murdering Serbs in Croatia. Still not a popular topic, as you can imagine. But when the explosion's over, I'll give Ispettore Caproni his get out.'

'It was in another country, and besides . . . the feller's dead.'

'What?'

'I mean there's nothing left to investigate. You'll tell your boss you have reason to think Captain Milić has departed this earth, never mind how you know.'

Giulio smiled. If nothing else, he was getting one up on his boss.

'He won't care how I know, but he'll find out it's true. And in the process he will call in his favours. And he won't need to work very hard. No one will want to know any more about this. If your friend Luca is out of the city, I'd say he's safe. Nobody's going to look for him now. If the man who killed an Irish priest is really a Croatian Fascist who was working with the Fascist police and Gestapo . . .'

'It's not a good look. Even for them.'

We left the bar and walked towards the Vatican.

'Do you like movies, Stefan?'

'It depends what it is.'

'Well, the Vatican doesn't show many movies. It's a first.'

He laughed and took two pieces of paper from his pocket.

'These are hard to come by. Vatican bigwigs and assorted diplomats. And the Gendarmerie. We have to go. "Pastor Angelicus." It won't be big on laughs.'

Somehow, somewhere, there's always an Irishman in it, even watching a film in the Vatican about the Pope. Pius XII was the Pastor Angelicus of the film's title, a name provided a thousand years earlier by St Malachy, Archbishop of Armagh, who prophesied the one hundred and twelve popes who would sit on St Peter's throne before the Last Judgement, along with a nickname for each. This Pope stood at one hundred and six on the list, which didn't leave long to go, but I assumed they worked on the principle that while an Irishman might come up with a vision that was inspirational enough, you wouldn't want to rely on the man much when it came to the timekeeping element.

It was an odd thing to sit in the dark and see so much of this Pope I hadn't even glimpsed, coming in and out of the Vatican City and St Peter's, not because I had any expectation of seeing him, but because it made me realise he was a constant presence. I was unexpectedly aware of that presence. I had somehow absorbed it without knowing. It wasn't that it meant anything, just that it was there. He was almost familiar. It was all familiar somehow. The film had a lot of statues of apostles and saints and angels. A lot of priests and cardinals and nuns and Swiss Guards and diplomats in tailcoats and breeches. There was a lot of ring-kissing and carrying-about on a chair and there were bigger and bigger crowds filling St Peter's Square and cheering the thin man on the balcony. And in between there was a lot of the thin man looking solitary and serious and ascetic. I saw only the pictures because the narration was in Italian. I got what mood I could from the music. I didn't know what I was meant to make of it. I wasn't strong on pomp, but that didn't mean I couldn't feel inspiration, even without believing. Maybe at another time I might have seen some sort of spiritual power set against the chaos beyond St Peter's Gates, but a couple of images of soldiers fighting and ships sinking, didn't do the job now. If the words I didn't understand said more about that, I doubted it was much more. It seemed a strange film to make with the world burning. But if that made me uneasy, I could see Giulio De Angelis felt differently. As the lights went up and everyone in the room stood to applaud, his eyes were shining. He could make a joke, but I knew there were tears in his eyes.

With the film over, the hall in which we had watched it was full of people talking enthusiastically. I talked quite enthusiastically myself, as the commissario had picked up all the inspiration I had missed. I imagined that not everyone there was inspired, but as I glanced around I couldn't help wanting to identify with the enthusiasts. Several men in German uniforms, not far away, looked as if they were making the same kind of polite noises I had just been making. Giulio laughed.

'Now you see the nest of spies in operation!'

'I can see a couple of SS men. Not their sort of movie, really . . .'

'The tall one is Obersturmbannführer Kappler. Head of the Gestapo and the SD. He runs the Via Tasso, of course. Your friend Hauptsturmführer Ritter's boss. With him, von Weizsäcker, German ambassador to the Holy See . . . and he's walking over to . . . there you have it . . . Sir D'Arcy Osborne, the British ambassador. One of the prisoners of the Vatican . . . he can't go outside the Vatican borders. You watch . . . they'll exchange a few remarks about the film and see if they can read something significant into what the other one says. It'll be short. It always is. I've watched them enough. But they make a point of saying something.'

'When it's about nothing.'

'Exactly. They'll all be at it.'

Commissario De Angelis turned away as someone spoke to him in Italian. I left him to the conversation and looked round the hall. Waiters were going round with glasses of wine. I took a glass and watched. I didn't know who any of the people in the room were besides the ones Giulio had pointed out. It was hard to relate any of this to where I had been only twenty-four hours earlier, or even to the streets of Rome. None of it felt solid. I looked back towards the men I now knew as the German ambassador and the British ambassador, sharing some small joke. Not every conversation I could see would be between two implacable enemies exchanging pleasantries and idle remarks over a glass of wine, but it was hard to imagine anything here was real in the way the world outside was real. Yet this was a place of truth. Wasn't that what the film was about? Now, in the buzz of conversation, weren't they all lying about something, even if that only meant saying nothing? I decided I wasn't up for it. I had several dead bodies in my head, that I hadn't managed to get out yet. Irrespective of whether they died for one side or another or no side at all, they weren't the right company for this place. I said goodbye to Giulio and left him still enthusing about the Angelic Shepherd.

The next morning, I made a decision. I wanted to get out. I needed to get home. I had no place in any of it. I was sick of it. But I had the job to do that the Department of External Affairs still insisted needed doing. And doing it would put me on a train quicker than anything else. Doing it would get me to Spain and Portugal and on a plane to England and then Ireland. And I had an idea, just about, that whatever kind of bollocks it was that sent me to Rome in the first place, it was bollocks that had to be finished. I didn't give a shite about the people who sent me. I didn't owe anything to Michael MacWhite, who didn't care anyway. I couldn't have given a fuck what it was Charles Bewley had up his sleeve to embarrass Joe Walshe or Éamon de Valera, or even Holy Ireland herself. Perhaps I was too used to being a foot soldier. What else was I? In the end, I would do what I was told. And the sooner the better.

I came downstairs and went to the office. Mrs Butler was sorting through the post. She looked up with something that bore a resemblance to a smile. I had worked out she wasn't a woman who overdid such things. She was warming to me.

'Can you get me someone on the phone, Mrs Butler?'

'Will it be in Irish or English?'

There was even something funny. I felt privileged.

'How's your German?'

I had her there. That was my decision. I'd started out thinking I might use some of Vittoria's friends to help me get into Bewley's apartment. That felt like a long time ago and it didn't work. But I was still a neutral. Either side would do for me. Hadn't I watched people who'd cheerfully turn a gun on each other making polite noises the evening before? It wasn't so hard. And I had a favour to call in.

'Hauptsturmführer Ritter at Gestapo Headquarters . . . Via Tasso.'

21

FORUM ROMANUM

I was unsure how Dietrich Ritter would deal with the favour he owed me. The real favour was the one Luca Horvat did him, in crushing a man to death. But I thought that if the Partisans had spent any time reflecting on that, they might have recovered their appetites and come to the conclusion that leaving SS men alive was a mistake. If I contributed something to Hauptsturmführer Ritter still being alive, it hadn't been because I much cared. I didn't. But whatever it was, and whatever it amounted to, I thought it would suffice. At the same time, it seemed wise to tread carefully. I didn't relish another visit to the Via Tasso, even with a get-out-of-gaol ticket. I couldn't know what Ritter's report said about me. Or if he was going to do me a favour at all. I also doubted he would want anyone else to know what passed between us. Instinct told me his account of events at the Villa Greca would be light on detail. I was the witness to the fact that he ended up looking like an arsehole. Whatever he'd added or subtracted, that wouldn't be the picture he had presented.

In a monosyllabic telephone conversation, the SS man agreed to meet me. He didn't seem keen that I came to Gestapo HQ either. We chose somewhere neutral. An empty place it was reasonable enough to walk in, at a time when no one else would be there. I met him late in the evening, in the Roman Forum.

The Forum was empty. It was dark, but there was a half-moon low in the sky. With the Forum sitting so low itself, beneath the level of the streets that surrounded it, the modern buildings that bordered it were barely more than a few lights scattered against a black backdrop. Seen like this, the ancient stones were more alive, more solid, than they had been in daylight. The past was closer. At any other time it might have been pleasant enough to wander with the ghosts, but the present was already there, waiting, in field grey, smoking a cigarette. SS Hauptsturmführer Ritter sat on the stump of a fluted column. I looked past him. A soldier leaning against an arch, some way off, holding a rifle. He wasn't hiding. He wasn't even threatening, but he was there. And there were probably a couple more.

'You're right, Stefan, much better than the Via Tasso.'

'There's quite a long list of places better than that.'

'You'd have been safe enough.'

'Well, we've been through a bit, Dietrich. It's not as chummy as it started out. And people do go in there and not come out. At least not how they went in.'

'I'd have an awful lot to explain if that happened. Wouldn't be worth it.'

He took out a packet of cigarettes and held it out. I moved closer and took one. He flicked his lighter. I bent to light the cigarette. I breathed in sour smoke.

'These are terrible.'

He laughed.

'German. One price of war. I keep the English ones for myself. Anyway, here we are. I assume this is a little chat neither of us might want . . . on record.'

'Let's say I'm getting picky about who I'm seen with, Hauptsturmführer.'

'Not as picky as you should be. You've made some unfortunate friends.'

'It depends how you look at it.'

He got up from the broken column he was sitting on.

'We should walk, Stefan. It's something, isn't it . . . to have it to ourselves.'

We walked slowly. At a distance, the soldier with the rifle kept pace.

'What happened to the woman, Signorina Campana?'

'I don't know.'

'She would be strongly advised not to reappear in Rome.'

'I'm sure she knows what she's doing.'

'They all know what they're doing. I doubt it's very helpful . . . at the end.'

He said it with a kind of lazy disdain. I wasn't sure he quite believed it.

'How helpful would you have found it, Dietrich? That could have been your end, couldn't it? At the Villa Greca. And you knew exactly what you were doing.'

The SS man said nothing. He owed me some part of his life. He owed even more of it to a drunken Croatian friar who might not have been a psychotic killer but probably was half mad. And he hated it. He hated what had happened. He hated me now, less for what I'd done than what I knew. There was a struggle I could see in his face, between the anger he felt and a debt he couldn't ignore. He wanted to show the contempt he was trained to, but there was enough left of what he once might have believed in as a sense of honour, to recognise that wouldn't do. He was almost humiliated by the way he had survived. That was why he agreed to meet like this, unseen. I was his humiliation. Maybe his comrades would smell it.

'You want something, Stefan. That's what you said.'

He dropped the philosophy. It was time for business.

'Yes. I think you owe me something, Dietrich. You owe me enough . . .'

He didn't answer. But the silence was consent.

'Charles Bewley. Your friend. Or whatever the word is.'

Ritter nodded.

'That's what it's about,' I continued. 'The Irish government has a problem, a disagreement, let's call it that . . . with Mr Bewley, who was ambassador in Berlin until nineteen thirty-nine. He was dismissed from his post for reasons I don't know much about. And who cares? I'd say the bottom line was that he thought working for your government was more important than what he did for his own. It's a habit he seems to have clung on to . . . though not at such an exalted level. However, when Charlie left the embassy in Berlin he took a lot more than his toothbrush and a change of underwear. He has a collection of documents in his apartment . . . that the Irish government thinks he shouldn't have. And they want them back. They've wanted them back for a long time. Whatever they contain . . . they are an embarrassment.'

Hauptsturmführer Ritter was almost amused. He shook his head.

'Indeed, who cares? I'm surprised Charles matters very much at all.'

'The documents matter, that's all. And I have the job of getting them back.'

'It sounds very trivial, Stefan, in the middle of a war. I can't imagine what sort of secrets your ambassador would have had in nineteen thirty-nine, that would be worth anyone's time now. Do you never leave Gulliver and Lilliput behind? I know we like to think Irish neutrality does some damage . . . to the English. And the English like to jump up and down and complain about the treacherous Irish. I know we have experts in Intelligence who earn a good living peddling the idea there's something useful in all that for Germany. But the truth is, it means fuck all.

I've never been convinced otherwise. When you lay the cards out, Irish neutrality or the squabble between Ireland and England . . . does anyone, on either side, give a fuck?'

'Maybe you have a point.' I laughed. 'But you're a hard man, Dietrich.'

'You want these papers? Get them. So what?'

'Mr Bewley regards them as a great prize, that's the trouble. I don't know whether it's because he wants his revenge on the Irish government at some point, served cold, as recommended, or whether he thinks it'll help him if the Allies catch up with him in Rome or wherever. Some quid pro quo in an interrogation room.'

Ritter didn't trot out the usual line about the Allies never reaching Rome.

'Why should I worry about this, Stefan? Charles is a low-level informant, that's all. He provides gossip about a few expatriates we keep an eye on. He has friends in the Vatican, but we have far better contacts. Trawling through what he comes up with takes more time than it's ever worth. He's barely worth the money.'

'You got more than that at the Villa Greca, Dietrich.'

'It doesn't happen often.'

'Maybe you get more from his chauffeur?'

'And maybe gossip isn't the priority it once was, Inspector.'

'With the Allies just down the road, you mean?'

Hauptsturmführer Ritter shrugged, but again, he didn't argue.

'Tell me what you want.'

'I need access to Bewley's apartment. I need to find the documents, get them out and take them to the Villa Spada. I've looked at breaking in. I even looked at getting someone else to break in. But there is a simpler way. A key to the front door. An apartment with nobody in it. And time. Time to search and time to take the material down the stairs and into a car. With no fuss, no mess, no interruption.'

'And you think I'm in the habit of facilitating burglaries?'

I thought Ritter might have joined in when I laughed. Somehow he kept a straight face. Maybe it's what the riding boots were for, exercising the high horse.

'Come on, Dietrich. The favour isn't even that. I already know Alfredo's one of your lads too. Though I don't suppose Charlie does. It was Alfredo who gave you the gossip that got you to the Villa Greca . . . with unlooked-for consequences.'

The SS man lit another cigarette. He didn't offer me one this time. The only consequence he was still thinking about was the one that had put him in my debt. It rankled. I could see it in the way he was shifting about. It clearly rankled like hell.

'I know Charlie has gone away for a couple of days, Dietrich.'

Ritter nodded. He knew too.

'North, I think, that's what he said to Mr MacWhite. He's moving out of Rome. I'd say he's twigged he could have some explaining to do if the British or the Americans ever cross his path. Is that what he told you? Or would he keep the rat-and-ship scenario to himself? I'd say very likely. What do you think, Dietrich?'

Ritter didn't bite. He probably had his own doubts about the ship.

'So, I want to get into Bewley's apartment. No questions. No risks. As a policeman, it would do me no good to get arrested, that's the thing. And I don't know what Mr MacWhite would think about that. Besides, I'd be uneasy about what might happen if I got arrested. You can probably appreciate that yourself.'

The Hauptsturmführer gave the first smile in some time.

'If I wanted you arrested, you'd be in a cell. I have no shortage of evidence, do I? You've helped a wanted killer to escape. You've colluded with Partisans and terrorists. Fuck diplomatic passports. If I wanted you shot, I'd have every reason.'

'But you don't want that . . .'

There was a part of him that did, but I still had the part that didn't.

'All you have to do is tell Alfredo to take a day off and go for a spin in Charlie's big red car. He needs to make sure the housekeeper's off too. Before he goes, he hands me the key to the flat. That's it. It's not a lot to ask, Dietrich, is it?'

The part of him that wanted to say, 'Fuck you!' put in an appearance.

'I have three men watching you . . . all I have to do . . .'

'You want to clear the debt, Dietrich. But just in case . . .'

I turned and lifted my arm. I called out.

'Giulio! You'd better be here!'

A voice answered in the darkness, echoing round the Forum.

'Una bella serata, signori.'

It was Commissario De Angelis. He stayed in the shadows.

'Who the fuck is that?' said Ritter.

'In Ireland we like to be sure twice. You know that one? Nobody really says it, but you'll get the point. I didn't want to catch you after a bad day at the office. I said I'd meet Commissario De Angelis . . . the Vatican Gendarmerie . . . for a drink. He fancied a stroll . . . a lifetime in Rome and he's never seen the Forum by moonlight.'

The SS man laughed.

'He has no jurisdiction here. He can't even carry arms outside the Vatican.'

'If he is armed, five minutes in the confessional and a Hail Mary or two will redress the sin. And you wouldn't want to shoot him as well. Two diplomatic incidents and two dead neutral policemen? Obersturmbannführer Kappler wouldn't score you very high for that, let alone Berlin. I know these things get sorted out, but not before you found yourself in a concentration camp. Or do I read it wrong?'

Ritter laughed again. This time he was genuinely amused.

'It's a pity you didn't spend more time in Germany, Stefan. You're more unpleasant than you think you are. You'd have made a very good Party member.'

'Forgive me if I don't take that as a compliment, Dietrich.'

'It wasn't meant to be one.'

If the moment of tension had been real, it was gone.

'That's almost a joke, Dietrich. And not a bad one.'

He was brusque and businesslike again, his decision made.

'Do it the day after tomorrow. I'll speak to Alfredo. I'll send a note to the Irish embassy that will give you a time to collect the key from him. There will be very few police around in that part of the city, and few soldiers, even in the Via Tasso. There is a special operation. When you drive back to Trastevere, avoid the Jewish Ghetto. There'll be road blocks. Anywhere else . . . no one will bother you.'

Hauptsturmführer Ritter turned away. He didn't look back as he spoke.

'The debt is paid, Inspector Gillespie. You'd do well to remember it!'

I watched him walk on. I took out a cigarette. Three soldiers, SS men, came out of the shadows, following behind him. After a few moments Giulio appeared.

'You look like you need a drink, Stefan.'

'I think several.'

We walked slowly towards the lights of the city.

'You know this will go back to your Ispettore Caproni,' I said.

The commissario smiled. 'Are those cigarettes English?'

'No, French.'

He gave a shrug of disappointment and took one, then he laughed.

'Ispettore Dirigente Caproni has taken early retirement.'

I showed my surprise on my face. It sounded strangely abrupt.

'In fact he left this afternoon.'

'Just like that?'

'Just like that. It was a sudden decision. He took it after the Secretary of State called on him. I've never seen a cardinal of that rank in the Gendarmeria. It's like a prime minister dropping in. They didn't talk for long. But shortly afterwards, the Ispettore and several other senior officers decided they'd given such excellent service that it was time to hang up their hats. They happen to be the ones with a soft spot for Mussolini and a lot of old friends in the Fascist police. But that's probably a coincidence. Still, what you might call a changing of the guard. The Holy Father must have felt the way the wind is blowing . . . on his morning walk.'

*

It was two days later that I arrived at Charles Bewley's apartment block in a van that the ambassador had asked the gardener, Salvatore Rosselli, to borrow for the day. That was the full extent of MacWhite's involvement. The how was my business. And once it was done the business was nobody else's business. An employee of the Irish embassy driving Irish documents to the Villa Spada was of no interest to anyone, even if I was stopped. The risk was at the apartment. And I assumed that Hauptsturmführer Ritter had made sure that had been dealt with. Once I identified the material in the flat, it was a removal job, and nothing more.

I stopped the van at the archway that led into the courtyard behind Bewley's apartment. The red car sat under the arch, gleaming as usual. If gossip was something the chauffeur specialised in, car-polishing came a close second.

Alfredo got out and walked to the van. He was out of uniform. He was dressed for his day out, in something that looked like he was heading for a golf course. He said nothing. He passed a key through the window of the cab. He turned away and went back to the convertible. He drove out to the street as I moved forward to pull into the courtyard. In the back were the golf clubs. He accelerated away with enough anger to leave at least some part of the car's tyres behind. As he did I saw a motorbike pull out from the other side of the street. The man riding it wore no helmet. He raised his hand in a salute of what felt like recognition. And although he was gone in seconds, I thought I recognised him. I drove on into the courtyard and parked the van by the door to the back stairs of the apartment. I walked round to the front of the building and went in. I climbed the stairs to Bewley's flat. But I was still thinking about the motorcyclist. I did know him. Then I remembered. He was one of the Partisans who had walked into the Villa Greca with a machine gun.

The study that led off the room I had sat in with Charles Bewley was meticulously ordered. One glance at the book-shelves that took up three walls was enough to know that the books were arranged alphabetically and by subject matter. Fiction and non-fiction would not tread on each other's toes. You didn't need to check it was true. It was the kind of library that looked as if no volumes were ever taken from the shelves. There were no untidy piles of books on the desk or on the table. Everything had a place. And that included a series of boxes that took up the bottom row of the bookshelves. The boxes were dated, by month and year. The earliest date was 1918-22. Many of the boxes held material for three or four years, and whatever it was, it was of no concern. From 1930 on there was a box for each year. I crouched down and pulled out the ones I was here for. The first was 1933, when Bewley moved from being the Irish Minister to the Vatican to take up his role in Berlin. I opened the box. It was full of manila files. I took one out. There were sheafs of letters and accounts. There were letters in English and German. There were documents topped with the harp of Ireland or the German swastika and there were all sorts of handwritten, personal communications too. I pulled out boxes to the year 1939. Similar stuff. They all contained the same kind of material.

My business was not with the contents, however. Whether all of it mattered in some way or there were documents here and there that did, my job was to take it all. The boxes weren't that big. Three or four trips up and down the back stairs would do it. I had what I was there for, but I checked to see if there was anything else. There were two small filing cabinets. They seemed to hold nothing but recent correspondence and bills, accounts and bank statements. There was nothing more I could see. It wasn't a busy study somehow. Full of books and documents as it was, it felt as if nothing much went on except keeping it all tidy.

I managed the boxes in three trips. I saw no one. I had been in the apartment less than an hour. I left it as tidy as I found it, except for the gaps on the bottom shelves of the bookcases. I took one more look round. There was nothing I had missed. I stopped by the window, looking down to the street. It was quiet but once I was out of the apartment, there would be nothing to worry about. I looked down at a book, open on a wooden music stand by the window. It wasn't music, though like music it had only a few pages. It was a poem. I could tell it was on show, a trophy. I turned to the start. It was called 'Atlantis'. It was by Bewley himself. Beneath the title were the words 'Oxford Newdigate Poetry Prize 1910'.

I returned to the pages that had been displayed on the stand. There was a pencil mark under three of the lines. I read them aloud, and my voice echoed in the empty room.

'This world is man's abiding-place,
Where God has kindled his soul's spark
For a short hour 'twixt dark and dark.'

The words were like the room somehow, at first glance they were solid, even appealing, like all those books that furnished the bookshelves, but as I spoke them they sounded emptier than they looked on the page. The whole place was like that, emptier than it looked and in some strange way darker than it looked. I didn't know how much of Charles Bewley's head was in the boxes I was taking from his study. But I wasn't sorry I wouldn't have to find out. There was nothing I could have said was wrong with the room I was in, but I was relieved to get out of it.

I drove the van back through the city, across the river, heading past St Peter's then down to Trastevere and the Villa Spada. I had the map of the main roads in my head. I had gone over the route dozens of times in my mind. But I was beginning to know my way well enough. It was quiet, as Dietrich Ritter had said it would be. There were no checkpoints anywhere. There were few police about, and apart from the tanks that stood at a couple of road junctions, hardly any German soldiers.

At the embassy Signore Rosselli carried Bewley's boxes of papers into Michael MacWhite's office and set off to return the van. The ambassador was out. Something had come up and he was at the Vatican with Tom Kiernan. Still, the job was done. In a couple of days I would be on a train. That was what I wanted. But I found myself thinking more about what I was leaving than I'd expected. I walked to the outskirts of Trastevere and found the café I'd sat in with Vittoria. I drank a bottle of wine I didn't really want and thought maybe I would come back one day. It was enough wine to let me think that, but not enough to make me believe it.

I returned to the Villa Spada to find Michael MacWhite. I thought he might have been pleased to see the boxes from Bewley's apartment piled in front of his desk. But he had other things on his mind. I wasn't looking for congratulations, but some recognition that the fucking thing was done wouldn't have gone amiss. He looked at the boxes with a mix of irritation and something that seemed more like disgust, as if he didn't want them in the room. I shrugged and turned to leave.

'I know it wasn't easy, Stefan. It's the day that's in it . . . what's happened.'

'What has happened, sir?'

'The Germans went into the Jewish Ghetto this morning. They cleared the place. They arrested everyone they could find, men, women, children. They have them penned up in the Palazzo Salviati, just up the fucking road. Over a thousand people. Jesus, no one can even get in to see them . . . Tom Kiernan's been at the Vatican . . . I don't know what's happening, but I can't believe something won't be done. They're saying the Jews will be put on trains . . . deported . . . to Germany.'

The ambassador hovered over the word 'deported' for some seconds. I knew enough to know he had good reason to. It carried a lot of weight. There it was, the special operation Dietrich Ritter had told me about in the Forum. The reason why it was so quiet in the rest of Rome. MacWhite shook his head. He still didn't quite believe it. I could only nod.

22

PIAZZA SAN PIETRO

I spent the next day doing nothing very much. Mrs Butler was arranging the tickets and travel warrants that would get me out of Italy and as far as Lisbon. The subject of Rome's Jews was on everyone's mind, but little was said. The ambassador had told me more about what had happened. An SS brigade had come from Germany, not so much to do the job as to make sure that the Germans already in Rome did it. The Italian Fascist forces were kept well away from it. They had their own racial laws, mimicking Germany's, and their own contempt for Italian Jews, but they were probably not up for the SS operation. MacWhite had watched all that through his years in Rome, and he seemed genuinely puzzled that this had been done. His abrupt lapses into silence, and a series of half-formed sentences this articulate diplomat found himself unable to finish, told me that he knew a lot more about what was happening to Jews all over Europe than he was going to say. I knew what I'd seen in Germany, and I knew I'd barely glimpsed behind the curtain. Maybe that bit of German blood that flowed in my veins gave me knowledge that didn't need much more information. But if I was less surprised than I should have been, the ambassador was struggling to take it in. The

Jews had given the Germans the fifty kilograms of gold, hadn't they? They paid what they were asked to pay. Wasn't it an agreement? He kept coming back to that as if, behind the business of extorting money from people who knew they were bargaining for their lives, there was some kind of contract law to honour. And wasn't Italy different? That's why the Germans had to bring in the SS soldiers. Even the Italian Fascists couldn't be relied on, not for what had just happened. And if Italy was different, this was Rome! The ambassador kept saying Rome, as if the word had a power of its own.

I had the same conversation several times that day, as MacWhite came in and out of the Villa Spada, from meetings at other neutral embassies and journeys to the Via del Corridori to consult the Irish ambassador to the Vatican. Twice I drove him there myself. He kept circling round the bewilderment he felt. He couldn't shake it off. It wasn't that he thought he or Tom Kiernan could achieve anything, but I could see he was expecting the Holy See to do something. That's why his circular conversations ended at that point and then trailed away. He was waiting. The second time we drove back to the Villa Spada, he said something was happening. A protest had been made to Obersturmbannführer Kappler. Someone had managed to get several Jews with Catholic baptismal certificates released. A German bishop was going to make the strength of the Vatican's reaction known to Berlin. It seemed there was need for caution in that respect. There were issues of neutrality that made a direct approach difficult. There were difficulties, real difficulties. MacWhite kept saying that word now. Then he stopped. He wasn't trying to convince me of anything, he was trying to convince himself. He hadn't.

Between MacWhite leaving the Via del Corridori and getting back to the Villa Spada, Tom Kiernan had been in touch with more news from the Vatican. It wasn't the news Michael MacWhite was waiting to hear. The Jews imprisoned in the Palazzo Salviati, still more than a thousand of them, had been moved to railway sidings across the city, where they had been put into cattle trucks, ready for deportation.

The next morning I got up to see the ambassador below in the garden with Salvatore. There was a fire burning and Michael MacWhite was throwing files and papers on to it. The boxes that stood in a row by the bonfire were familiar enough. Charles Bewley's years in Berlin were going up in smoke. I couldn't know whether it was everything I'd brought from his apartment. I knew the ambassador had spent the previous evening going through the documents. If there was anything left, there wasn't much. I walked downstairs and went out into the garden myself.

Michael MacWhite didn't notice me for a moment. I got a greeting from Finn and the usual wry nod from Salvatore that had become the full extent of our communication. He still seemed to think the two of us shared some joke I hadn't got my head round. It didn't bother him that I hadn't. The ambassador was going at his task with an energy I hadn't seen before. It wasn't enthusiasm, it felt closer to anger. He turned away from the fire, his face flushed from the heat, and saw me.

'I want you to go and see Bewley, Inspector.'

'Yes, sir. What for?'

'You can give him his fucking passport now. It's done.'

'He's back then?'

'He came back early. There was an accident. His chauffeur was killed.'

I took in the information and I had no choice but to make a connection. I saw Alfredo driving away in Bewley's car. I saw the man on the motorbike giving me that almost knowing salute. And I saw the same man with a gun at the Villa Greca.

'What happened?'

'A car crash, somewhere outside the city. That's all I heard.'

MacWhite turned back to the boxes and threw more files on the fire. For him it was information that had no significance. But I didn't believe in the car crash. At least I didn't believe in an accident. I had told Vittoria how Dietrich Ritter found his way to the Villa Greca. Alfredo's life hung on that. You didn't have to say much. He didn't say much. I didn't say much more. Not much could be enough.

Charles Bewley didn't ask me to sit down. I stood, as I had stood before, in the sitting room of the apartment. His eyes ran up and down me with a look that was working hard at showing the contempt he couldn't quite manage. There would be no patronising banter. He wouldn't spend time putting me in my place. There was too much else going on in that head. And most of it couldn't be spoken. What he really wanted to know was whether I had anything to do with the bare shelves in his study. He had to assume that somehow all those boxes, all those pieces of his ambassadorial years that were precious to him in some way, that he felt gave him some hold over people he despised, people who had damaged him . . . that his archive of spite had been stolen by those same contemptible pigmies. He had to assume that, yet he couldn't say it. And if I was involved, how could he even ask? One question would show the weakness that allowed him to be beaten. Because he was beaten, by his standards at any rate. However much or however little all those boxes of the past contained of value, he believed he had made them a weapon. Just to have them was a victory. They were a trophy, like the poem on the music stand.

'I've been away. I had to come back early . . .'

He had decided nothing would be said about the robbery. I saw in his face his own recognition that he was defeated. I wondered if Joe Walshe knew him better than Bewley realised. Maybe it didn't matter what was in those files. What mattered was what the ex-ambassador believed about them. If getting them back was about Ireland avoiding embarrassing truths, it was also a long-delayed exercise in spite in its own right. Charles Bewley had lost more than paper. He looked older, even smaller. The toothbrush moustache looked more ridiculous.

'I don't know if MacWhite told you . . .'

He was going to talk about Alfredo instead. I had to play along.

'He said there was an accident.'

'My chauffeur, Alfredo. He's been with me a long time.'

'I'm sorry.'

I had to say it. I was sorry. I just wasn't very sorry. There was no point pretending. I didn't like what had happened, but I wasn't sure I had much right to like it or dislike it, let alone beat myself up. However, I didn't require the details.

'I don't know how he came off the road. It was long and straight. Out in the country. No traffic. There was no other vehicle involved . . . his neck was broken.'

I just listened. I was obviously meant to show something.

'I'm clearly boring you, Mr Gillespie.'

There wasn't much I could say, short of telling him the truth.

'These things happen.'

'Jesus Christ, you're an arsehole!'

There was real anger in Charles Bewley's eyes. I could understand it too. What I had said sounded as trite to me. I would have been better saying nothing at all. They were empty, dismissive words that would have insulted anybody who cared about someone who had just died. And he did care, I could see that he did.

'Give me the bloody passport and get out. That's all you're here for.'

I took out the new Irish passport Mr Bewley had been waiting so long for. There was a smile. He had got what he wanted. It was a victory, even it wasn't such a big one. That's what he was thinking. It wasn't hard to read. It would do. They didn't want to give him a passport. In Dublin, Joe Walshe had done everything he could to block it. But they'd run out of excuses, as he had known they must eventually. He had persevered. He had beaten Walshe down. He had one thing to be pleased about. But the ex-ambassador to Berlin wasn't going to be pleased for long. I gave him a few more seconds. I had already looked at the passport. I'd seen what Michael MacWhite had written in the space provided for an occupation. There would be no room for Bewley to write in 'Irish Ambassador, Retired' as he had in his old passport. I didn't know if the words were MacWhite's own or if they had come from Joe Walshe himself. Either way the sentiment was an exercise in spite that, aimed elsewhere, Charles Bewley might have applauded. I watched him open the passport, smiling, then I saw the expression on his face as he read the words especially written for him, 'Occupation: A Person of No Importance'.

There was a long moment. Mr Bewley didn't look up.

'Get out.' He said the words quietly.

I hesitated. It was so quiet that I wasn't sure what he'd said.

'Go on, get out!'

It was only a little louder. But he looked up at me now. I could see that there were tears in his eyes. I didn't think they were for Alfredo. They were all his own.

I wasn't far from Bewley's apartment when a man approached me with a sheaf of postcards. He stood in front of me, grinning broadly, fanning the cards out. He spoke in English. I didn't notice that he didn't bother trying Italian or German.

'Some postcards, signore. Colosseum, Forum, Pantheon, St Peter's.'

'I've enough . . . maybe too many.' I laughed. 'I haven't even sent one.'

'Then you should, signore. Pronto, eh? This picture of St Peter's . . .'

'You're right, I should, but no more, thank you . . . I don't need . . .'

The man pushed the postcard of St Peter's into my hand.

'A present, Signore Gillespie. And no need even to write on it.'

He grinned again, put the cards into his pocket, and walked quickly away. I looked back, only then realising he knew my name, but he had already gone. The card in my hand was a photograph of St Peter's Square, colonnades and basilica. I turned it over. There was a scribbled message. 'See me here. Today. Pronto. O'F.'

The message was from Hugh O'Flaherty. He would know already what had happened in Tivoli. I couldn't imagine there was much more to say. I'd done what I could. It hadn't worked out well. Or maybe it had. I didn't know how the monsignor reckoned these things. I wasn't sure I cared. If he wanted to know about Brother Luca, there was nothing I could tell him. I wondered whether to bother finding the monsignor at all. He was much admired for what he did. I had every reason to believe he should be. Maybe I'd been unlucky to see the worst end of it. But O'Flaherty wasn't an easy man to say no to, even on the back of a postcard.

I saw him as soon as I approached St Peter's Square, walking from the Via della Conciliazione. The tall, spare figure, the black soutane, and the circular clerical hat that looked almost as comical on him as it had done on Brother Luca. He was pacing the length of the thick white line that stretched across the cobbles of St Peter's Square, from one set of colonnades to the other, treading the Vatican side carefully. He walked slowly, deliberately, looking down at a book. As I approached, he stopped. He said something to a German soldier, keeping pace on the Italian side of the line. The soldier laughed. O'Flaherty walked on, returning to his book. It was only as I came towards him, crossing the white line from Italy into the

Holy See, that he saw me. He snapped the black missal he was reading shut.

'What sort of fags have you got, Stefan?'

'Some French . . .'

'Jesus, gut-rotting stuff, aren't they? But I . . . have some Player's!'

He took out a packet of twenty Player's Navy Cut.

'There are two things you can't knock the English for, literature and cigarettes. You'd think the Lord in his wisdom could have managed it better than English Protestants making the only translation of the Bible a man might have half a mind to think angels had a hand in . . . but I'm forgetting the company I'm in.'

He held out the cigarette packet, smiling. I took one.

'We'll stick to the fags, Stefan. A denomination all their own.'

The German soldier who had been following Monsignor O'Flaherty along the white line was standing opposite us. Other soldiers patrolled the line, but he seemed to have the particular job of dogging Hugh O'Flaherty's footsteps. The monsignor stood at the very edge of the line and reached across with the Player's. The soldier looked round then stretched out and snatched one of the cigarettes.

'If I stepped over the line, he'd arrest me. If I ignored him and I walked more than a few yards towards the Via della Conciliazione, he might shoot. Or someone might.' He looked up, out from the square. 'At the moment I'm watched from some of those windows. And you'll see the black cars that sit there all day long, just beyond the colonnades. You know who they are. Let's walk, my son.'

The priest turned away from the white line, lighting his cigarette and stopping to light mine. We walked slowly, ambling, towards the basilica.

'I can't leave the Vatican, well, not in any recognisable form.

My friend Obersturmbannführer Kappler has had enough. That's what he says. He says I'm safe within the Holy See, but he can't be answerable for anything that occurs outside. It's not just what we're doing, it's the way we've been doing it. He thinks I've been taking the piss . . . whatever the German is for that. I think that's the worst thing for him. Not the people we're protecting, it's the two fingers that go with it.'

'So is that what you're doing, standing on the white line? The two fingers?'

'It sounds very childish,' said O'Flaherty. 'But it is enjoyable.'

He laughed. He put an arm round my shoulder.

'But everything has a purpose under Heaven, Stefan. I'm happy to become an obsession for a man who seems to be very easily obsessed. I'm happy to be watched and followed and shadowed, even inside the Vatican. All that effort and all that time and all those men. It gives other people a little space to be invisible.'

'You know I lost Brother Luca, Monsignor . . . he got away, but . . .'

'I know. I have no idea where he is. He will have to trust to God now.'

'He's not alone, is he?'

O'Flaherty took his arm away. He walked on, silent for a moment.

'I try to smile. I have to. I ask people to risk their lives. I have to. I do what I can. If I can do no more, I have to do that. That's simply how it is. It doesn't mean I sleep easily. It doesn't mean I have slept at all since the Germans went into the Ghetto. If some of us suffer, even if some of us die, there is still something worse. We are not on that train. Don't think I am unaware of that, not even for a second.'

'I'm sorry. That's not really what I meant, Monsignor . . .'

'Isn't it? Well, it should be. But it's not why you're here.'

'So, why am I here?'

'I have no idea, Stefan, except that Bishop O'Rourke asked me to fetch you.' O'Flaherty grinned. 'I think I'm one of the only people left who wants to be seen talking to him. He was always a curmudgeonly, irritable bugger, but if the Holy Father kept a naughty list, and maybe he does, God save us, Edward would be right near the top. He may look like an old man in a wheelchair, but as far as anyone in the Roman Curia is concerned, he is Bishop Mad-Bad-And-Dangerous-To-Know.'

'What does that mean?'

Hugh O'Flaherty just slapped me on the back again, enjoying his own joke.

Bishop Edward O'Rourke poured the red wine into two glasses. I was back in the dark, untidy room, crammed to overflowing with books and papers and dog-eared files. He wheeled his chair round from the table towards me and held out a glass.

'I'm confined to barracks you might say.'

'What happened?'

'I'm exaggerating slightly, Stefan. I am forbidden from entering most of the Vatican gardens, except for a few little bits on this side. I need permission to go into any of the Curia offices or the Papal Apartments or even the Sistine Chapel, where I might bump into the Holy Father at Mass. Since I can't get anywhere much, even in the Vatican, it's no hardship. But the gardens . . . that's very harsh. Still, to be fair to the powers that be, the gardens provided my avenue of attack.'

'What did you attack?'

'The Holy Father . . . not so much an attack . . . as a story.'

'It must have been some story.'

The bishop looked down for a moment. He sipped at the wine.

'Perhaps it is . . . and perhaps it isn't. I don't know if he'd heard it. If he hadn't, I think he should have done. Anyway, I went into the garden where he usually takes his walk, at a time when no one else should be there. It's a long time since I had a conversation with him. I have an old man's habit of saying the same thing over and over again. It's all the more irritating when it's something, the same old something, everyone knows but doesn't want to hear, let alone talk about . . .'

He turned the wheelchair to the window. He spoke without looking at me.

'So, I stopped him. I got out of my chair and I knelt, and blocked his path. I didn't say the same old things. I told him that as the Bishop of Rome he should think about another bishop, the Metropolitan of the Orthodox Church in Bulgaria. The Germans started to herd together the country's Jews, only this year, tens of thousands of them, to send them on these journeys they call deportations and transports and relocations. Train after never-ending train of cattle trucks. We don't see them, do we? I know priests who travel all over Europe. They simply don't see them. Yet now, we have to. But in Bulgaria there was a bishop who saw them, who stood in front of his own government and the Germans and the trains and said, no more. We won't let it happen here. The Church will not let it happen here. I will not let it happen here. And it didn't happen. I don't say none of it happened. I don't say no trains left. But I know hundreds of those trains didn't run. Tens of thousands lived because of it.'

Edward O'Rourke turned from the window and held up his empty glass.

'You have the legs, my son. And my need is great.'

I brought the bottle from the table.

'That's what I said. What we all know too well, didn't need saying. We have the proof of it whenever we care to look at it. These deportations are death journeys for more than can be counted, from every corner of Europe. I saw it first when I fled Poland, though I could never have imagined the scale of what would follow. Since then I have collected everything, every report, every story, every witness who comes my way. Not just Jews, so many others . . . but always it comes back to Jews. We have the information here. More than the Allies, maybe more than the Germans themselves. I have it. I have it all around me. I live with it now.'

He gestured at the room with a kind of hopelessness.

'But walk only a few hundred meters from this building, and you'll find the shelves stacked with ten times as much evidence. Shut away. Because to speak . . . to speak is to . . . I don't know what it is now . . . I've been told why we can't. I've been told so many times. I've been told how we can do a little good by stealth . . . and that to try to do more, especially to say more, would cause more harm than good. To Catholics and to the Jews themselves. I have tried to believe it too. Obedience obliges me to. But the cattle trucks full of Jews are in Rome. What are we doing? There they are. Stealth won't save them. But now I'm told we can hide more than they're going to take away. I'm told that's enough. But I said it wasn't. I said it on my knees to the Holy Father. Not long ago he walked through Rome's bomb damage, with the blood of the dead on his robes. I told him to go to the train and say, no, no more. The Church will not let it happen here. I will not let it happen here.'

The old man let his head drop. He looked up. There was a smile of sorts.

'Shall we say it didn't go down well?'

'What did he say?'

'He walked away . . . and I felt as if I had hit a suffering man in the face.'

The bishop wheeled himself to the table. He picked up a thick envelope.

'That's for me to resolve. I can do no more. So, you're leaving Rome?'

The mood changed. The bishop was brusque, almost businesslike.

'Tomorrow.'

'To France and Spain and on to Ireland eventually.'

'Eventually.'

'I'd like you to take a detour, Stefan.'

I laughed. I wasn't sure why. It was simply unexpected.

'A detour?'

'A favour if you like. For old times in Danzig. You can change your route?'

The conversation was continuing as if I had already agreed to something.

'I have a route. I'll have tickets by now.'

'I don't think you'll find it difficult. You know that from getting here in the first place. You go north to Switzerland, just to Geneva. It's almost on the French border anyway. A train from there will have you back on track soon enough. I'm told it may be faster. Trains in and out of Switzerland are still good. You need spend only one night in Geneva. No one will know you were there, except the man I want you to take something to. Seán Lester. As I said, for old times in Danzig. He's sitting out the war in the League of Nations' empty palace. An Irish face will cheer him.'

'I'm not sure what you're really asking . . .'

'I'm asking you to take this envelope to Seán Lester. Call it a digest of everything I know about what's happening. For those who think the rumours of death camps and the murder of millions are just that, rumours, there are names and places and dates and maps. For those who want to say it's all some sort of black propaganda that the Allies have invented, there are lists and numbers and details of the machinery they use to kill. It's as much as I can get into such a small space but some of it is on microfilm. It's more material than it looks And there are photos too. I thought the place to speak out would be here. I thought that when all the evidence had piled so high that it was shutting out the light . . . that the Holy Father would act. I am still waiting. All I can do . . . is send out what I have . . . and hope it's more than a message in a bottle. I can hope that Seán and what is left of the League . . . still have a voice.'

'And you want me to take it . . .'

'Why wouldn't I, my son?' O'Rourke chuckled. 'Surely you know you were sent as an angelic messenger. How else can I send it? No one's going to let me put this in a Vatican diplomatic bag. And how safe those are is anybody's guess. Things may be changing, but if Mussolini's people wanted a look at what was coming out of the Holy See, the general view is it wasn't difficult. And if the place is a nest of spies, it leaks like a sieve. And I can hardly stick a stamp on it and expect it to get there, can I? But you carry a diplomatic bag, Stefan. You can walk across a border and no one is allowed to open it, let alone search it. The only difference with this is that you'll be carrying something your government knows nothing about. You'll be abusing all the polished rules of diplomacy. And in advance, I give you absolution.'

The bishop laughed. He raised his glass. I didn't argue. I raised mine.

It was late when I got back to the Irish embassy, carrying the envelope I had agreed to take to Seán Lester in Geneva. I wasn't sure why I'd agreed. I'd looked at what was going on around me, I suppose, and it was hard to argue against doing something when nobody was doing anything. What that something amounted to, I couldn't know. Edward O'Rourke thought it meant a lot. All I knew was that it meant something to him. He had been looking into the darkness for a long time. I took his word for it. And then again, he assumed I would do it. He didn't really ask. Perhaps it was a favour for an old man I didn't owe any favours to. Perhaps I did it because I liked him. Perhaps it felt like one way of going home with less of the smell of dead bodies that I'd picked up along the way and couldn't quite shake off. Maybe there wasn't a reason. You can kid yourself there are explanations for every decision you make. Anyway, I was doing it.

'That you, Stefan?'

The door to the ambassador's study was open. Finn came out to the hall, wagging his tail. It had taken time, but now I was leaving, we were great pals.

'Have a drink!'

I walked in to find Michael MacWhite sitting in an armchair by a fire.

'It's getting colder. You might not think it, but it does get cold.'

There was a bottle of whiskey and a glass on a table. The bottle was half empty and the ambassador's voice made it sound like he had drunk most of it.

'Help yourself. You're off tomorrow.'

I nodded. He held out his glass. I topped it up after filling mine.

'It's Donal's funeral, at the Irish College. Will you make that?'

I sat down in a chair opposite him.

'I'll make the Mass.'

For almost a minute, MacWhite looked into the fire.

'The train has gone . . . taking the Jews.'

'I heard that.'

'I've been waiting all day for a message from Dublin.'

He drank again.

'Tom and I have sent telegrams. We got through to some of the other embassies by phone. They've passed the messages on as well. I expected something to come back. Something must have got through. They should come back . . . it's hard to get these things through . . . and it has to be from de Valera.'

I sipped the whiskey. I knew he didn't believe his excuses.

'We got a protest note out very fast when the Allies bombed Rome. It's Rome, that's the thing. It's happening here . . . as a

Catholic country, we have to speak. And as a neutral country too. We have earned that right. I know we have.'

The ambassador drained his glass. He took the bottle again.

'We should be making a noise about this, Stefan. Don't you see?'

He looked at me with something like passion in his eyes, and then he looked away. I knew him now, a little at least. The conversation would stop. Even drunk, the diplomatic hat would slip back on his head. He knew there would be no protest coming from Dublin, just as he knew that the protests from the Pope had already recognised the difficulties in any head-on collision with Germany. In the same way he had let that conversation simply fade away earlier . . . this one would follow suit.

'I got rid of Bewley's bloody boxes today.'

It seemed like a different conversation, but it really wasn't.

'Yes, I saw.'

MacWhite turned to the fire again.

'You know what was there? You know what the problem was?'

He looked back at me, shaking his head.

'Jews. The same thing. All those years ago. Pages and pages of it. Year after year of it. Hundreds of Jews who tried to get out of Germany to Ireland. People with Irish relatives. People with all sorts of connections to Ireland that meant they should have been given visas. He stopped them. Charles, I mean. There are sheaves of valid applications. He ignored them. He destroyed supporting documents. He turned down people who had a right to seek refugee status as if they'd been refused in Dublin. In fact, he just took the decisions on himself. He handed lists of people trying to get out of Germany to the Nazi authorities. He passed on details of bank accounts abroad. He gave them information about families and businesses that the Nazis didn't know had Jewish connections. And it went on . . . for fucking years.'

'Didn't anyone know?'

'No one knew the extent of it. I believe that. No one knew how close he was with the Nazis. That only came out when he was sacked. In those days, embassies had to improvise . . . communication was poor . . . we were very new at it. Things that wouldn't happen now . . . but you can't say no one in Dublin knew anything.'

The ambassador poured more of the whiskey. I held out my glass.

'Well, if you couldn't then, maybe you can now, sir.'

He nodded. He sat back in the chair, gazing into the flames. I drank down the whisky in one. I stretched out for the bottle. Finn, who had been lying in front of the fire, got up suddenly and jumped on to Michael MacWhite's lap. The ambassador didn't even notice. It was only then that I saw he was fast asleep.

I took my glass of whiskey and walked out to the hall, heading upstairs. I looked round as Mrs Butler came out of the office. She had been there all along.

'You're working late, Mrs Butler.'

'You might call it work.' She smiled. 'Is the ambassador all right?'

'Well, he's a bit . . . to tell the truth, right now he's asleep.'

'I'll see he gets up to bed.'

'Goodnight, Mrs Butler.'

'I didn't think it could come here, Mr Gillespie, to the City of God.'

I didn't know what she expected me to say. I wasn't big on faith at the best of times. In anything. It crossed my mind that if faith couldn't move mountains, it could close your eyes and keep them closed, with little effort. Even in the City of God. Perhaps particularly in the City of God. I didn't say that. I liked her. I wouldn't have minded finding space for the kind of shock she was feeling. I made a noise that was as near to agreeing with her bewilderment as made no difference.

287

The funeral Mass in the chapel of the Irish College in Rome was over. Father Donal Hyde had been decently sprinkled with water and incensed and the choir had sung the *Dies Irae* and the *Libera Me*. At the close we all sang the Irish national anthem, *Amhran na bhFiann*, which brought tears to those eyes that had not yet shed them for Donal. Mostly the congregation was made up of priests and nuns and various Irish expatriates who lived in Rome. Among the clerics there was red and purple scattered about to show some hierarchical willing. There was no Hugh O'Flaherty, who was unable to leave the Vatican without risking arrest. I sat with the two Irish ambassadors and the staff of the Villa Spada and Via del Corridori. One of them was missing, of course, but among the flowers on the coffin was a bunch of white lilies and a card with the words, 'Mio Caro Amico, Vittoria'. Wherever she was, she knew and she had found her own way to say farewell. Also there was Commissario De Angelis, back in his antiquated uniform, complete with sword, and performing the duty of respect I had performed enough times myself, attending a funeral that marked the end of a murder investigation. Neither he nor I had achieved much in that investigation, except to find out that the war that wasn't our war, was everyone's. But there weren't too many who wanted us to achieve much. More was buried with Donal Hyde than his body. He wasn't alone in that.

I didn't follow the mourners to the cemetery to see the body interred. There was a taxi to bring me to the Stazione Termini, where I would take the train no one but Edward O'Rourke knew I was taking to Switzerland, instead of the one to the French border I was meant to be on. I saw that the big, black car was still outside the Irish College, as it had been when I arrived with Michael MacWhite and Mrs Butler. The Gestapo made no particular secret about watching the comings and goings at Donal's funeral. It was a matter of routine interest, given his connections, though they must have known no one who really interested them would be there. A list of some of us who attended the Mass would go to the Via Tasso where it would likely end up on the desk of Hauptsturmführer Dietrich Ritter. It was the last time I would be on such a list, for what it was worth. It wasn't worth much. I was lucky to be alive, but there was a list of those who weren't so lucky. If that wasn't such a long list, it was one I might have been on. It was also one I had contributed to.

At the station, changing my ticket took time but nothing more. I felt no real anxiety about the material I was smuggling out of Italy for Bishop O'Rourke. I had delivered diplomatic documents before. No one had broken the code that said the bag that carried them couldn't be searched. It was another game. If there was something worth finding out, there were other ways to do it. And as far as Irish diplomacy went, maybe nobody thought it was worth the fuss. The bishop was right about that. I didn't think about any of that as the train exited the Stazione Termini. I was thinking about the day I arrived there and the woman who met me.

23

MISSA EST

Brother Luca, Alone

To begin with, Brother Luca walked towards the hills. He followed no roads. He crossed them from one field to another, from one olive grove to another, from one wood of pine and beech to another. He kept the hills ahead. The hills led to the mountains, the low, dark line where the sky began. The high empty places. It would be like Paklenica, when summer days were long and there were only the other children, and all they heard all day were the sounds of birds and animals. The running of the deer, and mad hares dancing if you watched long enough in a clearing, and where the trees were thickest the crashing of a wild boar you would never see. You might hear a screech in the sky and see an eagle soaring above. The high places were in his head. He could see them. To be there would be enough. And he would take nothing on his journey, no staff, no bag, no bread, no money.

He wore a set of overalls. The trousers stopped at his calves, but the man who wore them was fat and the jacket did just about button. He left the priest's long soutane at the villa. He kept only the round, broad-brimmed, black hat, in case of a hot sun and because he missed the Franciscan hood that once hid his head. But now he wasn't hiding. It was hard not to think of what hiding had brought about.

When it was dark and he couldn't see where he was going, he stopped. He was in a narrow valley that smelled of thyme. There was a stream and he listened to it gurgling until he was tired enough to lie down and sleep. He woke with the sun. Around him were a dozen scruffy, long-legged sheep, picking at the yellow grass and taking no notice of him. There was a shrill, insistent bleating, interrupted by the same sort of sound in a higher pitch. He looked past the bleating ewe to the lamb, caught up in a thicket by the stream and struggling unsuccessfully to get out.

Luca went to the thicket and saw that there was some barbed wire on a piece of rotting fence post that must have washed down the stream somehow. The wire was round the lamb's hind legs. It took only seconds to release the wire. The lamb scurried to its mother, unharmed. With nothing else to do the job, Luca's hands were bleeding. He knelt down and washed the blood away in the stream's water.

'You'll be hungry, my friend.'

Luca looked up to see an old man. He took him to be the shepherd. They made no introductions. They sat down together. The old man brought out bread and cheese and pickled chestnuts. They ate breakfast and drank from the stream.

Neither man talked much. The shepherd said the cheese came from the milk of his ewes, and while last year's cheese wasn't bad, this year's wasn't good. You never knew why that was. The sheep were giving less milk though. Maybe the cream just wasn't there. But with what was going on in the world, it was a surprise anything was good. You wouldn't think what happened far away would make a difference, but he knew it did. Things carried, like disease. All you could do was keep away. It's why he never went to Rome. It was twenty years since he went.

'But it spreads out, you can't stop it. You heard about Tivoli?'

Luca said nothing and the shepherd wasn't looking for an answer.

'The villa where the Irish priests used to come for the summer. Someone killed an old man and someone killed a policeman. I think the Germans killed the first one and then it was the Partisans. People say they'll come back and kill some more. I don't know if that'll be the Germans or the Partisans. One or the other.'

They finished their meal with an apple. The shepherd got up.

'So, what way are you going, my friend?'

Now he was asked the question, Luca was less than sure.

'The mountains, I suppose . . . it's what I was thinking . . .'

'Were you in Rome?'

The friar nodded.

'Then the mountains will look even better. I never hear anything from Rome that isn't worse than I heard the last time. My neighbour told me yesterday they've taken the Jews . . . the Germans he said . . . all the Jews . . . taken them somewhere. He didn't know why. I do know people don't like Jews . . . and I suppose there must be a reason. I remember at school there was a fart of a Jesuit who said a lot about Jews. Jesus, such a long time ago! What he said, I've no idea.' The old man turned his head and spat. 'I wouldn't want to offend you, my friend, if you're a man of faith, but I never came across a priest who didn't turn out to be a fucking arsehole.'

Luca looked hard at the shepherd now, for the first time listening.

'How do you mean . . . taken them . . . taken the Jews?'

'I don't know if I ever met a Jew. I don't think so. Would I know if I had? Anyway, that's all he said. They took them away. I don't even know how you'd do such a thing . . . are there a lot of them? Why? You take them from one place and put them in another . . . they need somewhere to sleep and food to eat. A lot of trouble for nothing. Wouldn't you think those Germans in Rome might have more to worry about? The English, Americans? Even the sheep know they're coming!'

The old man laughed.

'Not here. But if they do? My neighbour says they have a lot of money, the Americans anyway. They can buy my cheese, even the cheese that's not so good.'

Brother Luca didn't hear those last words. When it came to taking people away, he did know how it was done. And he knew a place to sleep and food to eat wasn't such a problem, at least not for long. He was in Zagreb when the Ustaše collected the Jews for the concentration camp at Jasenovac. And he remembered the joke. Jesus, there's just too much to do in this war and many hands make light work. For us, the Serbs and for the Germans, the Jews. And now he remembered the rabbi in Dubrovnik too, when he first had to run from the Ustaše himself. The man found him looking for food in the bins behind the synagogue and hid him for two days till he got the boat that took him out of Croatia to Italy. There was much he had forgotten. And now he remembered, he was sure that though he longed for the mountains, and the high, empty places, he was not ready for that. There was something else. He didn't know what, but he knew he was going the wrong way.

'I've made a mistake. What way should I go to find the road to Rome?'

It took Brother Luca all day to get to Rome. He made no attempt to hide himself. He had no thought anyone might be looking for him. He had forgotten that. Once he found the main road and the signs, he simply walked. He stopped once to ask for water, at the start of the sprawl that would take him into the city. There was a woman selling watermelons by the road. He asked her for a drink. She gave him the water, but she gave him bread and a wedge of the melon too. He would have blessed her, but he wasn't comfortable with that now. He felt he had lost that right. He felt, in truth, that he had lost it a long time ago. And he concluded that the woman needed no blessing. To give without being asked is a blessing in itself.

He came into the city when it was sunset. He went to the place he knew only a little as the Ghetto. He had walked through it a few times and never taken much notice. And walking through it now, in the darkness, it looked like any other corner of Rome that wove a few broad streets of old buildings together with a network of narrow alleys and cobbled courtyards. But it was strangely empty. And it was silent. He went into none of the houses he passed, but the doors stood open in a way that said there is no one here. And there was that unsettling quiet, everywhere, like no other place in a city he knew for the noisy, bustling energy of the Roman evening, when everyone came out into the streets. He saw only a few people and they disappeared as soon as they saw him. When a man did finally walk past and Luca spoke to him, the man said nothing in reply. He might have been invisible. But then, by the building that he could see was the synagogue, he met two priests. They came towards him, walking quickly, and talking very fast.

'Are you Jewish, my son?'

Luca shook his head.

'Do you have proof?'

'Proof? What proof would I have?'

'Do you live here then?'

'No?'

'Then go. Just go. No one knows if the SS will come back.'

'Where are they all, Father?'

'If you can't prove you're not Jewish, it's still not safe.'

'What will they do to them?'

'They have them locked up. In the Military College over the river. But tomorrow the Holy Father will put a stop to it. For now, get away. And pray!'

Brother Luca slept in a square, close to the Ghetto, not sure where he was. The next morning he woke to a strange, soft, calming sound that was all around him. As he sat up, he saw there were cats, hundreds of cats, so many that he wondered if he was still asleep and dreaming. That was the sound he had woken to. The purring of cats in the stillness of the early morning, with most of the city asleep. He sat for some time, watching the cats, mostly asleep, and trying to say a prayer that asked why he was here. He reached for the words of St Francis. If there was sustenance from Brother Sun and Sister Moon for all God's creatures, there would be sustenance for cats, he was sure of that at least. But where the prayer touched on him, it didn't come easily. No prayers had come easily since the Villa Greca. And none came now. In the end he got up and walked away, as the cats brushed past him and pushed themselves against his legs and then forgot him.

He found a fountain and drank water from it. If he was hungry, he was unaware of it. He walked the streets with no real purpose. When he found a church with open doors he went in and sat at the back, listening to the Mass but not feeling part of it any more. But he heard the prayers the priest said for the Jews who had been taken away from their homes and he remembered the night before. And as the Mass ended he stayed in the church, and as the priest walked towards the doors, he got up and asked him what he knew about the Jews. What was happening? Where were they? He wasn't sure why he was asking. But it seemed he had to. The priest was uneasy. Prayers were one thing, but he didn't like the conversation. He said he didn't know. But as he walked on he stopped and turned back. He had heard that trucks were moving the Jews from Trastevere. To a train at the Tiburtina Station.

The train was a long line of cattle trucks. It lay beyond the Tiburtina Station in a maze of sidings that were cluttered with goods wagons of all kinds. Along the length of the train there was a line of Waffen SS soldiers. Some of them walked up and down with machine guns and rifles that seemed to hang almost lazily from their arms. There was nothing here that needed anything other than the idlest sort of policing. That was reflected in the groups of soldiers and SS men in black who stood around in groups, smoking and talking. There was no anxiety here. There was even laughter. The job, after all, was done. There had been some firing the previous day, when they went into the Ghetto, but even that was only for show, to frighten the shite out of the fuckers and ensure order. And there was order. There usually was. There were lists and lists meant everyone knew what to do. Once the streets in and out of the Ghetto were blocked off, the Jews had nowhere to go. And those SS men who had been brought in from Germany, who didn't know their way around Rome, did know their way around Jews. Like everywhere else, people did what they were told. They were ordered to stay in their homes and they did. They felt safer like that, though what it meant was they had nowhere to try to run to when the time came. And when they were marched to the trucks, men and women and children, the very old and the very young, it didn't take much to keep them in check. A prod with a gun now and then and a slap and a kick to remind them who they were. Not much at all. There was a system. And there was hope. It was hope that was the real prod that kept it all tight. Hope said this is bad, this is worse than bad even, but if we do what we're told, it's only this bad. There's always what's worse. Hope is the hope that you avoid that. The bad, yes, but not the very worst.

The cattle trucks were full now. They stayed in the siding all morning. There were more than a thousand people packed into the wagons. More women and children than men, because everyone believed the soldiers had come to collect the men for forced labour, building the fortifications across Italy that were going to halt the Allies. So when the men ran, the women and children and the old didn't, because they had no idea the SS had come for them too. And when they did, it was too late. Germany, they were told, they were going to Germany. It would be a camp, of course, and there would be barbed wire and guards. But such places could be survived. Hard, yes, cruel, yes, and all the harder when none of them thought it could happen in Rome. Whatever the stories from elsewhere, and you couldn't believe all that, not everything, because some of it was simply unbelievable, they were Roman Jews, they were even the Pope's Jews as the old joke went, that wasn't quite a joke, but an article of uneasy faith, a safety net. Yet as some of the trucks that drove them from the Military College at the Palazzo Salviati stopped at St Peter's Square for German soldiers to take photographs, there would be no net.

Brother Luca sat on a pile of railway sleepers, across from the siding where the train was standing. He watched as a locomotive backed along the track and railways workers coupled it to the wagons. There was a handful of others who watched with him. He didn't know who they were, but he knew what they risked. There was a priest who said the rosary in silence. There were men and women who gazed at the train hopelessly. Some cried and some didn't. No one spoke. German soldiers stood between the onlookers and the train. They carried machine guns, but they had no more thought of using them than the officers in black who stood in a circle, checking paperwork and checking their watches and looking back at the train, as if to say, it's time, let's get on with this, lads, there's a schedule.

If there was silence from the small group of onlookers, the noise that came from the train was loud and continuous. It was a cacophony of shouting and pleading and crying and screaming and sobbing and even prayers. There was terror and indignation and despair and disbelief, still, in all that clamour. It came and went in waves. Sometimes it would fade away, almost completely, but then it would start again and it would grow louder and louder and more and more desperate until it faded again. Mostly the Germans took no notice. Most of them had heard it all before. If they weren't ignoring it, they were laughing at it. Two soldiers walked along, one waving his arms as if he was conducting, swigging brandy from a bottle, then conducting again. On his head he wore the square, black, tufted hat of a synagogue cantor. Round his shoulders was draped a fringed tallit, picked up in some apartment as it was cleared. The other, also clutching a bottle, had a long, twisted ram's horn, a shofar. As the first soldier conducted the terrible sounds in the wagons, he blew it. Each time he blew, a roar of laughter and applause spread among the guards. There was always a clown to lift their spirits.

Suddenly, Brother Luca saw a woman walking towards the train. Only moments before she had been standing next to him. He watched her with surprise. She showed no fear. And the Germans took almost no notice. A couple of officers glanced at her as she passed them and went back to their conversation. A soldier turned his rifle towards her, then looked uncertainly at his sergeant, who shrugged. The woman went on past the line of troops guarding the cattle trucks. They watched her but did nothing. She walked beside the train, shouting, calling. Luca thought she was calling a name, several names. Then she stopped. She pushed her face against a crack in the doors to one of the cattle trucks. She was talking to someone. And then she turned away and began to talk to one of the soldiers. Another soldier came across and shouted at her. There was an argument going on. An officer appeared and now he was arguing with the woman too. It went on for five minutes. Everyone was looking. A lot of the soldiers were laughing. It was some joke, apparently. Then the officer walked to the cattle truck with the woman and another soldier pulled something from the doors and pushed them back a little. And hands came out and the woman reached up and then she was gone, pulled inside.

The soldiers who were standing a little way from Brother Luca's pile of sleepers were laughing now as well. He got up and moved closer, listening.

'She says she wants to go with her husband. They fucking missed her in the Ghetto . . . she gets away and she turns up and says, I won't have it . . . let me on that fucking train . . . and the Sturmbannführer says, madam, you really don't want to go, I promise . . . and she says, yes, I fucking do . . . and so he says, anything to oblige!'

Brother Luca took this in. And he knew why he had to come to Rome. He knew what this was. He knew why the mountains had to wait. He walked forward to the train, following almost exactly in the footsteps of the woman. He attracted a lot more attention than she had. There were guns that moved in his direction. A man so big, coming out of nowhere it seemed, dirty and dishevelled, with a straggling growth of matted beard and clothes bizarrely small and tight, yet somehow moving through the line of soldiers with a strange grace . . . it was hard to know whether to laugh or to put a bullet in him. But no one did put a bullet in him. And no one stopped him. He stood, as the woman had stood, by the doors to the same cattle truck. He didn't argue. He waited for the same SS officer to come and tell him to fuck off. And when the same SS officer got his pistol out and there was a machine gun pointing at him in a way that was far from idle, he simply said that all he wanted to do was to get on the train to be with his brothers and sisters. He said he didn't know where the train was going, but he knew how the journey would end. Then he looked at the Sturmbannführer for what seemed, to the SS man, a long and uncomfortable time. The German officer, who was on the point of telling one of his men to shoot this madman, nodded instead. He would say later that one more for the gas chamber didn't make any difference, but that wasn't what he felt at the time. All he wanted, as he barked an order for the cattle truck's doors to be opened one more time, was to stop the man staring. At him. And almost into him.

The Franciscan friar scrambled into the cattle truck. The doors crashed shut. He smiled at the men and women and children who were gazing at him, for a moment bewildered by something other than the unknowing fear that enveloped them. No one knew him. No one knew why he was there. When he found a corner to sit in, they had already forgotten him. For just at that instant, the train jolted forward and then, slowly, it began to move. Brother Luca couldn't know the name of the small Polish town that was the train's final destination. But he knew what was waiting there. He couldn't stop it. He could only make it his destination too.

24

GARE DE GENÈVE

Zurich, Again

In the bar of Zurich's Hotel Storchen, two Irishmen sat by the window. They had met to discuss another Irishman, known to one but not the other, who was now lying in a Swiss hospital, somewhere between life and death. He had arrived at the Central Station in Zurich late the previous night, on a train he was not supposed to have been on. Shortly afterwards he was battered into unconsciousness by a soldier from a German train that should not have been in Switzerland at all.

There was calming water beyond the hotel windows, as so often in Swiss cities. Here it was the River Limmat that flowed through Zurich from its lake source. The Secretary-General of the League of Nations, Seán Lester, and the Irish ambassador to Berne, Francis T. Cremins, had known each other a long time, though never very well. Lester too had been an Irish diplomat in the fledgling service of a newly independent country. His government had sent him to the League of Nations with considerable pride. Ireland was a small nation that had taken on an empire and won, at least in part. It could now play a role on the world stage. But when the scenery changed abruptly, only a few years later, one world order was replaced by another. Ireland's horizons narrowed to its own shores.

From great hopes its concerns turned to mere survival. Seán Lester was left with the last fragments of the dismembered League. In Ireland he was already almost forgotten.

Francis Cremins was awkward. He had let contact with his fellow countryman slip, for no real reason and with no malice. It was as much laziness as anything. However, it was a long haul since the Secretary-General of the League mattered anyway. Lester said little for a time, enjoying his colleague's discomfort.

'I'm sorry it's been so long, Seán.'

'Don't be, Francis. You'll have a lot more to do than I have.'

Cremins didn't reply. It was a quiet rebuke. That was one of the reasons he was uncomfortable with Seán Lester. The man was never rude. He never raised his voice. But he had a way of making pinpricks out of the most ordinary platitudes.

'Anyway,' continued the ambassador, 'this is an unexpected mess.'

'I'm sure Mr Gillespie would echo those sentiments . . . if he could.'

Another pinprick, but sharper.

'I'm quite as concerned about him as you are, Seán.'

Lester simply smiled. He looked up and caught the waiter's eye.

'Café, bitte, Herr Ober.'

'You don't want anything stronger?' asked Cremins.

'Maybe later, Francis.'

The chargé d'affaires held up an empty glass.

'Noch ein Weinbrand.'

Seán Lester sat back in his chair. He looked out over the river beyond the window. It was a busy, urban scene compared to his own lake in Geneva. He liked this view better. Geneva was more beautiful, but it had wearied him for too long.

'I saw Captain Batz, the policeman who was at the station,' he said.

'So you know the rest then, Seán. I could only say so much on the phone.'

'Yes, only saying . . . so much . . . seems to be the order of the day.'

'How do you mean?'

Cremins' defences were up. Ordinary words, but still the pinpricks.

'Well, the doctor had nothing to say about what actually occurred, though he knows. For some reason his nurses are under the impression Inspector Gillespie had an unfortunate accident, though I'd say they know too. However, Captain Batz was good enough to tell me about the German train . . . and some Italian prisoner making a run for it . . . and an SS Scharführer knocking the shite out of Gillespie's head with a rifle. That about sums up the rest of it, wouldn't you say, Francis?'

'I wonder if we shouldn't discuss this upstairs . . .'

Francis Cremins spoke in a stiff whisper, irritated and embarrassed.

The waiter put down the drinks and walked away.

'You mean I should keep my voice down?'

'I think you can understand the diplomatic sensitivity, Seán.'

'It'll be even more sensitive if Gillespie dies.'

The Irish diplomat said nothing. He picked up his brandy.

'Anyway, I only got the short version, Francis. Captain Batz's boss arrived at that point and gave him one of those looks that implied he'd be a long time waiting for promotion if he said more. Oberst Fischer then announced that he could give me no more information, since the matter now came under the auspices of the Swiss Foreign Office and that, as Mr Gillespie travelled on an Irish diplomatic passport, the person I should talk to was . . . with ingenious circularity . . . you.'

'And that would be an excellent piece of advice, Seán.'

Francis Cremins' voice was stronger. He was on bureaucratic ground.

303

'I see.' The Secretary-General took out a cigarette. 'Or do I?'

'You'll need no explanations for why this is sensitive.' The Irish ambassador's voice was more confident. 'You know well enough that German trains pass through Switzerland all the time. Everyone knows it. There are agreements that have remained in place all through the war. They're still in place. With the Allies bombing Northern Italy and the Austrian passes now, traffic will get diverted unexpectedly. There may be even more traffic. It's not how it should be. It's not how the Swiss want it. But their options are very limited, even now. Sometimes these trains need to stop. They may need fuel or a change of engine.'

'And still in place, Francis, are all the rules about what can be carried. We don't kid ourselves that arms and armaments are not on those trains. But I doubt there are many people in Switzerland who think trains full of slave labourers are passing through Zurich while they're tucked up in bed. Let alone that they stop to check whether or not the odd dead body in a cattle truck could be carrying typhus.'

Cremins glared at Lester. His voice was back to the stiff whisper.

'As I understand it, these were Italian volunteer workers.'

'That's what they told you? Oh, dear.'

Lester laughed. It was bigger than a pinprick.

The Irish ambassador ignored it.

'This was not a regular train. It was not expected at Zurich.'

'Ah, an unlucky chance. An accident after all. Gillespie will be relieved.'

'If you have something to take up with the Foreign Ministry, Seán, I suggest you do it. As a neutral ambassador I am not in the business of pointing fingers about who says what and who does what here. Propaganda is for the belligerents.'

'I also spoke to the stationmaster,' continued the Secretary-General. 'No information on a man nearly killed at his station. As for a German train, no record.'

'I'm not responsible for what the Swiss have to do to solve a particular problem. However, I am responsible, whatever you think, for an Irishman working for the Department of External Affairs. So, you might tell me what on earth he was doing here. He left Rome to make his way home to Ireland. That's no easy task at the moment, but he is an experienced man. I've been in contact with our embassies in Rome and with Dublin. And no one has the faintest idea why Gillespie was in Switzerland, let alone why I didn't know he was in Switzerland. The only person who knew, apparently, was you, Seán. Is that right? He was coming to see you?'

'Yes, he was.'

'And why was he doing that?'

'Old friends. We met when I was High Commissioner in Danzig.'

This was information Cremins knew nothing about. It was unexpected.

'We shared an interest in Wagner. At least we met at a Wagner opera. It was memorable. Somebody was trying to kill him at the time. You remember things like that. I did. Of course, it did feel like murder was more remarkable back then.'

'I don't much care about the circumstances, Seán. Look at the fucking mess. The man had no right to come through Switzerland without letting me know, whatever he was doing. If he had done I would have sent a car. At least the consul might have met him at the station. And then none of this would have happened.'

Seán Lester wasn't listening. He was looking out of the window again. Cremins was saying what he had to say. He was a stickler. Lester remembered that.

'Did you know he stayed here, Francis?'

'What?'

'At this hotel.'

'Gillespie?'

'No, Wagner.'

'Is that all you've got to say?'

'No.' Lester's voice was sharper. 'I assume you have his belongings?'

It was another non-sequitur.

'His belongings? I have, yes, I think . . .'

Cremins stopped. It wasn't a non-sequitur at all.

'I'm sure you can do better than "think", Francis. Inspector Gillespie was carrying something. For me. A letter or a package. From another friend of my Danzig days. Bishop Edward O'Rourke, in the Vatican. I don't know if you ever came across Edward. He's retired now. A Russian whose ancestor came from Ireland to fight for the Czar. I forget which one. Edward was Bishop of Danzig. Of course, he was pushed out in much the same way I was. Do you know him at all?'

'I know who he is.'

'His letter will be in Inspector Gillespie's bag.'

Cremins was awkward again. He hadn't anticipated this directness.

'Come on. You're not telling me you haven't checked the diplomatic bag to make sure there's nothing important in it. There's every chance he was taking something back to Dublin from Rome. I have no idea. That's not my business, but it's very definitely yours. You'll have already been through everything by now.'

For a moment Seán Lester thought the other Irishman was going to lie. Cremins was certainly thinking about it. It might be charitable to assume he was too honest, but the simple truth was that he was a man who worked to instructions. When he didn't have any, he found it difficult to make decisions of his own.

'You'd better come upstairs, Seán.'

In Cremins' bedroom there was a small safe built into a wall. The chargé d'affaires unlocked it and took out a heavy manilla

306

envelope. All that was written on the front was 'S L Comitatus Genevensis'. He handed the envelope to Lester.

'That's all there is. Naturally, I opened it. Gillespie is a courier.'

'Your prerogative,' shrugged the Secretary-General. 'No complaints.'

Lester pulled out the contents. Sheafs of paper, stapled together. Some were original typed sheets; others were carbon copies or blue mimeographs. There were also photographs of documents; in a smaller envelope photographic negatives. Lester flicked through this with no sense that he understood what he was looking at. He put the material back and was left with a letter, a Vatican crest at the top.

Seán Lester laughed.

'Latin. You didn't bring a *Lewis and Short* with you, Francis? Well, at first glance you'd certainly put that down to Vatican business . . . of interest to nobody.'

'All I took note of was the addressee,' said Cremins curtly. 'You.'

'Ah, get away with you, Francis. Go on! What did you make of it?'

The chargé d'affaires had made very little of it in the limited time he'd spent with the envelope, but he didn't much like the few things he'd picked out in that cursory glance at the contents. He felt those few things in his gut rather than his head. Even the bit of Latin he'd taken in from Bishop O'Rourke's letter went to his stomach. There was death hanging over all this somehow, a lot of it. That was as far as he got. Good diplomatic instincts told him that he should go no further.

Having made his decision to give the envelope to Lester, Francis T. Cremins felt it had been the right one, for a moment at least. If he hadn't made much of the letter, he made even less of the accompanying documents, many in languages he didn't know. There was German, certainly, and Italian, but also what looked like Polish and maybe Czech. There was something about this envelope that was compromising. He doubted it would sit well with the officious neutrality of the Irish state. He had wondered if, even without referring back to Dublin, simply disposing of the envelope might have been a good idea. This man Gillespie had no right to carry this material, whatever it was, let alone give it the protection of the Irish diplomatic bag. It spoke of trouble. But now the envelope was out of his hands. Lester had given him no time to do anything other than hand it over. The problem was, if he mentioned its existence in his report to HQ, the Department would want to know more. Maybe it hadn't been the right decision after all. He had a growing feeling that the lie he almost told Seán Lester would have been a better bet. Not that the Secretary-General would have believed him. Lester wouldn't have let it go. There would have been a row. But maybe another lie would serve as well. As far as Dublin was concerned, like that German train, there wasn't any envelope.

'It's all yours now, Seán. I think we'll just . . . forget I even saw it.'

The Secretary-General nodded. Without either man fully understanding why, there was a quiet agreement that said they would not mention this exchange again.

★

Stefan Gillespie regained full consciousness three days after the events at the Central Station in Zurich that had taken it away from him. For much of the day before he had drifted in and out of something like consciousness, not knowing where he was or what was real around him, stuck in claustrophobic dreams that played out along the shifting border between what was inside his head and what was outside that he couldn't quite get to. Then, quite suddenly it seemed, he was looking at the light through a window and there was a woman's head that was out of focus and then very clear. And so was her voice, a soft, gentle Irish voice.

'Are you with us then, Mr Gillespie?'

He thought he spoke, but no sounds came. The woman got up.

'I'll get the nurse. And I'll find my father.'

She was gone. There was only the light from the window.

After four more days in the hospital, Stefan was well enough for an ambulance to take him to Geneva and La Pelouse, the house overlooking the lake, in the grounds of the Palais des Nations, that was Seán Lester's home. For most of those four days he slept. Lester came to see him daily, greeting him like an old friend. The Irish ambassador came once, more relieved that Stefan wasn't dead than pleased to see him. And some of the time Seán Lester's daughter read to him. And that was what was easiest for him. He was too tired to talk. He had put together what had happened, but there was still a kind of fog in his head that he needed to let clear.

Once it seemed likely that the Irish policeman, as he was always known in the Lester household, would pull through, Ann Lester had come from Geneva to help her father. She had read when Stefan was still unconscious too. She did it for no reason except that she was reading herself, to pass the time. She decided that whether he could hear her not, she would read aloud. He was amused to hear it.

'What were you reading?'

'It was *The History of Mr Polly*. Something to make me smile.'

'Did you finish it?'

She shook her head.

'Where did we get to?'

'Uncle Jim's coming for him.'

'Would that be "with a 'atchet"?'

She nodded, laughing.

'That must have done my nightmares a power of good.'

'Ah, but Mr Polly sticks, that's the thing.'

'He does, so. How would you feel about starting it again?'

At La Pelouse, Stefan Gillespie recovered quickly. The bruises, as the doctor had expected, slowly disappeared, and the more he made himself walk, the easier the pain of walking became. His hand and his lower arm were in plaster, but somewhere underneath the bones were knitting. And the fog had gone from his head. He still slept for more hours than he was awake and sometimes waking was still harder than it should have been. But the upstairs flat where the Secretary-General of the League of Nations lived in a kind of solitude with his daughter, was an easy place to be. No one expected him to do anything other than nothing if that's what he wanted, and a lot of the time it was. Talking was still tiring. The fog came back if he talked too long. But the Lesters made sure there wasn't much to say. They both knew the Wicklow Mountains well and small, insignificant stories that he had and they had were healing in themselves. And if Seán Lester wasn't talking about mountains, he was talking about rivers and streams. Fishing was his great love and, like a lot of fishermen, he assumed the world shared his passion. Talk of the war came in due course, because it had to. Because it was always there. And if there wasn't much the Secretary-General didn't know about dry flies, there was even less he didn't know about the war in Europe. If the League was only a shadow of itself, and there were only a few typewriters left to clatter away in its empty offices, it was still somewhere that all the business of war found its way to.

Much of the time Stefan sat on the balcony at La Pelouse and looked out at Lake Geneva. As his strength returned he ambled about the gardens and the lake shore. And sometimes he walked with the ghosts in the Palais des Nations. It was somewhere else he knew without ever knowing it. It was a familiarity made up of the detritus of newspaper reports and front-page photographs and radio news and the newsreels he saw in cinemas in Carlow and Dublin, but he still walked into the League of Nations' buildings for the first time without seeing anything surprising.

After ten days, he was ready to go home. He would make the journey with a walking stick, and there was a new cast on his hand, but he was well enough. And it was only a day before he left that he stood in the great Assembly Hall of the League of Nations, taking one last look at this place that had become such an unexpected part of him. He turned to see Seán Lester watching him and smiling.

'You know you're on holy ground, Stefan?'

'The hall?'

'No, not the hall. Just that spot, or a few feet away.'

Stefan, with no idea what Lester meant, waited for an explanation.

'It was one day, in nineteen thirty-six. I'd just said a lot of very reasonable and accommodating things about the Nazi leader of the Danzig, far too reasonable and far too accommodating in fact, and he replied with a stream of abuse about the Nazis who were being beaten up in the streets of the Free City and the Jews and the Communists and the capitalists and the decadent democracies whose only aim was to destroy the dream that was in every citizen of Danzig's heart, uniting with the Reich. And if it wasn't all those Jewish-Communist-capitalist bastards doing it, it was me, personally. There was a lot of that. Years of it. And years of appeasing, of course, and saying, well, they've got a point. And if they haven't, agree anyway.'

Lester looked round the hall, silent for some time.

'One man who didn't agree came into the hall that day. He stood close to where you are. He took out a pistol and shot himself. To say, "Do something!" That was about it. He was Czech. And he was a Jew. And for some reason, he saw what was coming very clearly. I don't know if that just took away everything he had except despair, or if he really thought his death would make us all do something. He left some letters in a briefcase, that showed, I think, that he hoped something would happen, that the League, or the British, or the French, or some vague and intangible feeling of goodwill and good sense would somehow . . .'

The Secretary-General stopped and lit a cigarette.

'There was no such thing. Only self-interest . . . self-interest that wasn't even that . . . self-interest was its own mistake and illusion. Anyway, the man's name was Štefan Lux. I'm probably one of the few people who even remembers his name. Lux for light. Look around. This is the light that failed. Come on . . . let's go outside.'

The two men walked out to the gardens and the lake.

'There have been a lot of briefcases over the years . . . that changed nothing.'

Little had been said in Stefan's time at La Pelouse about the envelope he'd brought to Geneva from Edward O'Rourke in Rome. He hadn't thought about that much. His job had been to deliver it and he had done that, whatever the unlooked-for consequences. But now, in the Secretary-General's words, he wondered if he heard something that gave the silence a more significant meaning.

'Is Bishop O'Rourke's envelope another briefcase?'

'It's hard to say that to you . . . after what it cost you to bring it.'

'But it's true?'

'In a way. It's full of all sorts of things I didn't know. Names, places, locations, dates. But I have cabinets full of the same things. Different names, different places, or the same reports he has, the same witnesses. It's not that no one knows. It's that there's no one to do anything. There's no one even to say no one's doing anything. That seems impossible. And Edward still believes it is impossible.'

'He's not alone,' I said. 'Everything I've heard now, I can't believe . . .'

'You can learn a lot from trains, Stefan. I play chess with a man who runs Swiss Railways in Geneva. He's always talking to his opposite numbers in France and Italy and Austria and Germany. He hears their gripes about schedules and timetables and getting the trains and the carriages they need. And you know what he hears? You'd think it would all be about war. Supplies, troops, tanks. It's a war that runs on railways. But there are other priorities. Trains taking soldiers into Italy to fight the Allies are delayed and cancelled. Trains taking food and winter clothes and shells to the Russian front are diverted. Trains sit in sidings all over Europe, not loading for war, but loading Jews who've never even picked up a gun. Those trains run on time. So, if you ever wondered what this war is for, the trains tell you what it's for. If there is a war the Nazis are losing . . . there's one they're winning.'

The two men stood still, watching the water and the mountains beyond.

'So, there you have it, Stefan. The briefcase, the envelope. Maybe I'm wrong. Maybe my old friend is right. I'd like to hope so. But hope was never enough before . . . it isn't now . . . it won't end till the end of the war stops it . . .'

'Is that what you told the bishop?'

'What I've told Edward is . . . I'm doing all I can. An old diplomatic standby. I know he's unwell. I think very unwell. I wish I had a decent lie for him. He won't die easier for knowing that when he finally had to shout . . . no one was listening . . .'

'He still thinks if the Vatican speaks out . . . if the Pope . . .'

'I know what he thinks. If all this truth is somehow pumped

out into the atmosphere, it will become so morally irresistible that it will force Pius to act.'

'Is that such a mad idea?'

'In a mad world, maybe mad ideas are worth more than I think,' said Lester. 'But I'm past second-guessing. I have become more sentimental than I was . . . when this Palace of the Nations was full of the world's leaders and I could believe all those debates and treaties and oaths and just a bit of solid decency . . . were enough to hold us together . . . when everything was pulling us apart. Now, I can't get further than thinking, do what's right. We didn't do it here. I didn't do it. We shut our mouths too. We thought that would work. We thought, well, it could be worse . . . then it was worse, much worse. That's all I have. Do the right thing. Could the Pope's voice change something? Maybe, maybe not. I don't have my old friend's faith in a feller in the white robe standing in front of a train . . . and yet . . .'

Seán Lester shook his head. It was a thought too idle even to finish.

'Would it do anything? I don't know. I only know we'll never find out.'

*

The train that would take Stefan Gillespie into France left the Gare de Genève. It seemed an ordinary station, an ordinary train. It was doing the business trains were meant to do. No policemen searched the passengers and checked their names on lists to see if they were wanted. There were no carriages full of soldiers. There were no tanks and armoured cars in the sidings. The train might have been pulling out of Dublin, to rattle along familiar tracks with the kind of lazy purpose only a country that had shut war out could countenance. But nothing could shut out the dark completely. Stefan knew that too well. He knew it because of what had happened to him,

314

but that wasn't all. He knew because of what was in his head. Things there were no customs barriers for. If the trains he travelled through Europe on had been hard work, they had been no more than trains. If they were slow, there was at least some empty space to do nothing in. He didn't mind that. But that was already changing as he left Rome's Stazione Termini. Now, looking at the tracks, the space wasn't empty. He had seen the lines of slow-moving cattle trucks before, everywhere he went. Every railway's workhorses, carrying anything, everything, anywhere, everywhere. He would see them again now, in their hundreds. He wouldn't know how many carried people, but he knew some would, some must.

All that, he was taking home. And when he got home, what would he do with it? He already saw himself in the big room in the Department of External Affairs that looked out on Stephen's Green, and Joe Walshe, Secretary of the Department, asking what the fuck he thought he was doing in Switzerland. He would say what the fuck he thought he was doing and would end up telling Mr Walshe he could fuck himself. If he kept at it, Walshe would be on the phone to Superintendent Gregory at Dublin Castle to tell him to send Inspector Gillespie back to his Wicklow hillside and his fucking sheep and if there was any question of a fucking pension it would be over his dead body. Stefan smiled as he heard Joe Walshe's fury. He might share one thing with Charles Bewley now. The sack. But it felt like time. It had been time for a long time. They wouldn't let him go, but now perhaps they couldn't let him stay. One thing he guessed though. Whatever the ruckus in Dublin, whatever way it ran, there would be no conversation about why he went to Geneva. If Walshe had anything to say on that, it would be to tell him to keep his mouth shut. And he might do. He might do anyway. What would he say? He thought of the building at the other end of Stephen's Green, Wesley College, his son's school. What would he tell Tom? He couldn't even begin to hear that conversation. It was enough that the thing tainted him. He needed to be in quarantine. Till then? If the words meant nothing, maybe there was only silence.

But there was something else Stefan Gillespie was taking home. And that was a different pain. It was his own. Its sharpness pushed away everything else that came into his mind. Nothing would stop it. He took a piece of folded paper from his wallet. It had come from Michael MacWhite the previous day. There was no point reading it again, but there was already no counting how many times he had read it. It would be read many more times. One day, his son would find it, in a box or at the back of a drawer, as he was tidying away the final clutter of his father's life. It would still be there. It would always be there. It was all he had of her now.

WITH MUCH REGRET STOP SIGNORINA CAMPANA
KILLED NEAR ROME YESTERDAY STOP YOU WILL
WANT TO KNOW STOP CANNOT GIVE DETAILS
HERE BUT HER FRIENDS ONLY CONSOLATION
IS VITTORIA WAS NOT CAPTURED ALIVE STOP

NOTES AND ACKNOWLEDGEMENTS

Dramatis Personae

Details of historical figures who appear in the story. At this time what is now the Irish Department of Foreign Affairs was the Department of External Affairs. Irish Ministers and chargés d'affaires at various embassies are often referred to as ambassadors, not always correctly. That title had only been available if an appointment was ratified by the English king. The Irish government mostly ignored this.

Seán Lester – Irish diplomat who was a major figure in the League of Nations. He served as the League's High Commissioner in Danzig but was forced out in 1937 by opposition from the Free City's Nazi government. He appears in the first Stefan Gillespie novel, *The City of Shadows*. As the League of Nations collapsed, Lester became the last Secretary-General. He stayed in Geneva throughout the war, with only a skeleton staff, knowing he was on a Nazi death list. In 1947 he handed the League of Nations' legacy to the newly formed United Nations. For his steadfast defence of democracy, he was rewarded with something close to contempt by the new power-brokers: the countries that had won the war they allowed to happen.

Ann Lester – Seán Lester's daughter was only eighteen, in 1942, when she travelled across Europe to keep her father company in his isolated and vulnerable Geneva outpost.

Michael MacWhite – Irish Minister to Italy (1938-50). I have located the Irish embassy at the Villa Spada, where it is today. In fact the Villa Spada was not purchased until 1946 and then as the base for the Irish Embassy to the Holy See.

Charles Bewley – Ireland's ex-Minister to Germany (1933-39), sacked and disgraced because of pro-Nazi activities. He stayed in Berlin, working for Goebbels; at that time he appears in the fourth Stefan Gillespie novel, *The City of Lies*. Later he moved to Rome. At the war's end he was arrested in northern Italy by British troops, imprisoned and interrogated. Once released he lived in Rome until his death. When arrested his Irish passport did describe him as, 'A Person of No Importance'.

Thomas J. Kiernan – Irish Minister to the Holy See (1942-6). He later held some of Ireland's most senior diplomatic posts, including US Ambassador. Although there is no room in this story, Kiernan acted as a go-between in the last years of the war, passing information from a Vatican source in Japan, via Dublin, to US Intelligence.

Delia Kiernan – As Delia Murphy, she was a well-known Irish ballad singer. She used the advantages of neutrality and diplomatic immunity to play a significant part in Monsignor Hugh O'Flaherty's Roman 'underground railway', smuggling and hiding fugitives from the Germans, including many Allied POWs and Jews.

Monsignor Hugh O'Flaherty – After Italy's entry into the war, Irish priest Hugh O'Flaherty was appointed by Pius XII to minister to prisoners of war. With the collapse of Mussolini's regime and

German occupation, O'Flaherty took a radical approach to what his POW ministry meant. He established an 'underground railway' to hide escaped Allied prisoners; in Rome, in monasteries outside the city, and in the Vatican and its extra-territorial properties. Over time this network involved Italian political figures, Jews and others fleeing the Nazis. The monsignor became a wanted man himself, though he continued to move about Rome, beyond the Vatican's security, in disguise. The coal-cellar escape in this story is based on one of O'Flaherty's own close shaves. He maintained two unlikely friendships in the years after the war; one with Herbert Kappler, the city's imprisoned ex-Gestapo chief, who had converted to Catholicism; the other with Charles Bewley, maybe another man in need of a confessor, or maybe just another Irishman out of his time.

Bishop Edward O'Rourke – An ancestor of O'Rourke's fled 17th-century Ireland to become a Czarist soldier and found a Russian aristocratic dynasty that never abandoned its Irish heritage or its Catholicism. Count Edward O'Rourke left Russia after the Revolution and later became Bishop of Danzig, established as a German-speaking enclave, almost surrounded by Poland, in 1922. In alliance with the Irish League of Nations High Commissioner, Seán Lester, the bishop defended his Church, the constitution of the Free City, and its minorities, against a Nazi government demanding unification with Hitler's Germany. The bishop appears in the first Stefan Gillespie book, *The City of Shadows*. O'Rourke and Lester were forced out of Danzig in the face of appeasement by their own institutions – the Catholic Church and the League of Nations. When Germany invaded Poland in 1939, Edward O'Rourke had to flee, probably for his life. He lived out the rest of his days in the Vatican, safe but largely ignored, especially with regard to Nazi atrocities in Poland, which he witnessed and continued to monitor. He died in 1943.

Francis T. Cremins – Permanent Representative to the League of Nations in Geneva (1934-40), and afterwards Irish Chargé d'Affaires, Berne, Switzerland (1940-49).

Mentioned in Dispatches

Historical figures who play a part in the story but do not appear.

Štefan Lux – Born in what is now Slovakia, Lux was a Jewish Czechoslovak citizen. He was a film-maker and writer. He shot himself at the League of Nations in 1938. If he was naïve to think he could shock the world into action, he was not alone in believing that accommodating Nazi Germany would lead to war and worse. Winston Churchill was also convinced the great powers (including the Soviet Union then) could stop Hitler. It was a bitter conviction that Churchill never lost.

Joseph Patrick Walshe – Joe Walshe was Secretary of the Department of External Affairs and, along with the Taoiseach, Éamon de Valera, was almost entirely responsible for foreign policy in the period of the Emergency (as the war was officially titled in Ireland). In these books I have generally accepted that de Valera's decision about Irish neutrality was necessary and right. At the same time I have illustrated the close working links between Irish and British Intelligence. However, I think de Valera's refusal to abandon the most rigorous, even bloody-minded interpretation of neutrality when it came to any public stance on the orchestrated murder of millions of civilians in Europe later in the war, which owed as much to Walshe's intransigence as to his own, was neither necessary nor right. Joe Walshe appears briefly in the fourth Stefan Gillespie book, *The City of Lies*.

Leopold Kerney – Minister to Spain (1935-46). He appears in this role in the third Stefan Gillespie book, *The City in Darkness*, where he plays a part in getting the ex-IRA leader and International Brigade commander, Frank Ryan, released from gaol in Fascist Spain. He helped save Ryan's life, but at the cost of handing him to German Intelligence. Kerney's links with German interests in Spain remained at the very least ambiguous, so much so that in 1943 the Irish government sent Intelligence officers to Madrid to look into what he was doing. They seem to have concluded that if he wasn't doing anything wrong, he still needed to stop doing it!

Acknowledgements

As ever, a lot of books contributed to this story, over a lot of years. I first read Rolf Hochhuth's play *The Representative* (*Der Stellvertreter*) in my teens. It remains a great work in a polemical tradition owing much to Karl Kraus's masterpiece *The Last Days of Mankind*. The play, which is as much about how individuals of faith face overwhelming evil as about any failings of the Catholic Church in confronting such evil, produced responses that dismissed it as simultaneously a vindictive, hysterical farrago and a selective rewriting of history of Machiavellian genius. Such refutations were often more hysterical and selective than anything in the play, though not all. But it is a work of art not history, though it stubbornly disrupts much of the history thrown together to demolish it. The play's importance lies in how it questions our confrontation with evil, inside the Church and outside, institutionally and individually, not in answers it doesn't attempt to give. Oddly the play, now largely forgotten, still provokes hysteria. Recently it was claimed the Stasi and KGB wrote it. Who knew they had such talent? I make no apology for *The Representative* being in my head fifty years on. The Church can still learn from the play; not because of accuracy or inaccuracy, but because of its humanity. Historical books that informed this aspect of the story, none of which are responsible for my failings, were many and varied. I mention only a few. Pierre Blet's *Pius XII and the Second World War: According to the Archives of the Vatican*, is a Holy-See-sanctioned collection of documents produced in part to refute Hochhuth's play. The claim, in the author's words, is that Pius was 'not silent but restrained', practising 'the quiet diplomacy of the possible'. The documents are selective and there was no access to great quantities of archive material; they do demonstrate deep concern on the part of the Pope and often great anguish. Carlo Falconi's *The Silence of Pius XII* offers very different documents, also, it must be said, chosen selectively; it is strong on Croatia, Pavelić, the Ustaše. David Kertzer's *The Pope at War* is one of the first books to examine Vatican archives released in 2020; these contain unseen material, including thousands of harrowing personal pleas by Jews all over Europe. This new material doesn't help the Vatican case that quiet restraint was the only option and anything else would have made matters worse. One book about the transportation of Roman Jews to Auschwitz that is essential reading is Giacomo Debenedetti's *October 16, 1943*. Only forty pages long, it is both a document of Holocaust history and a great literary work. On other topics: In *Switzerland, National Socialism and the Second World War*, the report of the Swiss Commission of Experts claims no trains carrying Italian workers transited the country after July 1943, so no Italian forced labour. However, documents from Swiss Federal Railways and German Railways dispute this. Elmer Bendiner's *A Time for Angels* provides a compelling account of the League of Nations' collapse and Seán Lester's lonely wartime sojourn in Geneva. Charles Bewley's bizarre and extremely selective *Memoirs of a Wild Goose* makes, as Stefan Gillespie anticipated, uncomfortable reading. The Royal Irish Academy's *Documents on Irish Foreign Policy* series records much of what was going on in the Department of External Affairs and in Ireland's several legations. But we can only read what is there; certainly not everything is.